SECRETS OF THE HEART

I will never abandon you, my precious Justin, Nick vowed silently as he gently kissed his son's golden hair. And I will try so very hard never again to cause you harm.

Nick wanted to harm no one, not ever, and most assuredly not someone he loved. His love for Justin had come as a wonderful surprise, a gift of joy that was far more than he deserved, and it had not occurred to Nick that he would ever love anyone but his son.

But now he did. And he saw, in her lovely emerald eyes, that she cared about him, too. Far too much. Elizabeth didn't seem to know that she deserved someone much better than he, someone whose heart was whole, not wounded—a heart that smiled with radiant joy, as hers did, not screamed with pain, like his.

It was a constant battle for Nick to prevent himself from becoming lost in her emerald eyes . . . and to stop his arms from gently drawing her lovely body close to his . . . and to forbid his lips from confessing to her all his secret truths.

It was a constant battle, but it was a battle Nick always won. Because he loved her. Because he knew with absolute certainty that it was best for Elizabeth if he stayed very far away . . .

KATHERINE STONE

PROMISES

ZEBRA BOOKS
KENSINGTON PUBLISHING CORP.

ZEBRA BOOKS are published by

Kensington Publishing Corp.
475 Park Avenue South
New York, NY 10016

Zebra and the Z logo are trademarks of Kensington Publishing Corp.

First Hardcover Printing: February, 1993
First Paperback Printing: September, 1993

Printed in the United States of America

Part

One

Chapter One

San Francisco, California
August 1991

Dr. Elizabeth Jennings abandoned all hope of further sleep shortly before dawn. She had been awake for almost two hours, far too excited—and anxious—to drift back to the tranquility of dreams. Today Elizabeth was going to assist Dr. Nicholas Chase with the transplantation of a small portion of a young mother's healthy liver to her infant daughter's diseased one. If everything went well, and it would because of Nick's immense talent, both mother and daughter would have a long life of health and love ahead of them.

Today's surgery wouldn't be the world's first living donor liver transplantation—that monumental surgery had been done twenty-one months before—but it would be the first such operation performed in San Francisco, and the first also in which Elizabeth would participate. The surgery wasn't new to Nick, of course. He had been a member of the surgical team in Chicago on that historic day in November 1989, and he had since become a leading expert on the lifesaving operation. Now, in just a few hours, Nick was going to introduce the extraordinary technique to his own surgical team at Pacific Heights Medical Center as well as to other Bay Area transplant surgeons who had been specially invited to observe the delicate and difficult surgery from the amphitheater above the operating room. Only one surgeon would be in the operating room with Nick, assisting him . . .

How Elizabeth wished she could believe that she had been handpicked by Nick because he valued her surgical skill, the decisive agility of her slender fingers combined with her unshakable calm in the OR, but she had no proof whatsoever that the great Nicholas Chase thought she had any surgical aptitude at all. He hadn't chosen her to be the second member of his two-member team, after all, he had simply inherited her.

Elizabeth was already on the faculty of the medical center's prestigious Department of Surgery when Nick arrived. She had been recruited because of her expertise in trauma, and once there, because the center's organ transplantation program was expanding, the transplant service chief had convinced her to become trained in that surgical subspecialty as well. Elizabeth had just completed that training when, eight months ago, Nick had arrived to become the new transplant service chief—and he had inherited her as his assistant, the person designated to work most closely with him, the other half of his two-person team.

Dr. Elizabeth Jennings was beneath Dr. Nicholas Chase in academic rank, of course. Nick was eight years her senior both in age and in surgical experience. But she was a good surgeon, perhaps even a gifted one. Still, with Nick she felt uncertain, as if he were uncertain of her, unsure of what to do with her and strangely wary. He was

8

always polite to her, a cool formal politeness that kept a vast distance between them despite the intimacy of the work they did together.

Somewhere in that cool wary distance, and all its uneasy silences, was Nick privately wishing that she had followed his predecessor—and her mentor—to Boston, so that he would have been free to recruit someone new, someone he really wanted, a choice not a legacy? Had Nick awakened early today, too, the peacefulness of his sleep disrupted by the smoldering displeasure that it would be she who would be assisting him with today's momentous surgery?

It was that anxiety, that tormenting worry amid the excitement she felt about the day that lay ahead, that finally drove Elizabeth from her bed. She would banish that worry, she decided, with hot tea and the splendor of daybreak over San Francisco Bay. Elizabeth had a view of that splendor, of all the magnificent and ever-changing dramas of sea and sky, from the living room of her Pacific Heights apartment. The worry would vanish with the golden dawn, she would force it to; and then she would focus all the energy and attention of her bright mind on the extraordinary task that lay ahead—mentally reviewing the scientific papers she had read, the diagrams she had memorized, the words Nick himself had said, as recently as last night, about the intricate technique, the precise timing, the potential catastrophes.

Elizabeth made tea then settled into a cozy chair in the living room and gazed outside. The tormenting worry about Nick would be conquered by the pale yellow rays of morning. But it was night still, the darkest hour before dawn, and she simply permitted all the thoughts and worries about him to surface, narrowing her luminous emerald eyes as if hoping to see them more clearly. But there was no clarity.

There were only the dark shadows cast by the dark, handsome, mysterious Dr. Chase.

Nick was the best surgeon Elizabeth had ever known. Everyone at the medical center knew that about Nick. Just as everyone seemed to know about his affairs with the hospital's most beautiful women. Nick's affairs were short-lived—and mysterious, occurring in darkness, breathless rendezvous of pleasure and passion that began at midnight and always ended before dawn. Dr. Nicholas Chase didn't seduce with romantic candlelight dinners, he didn't need to, nor apparently was there ever much meaningful conversation, just enough words from Nick to make it abundantly clear that he was not interested in love.

Elizabeth did not want to hear about Nick's love . . . sex . . . life. She did not want to learn that even his immense talent as a surgeon was eclipsed by his extraordinary expertise as a lover. But since the devastatingly sexy black-haired, blue-eyed doctor and his affairs were a favorite topic of conversation at the hospital, it was virtually impossible not to unwittingly overhear. And more than once, astonishingly, one of Nick's women had actually come to her, seeking her advice, as if she would have some special insight into his mysteries and secrets. She was Nick's partner after all, his shadow, his sidekick. Surely in the long emotional hours that she and Nick spent together, saving lives and losing them, he would have confided some truths about himself. Elizabeth would never have revealed such truths had she known them, but of course she knew nothing. Even in the most emotional

10

times, there had been only politeness from Nick—and distance and silence.

Elizabeth did not want to know about Nick's affairs. But she did: his breathtaking sensuality, his talent for pleasure, the reckless abandon of his passion—and yet the surprising care he took to be certain that the intimacy was safe, for all the new reasons—and for the oldest reason of all.

Nicholas Chase did not want to become a father, his beautiful women all agreed. Not that he would *be* a father of course, they added knowingly, predicting with absolute certainty that Nick would wash his hands of that responsibility as thoroughly as he scrubbed before a case in the OR.

That's not true! Elizabeth protested silently whenever she heard the confident pronouncement. If Nick fathered a child, he would be very responsible. She was sure of it. And she was sure, too, that the man who was such a good doctor, so caring and so compassionate with his patients, would be a wonderful and loving father.

Elizabeth defended Nick in silence, in her heart, in the same heart that ached whenever she inadvertently stumbled into a discussion about him. Did Nick know that such discussions took place? she wondered. Would it bother him if he did? Elizabeth hoped it would. It was so private, and it should have been so special. The women with whom Nick shared himself didn't want him, not really, not for keeps. They knew how dangerous he was, how wild and restless, how intense and demanding, how undeserving of their trust much less their love. Nick's lovers didn't want Nick, and Nick didn't want them—except for the night-cloaked moments of pleasure about which Elizabeth hated hearing so much.

Why would Nick give himself away so freely? Why would he devalue himself that way? It was as if he didn't believe there was anything important or special about him, as if he didn't matter at all. Nicholas Chase mattered very much to Elizabeth Jennings, even though it was painfully obvious that the feeling wasn't mutual.

Elizabeth had wondered in the beginning if it was possible that Nick actually felt threatened by her. Her remarkable academic and career successes rivaled his own stunning accomplishments at her age; and she, like he, had chosen to become expert in both trauma and transplantation surgery. Was Nick threatened by her accomplishments and her talent? Or was he simply annoyed by her boldly calm and competent invasion of the sacrosanct male domain of the operating room?

Neither, Elizabeth was forced to realize. Nick was neither threatened nor annoyed. It was the nineties, after all, and Nicholas Chase was a modern man, not a chauvinist. By night, yes, he had meaningless affairs with women doctors; but that was by mutual consent, an enthusiastic choice to share passion and nothing else. And by day, in the hospital, he consulted those same women physicians, wanting their medical opinions, listening with uncondescending interest to what they said and then daring to both agree and disagree.

It wasn't that Nick disliked women physicians. It was just, quite simply, that he didn't like *her*. The dark blue eyes that flirted with every other woman with such effortlessness that the seduction seemed almost instinctive had never been anything but subdued and solemn with her. Subdued and solemn and sometimes—when they were alone and Nick was so lost in thought that he seemed to have forgotten she was there—Elizabeth caught glimpses of powerful currents swirling beneath the sensual calm, flickers of secret and turbulent emotions in the ocean blue depths. What she saw, what she believed she saw, was pain, uncertainty, and a sadness as dark and deep as the blue itself.

She had to be mistaken. Nick was confident, arrogant even, and deservedly so, both personally and professionally. Confident and arrogant, alluring and dangerous—not anguished, not uncertain, not sad. It had to be an optical illusion created by his tall, dark, handsome shadow and further blurred by her own emotions about him . . .

"Hopeless," Elizabeth whispered to the night-black sky that was now beginning to yield to the pale yellow rays of morning. A soft smile touched her lips as she realized the word she whispered was, like the awakening dawn, a glimmer of light and truth. Her relationship—*relationship?*—with Nick was hopeless. Of course stunningly gorgeous Nicholas Chase would never find stunningly wholesome Elizabeth Jennings desirable. But she wished, oh how she wished, that he would like her.

"Completely hopeless," she repeated softly as she left the coziness of the chair to make a second cup of tea, one to last until the sky was bright gold and it was time to shower and dress before making the two-minute walk from her apartment to the medical center.

While waiting for the water to heat, Elizabeth gazed thoughtfully at the mug her hands had found in the pre-dawn darkness. It was her favorite, a festive scene of brightly colored balloons floating amid swirls of confetti and personalized with the exuberant command, emblazoned in brilliant fuschia: ELIZABETH! CELEBRATE!!

The mug had been one of two gifts given to her by her

best friend in celebration of her twenty-first birthday. Larisa's other gift had been a bottle of Courvoisier. "Because, Liz," she had announced, her voice solemn but her eyes sparkling as she spoke the nickname no one else ever had, "you're twenty-one years old now. You have to at least *taste* alcohol!" Even then both Elizabeth and Larisa had known that of the two gifts the mug would get the most use. And indeed now, nine years later, the bottle of vintage cognac remained almost full—and the mug was still Elizabeth's favorite.

Elizabeth sighed softly as she looked at the mug and remembered that twenty-first birthday . . . and the triumphant years that had followed for both of them . . . and the three years that had elapsed since she had last heard from Larisa. No, that was wrong. It had been three years since Elizabeth had mailed her last letter to her best friend, but it had been three and a half years since Larisa had last communicated with her. Elizabeth very much missed the letters punctuated with exclamation points and smiling—and frowning—faces; and she missed even more the late night phone calls that had stopped even before the letters but had once been an effortless flow of quietly shared secrets and dreams interspersed with soft cascades of merry, and so uncomplicated, laughter.

As Elizabeth poured the hot tea water into the mug and thought about the uncomplicated laughter, she imagined a scene between her best friend and the man who had so complicated her own life. Even Nick, a connoisseur of beautiful women, would be dazzled by Larisa's beauty. Even he would be captivated by the brilliant blue eyes that would appraise him with provocative boldness.

Larisa's appraisal of Nick would be unhurried, a leisurely and pleasurable perusal, and when at last she was finished, she would tell him with unblushing candor that

14

she approved of his rich coal black hair and his seductive dark blue eyes and the proud strength of his sculpted features and the devastating sexiness of his lazy smile.

"Well, Nick, you are indeed as advertised—really quite gorgeous," she would say. Then, after Nick's dark blue eyes had eloquently returned the compliment in kind, she would continue, "I have some questions for you, Doctor. Most of them are Elizabeth's questions, but I do have one of my own, which I'll save for last. So, let's see. What are you, confident and arrogant, or uncertain and sad? You look confident and arrogant to me—and very dangerous. But even though I see only seduction in your blue eyes, Liz has told me that sometimes she has seen pain. And I can't simply discount her impressions, you see, because her instincts about people are usually pure gold. Although, admittedly, she is so generous that she has been known to find good where no one else can . . ." Larisa's focus would drift for a moment, from her search for the real Nicholas Chase to thoughts of her friend—her own relentless teasing that Elizabeth always saw the best in people, and her immense pride in her generous friend for doing so.

Then she would concentrate once again on Nick, and still seeing for herself only the arrogant confidence of a stunningly handsome man, she would demand, "What is the story with these meaningless affairs that occur only in darkness? Oh, don't get me wrong. I don't care that they're meaningless. But what is this prince of midnight nonsense? A ploy to add more danger, more romance, more drama? You don't need the extra theatrics, Doctor Chase. In broad daylight, in the harshest of lights, I am quite certain that you could seduce." Larisa would smile radiantly at the inscrutable blue eyes and when it became abundantly clear that they were going to remain inscrutable to her forever, she would give a resigned sigh and say, "Well. I can tell that even if there is some deep secret anguish you aren't going to reveal it to me. So, let me ask my question."

The provocative teasing would leave Larisa's voice then and her beautiful face would become thoughtful as she asked with quiet bewilderment, "Why don't you like my friend?" And then, in the long silence that would surely follow, the thoughtful blue eyes would flash with anger and when she spoke again it would be with icy indignation, "How *dare* you not like Elizabeth!"

Elizabeth gave a soft shake of her dark brown curls at the image of Larisa, free-spirited and provocative, irreverent and bold, fiercely loyal and mother-bear protective. That was the Larisa who had been randomly assigned to be her freshman roommate at Berkeley. It had been the frisky trick of some wily computer, matching—*mis*matching—glamorous and sophisticated Larisa Locksley with naive and unglamorous Elizabeth Jennings. But they had become best friends throughout the three years each had spent in college and best friends after despite the continent of separation and divergence of life-styles that occurred when Larisa had moved to New York to become a top fashion model and Elizabeth had remained in San Francisco to attend medical school.

And when, six years ago, Larisa had joyfully announced her engagement to the very handsome and staggeringly wealthy thirty-year-old Julian Chancellor, and had wanted her best friend to be her maid of honor, the June wedding had been arranged to accommodate Elizabeth's rigorous on-call schedule as a surgery resident at the grueling and prestigious program at Parkland in Dallas. With careful planning she had been able to get away for twenty-four hours, arriving in New York just in time for the rehearsal dinner at La Côte Basque in Manhattan and leaving the Southampton Club on Long Island the following afternoon just moments after the bride and groom themselves had bid adieu to their wedding guests. The twenty-four hours had been a festive whirl of dazzle and elegance, crescendoing to the picture-perfect garden wedding—and yet Elizabeth had returned to Dallas with a feeling of sadness, an ominous and unshakable impression that Larisa's vibrant spirit had seemed a little subdued.

Elizabeth didn't see Larisa again. But for the next three years there were phone calls and letters, and with each ensuing one the impression became even stronger: her bright, funny, outrageous and courageous friend was fading. During college Elizabeth had always sensed that despite the many secrets Larisa had shared with her, there were important ones that she hadn't—and Elizabeth had never pushed. Were there new secrets now? she wondered as she felt Larisa fading. Secrets that Larisa either could not or would not share?

Elizabeth respected Larisa's privacy. She only offered her support and her friendship. But still Larisa withdrew. The phone calls stopped, and the letters became shorter as the gaps between them became longer. Finally, when four of her letters to Larisa went unanswered over a six-month period, Elizabeth herself stopped writing, not out of pique, but because it was so obvious that Larisa no longer wanted to continue the correspondence.

Maybe Larisa hasn't faded, Elizabeth told herself. Maybe it is simply time for our surprising friendship to fade. The thought saddened Elizabeth, but not nearly as much as the image of a faded Larisa did.

Although she had never actually said so, Elizabeth knew that the childhood of which Larisa had so rarely spoken could not have been a happy one. And she wanted happiness for her best friend. Happiness—and love. For as long as Elizabeth had known her, there had been men in Larisa's life, but until Julian the relationships had always been fleeting. Larisa had kept them that way, ending them quickly but never cruelly, always genuinely surprised when even the most gentle rejection had caused rage, as if she believed that the man had never really wanted her, only her astonishing beauty.

"Julian loves me for me," Larisa had confessed to Elizabeth shortly before her fairy-tale wedding, a soft confession of disbelief and joy.

Elizabeth had been so thrilled for Larisa, and so very eager to meet the man who had brought her friend such happiness at last. But when she met the handsome and powerful Julian Chancellor, Elizabeth had been swept by a strange uneasiness. She hadn't been able to free herself of it, nor had she been able to clearly define it. All she knew was that when she met Julian the invisible rose-colored glasses, about which Larisa had always teased her, had been quite firmly in place, and she had been prepared, as always, to see only the very best. But even though Elizabeth could not define what she had seen, and most surely had never communicated her uneasiness to Larisa, there was something about Julian Chancellor that had sent shivers of ice through her.

Then—and still.

Elizabeth melted the icy shivers now by curling her fingers around the warm mug and smiling at the brilliant fuschia command.

Celebrate, Larisa, she commanded silently in return. I hope that I was very wrong about Julian. I hope that he has given you all the wonderful love and happiness that you deserve and that at this very moment, as you are awakening a continent away in your penthouse in Manhattan, your heart is overflowing with joy . . .

Chapter Two

Manhattan
August 1991

Eight-thirty, read the Lalique crystal clock beside the bed. Far below the Fifth Avenue penthouse, Manhattan was awake and already very hot and humid beneath the glaring August sun.

Eight-thirty! Larisa was seized with panic as the realization settled. At three, when she had been certain that Julian had truly gone, she had crawled to the bathroom and taken a long, hot, necessary shower. She had wanted to leave then, but she had been far too weak, far too dizzy. She had needed to lie down again, just for a few moments, just a brief rest . . .

But she had fallen asleep, and now five precious hours had passed, and what if Julian was putting his key into the front door lock at this very moment? What if he was closer even than that, his footsteps softly muted by the plush carpet?

Julian won't return, Larisa bravely told her racing heart. He won't return until this evening, as usual. As usual . . . as if nothing had happened. He will spend today negotiating new multimillion-dollar deals, and perhaps negotiating the recapture of whatever real estate deal it was that he had lost yesterday—a loss which had triggered such violence and such rage.

Julian won't return, Larisa assured herself bravely. But still, I have to get up and pack and leave—*now*.

In the wonderful dreams Larisa had dreamed during the past five hours, both her body and spirit had been strong, not damaged, and together they had already taken her very far away. But those were dreams, wonderful dreams, and she was awake now, still in the penthouse where Julian might return, still needing to leave.

As she became more wakeful, the courageous woman in her dreams seemed to vanish and the bright light of day exposed the wonderful dreams for what they had actually been: impossible ones. How could she possibly leave him? She was bound to him, wasn't she, tightly and forever? Oh, yes, the chains that bound her to Julian were quite invisible, but they were also very real—terribly, painfully real. Julian owned her, all of her, her heart, her spirit, her body, her destiny. Larisa knew exactly what Julian owned, what he possessed and controlled, because his possessions were gifts of love and trust that she herself had given him; and she knew exactly how much he owned—*everything*—because it was she who had given him everything she had to give.

The invisible chains were all that were necessary to imprison the invisible woman she had become. She was without any substance whatsoever, lighter than air, floating, floating. Larisa's mind floated now, blurred by the vicious blows to her head, and in a moment she would float back to those wonderful courageous dreams . . .

No! The cry came from very deep within her, from some resilient place that didn't belong to Julian because all this time it had been hidden even from her. The voice continued with nurturing calm, *You can sleep later. But right now you must get up. You must act out the scenes you have so carefully rehearsed in your dreams. Right now!*

Larisa obeyed the voice. Too quickly, she realized as the room began to whirl violently when she sat up. But the whirling was more than simply a too hasty change of position. It was part of her, inside her. Inside her head because of the blows? Or inside the slender abdomen that screamed in silent pain, as if in horrified witness to hidden pools of blood? Whatever its source, Larisa realized that the whirling was going to travel with her on her journey. She spent a few moments getting used to it, accepting it. When she finally stood, she wobbled again, and waited again, adjusting. Then, when the whirling was under her control, even though it hadn't abated, she simply willed herself to become the brave woman about whom she had dreamed.

Larisa moved slowly, conserving energy, but she moved decisively, too, reliving the scenes that had already been so successfully enacted in her dreams. She needed to dress elegantly. She was the ravishingly beautiful wife of billionaire Julian Chancellor, after all, and it was essential that anyone who happened to see her as she made her escape not ever guess that anything was amiss. She needed a summer travel outfit, and she had many, but today there were other requirements as well. Today whatever she wore had to conceal the purple bruises on her snow-white limbs and it had to drape softly, loosely, on her ravaged body. Larisa selected a long-sleeved teal silk blouse and matching silk harem pants, accessorized, at least until she was far away from eyes that might recognize her, by a gold chain belt around her slender aching waist.

The outfit was fine, elegant and concealing, but what about her beautiful recognizable face? Would she be able to wear her trademark hairstyle, her magnificent red-gold hair swept off her face and twisted into a lustrous knot atop her head? That was the hairstyle Manhattan had come to expect. For the past six years the luxuriant fire-kissed golden mane for which she had been so famous during her modeling days had been hidden entirely from public view, allowed to flow freely only for Julian. He had insisted on it.

Would it be possible for her to fully expose her face today as always? Larisa wondered as she approached the mirror with trepidation, so very fearful of what she might see—or might not see. Eighteen years ago, after the first time she had been brutally betrayed, whenever she had looked into a mirror, she had seen nothing. Where her face should have been, there had been no image at all, only a blurry oval shadow. The facelessness then had lasted for almost four years, and even when she had finally been able to see her reflection again, what Larisa had seen was only an extraordinarily beautiful mask, a ravishing disguise that would enable her to move through the world with an aura of glittering confidence despite her true uncertainty and fear. The remarkable face, the exquisite masquerade, had made Larisa Locksley rich and famous. And it had made Julian Chancellor want to own her. And sometime in the past year or two—or maybe three or even four—there had been days when Larisa would look into a mirror and see again only the blurry oval shadow.

As a teenager, Larisa had been unable to conquer the shadowy facelessness. She had never even wanted to. But in the past few years, she had learned of necessity how to force her image to come into view. That was what she did now, watching her face surface from the dark depths, cringing when she first saw her eyes, so haunted and hopeless, then resolutely leaving them to begin the careful search for bruises.

There were swollen lumps on both sides of her head, warm, tender gravestones that marked the death of her love. But those lumps were beneath her golden-red hair. No one would notice them.

And her face itself? It was quite undamaged—except for the haunted hopeless blue. Julian had been terribly careful not to damage his most prized possession. Larisa trembled at the thought and its hideous meaning. Had Julian really known what he was doing? Had there actually been thought and control in his rage? She didn't know, didn't want to know. She only knew that she was grateful that her face had been spared his brutal violence.

Grateful? Yes, because it meant she could leave today. And there was more gratitude—to whoever it was who had tricked Julian out of the property he had obviously wanted so desperately and lost. Larisa had known nothing about the real estate deal, and still didn't, except that apparently clever and devious Julian, himself a master of trickery, had been outdone, and that had enraged him, and somehow, inexplicably and irrationally, he had shifted all the blame of his defeat to her. The blame, the rage . . . and the punishment. He had punished her with words first, a vicious assault that left her heart in a thousand weeping pieces, and then he had punished her further, physically, mercilessly ignoring her terrified pleas and finally possessing her against her will—as if she had no will, as if she was his to own, to harm, to control, to destroy.

She *was* his, a gift of love from her to him, because she had loved him, and had needed his love, and because she had so desperately needed to believe that she had been

24

right to trust him. She had acceded to Julian's every wish, his every whim, betraying herself in the process, somehow convincing herself that each demand was merely a romantic request of love. She had abandoned the modeling career she had loved—yes, willingly!—because Julian had wanted her to be available to him and his insatiable desire for her at all times. He had wanted her to abandon even more, everything that had come before him: her career, her friends, all ties with her past. Was it a romantic request, a wish for her life and her happiness to begin with their love? Or a blue-blooded request, the *Mayflower* descendant wanting to erase forever the memory of his bride's decidedly underprivileged lineage? Or was the request simply a controlling demand, wanting all invisible bonds to bind her to him and him alone?

Larisa had convinced herself that Julian's requests were romantic ones. Without hesitation she had abandoned her career and the friends she had made during her years as a model . . . and finally, three and a half years ago, she had even abandoned the only friend who had ever really mattered. Had she really severed her relationship with Elizabeth to please Julian? Or had it been in truth because something deep inside her hadn't wanted her best friend to know what had become of her, what she herself had *allowed* to happen to her?

Julian took, and Larisa gave, giving herself away, betraying her own heart and spirit with each new gift, dying a little more every day—and yet resolutely denying the truth because her need to believe in his love was so great. She might have lived—and died—with Julian forever. But after last night . . .

She had been raped once before, when she was twelve. On that distant night of terror there had been no one to protect her from the violence or to rescue her from the

25

anguish of its aftermath. When Julian raped her last night, he had raped once again the innocent little girl who dwelled within her still. Despite her pleas, Larisa had been unable to protect either herself or the fragile child inside against Julian's violence. But now, gently yet firmly guided by the strong and courageous woman of her dreams, she was going to rescue them both from further anguish and harm.

Larisa was grateful to whoever it was who had tricked Julian and unmasked his brutal rage.

Because now she knew all about Julian and his love.

Now she could deny the truth no longer.

Larisa felt as if she were moving in slow motion through a whirling world of pain and fear. The pain was constant, a fiery legacy of Julian's venom, but the fear came in terrifying waves, crashing with each new sound, however slight, and lasting until the sound—the traffic far below, the air conditioner exhaling its cool air to offset the oppressive heat—was identified as being not Julian.

For a brief hopeful moment, Larisa wondered if Julian might be relieved if he returned and discovered she was leaving. *No*, the answer came swiftly, carried by yet another crashing wave of fear. Julian would be enraged. And the rage she had witnessed last night, when he had simply lost a piece of property he had wanted to add to his already vast empire, would be trivial compared to his rage at the loss of his wife.

Move more quickly! she urged her weak and whirling body.

She was dressed now and looked presentable, elegant. She needed only to pack and get whatever money she could find in Julian's desk. Neither would take long. Quickly and without sentimentality, she put an assortment of designer clothes in her suitcase, leaving room on

26

top for the few items of clothing that were important to her, the few comfortable and treasured friends she had kept hidden from Julian.

Hidden? her mind echoed. Shouldn't that have been a clue? Doesn't hiding things from your husband seem like a marriage with problems?

She had hidden such trivial things: her well-worn, much beloved jeans from college, a blue sweatshirt with BERKELEY emblazoned in gold, the tattered cotton bathrobe and nightgown she had worn when she and Elizabeth stayed up all night sharing secrets and dreams. The clothes were rags, but they were the only friends from her past that still survived.

After the college clothes were packed, there was still a little room left in the suitcase. On impulse, or perhaps it had already been planned in her dreams, Larisa retrieved the long gown of flowing white silk—hidden also—from a far corner of her closet. She had loved the gown the moment she had seen it. So romantic, she had thought. So innocent, so pure, its delicate pearl and silver beads glistening like dewdrops on roses. How eager she had been to show her romantic discovery to Julian. How perfect it was, she had thought, for the enchanted evening before their fairy-tale wedding.

But Julian hadn't liked the beautiful gown. He had already decided what she would wear that night, a designer gown that tastefully yet undeniably celebrated the perfect body that would soon be his, provocative and luscious, not innocent and pure. Julian had wanted Larisa to wear his choice, and of course she had. But what if, on the eve of their wedding, she had said no? Would Julian have forced the issue? Might she have known the truth even then?

Larisa had hidden her college clothes and the never-worn gown from Julian for six years. Had he discovered those treasures of her past, he might have been annoyed, contemptuous of her silly sentimentality. But, she thought as she removed four small pink packets from their hiding place between layers of silk and satin in her dresser drawer, if Julian knew I had these . . .

A shiver of ice passed through her as she stared at the birth-control pills, the tiny reminders of such foolish hope and such shattering loss. How she had wanted children, his children, *their* children. How joyful, how hopeful she had been when the gynecologist she had consulted four months before her wedding—because she had known she must—had told her, "Yes, there is definitely very significant damage to the Fallopian tubes, but it's virtually impossible to predict to what extent that damage will affect your fertility. I have personally cared for women with similar tubal damage who have had totally normal pregnancies." Her past, that long ago night of terror, would not come back to haunt her, Larisa had told herself. She would have normal pregnancies, and she and Julian would have babies conceived in the greatest of love and raised by parents who would love and protect and cherish them—as parents should.

Larisa never told Julian that she was trying to get pregnant. She had wanted to surprise him, believing he would be thrilled, imagining the joy on his handsome face at the wonderful news. And she had hidden her own sadness from him as month after month—and then year after year—she failed to conceive.

After five years, the diagnosis seemed quite secure: she was infertile. There might be surgical and *in vitro* techniques that could be tried, of course, but it seemed very certain that she would never become pregnant without such sophisticated intervention. There was no reason whatsoever for her to use birth control.

But that was what she did, beginning nine months ago, because that was when something deep inside told her, warned her, that it would be disastrous to start a family with Julian. He wasn't ready, *they* weren't ready, to be the kind of parents she wanted for their babies. It would have been a miracle for her to conceive after five years of trying unsuccessfully—and Larisa had no reason to believe in miracles—but nonetheless she began taking birth-control pills to prevent the miracle she had once wanted with all her heart.

And when, six months ago, for the first time in their marriage Julian had told her he wanted children and wanted her to begin trying to get pregnant right away, she had agreed without protest—and each day, without fail, she had continued to take a pill from the carefully hidden pink packets.

He would kill me if he found these, Larisa thought with terrifying confidence as she put the pink packets in the suitcase on top of the lovingly folded white silk gown. She would finish the current cycle of pills, she decided, to make certain that last night's violence hadn't created a physical bond to Julian in addition to the invisible ones. Then she would throw the rest of the packets away. It was impossible to imagine ever making love again, and even if that impossible day ever came, she knew she didn't really need contraception.

Larisa closed the suitcase, her packing complete, then left the bedroom in search of the cash she would need to make her escape. She was married to one of the richest men in America, but she had no credit cards, no check-book, no access to any money at all beyond what Julian

29

kept in his desk in the penthouse's elegant wood-paneled library.

Larisa had been financially independent—until Julian. He had wanted to take care of her as no one had ever wanted to before, providing everything for her, freeing her from such trivialities as bills and checking accounts. And she had allowed Julian to provide everything, believing the romantic illusion of freedom, when in fact she was a prisoner, a pampered princess in a most luxurious prison, trapped by the decisions she herself had made in the name of love.

She hadn't felt trapped until now. Just her signature—Mrs. Julian Chancellor—could buy her a fortune in clothes or gems in any boutique in Manhattan, or a gourmet meal drenched in Dom Perignon at Le Cirque or La Côte; and there had always been enough cash, far more than she had ever needed, in the desk drawer. Julian liked to carry cash, to bestow lavish tips or pay outright for extravagant meals when he felt like it. The amounts of money he routinely carried, hundreds or even thousands of dollars, would be quite substantial for most men, but they were virtually spare change for a billionaire.

Still, at first, Julian had resisted the idea of leaving money for Larisa. Her name—the name that proved she was his wife—was surely all she would ever need to get whatever she wanted. But what if I want to leave a cash tip? she had asked. Or what if I want to buy a warm pretzel smothered in mustard from a corner vendor? Or what if, she had whispered softly, I want to surprise you with new sexy lingerie? That's a surprise I want to share with you, Julian, not with your accountant!

Julian had acceded to Larisa's wish on this one small point. She was to help herself to the money in his desk, he told her. And over the years she had, to leave tips and buy pretzels and presents—and to pay for her birth-control pills.

Now Larisa needed the money from Julian's desk to help her escape from him.

But what if Julian had taken it all with him when he left last night? Well . . . she did have a contingency plan. She would pawn the flawless eight-carat diamond engagement ring she wore. The plan was workable, but terrifying. It would necessarily involve others in the scandal of their failed marriage and blue-blooded Julian Chancellor hated the taint of scandal almost as much as he hated losing things he wanted.

Larisa sighed a soft breath of relief as she opened the desk drawer and saw the neat stack of bills—twenties, fifties, hundreds. She took the entire stack, her slender fingers flipping through it as she returned to the bedroom to get her suitcase, and even more relief pulsed through her as she realized the amount: four thousand three hundred and fifty. She would be able to get very far away.

Before leaving the bedroom, Larisa removed the magnificent diamond engagement ring, a Chancellor family heirloom, as well as her gold and diamond wedding band. She put the rings and her set of keys on the antique bureau nearest Julian's dressing room. She had no intention of leaving a note. The rings, the keys, the still-open door to her closet would send an eloquent message that she had gone.

After moving the suitcase from the bedroom to the penthouse's marble foyer, Larisa placed a call to the building's bellman. Mrs. Julian Chancellor did not carry her own suitcase to the curb, not even when she was making her desperate escape. When the bellman arrived, he took the suitcase without question or comment. Like all the staff of the luxury apartment building, he was discreet, carefully trained never to initiate a personal conversation, not even a polite query about her destination. There was nothing unusual about her leaving alone for a trip, of course. She often answered Julian's impulsive summons to join him in Paris or London or Rome, and sometimes, when he was away, she would go by herself to the sanctuary of one of the world's most tranquil spas.

Nothing unusual, but still Larisa's heart quivered. What if Julian had left instructions to be notified immediately if his wife even tried to leave the building today?

Paranoia! she told herself, although the quivering didn't abate.

When they reached the street level, the bellman offered to call one of the fleet of limousines always available to the Chancellors.

"Oh, no, thank you," Larisa answered with an easy gracious smile as her blue eyes fell gratefully on an already waiting taxi. "A cab will be just fine."

"Air France, please," Larisa told the cab driver as they neared Kennedy. Later, if anyone wanted to know, the driver would recall that he had driven Mrs. Julian Chancellor to the Air France terminal, presumably to catch the Concorde to Paris.

With painful yet forcefully confident strides, Larisa carried her suitcase into the terminal, past the check-in counters and into a nearby restroom. Once there, she removed the golden pins that secured her famous topknot, freeing the silky mane of golden-red hair to tumble halfway down her back and softly veil her beautiful face. Next she unclasped the gold belt, transforming her outfit from sleek to baggy. Then she stood in front of the mirror and forced her image to come into focus. She no longer looked like stylish and elegant Larisa Chancellor. She looked like what she was, a weary traveler.

Far too weary, she realized, to carry out the next phase of her plan, to catch the shuttle bus to the United terminal and take the first available flight to anywhere. Far too weary . . . and so weak . . . and, despite the oppressive heat of the day, so terribly cold.

Her ever-weakening body urged her to lie down on the tile floor, here and now, and simply close her eyes and float off to her wonderful dreams. Larisa fought the almost overwhelming urge with terrifying images of what would happen if she succumbed to it. She would be found and rushed by ambulance to Memorial Hospital in Manhattan. Someone would call Julian, to gently notify him of the brutal assault on his beautiful wife that had apparently occurred at the airport, and after that there would be even more violence.

Fueled more by sheer fear than by any strength left in her fragile body, Larisa walked back outside and boarded the first motel courtesy van that appeared. During her years as a top fashion model, when her famous name and face were recognized around the world, Larisa had often traveled under assumed names, embellished by the appropriate foreign accents. Then it had been a game, amusing and without significant consequence if the charade failed, but it wasn't a game now. It was absolutely necessary that the motel clerk not identify her. Her soft French accent and halting English had to convince him that she was indeed Chantal Chandon, a possibly beautiful Frenchwoman hidden behind sunglasses and a shimmering red and gold curtain of hair who was probably meeting a lover for a clandestine affair. Whether the clerk was convinced or simply totally disinterested, Larisa didn't know; but, after paying him in full in cash for one night's lodging, she left to find her room with the wonderfully comforting impression that he would forget all about her the moment she was out of his sight.

Then she was in the room. First she threw the deadbolt lock that would protect her from intrusion from the outside world. Next she turned off the air-conditioning, because she was so cold, shivering now; and then, after exchanging the elegant teal silk for her beloved tattered nightgown, she curled in a tight ball beneath the covers of the bed. Soon, she told herself, very soon there would be warmth. Without air-conditioning, the small room would rapidly acquire and hold the humid heat of the steamy August day.

The warmth did come quickly, and as it enveloped her, Larisa allowed herself at last to drift to the memories of the wonderful dreams in which she was already safe and strong and far away. This is as far as I can get today, she reminded herself gently. And maybe this is already too far, she realized as she felt the dramatic effect of the sultry air on her body. The heat was making her even weaker—and so very dizzy even though she was lying down. Maybe she would die here, a warm, safe, peaceful death. Or maybe when she didn't leave the room as promised tomorrow, someone would break through the deadbolt lock and discover that her unconscious and battered body still had a little life, and she would be rushed to the care of a trauma surgeon.

The thought wasn't as terrifying now as it had been earlier, because now the trauma surgeon had a face: the lovely face of her best friend, her only true friend ever, the friend she had abandoned. A soft smile touched Larisa's lips as her mind filled with distant images of Elizabeth. There they were, Liz and Lara, walking around campus together, Elizabeth raving about the magnificence of the sky even if it was gray and scowling, or marveling at the delicate fragrance of the flowers they passed even though all that anyone else could detect were the city scents of pollution and fumes. That was Elizabeth, seeing the silver lining in the darkest of clouds, finding the perfume amid the heavy breath of diesel. Happy, joyous, optimistic— and quite oblivious to the grim realities. Larisa hadn't been oblivious, of course. Long before college she had known that most dark clouds didn't have silver linings, and that sometimes the most delicate of flowers died because there was no one who cared enough to rescue them.

Even at age eighteen Larisa hadn't been oblivious to the realities of clouds and flowers, nor had she been oblivious to the eyes that had followed the two of them on their journeys around Berkeley. The stares she herself had drawn had always been filled with unconcealed desire, lustful, possessive, wanting her extraordinary beauty and yet somehow contemptuous of it. And the stares Elizabeth had drawn? People of all ages and both sexes had simply smiled at her. She was everyone's long-lost sister or daughter, happily returning to them at last, a boundless source of warmth and comfort and joy.

How comforting it would be to be a patient in Elizabeth's gentle care. Larisa thought of herself in that role now, a trauma victim presenting herself to Elizabeth's emergency room. The intelligent emerald eyes would offer a warm greeting of welcome, and then the delicate but confident hands of the talented seamstress would gently examine the ravaged body that lay before her. And when Elizabeth had finished her gentle and careful exam, she would say with quiet yet reassuring candor, "I think you may have internal injuries, Lara. I'll need to operate to repair the damage."

35

"All right," Larisa would answer. "But, Liz, what about the other trauma, to my heart and my soul?"

"I'll help you with that trauma too, Lara. I promise I will."

As Larisa drifted off to sleep, or perhaps to death, she imagined a distant time when she would awaken again and call her best friend. Elizabeth should be in San Francisco now. At least, that had been her plan in the last unanswered letter Larisa had received three years ago. As soon as she completed her chief residency in trauma surgery in Dallas she would join the faculty of Pacific Heights Medical Center. There had been other news in that letter, personal not professional—a cardiologist who Elizabeth had been dating for several months. "It's possible," Elizabeth had written, "—and only *possible*, Lara!—that he will follow me to San Francisco."

Had Elizabeth's cardiologist followed her to the City by the Bay? Larisa wondered. Had Elizabeth truly fallen in love at last? Did those gentle and accomplished surgeon's hands now wear a gold wedding band? That was all Elizabeth would choose to wear, Larisa was certain of it. Elizabeth would wear a plain gold band, a simple yet compelling symbol of the deepest commitment and love—not the glittering jewels Larisa had worn, symbols of nothing, dazzling illusions that were decorative only . . . as she herself had always been.

Chapter Three

"Is little Molly all right?"

"How is Mary Ann?"

Variations of those two questions greeted Pacific Heights Medical Center's transplant team as they entered the hospital's largest conference room to meet with members of the news media shortly after the completion of the historic transplant surgery. The largest conference room was necessary. The Bay Area's news corps had assembled in full force to learn what had happened to the sunny infant Molly and her brave mother Mary Ann, both of whom had become well known and much beloved by the reading and viewing public in the weeks preceding the surgery.

The press conference had been partially scripted in advance. The center's director of public relations would make the opening remarks—a brief summary of the surgical technique, a reminder that this was the *first* such surgery to be performed in San Francisco, an overall introduction of the entire transplant team, and a few specific introductions as well. After the opening remarks and introductions, the director would turn the podium over to Nick to answer specific questions about the surgery.

The director realized at once that if he wanted to have the journalists' attention for what was essentially but importantly a public relations promo, he needed to give them the good news first. So he began, "Both Molly and Mary Ann are fine. In a moment I'll let Doctor Chase give you the details, but first I would like to draw your attention to the packet of information you each have received . . ."

Elizabeth listened vaguely to the director, so that she would be ready to smile on cue when he introduced her; but mostly, her heart still racing with exhilaration, she thought about the surgery. It had all gone so well. There had been virtually no words exchanged between herself and Nick—none had been necessary, of course, because he had explained the procedure with such clarity beforehand—so they had operated in silence . . . and it had been a perfectly choreographed dance of their talented hands, moving together in graceful harmony, without a falter, without a single false step . . .

"The surgery was performed by Doctors Elizabeth Jennings and Nicholas Chase. Doctor Jennings is an associate professor of surgery with training in trauma as well as transplantation surgery."

It was time for Elizabeth to smile. And somehow she did, even though her racing heart almost stopped. The director should have said, "The surgery was performed *by* Doctor Nicholas Chase *with assistance from* Doctor Elizabeth Jennings." True, Nick had permitted her to do far more of the intricate suturing than she had ever dared imagine he would. In fact, it was she who had placed almost all of the tiny critical stitches that bound Mary Ann's tissue to Molly's. Was it silent—and thrilling—

proof of Nick's confidence in her after all? she had wondered for a brief hopeful moment. No, she had reminded herself swiftly. Nick had simply been doing his job, fulfilling his teaching responsibilities to his junior faculty and making very certain that all members of his transplant team—be they chosen or inherited—knew the techniques perfectly, so that PHMC could become the major West Coast transplant center Nick wanted it to be.

Nick was the maestro, and she was his pupil, and just as she had been celebrating their magnificent dance, her mind spinning in pirouettes of pure joy, the memory of the breathtaking performance had been abruptly undermined—during its curtain call!—by this indisputable *faux pas*. She had been remembering the silent grace, marveling still at the wondrous harmony of their hands, thinking about operating with him again and again, and now . . .

Now the director had given the master and the novice equal billing.

Was Nick infuriated by the mistake? It seemed so careless, and so surprising. Surely Nick had read over the words the director would speak at the press conference. Had he just checked for technical accuracy, not imagining there would be such a breech in surgical protocol?

The bright lights of the television cameras moved quickly from her face to Nick's. He smiled as he was introduced, his sexy half smile, and it was absolutely impossible to tell from his calm dark blue eyes if he was angered, or perhaps even enraged, by the director's extraordinary blunder—just as it was absolutely impossible to detect anything but polite calm in the voice that addressed the press a few moments later.

"The surgery on both mother and daughter was uneventful," Nick began. "There were no intraoperative complications whatsoever."

"Now what, Doctor?"

"Now the vigil begins, especially for Molly. There are the usual postoperative concerns, notably bleeding, for both of them, but for Molly there are the immunologic and physiologic issues as well. She has been given immunosuppressive therapy to minimize the risk of rejection of the transplant, but the question remains: Will her immune system accept the transplanted tissue? And, if so, will the new liver become functional?"

The press conference lasted thirty minutes. The reporters wanted all the remarkable details about the surgery, and they also wanted as much footage as possible of the handsome surgeon—his long-lashed dark blue eyes, his tousled coal-black hair, the patch of bare chest that was now so tantalizingly revealed by the deep V in his royal blue surgical scrubs. They all knew that their viewers had fallen in love with the sexy surgeon who had been interviewed during the weeks preceding the historic surgery, the Dr. Nicholas Chase who wore a crisp white coat over a starched shirt and conservative tie. But now the cameras captured an even better, even more enticing image of him . . . a wild and alluring image that made the inevitable and compelling mental transition from operating room to bedroom almost effortless.

Following the press conference, Elizabeth and Nick made rounds on Mary Ann in the surgery ICU, and Molly in the pediatric ICU, and their patients on the wards, and then Mary Ann again, and then Molly. Mother and daughter were rock steady, vital signs normal and postop lab values all excellent.

"Well," Nick said when he and Elizabeth had finished rounds and were standing in the nurses' station in the pediatric ICU. "I think I'll go get changed."

Nick's words were not, Elizabeth knew, an invitation to walk with him down the three flights of stairs to the surgical dressing rooms. Nor, she knew, would she answer by boldly announcing that she would accompany him— even though it was an opportune time for her to change, too. Opportune, because everything was under control, but not essential, because she was on call tonight and could change at any time—and Nick was doubtless getting ready to leave.

Dr. Nicholas Chase wasn't officially on call tonight, but he would expect Elizabeth to page him immediately if even the slightest problem arose. Page, not telephone, because although Nick had given her his unlisted home phone number, he had told her that he would have his pager with him at all times. He preferred, apparently, to be summoned by the soft beep of a pager rather than the harsh ring of a telephone; and he preferred, apparently, to be able to return the page when he chose, rather than being forced to answer the ringing intrusion at an inconvenient moment. Nick always answered Elizabeth's pages promptly, even in the middle of the night; and she was quite happy that she had never needed to dial the phone number he had given her. The pager seemed less personal, less intimate, even if the only privacy she was invading was a sound sleep.

Now Nick was going to change, and she needed to change too, and with any other surgeon with whom she had accomplished so much, such a flawless surgery, such a wonderful outcome so far, Elizabeth would have simply announced that she would walk with him. And they would have talked, allowing their exhilaration to surface, just a little, sharing the triumph and quietly confessing to the feelings of immense relief and gratitude they both felt. But if she accompanied Nick now, Elizabeth knew there would be only silence. Polite silence, yes, and perhaps an awkward smile or two, but silence nonetheless. Nick would be silent as always, and she would be too, because as effortlessly as she found words for the rest of the world, it seemed quite impossible for her to ever find precisely the right ones to speak to him.

"I think I'll go to the ward," she murmured finally, realizing as she spoke that once again she had not found the right words. She had no reason to go to the ward. She and Nick had just finished rounding there, and both knew perfectly well that all their patients were quite stable and that there were no worrisome loose ends whatsoever.

"Okay," he replied, his polite dark blue eyes solemn and not questioning. "I'll see you later."

Halfway across the ICU, Nick's long graceful strides came to an abrupt halt, his path purposefully, teasingly blocked by Sara, the beautiful British pediatric anesthesiologist who had done the anesthesia for Molly. Elizabeth didn't hear their words, but she saw that there was animated conversation, not awkward silence, an effortless flow embellished by provocative smiles and flirtatious eyes. And when they parted, Nick to change, and Sara to do the final postanesthesia check on Molly, the smiles lingered, perhaps in anticipation of a midnight rendezvous to celebrate.

Once Nick finally disappeared beyond the double doors that separated the ICU from the rest of the hospital,

Elizabeth began her walk toward the same doors. Where are you going? she asked herself. You don't really need to go to the ward, remember? That was just a flimsy excuse. Everything is under control now, a momentary calm in the center of what may be a nighttime of never-ending storms. You really should be walking to the dressing rooms with Nick, thinking of intelligent and insightful things to say to him—and saying them.

Elizabeth felt a little lost. There were rarely moments in the hospital when she had nothing to do. Surely there was something, just a ten-minute task until Nick was safely in the men's dressing room and she could sneak into the women's. As her mind searched, she was suddenly rescued by the soft insistent ring of her beeper. The calm was over. She was needed. Good.

"An outside call, Doctor Jennings," the page operator told her when she answered her page. Then, addressing the caller, the operator said, "I have Doctor Jennings on the line now. Go ahead, please."

"Elizabeth? I didn't realize they'd actually get you . . . I only asked if you were on the staff . . . I was just going to leave a message if they said yes." The words had come in a rush, and now Larisa stopped, breathless and whirling as flames of fire blazed inside her.

"Larisa?" Elizabeth spoke with soft, hopeful surprise to the faraway voice. The voice was a mere shadow of the once so vibrant one, and Elizabeth was swept with worry at its frailty; but she forced the worry from her own voice, filling it with warmth and welcome, and repeated, "Larisa? Is that you?"

"Yes." Larisa was curled beneath the covers in the motel room, very cold still despite the ambient heat and her own fiery pain. But at the gentle welcome in Elizabeth's voice a wave of true warmth washed through her. She clutched the receiver, the lifeline to that wonderful and hopeful warmth, even tighter in her pale white hands. "It's me. A voice from the past. Hi."

"Hi. This is so amazing. I was thinking about you today." Thinking about you, worrying about you, hoping that my worries were without substance. "Talk to me."

"You can talk now? You don't have any trauma cases at the moment?" Except for me? Except for the friend who has been such a terrible friend, but who, because you are so generous, you seem to have instantly forgiven.

"No, well, as a matter of fact, tonight I'm on call for the transplant service."

"I thought you'd trained in trauma."

"I did, and I take trauma call too." Elizabeth laughed softly. "Long story."

"But as always you're doing twice as much as even the most supernormal human being could do," Larisa said, her frail voice gaining strength as it filled with fondness and pride for her remarkable friend. "I haven't forgotten your double major in biology and chemistry in college. Your reason then, as I recall, was that both were so interesting and challenging that you simply couldn't choose one over the other."

"It's the same with trauma and transplant," Elizabeth admitted. After a moment she added with quiet reverence, "Today, Lara, I got to assist with a living donor liver transplant. We transplanted tissue from a mother about our age to her eight-month-old daughter."

"Oh, Liz," Larisa replied with matching wonder. "And . . . ?"

"And so far they both are fine. It's really an extraordinary surgery. However, don't let me get going on the miracles of transplantation surgery or we'll never talk about you."

I don't care if we never talk about me, Larisa thought as she clutched the receiver even tighter and curled more deeply into the so very comforting faraway warmth. "I want to hear all about the miracles of transplantation—and all about you."

"Then before we sign off tonight we'll arrange a time for one of our famous all-night talks, but for now that's me in a nutshell. Trauma and transplant, and still quite unmarried."

"The cardiologist from Dallas?"

"That lingered, long distance, for almost two years. About eight months ago, we decided it just wasn't meant to be." Eight months ago . . . when Nicholas Chase arrived. Clamping down firmly on the frisky thought, Elizabeth added breezily, "So, I'm not involved with anyone now, completely devoted to my career."

"And your family?" Larisa prompted, knowing that soon, too soon, the conversation would shift to her . . . and wanting to linger as long as possible in the happy, accomplished, and so wonderfully *non*sordid life of her best friend. "Your parents and Mark?"

"They're all fine. My parents are finally taking the sabbatical they've been talking about for years. They left last week for London and will be there until next June. And Mark's with a very good law firm here in the city. He's fine, and Wendy's fine, and their girls are wonderful, nine and eleven already, happy and healthy. So, that's it. Everybody's fine," Elizabeth said with finality. Then, continuing gently, she urged, "Now, tell me about you, Lara. Something's happened, hasn't it?"

"Yes," she admitted softly as a war raged inside her. It

was a battle of warmth and ice—the safe wonderful warmth of her best friend . . . and the terrifyingly dangerous icy memories of the man she had married. Speaking bravely to the warmth, she confessed, "I left Julian today, Liz. He's probably realizing just about now that I'm gone."

"And you're not going back," Elizabeth said with quiet calm, a statement, not a question. You're not going back to the man who claimed to have loved you but who somehow caused your wonderful vibrant spirit to fade away.

"No," Larisa agreed, her voice not nearly as confident as her friend's. She had come this far in her impossible dream of escape, but the invisible chains were there still, reminding her that she was owned, not by herself but by another, and reminding her, too, that even though they had slackened briefly, permitting her to indulge in this fantasy of escape, soon they would constrict again, more tightly than ever, a suffocating punishment for her courageous folly. *No. I own myself! Yes, I did betray myself once. I gave Julian everything he wanted of me, even parts of myself that I should have known to protect and cherish. But I will never betray myself again. Please let me have a chance to prove that!*

"Lara?"

"No," she repeated quietly. "I'm not ever going back to Julian."

"Good. So, where are you now?"

"In a motel at JFK."

"Planning to take the first flight in the morning to San Francisco, I hope."

"Oh, I—"

"Actually, if you get a flight that is due in tomorrow night, like about eight, barring an emergency I should be able to meet you. I have a very spacious apartment, including a large second bedroom that is completely unused. Admittedly, it's not decorated, but it does have a perfectly good bed, and even a dresser and a chair, and it's yours for as long as you want it."

"Oh," Larisa whispered. "That sounds so good to me."

"It sounds good to me, too. So *come.*"

"Okay," Larisa said to her friend. And then, speaking also to the invisible chains and icy memories, she added bravely, "I will."

"Terrific. If you want to take an earlier flight, to get out of New York as soon as possible, the apartment has a doorman on duty at all times so I can easily arrange to have him let you in."

"No," Larisa answered swiftly, wondering if even by tomorrow afternoon she would be strong enough for a six-hour flight. I will be strong enough by then, she promised herself. I will be. "Arriving about eight tomorrow night will be fine—perfect."

"Okay, well, let's see. Call me back when you know the flight information. If I'm tied up, you can leave a message with the page operator. And, in case we don't talk again, and on the off chance that I'm not at the gate when you arrive, just call here from the airport. The page operator will know why I'm delayed and she'll have all the details of a contingency plan. Okay?"

"Yes, okay. And Liz? Thank you."

"Of course!"

"Oh, and I don't think he will, I imagine he thinks

47

you're still in Dallas"—*unless he read the letters you wrote me*—"but if Julian calls—"

"Don't worry. I'll tell him I haven't heard from you for over three years."

Chapter Four

By five-thirty Friday afternoon, Elizabeth was finishing her last progress note of the day. Molly and Mary Ann both continued to be remarkably stable, as did the patients on the ward. Elizabeth knew how well they were all doing because she had spent most of last night and today watching them, checking on them over and over again, troubleshooting small problems so that they would never grow into large ones.

As an attending physician, Elizabeth was expected to take call from home, not at the hospital. There were residents, fellows, and a Code Blue team in the hospital at all times, after all, not to mention the fact that she could get to the center's ICUs and ER as quickly from her own apartment as she could from some parts of the gigantic medical complex. But still, unless there was a compelling reason for her to be at home, Elizabeth usually spent most of her on-call nights at the hospital, as she had last night, just in case.

She had returned to her apartment at dawn to shower and change, and to give the apartment a quick once-over-lightly in case she didn't have a chance to later in the day. But now it was only five-thirty, and Larisa wasn't arriving

49

until eight-fifteen, so she had plenty of time to buy flowers, and run the vacuum she hadn't run at daybreak, and give everything a final dust and polish.

Lots of flowers, she decided, smiling softly as she closed the metal cover of the chart, the last progress note of the day now complete.

"Elizabeth?"

Her soft smile vanished at the sound of his voice, and her entire body went on alert, as it always did when she was with him, muscles tense, stomach churning, heart racing. She was sitting on a stool in the nurses' station, and he was standing, towering above her. With any other man, Elizabeth would have remained seated and simply looked up to greet him, her emerald eyes sparkling with warmth and welcome. And, she well knew, with any other woman, Nick would have casually leaned toward her, a dark blue greeting of pure seduction.

But he wasn't any man, so Elizabeth stood at attention.

And she wasn't any woman, so Nick backed away a little as she stood, creating more space, more distance, between them.

"Yes, Nick?"

"Something . . . important . . . has come up, Elizabeth," he began haltingly. "I wondered if it would be possible for you to take call for me tonight?"

Was he trying to charm her at long last, filling the sensuous dark blue with sheepish apology at his surprising last-minute imposition? Elizabeth saw apology in Nick's eyes, but not a flicker of charm. In fact, what she saw, what she believed she saw, was almost heart-stopping worry—and fear. Another optical illusion surely, but still she answered softly, "Oh, sure, of course I can."

"It's more than just covering transplant, Elizabeth. I'm on second call tonight for trauma as well. If it's not convenient, I can see if Bill or Ed can cover."

"No, it's fine, Nick, really."

"Thank you," he said quietly, the immense relief obvious in his troubled eyes. "I really appreciate this, Elizabeth. You're scheduled to be on on Sunday, aren't you? Why don't I take call for you then?"

"That's not really a fair trade for you, Nick. I'm on first call for trauma on Sunday and it's a weekend."

"I consider it more than fair. Okay?"

"Okay," she said, agreeing only because she sensed his sudden restlessness. He was obviously very eager to leave, but he wanted to settle the trade with her first. "That's fine, Nick. I'll notify paging of the changes."

"All right." His eyes met hers and for a moment the restlessness vanished and there was pure gratitude; and there was something else in the intense dark blue depths, a deep and powerful current that she couldn't identify but which made her tremble . . . and which somehow touched his voice with exquisite softness as he said, "Thank you, Elizabeth."

"You're welcome, Nick."

Elizabeth remained standing at attention as she watched Nick disappear along the linoleum corridor, his long strides taking him swiftly toward whatever, *whoever*, was so important that he had made the surprising request. Had Nicholas Chase finally found a lover for whom he truly cared? A beautiful woman who was so important to him that when she requested an entire evening with him, a romantic candlelight dinner in prelude to their late-night hours of breathless passion, Nick had instantly complied? Yes, apparently he had found such a woman,

Elizabeth decided. And, she thought, whoever she was, Nick obviously cared about her very deeply.

After Nick had vanished from her sight, Elizabeth sighed softly and settled once again onto the stool. She needed to notify paging of the changes in the on-call schedule—and also to tell the page operator that she was expecting a call from Larisa later on. Elizabeth might be scrubbed in the OR when Larisa's plane landed, or she might be at the apartment arranging flowers, but one thing was certain: she wouldn't be at the gate to greet her friend when she arrived. Second call for trauma meant that she had to be within minutes of the hospital at all times.

You really are a bastard, Nicholas Chase. The thought came with a rush of anger but without a flicker of surprise. Dr. Stephen Sheridan was quite confident of his assessment of his colleague. The trouble was that Elizabeth didn't share the sentiment. Which was why, when Stephen walked into the nurses' station just in time to overhear the exchange between Elizabeth and Nick, he hadn't intervened. And which was why now, even though Nick had gone and Elizabeth was making a phone call, Stephen still hadn't approached her.

He needed to be a little more calm. He needed to remember the necessary truce that he and Elizabeth had declared on the subject of Nick.

The truce was necessary to preserve the friendship that was so important to both of them, a friendship that had begun years before, when Elizabeth had been a fourth-year medical student and Stephen had been her attending physician on the oncology service. He had heard about her even before meeting her, the star student who was nice in addition to being brilliant; and Elizabeth had heard, too, in advance about him, the stunningly handsome heir to the Sheridan publishing fortune who had chosen to dedicate his life to the mysteries and challenges of medicine instead of to the luxuries and pleasures to which his vast wealth had given him carte blanche from the moment of his birth. Stephen had known before he ever met Elizabeth Jennings that the faculty considered her the most promising student they had seen in years; and Elizabeth had known before she ever met Stephen Sheridan that everyone believed that eventually he would conquer the obstacles that remained in the quest for the cure for cancer.

Stephen and Elizabeth had met during attending rounds; and later that night, while she had been roaming the oncology ward, keeping vigil over her—their—patients, just in case, she had run into him, having left his nearby laboratory to do the same thing. And they had talked, as colleagues, not as student and teacher, sharing their passion for science, musing together about the mysteries yet to be unraveled and the problems yet to be solved.

They had talked often during that month, late at night; and a few months later Elizabeth left for her surgical residency in Dallas; and she and Stephen didn't see each other again until she returned to PHMC five years later. Then they simply picked up where they had left off, running into each other on the wards late at night and talking for hours about the exciting challenges of their chosen careers. It was Stephen who had been most encouraging in her decision to pursue the specialty training in transplantation surgery. Dual specialties were often complementary, he had offered, citing his own dual training in immunology and oncology. And besides, he had added, since he was one of the two immunologists who managed the immunosuppressive therapy for the transplant recipients, if she became a transplant surgeon, they would be caring for patients together again.

At some point, the late-night conversations between Dr. Elizabeth Jennings and Dr. Stephen Sheridan shifted from professional to personal—a transition that was so seamless and so welcome that they both simply acknowledged it with gentle smiles. And now Elizabeth and Stephen were respected colleagues; and they worked together to care for such precious young lives as that of Molly, for whom Elizabeth had expertly placed the precise stitches and for whom Stephen had with matching precision and expertise selected doses of immunosuppression carefully balanced to help without causing harm; and they were very good friends.

Stephen felt protective of her, and he very much wanted to shield Elizabeth from the hurt and uncertainty caused by Nicholas Chase, but it was impossible. Every time he even casually alluded to one of Nick's flaws, not the least of which was the way Nick treated *her*, Elizabeth bristled and leapt immediately to Nick's defense. So they had declared a necessary truce on the topic of the blue-eyed surgeon.

But no white flags were unfurled inside Stephen now as he watched Elizabeth make the call to the page operator. No white flags, just pure anger. Nick was taking advantage of her kindness! True, although Stephen himself knew that Larisa was arriving this evening—Elizabeth had told him when she stopped by his research lab at midnight last night—Nick undoubtedly didn't. Nor did Nick know how worried Elizabeth was about her friend, how fragile she had thought Larisa sounded, how eager she was to be at the airport to greet her.

Now Nick had undermined that plan. Not on purpose, admittedly, but Nick's arrogant selfishness angered Stephen nonetheless. Nick had known Elizabeth would agree to cover for him, because even a man as self-absorbed as Nicholas Chase had surely noticed how much lovely Elizabeth Jennings cared about him. Nick noticed it, and cruelly dismissed it, until he needed her help, as he apparently did tonight . . . then he simply used Elizabeth's caring about him to his own advantage.

Such a bastard, Stephen thought, not feeling any more calm at all, but crossing to Elizabeth nonetheless because her phone call was completed.

"Hello there."

For the second time in just a few minutes, Elizabeth recognized the familiar male voice coming from overhead. But this time, the voice triggered welcome, not heart-racing wariness, and this time she simply swiveled on the stool and smiled as she looked up into the long-lashed dark brown eyes of her very handsome friend. Stephen was the hospital's *other* tall, dark, and sexy thirty-eight-year-old bachelor. Both men sent powerfully compelling messages of intelligence and sensuality; but if Nicholas Chase was a blue-eyed panther, restless and wild, untamed and untamable, Stephen Sheridan was an elegant thoroughbred, sleek and stylish and with the most impeccable of bloodlines.

"Hello there," Elizabeth echoed softly. Then, tilting her head inquisitively, she added, "You look worried."

"I was thinking about the administration of LKC I'm giving tonight."

LKC was Stephen's creation, an innovative immuno therapy that combined interleukin-2 with activated kille cells, not a cure yet, not *the* cure, but the most majo advance to date in the war against cancer. Infusions o LKC were always anticipated with a mixture of solemnit and hope. Lethal anaphylaxis could occur at any tim during the infusion, but even the fear of that catastrophi complication was offset by the therapy's extraordinar potential benefit. For some reason Stephen seemed un usually worried about the dose of LKC he would adminis ter this evening.

"Is there something particularly problematic about thi evening's infusion, Stephen?"

"Not the infusion, just the timing. We're scheduled t begin at seven, and it will take about three and a ha hours, during which time I can't leave the patient's bed side."

Elizabeth looked at her friend with surprise. She knew all this. "And?"

"And Larisa's plane is due at eight-fifteen."

"And you overheard my conversation with Nick an know that I can't meet her so you're trying to figure how you can." Elizabeth's emerald eyes sparkled as she aske the dark brown ones, "Did anyone ever tell you tha you're an awfully nice man?"

"You're the one who's nice—far too nice." Stephen added quietly, "You could have told him no, you know.'

"Well." Elizabeth shrugged softly. "It seemed very im portant, whatever it was."

"So was meeting Larisa at the airport. You told me sh sounded very fragile."

"Yes, she did, and I had hoped to have been able to be at the airport to meet her. But we have a contingency plan. She can take a cab to the apartment and maybe it will be so quiet tonight that I'll be there when she arrives. You can't reschedule the infusion, Stephen," Elizabeth added quietly, even though "won't" would have been a more correct word than "can't." Stephen could reschedule, but Elizabeth knew that he wouldn't; and neither she nor Larisa would have wanted him to. It would be too unfair, too emotionally difficult for the patient for whom Stephen's wonder therapy could mean either a dramatic prolongation of life—or a dramatic death despite the fact that Stephen would be at his bedside, ready to leap into action, and the Code Blue team would be nearby and on alert.

"I would if I could."

"I know you would, Stephen. Thank you."

"For the record, in the interest of at least noting events as they happen, you have to admit that it was an incredible imposition for Nick to have asked you to cover for him at the last minute."

"He probably guessed I wouldn't have any major conflicts, even though it's a Friday night," Elizabeth said thoughtfully. Then, as she saw sudden anger on Stephen's handsome face in response to her honest—and not the least bit self-deprecating—observation, her emerald eyes danced merrily and she added lightly, "Stephen! It's true, after all. If Larisa hadn't called out of the blue, I wouldn't have had any conflicts tonight."

"Well, again for the record—are you paying attention, Elizabeth?—Nick did not ask you to cover because it's Friday night and he figured that you would be available."

"Oh, no?"

"No. Whatever else the man is, and we won't get into that at the moment, Nicholas Chase is *not* an idiot. He knows very well that you're the best surgeon in San Francisco—and parts east."

Elizabeth's beautiful emerald eyes filled with gentle fondness for her very good friend as she laughed softly and said, "Dream on, Doctor!"

Chapter Five

"Nick," Margaret whispered with obvious relief when Nick appeared in the kitchen of his—their—Pacific Heights home. A warm smile briefly brightened Margaret's youthful seventy-four-year-old face, but it lapsed quickly back to the expression of worry that matched the worry Nick had heard in her voice when she had called to urge him to come home, soon, if he possibly could. "I'm so glad you were able to get away."

Margaret Reilly was not an alarmist. Although she had been unable ever to have children of her own, as much as she had wanted them, Margaret knew children, especially sick ones, very well. For fifty years of her life, she had been a pediatric nurse. During her long career, she had worked in all possible settings—well-baby clinic, and inpatient ward, and emergency room, and intensive care—and she had seen children of all ages and in all extremes of sickness and health. And tonight Margaret saw in the glassy blue eyes of the precious little boy who was in her charge something that truly terrified her.

It was as if Justin had given up hope.

"How is he?" Nick asked. His own eyes, the same dark blue as the young glassy ones, were filled, too, with terror.

"He's the same as when I called you, Nick. I was just about to try some more ginger ale. I haven't been able to get him to drink anything and his temp is still very high. I haven't given him aspirin of course, because even though it seems like the same summer virus that the other neighborhood children have . . ." Margaret didn't finish the worry. She didn't need to utter aloud the concern that Justin might have a chicken pox prodrome, in which case aspirin could be dangerous, perhaps even lethal. She and Nick both knew all too well about Reye Syndrome and all the other diseases that could come without warning and steal beloved children from their families. Margaret looked at Nick's worried blue eyes and felt his restlessness. He wanted to hear her experienced assessment, but mostly he wanted to dash upstairs to the bedroom that was closest to his own. "Go ahead, Nick. I'll get the ginger ale and join you."

Justin was a small motionless mound beneath the patch-work quilt that had been lovingly made for him by Margaret. *So still.* That was what Margaret had said when she had called, "He's so quiet, Nick, and so still." As Nick neared his son's bed, he saw a second small motionless mound beneath the quilt: Mr. Bear. Once that fluffy friend had been as big as Justin, bigger even, but as Justin had grown—healthy and happy and oh so quickly!—Mr. Bear had become smaller. But he was still very much loved by the little boy, and he was cradled now, clutched tightly, in Justin's small arms.

Nick knelt beside the bed and gazed for a moment at the flushed face of his four-year-old son. Justin's eyes were closed, but he wasn't asleep, only very still. Gently, so

60

gently, Nick touched a cool loving hand to his son's hot forehead and whispered softly, "Jussie?"

The dark blue eyes that Justin had inherited from his father fluttered open, unfocused at first and disbelieving. And then, as he focused on the eyes that gazed at him with such love, his small arms released their clutch of Mr. Bear and extended with an eagerness that was almost desperation to Nick.

"Daddy!"

Nick curled Justin's small hot body close to his own and gently kissed the fever-dampened silky golden hair as he asked tenderly, "How's my little boy? Are you sick?"

Justin nodded against Nick's caressing lips and curled even closer to his father. Nick closed his eyes briefly, an emotional moment of silent gratitude and relief. He would examine his son very carefully, but the young blue eyes were alive now, and when Nick finally opened his own eyes and saw a relieved and smiling Margaret, he knew it was as she had said, just an innocuous summer virus.

But there was more, what Margaret hadn't said but what they both knew: it was just an innocuous summer virus, but it was complicated by ancient fears for which Nick would never forgive himself.

"I love you, Jussie," Nick whispered gently. "I missed you. Did it seem like I'd been away for a long time? Yes? Well, I kissed you goodbye this morning, but you were still asleep, so you don't remember."

"He just needed his daddy," Margaret said softly. Justin loved her and trusted her, but tonight, because he was sick, he had needed the most important person in his life—his father.

"I guess so," Nick agreed quietly, astonished that he

could mean so much to anyone, least of all this precious little boy.

"Can you stay long, Nick?" Margaret asked before withdrawing to give Nick and Justin privacy.

"I can stay all night. Elizabeth agreed to take call for me."

The mysterious Elizabeth, Margaret mused thoughtfully, with a motherly mixture of fondness and curiosity. There was always such softness in Nick's voice when he spoke of her. And, a month ago, when Margaret had finally decided to simply ask him quite bluntly what Elizabeth was like, Nick had replied quietly and without hesitation, "She's remarkable." Margaret had been very tempted to drop by the hospital to meet the remarkable Elizabeth, or even to suggest that Nick invite her to dinner sometime. But she did neither, because she knew how determined Nick was to keep the important truth of his personal life—the existence of his beloved son—completely separate and private from his work. Margaret had hoped to at least catch a glimpse of Elizabeth Jennings on the television coverage of yesterday's press conference. But on every channel, the producers had all made the same editorial decision: to show as much footage as possible of the tousled black hair and seductive dark blue eyes of Nicholas Chase.

So Margaret was left simply to wonder about the woman surgeon with whom Nick spent so much of his life and about whom he spoke so often—probably far more often than he realized—and always with such softness.

"That was very nice of her," Margaret said finally.

"Yes it was," Nick agreed quietly. "If something comes up with Molly or Mary Ann, she'll page me of course, but I don't expect either of them to have problems. Which

62

means that I don't have to go anywhere. I can stay right here all night long."

Right here was exactly where Nick planned to stay, all night long, holding Justin, reassuring his little boy that he was loved, so very loved, and that he would never be abandoned again.

Justin wouldn't remember the first six months of his life, not consciously, and sometimes, because Justin seemed so happy and well adjusted, Nick allowed himself the luxury of believing that the wounds of those first six months were magically healed, without any scars whatsoever. But Justin's stillness tonight, his bewildered fear, proved that there were scars still in his small heart, a deep terrifying memory of the time in his young life when he had not been loved . . .

"You—we—are going to have a baby." Glenna's eyes flashed triumphantly as she made the shattering announcement. "So, Doctor Nicholas Chase, now try telling me that our relationship is over."

"Why?" Nick asked with quiet horror. "Why would you do this to yourself, to us, and most of all to an innocent child? Tell me why, Glenna. Please."

"Don't you think we'll make a nice happy family, Nick?"

"We aren't happy together now, Glenna," Nick reminded her solemnly. "We never will be."

"Oh, Nicky," Glenna purred. "We fight. We say cruel and hurtful things to each other. But maybe this mock hatred is really just denial of how much we love each other."

"We don't love each other, Glenna."

Nick knew about himself that he was incapable of love,

63

and the many women with whom he had been involved had always seemed to know that, too. They were drawn to him by his looks, his wildness, his dangerous yet compelling sensuality, but a deep instinct inevitably warned them to play only—and never to care—and certainly never to expect nor want more from him than the talented caresses of his eyes, his lips, his hands, and his body. Women seemed to know neither to want nor expect Nick's heart. They seemed to sense, quite correctly, that it wasn't worth having.

Until Glenna, all the women in Nick's life had been smart enough to stay emotionally very far away. Glenna should have known to stay far away, because Nick's relationship with her had been even more cold and uncaring than most. But instead, she had obviously quite intentionally chosen to create a permanent bond between them. Some deep flaw in her, perhaps as deep and self-destructive as his own flaws, had compelled her to this terribly selfish act.

What was it that she wanted? Nick wondered. Not love, obviously. Money and prestige, perhaps? The luxuries that would be hers as the wife of a rich and famous surgeon? Yes, he thought. That was probably it. But at what cost to herself, to all of them?

"I know for a fact that I have no business being a parent, Glenna." With quiet sadness for the innocent new life that was growing inside her, Nick added, "And I'm not sure that you do."

"Thank you for your confidence," Glenna bristled. Then, raising her beautiful chin, she announced defiantly, "I am having this baby, Nick."

"I'm not asking you not to. I'm just telling you that I don't think that it is in anyone's best interest—not yours, not mine, and certainly not the baby's—for me to be part of its life."

"Maybe not. But, Nick, you owe it to your unborn baby to at least try."

Nick and Glenna weren't in love, and didn't really even like each other, and yet they married. The marriage lasted just long enough for Justin to be born to parents who were legally married and to be given Nick's last name. According to the courts, the marriage of Nicholas and Glenna Chase lasted five months. But, in fact, they only lived together for the first two, after which time Glenna angrily accepted defeat.

"You didn't want it to work, you bastard!"

"I couldn't make it work, Glenna, and neither could you."

"And what about the baby?" Glenna asked. Then, answering her own question, her voice filled with icy warning, "I want it to have all the privileges that are its due as the child of a wealthy and successful surgeon."

"All right," Nick agreed softly, as his mind cried silently, but what about love? If he gave Glenna all the money she wanted, would she love the innocent life she carried?

She claimed that she desperately wanted the baby, and claimed, too, that she already loved it deeply. Nick prayed that that was true. He knew, without a flicker of doubt, that even given Glenna's selfishness, the baby would be far better off with her than with him. He had no illusions whatsoever about his own ability—inability—to love. It would be best for his unborn child if the only role he ever played in its life would be to provide money. And that was what was agreed. Glenna would have custody, and she and the baby would receive the lion's share of Nick's earnings until the child was an adult. The divorce settlement was agreed upon before the baby's birth and would be signed and filed promptly thereafter.

Assuming, Nick decided privately, that the baby is even mine.

Justin Chase was born in the Chicago hospital where Nick was a surgeon and where until their marriage Glenna had been a nurse. Glenna had quit working the day they married, but she had kept in close touch with her friends at the hospital, bitterly revealing to them in sordid detail the disintegration of her relationship with Nick. By the time Justin was born, anyone on the staff who cared to listen had heard all about Nick's crimes, his broken promises, his cruel indifference to Glenna, his cavalier disregard for his unborn child. The assault was one-sided—Nick endured the unconcealed glowers and offered no defense—but even with rebuttal Glenna's version would have been believed without question. Nick had a long history of stormy romances. Glenna, it seemed, was simply his latest victim. Glenna *and* the unborn baby.

Only Margaret Reilly staunchly defended Nick. Then the head nurse in the hospital's pediatric ICU, Margaret had known Nick since shortly after his arrival at the hospital as a surgery intern over ten years before. It was her husband Edward, a gifted pediatric surgeon, who had actually met Nick first—and who had immediately recognized in the taciturn young intern a surgical gift similar to his own.

Edward and Margaret Reilly had spent the first half of their forty-five-year marriage hoping for a family. But the small lives on which Edward operated and for whom

Margaret so lovingly cared were the only children they were ever to have. Then Nick arrived, and without knowing it, and certainly without willing it, he tugged at their generous and loving heartstrings. He was so bright, so sensitive, so talented—and yet so troubled, so self-destructive, so obviously without any respect for himself whatsoever. Edward and Margaret each spent long emotional hours working side by side with Nick, Edward in the OR, Margaret in the ICU, and both would have quite happily welcomed him as a son. But he was withdrawn, and the Reillys themselves were both quiet and unassuming, and it wasn't until tragedy struck that it became apparent that they had reached him after all.

On that snowy November night, during evening postop rounds, Dr. Edward Reilly suffered a fatal heart attack. It was Nick who caught him as he collapsed, and Nick who held him so gently, comforting him as a loving son would comfort his beloved father. And it was because of Nick that in the moments before he lost consciousness, Edward felt great happiness and peace.

The Code Blue team arrived swiftly, and everything was done correctly, but it was not possible to save Edward's life. Nick held his lifeless body again, after he died, and then, because she needed to be told in person by someone who cared deeply about both of them, Nick drove through the snowstorm to the Reilly home in Winnetka to tell Margaret. He held her as she cried, and even though she never saw them, there were tears in Nick's eyes, too.

In the five years between Edward's death and the birth of Nick's son, the relationship between Margaret and Nick appeared unchanged from what it had always been. They were colleagues, working together to save small lives, nothing more. But there was more, a deep silent bond, a caring that compelled Margaret to staunchly defend Nick against his many critics and to go to him to tell him personally when Justin was born.

Margaret found him in his office.

"A healthy little boy, Nick," she said gently.

"I'm glad he's healthy, Margaret." *I hope he will be happy.*

"Are you going to see him?"

"No."

"Nick . . ."

"There's really no point. It would serve no purpose whatsoever." Nick's solemn dark blue eyes were resolute and unyielding. They had to be, because he could tell that Margaret was about to tell him what she thought: that he should see his son, that he should be a father to him, that he would be a *good* father.

Their eyes met for a long silent moment, and it was only when Margaret saw fear in the dark blue that she finally relented.

"Okay, Nick," she said quietly.

"Thank you," he answered with matching quiet. Then he asked, "Will you do something for me, Margaret? Will you get some of his blood for tissue typing?"

"Do you think he might not be yours?"

"I just want to be sure."

"All right," Margaret agreed. She knew Glenna, and she knew that with Glenna anything was possible. She found herself hoping that the newborn infant wasn't Nick's after all, hoping that he could be spared the guilt that she knew would torment him always.

"Maybe you could just arrange to have them take a little extra when they're getting the routine bloodwork . . ."

"You don't want to have him stuck unnecessarily."

"I have no wish to hurt that little boy, Margaret." Nick

held up his hands to stop the words he knew he would hear, the gentle plea for him to be the father he knew so well he could not be.

"I know that you don't, Nick."

Nick had a sample of Justin's blood and one of his own run in the highly specialized immunology lab that provided detailed tissue typing data for the transplantation program. The match was astonishing, a genetic similarity that was a transplant surgeon's dream. If ever his son needed a blood transfusion, or a new kidney, or a bone marrow transplantation . . .

Nick made certain that his attorney communicated that important bit of information to Glenna's attorney. Some day, perhaps, there might be a time when Justin would benefit from his genetic similarity to his father. It was a remote possibility, and obviously one that, for Justin's sake, Nick hoped would never come to pass, but it was the only silver lining he could find in the astonishing match. Mostly, the remarkable genetic similarity made him very sad. He would not wish his own genetic makeup on anyone, especially not an innocent child. Even though he was protecting his son by staying far away from him, had he unwittingly given him a genetic inheritance that would destine Justin to live with the same demons that had plagued Nick for his entire life?

No, Nick told himself. Surely environment played a role. Glenna didn't drink, had no drug dependencies whatsoever, and she would have all the wealth and luxury that were so clearly important to her. She didn't need to work, which meant she could be at home with Justin, loving him, making him feel safe and wanted, giving him a boyhood so different from the loveless and so very silent childhood Nick himself had lived. The silence of Nick's childhood had had many facets, sometimes brooding, sometimes demanding, sometimes filled with such anger that it would finally explode in a vicious burst of condemnation. The silence had been multifaceted, but never once, not in all the years Nick had lived with his perfectionistic alcoholic father, had the silence been peaceful.

Nick had made brave solemn promises to himself that he would not become his father, nor would he make the mistakes his father had made. But Nick was very much like the father he loathed, and now he had repeated the greatest and most grievous mistake his father had ever made: he had had a son.

But Justin's life would be different.

It already was different.

Because Justin would never know the dark moods, nor the screaming nightmares, nor the relentless perfectionism of his own alcoholic father.

Love him, Glenna, Nick pleaded with silent desperation as he stared at the lab data that proved without a doubt that Justin was his. Make him feel safe and happy and loved. And please, *please,* don't ever doom him to the terrifying monsters that lurk in the many sounds of silence.

"I need to see you." Glenna didn't bother to identify herself. She knew Nick would recognize her voice; and he did, even though it had been over six months ago, shortly before Justin's birth, since he had last heard it. He had sent the large monthly checks to her without fail, in fact usually ahead of schedule, but still her voice sounded ominous, filled with censure and warning.

"All right," he agreed quietly. "I should be through

70

here by seven this evening and have the weekend off. Tell me when and where."

"Your apartment at eight tonight."

Nick reached his Lake Shore Drive apartment thirty minutes before Glenna was due to arrive. It gave him enough time to shower and change—for himself not for her—and as well to pour the first glass of what would be a weekend of Scotch. Since he wasn't on call, he would spend the entire time drinking, in silent solitude, stopping early enough Sunday evening that his brilliant mind and talented hands would be clear and steady when he returned to the hospital on Monday. Dr. Nicholas Chase was never, ever, intoxicated when he was responsible for patients, either at the hospital or on call at home. He never had been, nor would he ever be. And he was rarely, never, sober when he was responsible only for himself.

Most people would not have known when Nick wasn't sober. Not since his teens had he ever appeared to be drunk. What they would have noticed was simply that he was withdrawn; and had they been able to penetrate the brooding silence and somehow convinced him to explain why he drank, Nick would have told them the truth: to numb the pain, to forget the memories, to escape the nightmares that haunted him even in the brightest light of day.

Nick drank, whenever it was safe for him to do so, whenever the only person on earth to whom he was accountable was himself.

The intercom buzzed at eight P.M., and Glenna was announced by the building's security guard. As he waited for the elevator to carry her the twenty-four floors to his apartment, Nick swallowed half of the full glass of Scotch

71

that he had just poured. It was a lot of alcohol, swallowed quickly, but it had virtually no effect. His tolerance to alcohol was very high. He would need much much more to even begin his most necessary escape from pain.

Which meant that the images Nick saw when he opened the apartment door were very clear, very vivid—and terribly painful: Glenna's expensive new clothes, her flashing defiant eyes, the bulging canvas bag slung over her shoulder, the blond-haired infant propped against her hip and held firmly in a position that faced him away from her instead of being nestled gently, protectively, against her.

"He's yours now," she announced harshly, accusingly, as if everything that had happened had been Nick's idea and Nick's fault. "I can't take care of him anymore."

Nick saw the truth of Glenna's words in her eyes. There was defiance there, but frailty too. Perhaps she had tried to love her baby and failed. Or perhaps she hadn't really tried at all. It hardly mattered. What mattered was that it was painfully clear that the role of loving mother was simply too much for her. Maybe Glenna had expected the baby to provide whatever it was she so desperately needed, to magically fill an emptiness inside her, just as she had expected Nick to fill that same void. But the baby, Nick's baby, had failed her—just as Nick himself had—and Glenna obviously bitterly blamed the small infant for that failure, just as she had bitterly blamed his father.

Nick looked at Glenna for a moment, long enough to realize what had happened. Then his gaze was powerfully drawn to the small bundle held firmly against her hip. Justin was very still, very quiet, as Nick himself often became—as he made himself become with alcohol. And, like an alcohol-numbed Nick, Justin simply stared into space, his eyes unfocused and unseeing. As Nick gazed at his son's profile, Justin turned toward him, his dark blue eyes bewildered and empty, but not searching. He seemed to know that there was no reason to search, that there was nothing out there: no laughter, no love, no joy.

Nick didn't make a conscious decision to move, but suddenly he reached for the little boy . . . and then Justin was in his arms, curled tightly against his chest, quiet still, bewildered still, but making no move to twirl to see his mother, no squirming effort to free himself from the grasp of the stranger who held him so closely that his small ears could hear the thundering pounding of the stranger's angry heart.

Once free of Justin, Glenna removed the canvas bag from her shoulder. "The rest of his things and his crib are in the lobby. The security guard helped me unload everything, so you might want to tip him. I haven't been compensated enough yet for the last six months of caring for your baby, Nick. I'm planning to leave Chicago, so I'll need money for the move and to support me while I look for a new job. My attorney—"

"Get out."

"I mean it, Nick," Glenna countered bravely, although her voice wavered as she met his icy blue eyes. "I tried, but you didn't give me enough. I needed more."

"I mean it, too, Glenna," Nick said with controlled rage. "Get out. Now."

For a very long time, Nick just held his son, unable to speak, unable to stop the tears that spilled from his own eyes. Tears had flooded his eyes only once as an adult, the night Edward Reilly died. And before that? Nick didn't remember. Surely he had cried as a small boy, until he finally understood that tears didn't drown the fear or the sadness or the pain.

Nick cried now, and when the warm surprising wetness on Justin's golden head made him look up at his father, Nick whispered softly, "Hello, little Justin. I'm your daddy."

I'm your daddy, and oh, my Justin, what great damage have I unwittingly done to you? I truly believed that it was best for you to be with her, so much better than being with me.

If his son could have chosen his parents, Nick thought, he most assuredly would have chosen neither himself nor Glenna. But Justin couldn't choose, and now there were no options left for him, and the realization filled Nick with sadness and fear. People entrusted their lives to Dr. Nicholas Chase, of course, and for the hours and days that they were in his care, Nick never betrayed that immense trust. And the care he gave those patients? He had on occasion heard himself described as sensitive and compassionate, but Nick believed that the only care he truly gave his patients was technical—the agile artistry of his talented hands, the compulsiveness of his bright perfectionistic mind—and not, not ever, emotional.

The little life cradled in his arms, the small human being who had already been so badly wounded, desperately needed all the emotional care he could get. Justin needed love, and all Nick could do was make a solemn vow.

I will be the best father that I possibly can be, I promise you. I will never abandon you again, Justin, and I will try, oh, how I will try . . .

* * *

Nick held his son all that night, and all the next day, and all the next night, and all the next day, never breaking the physical bond, not for a moment. And he talked to his son, speaking with a softness that his voice had never held before, reassuring the small quiet life and confessing truths about his own childhood that he had never before spoken aloud.

At midnight Friday, Nick thought, just maybe, there was the faintest glimmer of life in the dark blue eyes that had been staring at him. Six hours later, when Justin awakened from where he had slept all night—curled against Nick's chest while Nick remained awake and watchful—he greeted his father with a look of surprise, but not fear, and after a moment his small hands reached up tentatively and patted Nick's unshaven face. On Saturday afternoon, Justin smiled, just a little, just enough to flood Nick's eyes with tears of joy, even though he knew how very fragile it was and that perhaps there had already been damage that could never be undone. And on Sunday, as Nick bathed him, as they bathed together, Justin laughed, a few surprised notes, rusty and uncertain, but the most wonderful sound Nick had ever heard.

Glenna had brought Justin's belongings—food, blankets, clothes, diapers, crib . . . but no toys. Nick's apartment was now cluttered with those symbols of his son, but the apartment still seemed sterile and colorless, the way Nick always kept it for himself, a place to be silent and numb. But there would be no silence here ever again. And no numbness, either, Nick thought as he poured out the never touched second half of the glass of Scotch that he had begun to drink moments before Glenna arrived. He would never drink again—not as long as he was responsible for this fragile, innocent, wounded little life.

After their bath and Justin's lunch on Sunday, Nick

took Justin to the Water Tower, Michigan Avenue's famous shopping complex, located just a few blocks from Nick's lakeside apartment. He bought many brightly colored mobiles, blocks, and balls, and one big soft brown thing—because Justin's blue eyes had fallen on it the moment they walked into the store and had kept returning to it—Mr. Bear. Mr. Bear was the last purchase Nick could make if he was to carry his son and all the toys, and it was time to return to the apartment anyway because it was late Sunday afternoon and beginning at dawn tomorrow, Nick had patients who were even now, on the eve of their operations, counting on his talent and expertise.

It was time for Nick to make the call he had been planning to make since late Friday night.

If he had ever asked for help in his entire life, Nick didn't remember when it had been. But he must have asked at one time, long ago, perhaps in the same silent anguished way that his son was asking now. His own pleas, his own silent screams of loneliness and fear had gone unanswered. Justin's would not, not anymore.

As Nick thought about the call he would make to ask for help for himself and his son, he was amazed at how easy it felt . . . because of who she was, because she was so generous and so kind. He had called her several times in the two months since her mandatory retirement at age seventy that they had both tried to fight. The conversations had been awkward, even though she had talked cheerfully about the things she might do: buy a condo in Florida, perhaps, or take a cruise around the world. She had lots of money, of course. She and Edward could have retired long ago, but they had both chosen to work because they had loved it—because they had both loved caring for the children.

The conversations in the past two months had been

awkward, and now Nick was calling to ask for her help, and he had never asked for anyone's help before . . . but the call didn't feel awkward at all.

"Hello, Margaret, it's Nick. I have some news."

"Oh?" Then, because she heard such tenderness in his voice, she offered quietly, "It sounds like good news."

"Justin is with me, Margaret. He's going to live with me from now on." Nick fought a rush of emotion, then continued solemnly, "It was a mistake to let him live with Glenna. He's in a shell, a protective shell . . ."

"You'll lure him out of it, Nick. I'm sure you will. And I will do whatever I can. I mean that. Anything."

"Well . . . I have to go to work tomorrow. I don't want to leave him, but I have to. I have a lot of vacation time that I can take, but it will be a couple of weeks before I can clear my schedule. Anyway, I've spent the weekend just being with him, instead of trying to find someone to look after him while I'm at work."

"Because you already knew you had someone. I would love to take care of Justin, Nick, and I will for as long as he needs me . . ."

Justin needed them both—the loving seventy-year-old woman who had always wanted a child and the father who had always doubted his own ability to love and yet meant everything to his son. Together, Nick and Margaret helped the damaged and neglected infant become a sunny toddler and then a happy, well-adjusted little boy. It didn't happen overnight, and for a very long time, Nick and Margaret had feared the deep wounds would never heal.

Margaret was with Justin almost constantly and Nick was with him as much as possible. When Nick had to be away—at work, and later, when he and Margaret agreed that it was emotionally safe for Justin, on the trips he made to share his unique expertise with other surgeons—Justin still heard his voice. Nick called home often, and even before Justin himself could speak, he recognized his father's voice and was reassured and comforted by it.

As a boy, Nick had never been touched, neither in love nor in anger. In the middle of the night, when he had awakened with nightmares and the vicious monsters of his dreams had come alive, he had trembled in the terrifying darkness, wanting to scream aloud but afraid to shatter the inviolate silence, waiting instead to be devoured. Nick touched his own son, gentle caresses of reassurance and love, and at night when Justin slept, Nick sat beside his crib, wakeful and watching, prepared to comfort the moment the small blue eyes opened. In the beginning, there were nights when Justin did awaken and was instantly greeted by his father's soft words and gentle touch; but eventually Justin slept all night long, his golden lashes fluttering occasionally with dreams that brought soft smiles to his lips, not troubled frowns to his small brow.

Justin slept peacefully, blissfully, unlike his father whose sleep had been tormented by nightmares forever. Nick's nightmares and the childhood memories that had given rise to them were so interwoven that the real and imagined had long since become irrevocably blurred. Had he really been the one to discover his mother's lifeless body? In his bloody nightmares of agonizing helplessness and horror, he had been the one. And had she really slashed her wrists so deeply and so savagely that her death was a swift and absolute certainty? Had she really needed to find such desperate and irreversible escape from her small son? *That*, the reason she had killed herself, had been mercilessly carved into his young heart. Even before her pale lifeless body had been taken away forever, his father had first spoken the words he would speak over and over and over again: "Look what you made her do, Nicholas. *Look.*"

The belief that his mother's death had been his fault, that there was something so unworthy and unlovable about him that she had killed herself to get away from him, became a fundamental truth of Nick's life. But as he held his own son, loving Justin so much, Nick knew that a little boy—he had only been three at the time—could not have driven his mother to suicide. She obviously had been plagued by her own demons, just as Nick was plagued by his, but hers had been so strong, so painful and so powerful, that she had even abandoned her baby.

It was impossible for Nick to imagine abandoning Justin, no matter how strong or painful or powerful his own demons became. He would live with them, as he always had, but now, without the numbing escape of alcohol, his badly injured heart would be exposed at all times, its wounds raw and weeping. Nick's demons weren't vanquished by his immense love for his son. In fact, the pain was worse than ever before, because now he was more aware than ever of the unspeakable harms that had been so willfully done to him as a child.

The pain was worse and so were the nightmares and Nick needed to find new ways to escape and to numb. At first, in the middle of the night, while Justin and Margaret were sleeping and he himself was driven gasping from sleep, Nick would run. He ran as fast as he could for as far as he could, until every cell in his strong lean body screamed with exhaustion and the physical pain surpassed the emotional . . . and then, to make the most welcome escape last a little longer, he would run even farther.

Eventually, Nick found other forms of physical release as well, satiating the gnawing sexual hungers of his strong healthy body with late-night forays into passion and pleasure. He was more careful than ever neither to harm nor mislead the women with whom he shared his sensual talents; but still, he knew, he was regarded as cruel, cavalier, and dangerous. He *was* dangerous, of course. Already once in the name of love he had caused great harm . . .

As Justin stirred in his arms now, the memory of the great harm he had so unwittingly caused his son came rushing back. Nick had allowed himself to believe that his happy and well-adjusted son had magically and totally recovered from the first six months of his life. But today had proven that the wounds were still there, buried very deep in his small heart. They had been exposed by the virus that had made him sick and vulnerable, and his dark blue eyes had been so terrifyingly bewildered, just as they had been the first time Nick had ever seen him. Bewildered, and so fearful of abandonment.

I will never abandon you, my precious Justin, Nick vowed silently as he gently kissed his sleeping son's golden hair. And I will try so very hard never again to cause harm.

Nick wanted to harm no one, not ever, and most assuredly not someone he loved. His love for Justin had come as a wondrous surprise, a magical gift of joy that was far more than he deserved, and it had not occurred to Nick that he would ever love anyone but his son.

But now he did. And he saw, in her lovely emerald eyes, that she cared about him too. Far too much. Elizabeth didn't seem to know that she deserved someone much better than he, someone whose heart was whole not wounded—a heart that smiled with radiant joy, as hers did, not screamed with pain, like his.

It was a constant battle for Nick to prevent himself from becoming lost in the beautiful and so welcoming emerald . . . and to stop his arms from gently drawing her lovely body close to his . . . and to forbid his lips from confessing to her all his secret truths . . . and to vanquish from his damaged heart the foolish yet so wondrous wish that with her the impossible could be possible after all.

It was a constant battle, but it was a battle that Nick always won. Because he loved her. Because he knew with absolute certainty that it was best for Elizabeth if he stayed very far away.

Part

Two

Chapter Six

San Francisco
August 1991

Elizabeth was scrubbed in the OR when Larisa called the hospital from the airport at eight-thirty. The page operator was expecting her call and pleasantly relayed the messages from Elizabeth—the address to her apartment, the assurance that the building's doorman was expecting her, and the hope that she herself would be home shortly after ten.

Forty-five minutes later Larisa was alone in her friend's apartment, and the anxiety that had traveled with her since the moment she emerged from the motel room at Kennedy magically vanished. She had made it. She was here, in this bright cheerful apartment, and she felt so safe—at last.

Her bedroom was, as Elizabeth had warned, quite un-decorated, except for its spectacular view of downtown San Francisco and the bay beyond—and except for an elegant pale pink rose that rested gently on a pillow on the bed. The bed . . . throughout the transcontinental flight Larisa had promised her dizzy and aching body that as soon as she reached her destination she would lie down. But now the relief at having successfully made the long journey gave her a brave and euphoric burst of energy.

Besides, she thought, Elizabeth will be home soon.

Larisa left her bedroom in search of the kitchen, to heat some water for tea. En route she paused briefly at the open door of Elizabeth's bedroom. The room was a mirror image of hers, but its views were toward the west—to the medical center and ocean and sunset—whereas her easterly views were of city and sunrise and bay. On the floor were neat stacks of medical journals and scientific papers-in-progress, and the walls were adorned with framed photographs of happiness and hope—a sailboat skimming across a sapphire sea, rainbows appearing through a sky of storm clouds, a forest dressed in the white laciness of freshly fallen snow.

So very Liz, Larisa thought as she left Elizabeth's bedroom and crossed the living room to the kitchen.

Her plans to heat the water were preempted the moment Larisa saw the flowers. There were a great many of them, a bountiful bouquet of fragrance and color. Their stems were soaking in the sink and on the nearby counter were scissors, sugar, and an assortment of vases—from Lalique crystal and Lenox china to a handcrafted pottery pitcher and an empty wine carafe. Elizabeth had obviously been in the process of arranging the flowers when she had been called back to the hospital.

Smiling softly, Larisa approached the sink full of flowers and began the creative task herself.

Which was where she was still, filling the final vase, when Elizabeth arrived home twenty minutes later. The sound of the running tap water prevented Larisa from hearing Elizabeth come in the front door, so Elizabeth's first glimpse of her friend was of Larisa's back, the glittering golden **red** mane that fell halfway to her waist, the once-familiar baggy jeans and Berkeley sweatshirt, the ballerina-graceful movements of her arms and hands as she placed the flowers in the vase just so.

When Elizabeth finally spoke, she did so very softly, not wanting to startle.

"Lara?"

But when Larisa turned and Elizabeth truly saw her best friend, it was she who was startled. For over six years she had worried that Larisa's wonderful vibrant spirit had begun to fade—and now it seemed as if even more of her friend had faded. She and Larisa were exactly the same height, but now Larisa seemed smaller, and so frail, a delicate porcelain doll paradoxically clothed in a sweatshirt and jeans. Porcelain? No, Elizabeth realized. The once creamy richness was gone from Larisa's skin. It was snow-white now and almost translucent, a gossamer thin covering over her fragile body.

Elizabeth gazed at her, suspended for a moment between her impulse to rush to her as her friend and her concern as a well-trained trauma surgeon about the cause of the extreme pallor and frailty. Friendship triumphed—at least for now.

"Welcome!" she said, embellishing her warmly enthusiastic greeting with a gentle hug.

"Thank you," Larisa whispered. Elizabeth's hug was very gentle, as if she knew she might break, and Larisa had seen the flickers of emerald worry in her friend's intelligent eyes. So she said as brightly, as lightly, as possible, "I know I look like death. This has all been a bit of an ordeal."

"You're awfully pale, Lara."

"Too much stress, too little sleep, and no sun," Larisa explained with a shrug. It was, at least, a partial truth.

After a moment she confessed softly, a pure and happy truth, "But I'm already better, Liz, just being here."

"I'm very glad you're here," Elizabeth answered, deciding to push no further now, and forced to let the subject drop anyway because her best friend's attention was suddenly focused on *her*.

For several moments Larisa simply stared. She was gazing at the same Elizabeth, of course—fresh and natural and so wonderfully radiant. But the lovely girl-next-door look was gone, replaced by a softly feminine and alluringly womanly beauty. The rich dark brown hair that had always curled naturally and luxuriantly—albeit randomly—was styled now, rich and luxuriant still, but swept into magnificent lustrous swirls; and the wide clear emerald eyes, always so luminous and sparkling, were subtly enhanced now, luminous and sparkling still, but intriguing, bewitching, hypnotic; and even though Elizabeth was dressed simply, the lines of the dress were elegant and the fabric was the color of fire, not the brown or blue she had always worn before.

"*I* may look like death," Larisa began finally, her own beautiful bright blue eyes suddenly alive and sparkling. "But you, Elizabeth Jennings, look positively glamorous."

"I don't know about glamorous . . . but maybe a little better. I gave myself a New Year's makeover." Her resolution to look as good as she possibly could *did* coincide with the new year—but in truth the more pertinent coincidence was the scheduled arrival of the new transplant service chief, Dr. Nicholas Chase, on January fifteenth. Elizabeth had already met Nick, when he had interviewed for the position in early December. He had been touring the medical center, and she had been emerging from the operating room, having operated all night, rumpled and tousled—and so very aware of how bedraggled she must have looked to the appraising dark blue eyes. "There's a wonderful place in Union Square called 'Sydney's, Of Course.' It's a combination clothing boutique and salon, so you can simply walk in and have a complete fashion overhaul—clothes, hair, makeup, the works. Which is what I did."

"Well, you look absolutely terrific." Impulsively reaching to touch a rich dark brown swirl, Larisa added softly, "Those curls."

"Attributable to an interested and creative hair stylist—and, of course, the magic of mousse," Elizabeth explained with a smile, even though her heart ached with renewed worry because the hand that had fondly touched her exuberant but stylish curls had been so pale and trembling. Smiling still, she suggested gently, "Why don't we sit, Lara? I've been on my feet for hours. I'll just put on some water for tea and we can plop down right here amid all these beautifully arranged flowers."

Without waiting for Larisa's concurrence, Elizabeth put her suggestion into action, filling the tea kettle and gesturing for her friend to sit at the small kitchen table.

"That's a very nice dress," Larisa said when they both had mugs of tea and were seated. "The color is really wonderful on you."

"I remember a very dear friend subtly suggesting for years that I might try brighter colors." Elizabeth smiled at the very good friend and then continued, "This dress, in fact my entire new revised wardrobe, is thanks to a woman at Sydney's named Christine. She's like you, Lara. She has a remarkable eye for color and fashion and style that I've just never had."

"I'm not exactly a fashion plate at the moment, although I do love this old outfit."

"So do I, and I have an identical one in my bedroom.

89

Someday we may have to put on our matching outfits and prowl around the old alma mater and reminisce. This weekend's out, I'm afraid, because even though after tonight I won't be officially on call again until Monday, I want to stay fairly close by, because of the liver transplantation we just did."

"It's fine with me to stay right here and drink tea in this cozy apartment."

"And stay up all night talking, like the good old days?"

"That sounds wonderful. I guess it's pretty obvious from my outfit that I'm already regressing." Larisa sighed and admitted softly, "I suppose what I'd really like to do is go back about ten years and start all over again."

"Ten years? Would you really want to undo your modeling career?"

"No. I did love modeling. But if I could just have another shot at the last six . . ." Larisa looked at her friend's sympathetic emerald eyes and confessed quietly, "I'm too tired to talk about Julian tonight. Let's stick to happier topics, okay? Like how terrific you look."

"And how I'm on call!" Elizabeth said with a soft laugh as she rose to answer the suddenly ringing telephone.

The call was from the hospital, but it was Stephen, not the ER. The LKC infusion had been completed without incident, and now, having been accepted by the patient's immune system, the new warrior cells were hard at work in his body, waging their valiant battle against the tumor—and Stephen was calling to see if Larisa had arrived.

"Yes, she's here, safe and sound," Elizabeth answered, smiling at Larisa even as she wondered at the truth of her own words. Was Larisa safe? And sound? "We're in the kitchen, surrounded by flowers, drinking tea."

When Elizabeth's brief conversation was over she explained, "That was Stephen Sheridan. He's an immunologist at the center, and a good friend. I hope you don't mind that I told him you were coming. I know he won't tell anyone."

"No, I don't mind." Then, remembering the warmth and familiarity in Elizabeth's voice as she had spoken with Stephen, Larisa smiled and prompted boldly, "A good friend?"

"A very good friend. Stephen is a very nice man."

Nice, Larisa mused. Elizabeth had always attracted nice men—nice, kind, generous, as Elizabeth herself was. And the men *she* had always attracted? They had never been nice. Like Julian, they had always wanted to possess her, to conquer and control her. Were there two entirely different kinds of men on earth? Larisa wondered. And was it her destiny to forever attract the ones who were cruel, and unkind, and selfish?

"Is Stephen married, Liz?"

"No, Mademoiselle Matchmaker, but he is involved."

Eager to hear all about Elizabeth's life—and Elizabeth's friends—Larisa pressed with genuine interest, "With who?"

"Her name is Madolyn Mitchell. She's an anchorwoman for one of the local stations. *The* anchorwoman, actually. She does the newscasts on weeknights at five and eleven and commands something like seventy percent of the audience."

"It sounds as if she could move on to a bigger market than local television."

"She's planning to. In fact she's in the midst of discussions about a network position in New York right now."

"Would Stephen move to New York with her?"

"Oh." Elizabeth frowned thoughtfully. "I don't know. I don't think so."

"It sounds as if you don't think he should."

"Oh, well, I don't know." Elizabeth shrugged. She and Stephen had had many honest conversations about their love lives—and the fact that despite careful searches neither had ever found a compelling love—and in the almost six months that Stephen had been dating Madolyn, he hadn't amended that fact. "I guess I've never thought Madolyn was right for Stephen—not that I have anyone else in mind!—but I suppose the truth is that she may be exactly the kind of woman he needs. She's almost as dedicated to her career as Stephen is to his, and maybe someone who doesn't expect too much of him and isn't too great a distraction for him would be best."

"I still get the distinct impression that you simply don't think Madolyn's the right woman for your very good friend. And you're probably right, Liz," Larisa affirmed with quiet confidence. "You're pretty good at being able to tell who would make your friends happy—or unhappy." Larisa paused briefly then asked, "You never really liked Julian, did you?"

"I barely knew him, Lara."

"I know, but still . . ." Larisa wanted to know what it was that Elizabeth had seen so quickly in Julian and that she herself had missed seeing for so very long. She wanted to know how Elizabeth spotted the nice men, and the not so nice ones, and if perhaps her friend could share that wisdom with her. But asking those questions now would lead to topics that she was far too tired to discuss.

The telephone rang and Larisa smiled as, for the second time tonight, a possible discussion of Julian was saved by the bell.

This time the call was from the emergency room. Elizabeth was needed. The first-call trauma attending was scrubbed in OR with a gunshot wound to the chest, and they had just received word that a badly injured victim from an MVA—motor vehicle accident—was en route.

"You'd better go!" Larisa exclaimed after Elizabeth had hung up and explained the call.

"The ambulance is still twenty minutes away and I can get to the hospital in less than two. But this will probably keep me busy for the rest of the night. I have to make rounds on the transplant service in the morning, so you won't see me again until at least noon."

"At which time you'll need to crash."

"I might take a brief nap, but I'll be fine. I actually have an appointment with Christine at Sydney's at five tomorrow. Four weeks from tomorrow there's going to be a black-tie ball at the Fairmont celebrating the ground-breaking for the new Immunology Institute—of which Stephen will be the director—and I need a formal gown." Elizabeth tilted her dark brown head and added, "Four weeks from tomorrow is also September fourteenth."

"Your thirty-first birthday!"

"Yes—which is all the more reason for me to try to look as good as possible that night. Would you like to come to Sydney's with me? Or are you planning to keep a lower profile than that?"

"I'm recognized in Manhattan, in certain exclusive boutiques and restaurants, but I can't imagine anyone here would recognize me. Aristocratic Julian always thought it was incredibly crass, incredibly *nouveau riche,* to have our photographs taken for society pages of magazines or newspapers, and it's been over six years since I last modeled."

"Not that any of the pictures taken of you as a model ever really looked like you."

"You didn't think so?" Larisa asked, surprised. "I know the look changed from photograph to photograph—

changes in hair and makeup and camera angle—but I always thought there was a similarity between them."

"The photographs were similar, but I never saw one that I thought was really you—the *real* you."

The real me, Larisa thought with a shiver. Of course there had never been such a shot. Or if there had, the photographer who had taken it would have promptly destroyed the negative, wanting no record of the embarrassing fact that he had actually made the ever-dazzling ever-confident supermodel Larisa Locksley look vulnerable and afraid.

"Well, anyway," Larisa continued hurriedly after an uneasy moment. "Even if someone happened to recognize me, it wouldn't be a problem. Only Julian knows that I'm missing and he wouldn't tell a soul. He absolutely hates scandal, even the whisper of it. If he needs to explain my absence, he'll say I'm off at a spa somewhere."

"Good. So, you can come to Sydney's with me. I'm eager for you to see the boutique and to meet Christine."

"Me too."

"I'd better go. Make yourself at home and get a good night's sleep. Tomorrow, after we've gone to Sydney's, we can talk about Julian . . . if you want to." Elizabeth saw both hope and apprehension on Larisa's pale beautiful face at the suggestion. Once the young Liz and Lara had shared their secrets and their dreams, trusting each other without question. On impulse, Elizabeth offered a secret of her own, "And tomorrow I'll tell you about Nick."

"Nick?" Larisa smiled. *"Nick?"*

"I don't know why I said that! There's really nothing."
Nothing and everything.

"Great." Larisa laughed softly, a joyous giggle that felt quite rusty, because it had been so very long, but which also felt quite wonderful. "I can't wait to hear every meaningless detail!"

Chapter Seven

It's as if she knows how weak I am, Larisa thought as Elizabeth drove to the valet parking in front of Sydney's instead of searching for a more distant parking place. She was weak still, despite a wonderfully deep and dreamless sleep, and the embers of pain that smoldered in her abdomen threatened to burst into flames. But she had wanted to accompany Elizabeth to Sydney's, had been determined to.

"The grand entrance," Elizabeth explained with an easy smile as she slowed the car to a gentle stop.

Their car doors were gallantly opened by two valets, and in just a few short steps they were inside Sydney's. And it was, Larisa decided, like being in a magnificent garden of fragrance and fabric. The intoxicating fragrance came from hundreds of roses artfully arranged in elaborate crystal vases, and the wonderful clothes were arranged as beautifully as the flowers in bright colorful bouquets of elegance and style. There were mirrors in this lush garden, and a sparkling fountain, and glittering crystal chandeliers. Champagne and cappuccino were served in the atrium and romantic songs of love softly filled the rose-fragrant air.

Sydney's, Of Course was very busy on this Saturday afternoon, and yet the boutique had been so brilliantly designed that there was a feeling of endless spaciousness and intimate privacy.

"This is wonderful," Larisa said after a few moments of silent admiration.

"Wait until you see the dressing rooms. They're very large and totally private. Each one is actually two rooms—one for changing and one for viewing. The viewing room has realistic mirrors and lighting as well as comfortable sofas for guests, such as yourself, to wait between showings. I just need to check with the receptionist to see what room we're in. Christine's probably already there arranging the gowns she has preselected."

"This is very good," Larisa murmured appreciatively. "Someone was really thinking when this place was created. Sydney, I suppose."

The dressing room was on the second floor, and yes, the receptionist confirmed, Christine would be there when they arrived. As she followed Elizabeth toward the wide circular staircase that swept up to the second floor, Larisa felt a clutch of fear. Her energy had held as they had wandered slowly among the bouquets of clothes and roses, but could she really climb the stairs? There was an all-glass elevator beyond a sparkling fountain, but . . .

It's only one flight, Larisa told herself. I can make it. If I become breathless halfway up, I can always stop on the pretext of wanting to gaze back at the colorful panorama of the first floor.

Halfway up, as she was thinking about doing just that, Larisa was rescued by the sudden appearance of a violet-eyed raven-haired beauty who was descending the stairs as she and Elizabeth were climbing up.

"Elizabeth!"

"Hello, Madolyn," Elizabeth greeted warmly. After a brief hesitation, she said, "Madolyn, I'd like you to meet Larisa. Larisa, this is Madolyn."

To protect Larisa's privacy, Elizabeth had purposefully omitted last names from the introduction. But, Larisa knew, this *had* to be the Madolyn with whom Stephen Sheridan was involved. She had a star quality about her, and a face that surely loved the camera. As she and the anchorwoman exchanged polite hellos, Larisa felt herself being scrutinized. Madolyn didn't seem to recognize her specifically, but she obviously identified her in general—a stunningly beautiful woman who was by definition some sort of competition. Larisa felt the heat of Madolyn's stare as the remarkable violet eyes searched intently for some indisputable defect in the dazzle, some flaw that made Larisa less beautiful and less desirable than she. Larisa was used to such appraisals, and the smoldering hostility that invariably accompanied the discovery that there were no defects or flaws—no physical ones that is.

Why are you looking at *me?* Larisa wondered. I'm no threat to you at all. If you want something to worry about, worry about the obviously very close and very important friendship between Stephen and Elizabeth.

"You're leaving Sydney's empty-handed, Madolyn?" Elizabeth asked finally after the violet eyes and bright blue ones had met for several unflickering moments.

"It only looks that way," Madolyn said, shifting her gaze from Larisa to Elizabeth and obviously relaxing as she did so. She gushed breathlessly, "Actually, I've just spent the last hour selecting fabric for the gown Christine is making for me for the Fairmont ball. She designed it herself—with my input of course—and it's going to be *wonderful*. I wanted something very special because it will

98

be such a special night for Stephen. Promise not to tell him, Elizabeth? I want it to be a big surprise."

"I won't tell him, Madolyn."

"Good, thanks. Well, I have to go. Stephen and I are meeting at the Cliff House at six. Nice to have met you . . ." Madolyn paused for just a fraction of a second, just long enough to give the unmistakable impression that her bright and impeccably trained journalistic mind had not bothered to remember Larisa's name. Then she added sweetly, "Larisa."

As Madolyn continued down the staircase, Larisa and Elizabeth walked up the remaining half flight. Larisa's energy had been rejuvenated by the brief rest as well as by the instinctive rush of adrenaline released by Madolyn's intense scrutiny. Still, she waited to speak again until they had reached the top of the stairs and were walking toward the designated dressing room.

"So, that was Madolyn," she said with a sly smile. Then smiling more broadly, she asked, "Remember when we were in college and you actually believed that if you couldn't say something nice about someone you shouldn't say anything at all? You always found something nice to say, of course, and I spent three years having to lock my lips." Larisa's delicate fingers duplicated the gesture she had made so often in college, the twisting motion of turning a key to keep her lips from speaking aloud whatever clever but not so nice thought danced in her mind. Her blue eyes sparkled now as they had sparkled then. "I can tell you still subscribe to that code, Elizabeth Jennings."

"Not really. Not *always*," Elizabeth told the sparkling blue eyes that now sent a challenge: No? Then prove it! "Okay, I admit, I'm not crazy about Madolyn. Okay, okay, I'll say it: Stephen could do much better. There!" Elizabeth laughed softly, then her emerald eyes became thoughtful as she added quietly, "I remember that in college you pretended that you could always think of something not nice to say about virtually everyone—but the truth was that you were the first to rush to the defense of anyone who needed defending."

"Well, I think Madolyn can defend herself quite admirably."

"Agreed. I do, however, think that it's very nice that she's having Christine design a gown for her. I think that's something that Christine will enjoy doing very much."

"I'm quite sure Madolyn is doing it for Madolyn, not for Christine. However," Larisa added fondly, "the search for—and discovery of!—the silver lining has been duly noted."

"Thank you." Elizabeth tilted her dark luxuriant curls in acknowledgment, then predicted seriously, "You're going to like Christine, Lara. She's the kind of person who you would have instantly rushed to defend in college."

In fact Larisa *had* instantly rushed to defend Christine in college.

"Larisa?" Christine asked as soon as Larisa and Elizabeth entered the private dressing room.

"Yes." Larisa smiled warmly, reassuringly, at the very pretty woman who had greeted her with soft surprise and shy uncertainty. Christine's involvement in fashion made it quite likely that she of all people in San Francisco might recognize Larisa as the once-famous high-fashion model. But Christine's quiet greeting had seemed more personal than professional. "I'm sorry, Christine, have we met?"

"I'm not sure we ever actually introduced ourselves, but twelve years ago, when we were both freshmen at Berkeley, you once helped me very much—far more than

100

you realized at the time." Now it was Larisa's turn to look surprised, and a little uncertain, and Christine's turn to warmly reassure, "Maybe you won't remember the incident at all, but, if you don't mind, I'd like to tell you my memory of it."

"Okay."

"Well . . . there was a design seminar taught by a man named David Andrews."

David Andrews, Elizabeth's mind echoed silently. The name was quite familiar to her, but it was a familiarity that was far more recent than twelve years ago. Could it possibly be the *same* David Andrews?

"David Andrews," Larisa murmured after a moment, echoing aloud the name that spun silently in Elizabeth's mind. David Andrews had been a campus legend. Twenty years older than the average college freshman, the very sexy art professor nonetheless had a steady stream of young women determined to seduce him. But he stayed very far away from his students, a restraint that only made him all the more desirable: sexy *and* ethical, the perfect romantic hero, nobly depriving himself of the passion he most surely wanted because propriety mandated it. As Larisa thought about it now, a far more likely explanation for David Andrews's restraint seemed obvious: what possible interest could a gorgeous thirty-eight-year-old man have had in giggling eighteen-year-old girls? "Yes, I remember him. He was supposed to be a sensational teacher, but also incredibly sexy, which was why there was always such competition to get into his design seminars. Only one of the seminars was even open to freshmen and you had to show up bright and early in the art department office on registration day to have any hope of getting in."

David Andrews's name had triggered distant memories, and now as Larisa looked closely at Christine even more memories flooded back. Christine's glittering spun-gold hair had been very long then, waist length, a shimmering golden veil that had concealed all of her pretty face—except for her remarkable lavender eyes. The dazzling golden hair was shorter now—and knotted into a sedate chignon—but the luminous lavender eyes were the same. Smiling now at those eyes, Larisa said, "We were both there, in the art department office, waiting to sign up for the seminar."

"Yes, that's right," Christine said, obviously pleased that Larisa had remembered. "There were six of us waiting, and as we waited the other girls shared their reasons for wanting to take the seminar—basically because of David, of how attractive he was. But that wasn't your reason. You wanted to take the seminar because you were going to be a top fashion model and you wanted to learn all you could about color and design."

"And then one of the other girls asked you for your reason," Larisa said quietly, now vividly remembering the scene. There had been such apprehension in the beautiful lavender eyes as Christine had steeled herself for the scorn of the others. She was so obviously shy, so decidedly *un*glamorous in the drab clothes she wore. She was no more the other girls' image of a future fashion designer than she was the image of someone who would have had designs on the handsome teacher. Christine had been apprehensive, but the remarkable lavender had filled with shy yet proud defiance as she had made her startling pronouncement. "And you said that you were going to be a fashion designer."

"Yes," Christine replied softly, grateful still after all these years for what Larisa had done next—and so swiftly that there hadn't been even a heartbeat of stunned awkward silence. "And you said that you hoped that one day you would have the opportunity to model my designs. That was so nice of you to say, Larisa. And then a few minutes later, when we were told that there were only five places available in the seminar, you withdrew your name so that I could get in."

"And you took the seminar, and now, according to what we just heard from Madolyn Mitchell, you're designing beautiful evening gowns."

"I took the seminar, and now I'm designing at least one gown, which I hope will be beautiful." Christine paused and then said softly, her lavender eyes glowing, "But the most important thing that happened because of what you did that morning was that I met and married David."

"Did you? Good for you." Good for David, Larisa added silently, feeling sudden respect for the man she had known only by rumor. David Andrews had effortlessly resisted the provocative advances of all the giggling eighteen-year-olds. But he had been unable to resist the shy and proud—and so serious—Christine. "I remember hearing that he had gotten married. No one really knew any details."

"No. We had to be very careful, because he was a teacher and I was his student. We actually saw each other only in class while I was in his seminar, but we both knew. When the course was over, David asked me if I would mind not enrolling for a second term." She added softly, "And then he asked me if I would marry him."

"How romantic." Larisa looked then from Christine to Elizabeth. She expected a knowing smile from her always optimistic friend at the fairy-tale romance; but there was no smile on Elizabeth's serious face and her emerald eyes were strangely distant, troubled even. After a confused moment, Larisa turned back to Christine, and as her gaze

103

drifted from the smiling lavender eyes to the gold wedding band on Christine's delicate hand, Larisa herself offered the happy ending she had expected Elizabeth to provide, "And it's been wonderful."

"We had eleven wonderful years," Christine agreed quietly. A frown clouded her lovely face. "David died a year ago."

"Oh, no. Christine, I'm so sorry."

"It's okay, Larisa," Christine assured swiftly. "I'm the one who brought it up—and I *wanted* to. I've always hoped that there would be a day when I would see you again and be able to thank you for your kindness to me that morning. It meant so much. I was terribly shy then, and it was so nice of you to leap to my defense. And when you withdrew your name so that I could get into the seminar . . . well, it's because of your kindness that I met David. I think it's an amazing coincidence that you and Elizabeth are friends."

There is another coincidence, Elizabeth thought as she silently struggled with that coincidence and her decision about whether or not to reveal it. She hadn't been specifically involved in the care of David Andrews, but she had known a great deal about the talented artist who had been inexplicably stricken with liver cancer. David had been the first recipient of LKC. Having failed conventional chemotherapy, he had been literally dying when the decision had been made to try Stephen's new and innovative immunotherapy; and with that revolutionary therapy, David had lived, quality life, for another year.

Everyone at the medical center—and oncologists around the world—knew about the dramatic scientific breakthrough. But that was pure science, without a patient's name attached. Elizabeth had learned David's name from Stephen; and during that final year of David's

104

life she had heard it often, because Stephen had shared with her both the hope and the sadness he had felt for his patient—and for his courageous young wife. But if Stephen had ever referred to Mrs. David Andrews by her first name, Elizabeth didn't remember it; and even had she known that Christine's last name was Andrews, she doubted that she would have made the connection.

Christine knew of Elizabeth's friendship with Stephen, as well as of Madolyn's intimate relationship with him, and yet she had said nothing about her own connection to him. Christine had chosen not to mention the coincidence, and that was obviously her choice to make.

But now Elizabeth had her own choice to make, and she decided that she felt uncomfortable keeping silent.

"Your husband was a patient of Stephen Sheridan's, wasn't he?"

"Yes," Christine answered. She turned to Elizabeth, her lavender eyes hopeful, and said softly, "I didn't realize that you had known David, Elizabeth."

"I didn't know him. I only knew of him—through Stephen." Elizabeth drew a soft breath and, her emerald eyes gently apologetic, explained, "Sometimes it's necessary, emotionally necessary, for doctors to talk to each other about patients, even if they aren't both actually involved in that patient's care."

"I don't mind that he talked to you about David," Christine assured quietly. "I know how dedicated he is, and how much he cares, and how wonderfully he cared for David. I suppose I should have asked if you knew about David, but I guess it just seemed less . . . complicated . . . not to. No one at Sydney's knows anything about him. I started working here a month after his death and—"

"And it's very private," Elizabeth said softly. "And it will stay that way."

"Thank you."

After a long but not awkward silence, during which the three women exchanged smiles of understanding and trust, Larisa finally enthused, "I'm so impressed with the outfits you've put together for Elizabeth, Christine. I can't wait to see the gowns you've selected for the ball."

"They're in the changing room. I think there are several that will look wonderful on you, Elizabeth, but if you don't agree, I'd be very happy to design something for you, too . . ."

It was quickly apparent that it would not be necessary for Christine to design an evening gown for Elizabeth. Every gown she had selected did, in fact, look quite wonderful. As they discussed which was the best of the best, the most ravishing and glamorous, the thoughtful analysis was liberally sprinkled with the fond smiles and gentle teases of friendship.

Eventually they reached a consensus: the coral silk chiffon. The bright, rich color was absolutely perfect for Elizabeth, Christine and Larisa agreed. And, they concurred, the gown's long elegant lines artfully accentuated her long and elegant figure.

Larisa herself had a strong sense of style and color, but she saw in Christine a true gift: the appreciation of what looked best coupled with the creative flair to make it look even better. As she sat on the sofa in the salon's private viewing area watching Christine's lavender eyes focus intently on the issue of which shoes best accessorized the gown, Larisa thought about what she had said to Christine on that long-ago morning in the art department at

Berkeley—the hope that one day she would have the opportunity to model one of Christine's designs.

Larisa knew it was a hope that would never come true. Christine might become a famous designer, of course. She was only thirty, after all, and so clearly gifted. But Larisa knew that her own modeling days were over. Even though the world had enjoyed watching supermodels Christie Brinkley, Lauren Hutton, and Cheryl Tiegs age beautifully, Larisa Locksley had been out of the public eye for over six years. No one was bonded to her, and the contrast between the woman she had been six years ago and the woman she was now would be too harsh.

The problem wasn't her body. When strong and healthy, her shape was still as sleek and provocative as ever. Julian had insisted on it. No, Larisa knew, the problem was her eyes. Before Julian, she had been able to make the brilliant blue glow with hope and joy. She had learned the radiant look from Elizabeth, for whom it was entirely authentic, a happy and optimistic vision of the bountiful promises of life. Her best friend's beautiful luminous emerald eyes sparkled still, but Larisa knew that she could no longer mimic the joyous look. Her own blue eyes had seen far too much now, and they sent messages over which she had no control . . . haunted messages of hopelessness . . . of dreams shattered and love betrayed.

Chapter Eight

The day was still warm and sunny when Elizabeth and Larisa emerged from Sydney's. As they stood in the late afternoon sunshine awaiting the arrival of Elizabeth's car, Elizabeth asked her friend what she would like to do with the glorious summer evening that lay ahead. A picnic supper in Ghirardelli's waterfront park perhaps? Or seafood salad on Fisherman's Wharf? Or a leisurely stroll along Pacific Beach at sunset?

I can't do any of those things, Larisa thought. Her now exhausted body trembled with weakness and the embers in her abdomen had become a fire that threatened to rage out of control. Instead of Ghirardelli or the wharf or the beach, perhaps she should ask Elizabeth to take her to the medical center to determine the extent of her trauma, to see if there had been life-threatening injuries to vital organs other than the one of which she was already fully aware: her heart.

No, Larisa told herself. She was fatigued now, wobbly and in pain, but overall she had been better today than yesterday, and tomorrow she would be even better still, and on Monday, while Elizabeth was at work, she would walk to the nearby pharmacy to buy iron and vitamins.

And, by next weekend, she would be able to accompany Elizabeth to their once-favorite haunts.

But not now.

"Aren't you tired, Liz?" she asked softly. "You were up all night and you only had a short nap."

Elizabeth looked thoughtfully at the friend who had always before been the one with unlimited energy. Despite the pale whiteness of her once rich creamy skin, in the dressing salon at Sydney's Larisa had seemed almost like her old self—funny, clever, and lively. But, Elizabeth realized now as she looked closely at the strain on Larisa's beautiful face, the glimpse of Larisa-past had come at great expense.

"Are you okay, Lara? I know you've been under a great deal of stress . . . but I wonder if there's something more." Elizabeth tilted her head and guessed gently, "Pregnancy, maybe?"

"I'm definitely not pregnant. And I am okay." *I will be okay.* "I'm just tired, Liz, that's all."

The beautiful strained face sent a message of courage— and of fear—and Elizabeth respected her friend's obvious wish that she push no further. So she simply smiled and confessed, "Well, I'm tired, too, in a cozy sort of way. Why don't we just pick up some food on the way home, change into our bathrobes, and talk until we fall asleep?"

In college, Elizabeth and Larisa had shared their secrets, their wishes, and their dreams. Now, as they sat in the living room of Elizabeth's apartment and watched the golden splendor of the sun as it fell into the Pacific, they remembered that time of sharing . . . and they remembered the dreams.

From the very beginning, Elizabeth's dream had been

to become a doctor. When Larisa had pressed for more parts to the dream, eighteen-year-old Elizabeth had confessed that yes, she did want to fall in love someday, and yes, she wanted to get married and have children. Larisa took the simple facts of Elizabeth's dream and embellished with enthusiasm fueled by the heartfelt conviction that everything her generous and optimistic friend dreamed for herself *should* come true.

"You had me living in a charming white-and-yellow house surrounded by white-and-yellow roses and a picket fence," Elizabeth said as she recalled vividly the richly textured portrait Larisa had painted of her future. "I was going to have an office in the house—so I could be a doctor, a wife, and a mother all at once—and while I was doing all that, you would be gallavanting around the world, modeling the latest fashions and having a never-ending series of glamorous, amorous adventures."

"Glamorous, amorous," Larisa echoed quietly. She had known so clearly in college that she would never fall in love. She believed in love and romance for Elizabeth, of course, but never, not ever, for herself. There would be men in the glamorous life she would lead as a high-fashion model, handsome and dashing men with whom she would share grand adventures, but there would never be love. That had been her plan. Now she thought, I should have stayed with that plan. "And every so often I'd come visit you and dazzle your children with discreetly edited versions of my adventures. And eventually, when there had been enough adventures, I'd come to stay, probably forever, and simply sit on your veranda sipping lemonade amid the roses and writing my best-selling memoirs."

"We never exactly decided where that charming house was, did we?" Elizabeth asked. "Somewhere pastoral and folksy, a perfect place for raising children, but with virtual

110

instant access to every advance modern medicine had to offer."

"Of course! And it had lots of snow in winter, for sleigh rides and ice-skating and twinkling lights of Christmas, but in summer, when I was sipping lemonade and writing my steamy memoirs, it was the South at its most hot and sultry." Larisa shrugged softly. The lovely place she had so enthusiastically envisioned for them in which to share their dreams didn't exist. And the dreams themselves? She had become the model she had dreamed of becoming. And Elizabeth had become the gifted surgeon. But what about the other parts of Elizabeth's dream? Larisa tilted her head thoughtfully and asked quietly, "Have you ever fallen in love?"

"I guess not. Whatever falling in love is." Elizabeth smiled, and then confessed, "I've wondered if it's actually happened and I just didn't realize it because I was expecting so much—too much, some impossible fantasy. I've always told myself, no, when it happens, when you really fall in love, you'll know. It will be so compelling—and so wonderful—that there will be no doubt."

"Isn't it strange, Liz? Of the two of us, you were the only one who truly believed in love. And yet somehow I convinced myself that I had found my fairy-tale prince. The real truth is that Julian found me. He'd seen my photographs and wanted to meet me. I knew that at the time—and I suppose I should have known that I was just another trophy for him—but I allowed myself the foolish delusion that he loved me for me." A frown saddened her beautiful pale face. "I'm not sure he ever really did."

"Marriage can begin with great love and still falter, Lara."

"Yes, well, it definitely faltered. Or maybe I was the one who faltered," she added quietly. "Maybe Julian did love me at one time and I somehow disappointed him."

"I doubt that."

"I have to accept at least half the responsibility for the failure of my marriage. And I do, even though I'm not yet sure exactly what it was I did wrong." *I gave him everything I had to give—and it was too much of myself to have given away—and yet still it was not enough for him.* Larisa sighed softly. "I guess it's pretty obvious that it's too soon for me to talk about this coherently. It's all still a confusing blur. But one thing isn't confused." Her worried blue eyes met the sympathetic emerald ones, and drawing strength from Elizabeth's strength, she vowed solemnly, "I'm not going back to him."

"Good." Elizabeth smiled and suggested gently, "I think maybe the sooner the marriage is officially over, the easier it will be for you to go on."

Larisa shuddered involuntarily as she remembered Julian's violent rage over the simple loss of a piece of real estate. After a moment she said, "I'm not sure that Julian will ever give me a divorce, Liz. He hates to lose anything that he believes should belong to him."

"Julian doesn't have a choice about giving you a divorce, Lara. If you want a divorce, you can have it. The choice is yours as much as Julian's."

Choice. The word echoed in Larisa's mind like the most rare and wonderful of delicacies. Choice hadn't been a part of her life for the past six years, despite her world of riches and luxury. Even leaving Julian hadn't truly been a choice, only the deepest instinct for survival compelled by the anguished cry of an innocent girl who had been brutally betrayed once again.

"Julian is very powerful. He'll get the best attorneys. It may be very difficult for me even to find someone who is willing to do battle with him."

"You already have someone," Elizabeth countered. Her clear emerald eyes sparkled and her voice filled with sisterly confidence and pride as she elaborated, "You have my brother."

"Mark? He's doing divorce law?"

"Yes. It began by accident when the divorce attorney in his law firm left unexpectedly, in the midst of a very bitter action. Mark was asked to fill in, and it turned out that he had a remarkably calming effect, managing to guide even that acrimonious divorce to an almost harmonious dissolution. As a result, he's now handling all the firm's divorce cases."

"It doesn't surprise me that Mark does it well," Larisa said softly. *Harmony and fairness are Jennings family traits.* "But doesn't he find it distasteful? Divorce is such a failure."

"I think Mark finds it challenging and rewarding to help make what is such an emotionally difficult situation as painless as possible."

"Just like what you do with dying patients."

"Oh, well, I don't know. Anyway, Mark has become a little famous in legal circles for his success with divorce cases. He's handled some of San Francisco's biggest and most difficult ones. He's also handled a few in Hollywood, ones in which no one even knew the divorce was happening until the press agents quietly announced that it was a done thing. Mark believes very strongly that divorce should be private. He refuses to take cases in which either party wants publicity—newspaper headlines, Larry King, Phil Donahue, that sort of thing—and you've already told me that Julian hates even the whisper of scandal." Elizabeth smiled triumphantly. "So Mark is the perfect choice."

Mark. Larisa had met him only moments after she had met Elizabeth. Mark, then a third-year law student at

Hastings, had been the protective older brother, showing up in his little sister's dormitory room to make sure everything was all right, including her new roommate. Larisa's reaction to handsome and confident Mark Jennings had been her reaction to all men: a wariness that had manifested itself as haughty contempt. In fact, Larisa had trusted no one then—neither men nor women. She had learned to trust her warm and generous roommate, of course, and eventually she had even been friendly to the older brother who was so protective of Elizabeth—a protectiveness that would have extended to Larisa had she permitted it to. But Larisa wouldn't allow Mark to protect her, and there had always remained a little distance and uncertainty between them. Mark didn't really approve of her, Larisa had decided. She was far too wild, too provocative, and too brazen for his innocent little sister.

Larisa knew that Julian and his attorneys would say whatever was necessary to persuade her attorney that a divorce was simply out of the question. Did she want Mark, who already disapproved of her, to hear the lies she knew they would speak? That her obviously erratic and emotional behavior was perhaps best explained by her addiction to cocaine? Or that she was sexually wanton and had had numerous extramarital affairs? Mark would tell her what Julian had said, and then she would have to confess to him that at the center of each lie there was in fact a little bit of truth. Yes, she would tell him, on occasion she *had* used cocaine; and she might even add that although she hated using the drug, there were times when it made everything much easier. But she would be far too ashamed to admit to Mark that she had only used the illicit snow-white powder when Julian had forced her to, because she had had too little will—and far too much of a wish to please him, *to have him love her*—to ever say no to him.

And her sexual wantonness? Larisa had satisfied Julian's every sexual whim, and more and more he had insisted that cocaine become part of their lovemaking, and she had perhaps been wanton with him. But she had never had an affair, never even considered it. Julian had had affairs, many of them. She might confess that to Mark, another admission of her own failure, but she would never be able to tell him or anyone about the last night with Julian. She was far too ashamed to admit that greatest failure of all—the betrayal of herself, the giving away of herself until there had been so little left, so little respect or value or worth that Julian hadn't hesitated to possess her violently and against her will.

Larisa had no doubt that Mark Jennings had a gift for serenely handling even the messiest of divorces. She could even imagine him being quite undaunted by Julian and his slick and powerful attorneys. But did she really want Mark to know about her foolish romanticism, her terrible mistakes, her unspeakable shame?

"Mark will be deeply offended if you don't at least talk to him," Elizabeth said as if in response to Larisa's silent question. "Even if you decide not to have him represent you, you should trust him to give you good advice."

"I *do* trust him. It's just that this is all so sordid."

"He'll want to help," Elizabeth countered firmly. Then, with a note of finality, she added, "So. That's settled. We'll call him at home tomorrow morning and set up an appointment for sometime this week."

"Okay," Larisa agreed softly as she thought, I'm so needy. I always have been. And Elizabeth and Mark have always been so willing to give. Someday, maybe, please, I'll be able to repay them for their kindness. "Thank you."

115

"You're welcome!" Elizabeth smiled and added sympathetically, "I know there's a lot about what happened with Julian that's still just pure emotion. You want it all to make sense, and maybe someday it will. But, Lara, maybe it won't. I'm not sure feelings can be wrapped up in neat little packages. Sometimes relationships simply fail no matter how much you care or how hard you try to make them work."

As Larisa saw the gentle sadness in Elizabeth's emerald eyes and heard a wistful softness in her friend's voice that she had never heard before, she realized that Elizabeth's gentle words of wisdom were very personal. But, as far as Larisa knew, none of Elizabeth's relationships had ever failed. They had just faded, gradually losing brilliance like the sun falling from the sky. True, as might accompany the final adieu to the warmth and goodness of a glorious summer day, there had sometimes been a gentle sadness, a wistful regret that the golden sunshine couldn't last forever—but there had never been a sense of failure.

Until now.

After a moment Larisa guessed softly, "Are you talking about Nick?"

"Oh! No." Elizabeth frowned thoughtfully before confessing quietly, "Well, maybe I am. My relationship with Nick has been a failure, but it's not a grand love affair gone awry. The truth is that Nicholas Chase has never even liked me."

"If Nicholas Chase, whoever he is, doesn't like you, then there's something fatally wrong with him."

"No. There's nothing wrong with Nick."

"And there's nothing wrong with you," Larisa reminded fondly. "So, tell me about him."

"Okay." Elizabeth drew a soft breath and then began, "He's a gifted surgeon, the most talented I've ever known, and he is also a wonderfully sensitive and compassionate physician. But . . . he and I just don't connect. We never have. In the past eight months I've probably spent more hours with Nick than I've spent with any other man. We've been together, literally, for up to thirty-six hours at a time, working together, saving lives and losing them. With anyone else there would be something personal, an acknowledgment at least of the emotion of what we're doing."

"And the ice man won't talk about his emotions?"

"Not with me. Nick and I don't talk at all, unless it's a necessary conversation about one of our patients."

"But you're so easy to talk to! You're always so interested and open, and you always have such cheerful things to say."

"Thanks. But with Nick I feel very uncomfortable. Every time I think of something light and cheerful that I could say, I decide against it for fear that he would consider it silly or foolish."

"I don't get it, Lizzie," Larisa said softly. "The man sounds perfectly awful."

"But he isn't awful, Lara, that's the point. And with everyone else, he's very charming and personable."

"Then there's a piece missing, something you haven't told me. Everyone likes you." Larisa hesitated a moment, then suggested quietly, "Maybe he's secretly in love with you."

"Oh, no." Elizabeth's cheeks flushed pink. "I can assure you that he's not."

"I think you'd better tell me all about Doctor Nicholas Chase—from the beginning."

Larisa listened in intent and interested silence as Elizabeth recapped the past eight months: how Nick had inherited her, his too-talked about midnight affairs with the hospital's most beautiful women, the emotional distance he had kept from her from the very beginning, and her secret worry that Nick didn't respect her as a surgeon and wished that she would simply disappear. . . .

"But he has to know that you're an excellent surgeon— because you are! You've had enough people tell you that over the years and surely it's something that you know yourself."

"Yes. I am a good surgeon," Elizabeth admitted quietly. "I do know that. My patients do very well, but . . ."

"But because of this Nick character, you're beginning to doubt yourself." Larisa's own self-esteem had been very fragile for a very long time and with very good reason. And even though it had been terribly painful when her delicate and precarious self-worth had been so brutally shattered by Julian, it made sense. It was even, somehow, all right. But it was not all right for someone to shake the confidence of the lovely and so worthy Elizabeth Jennings. "Don't ever doubt yourself, Liz."

"I'm trying to resist doing just that," Elizabeth said, smiling gratefully at the mother-bear protectiveness of her friend. "I'm trying to be scientific and analytical about the situation, but the truth is I've actually been thinking about looking for a job somewhere else."

"But you love San Francisco! Not only is it your home, but you're at a prestigious institution, doing trauma *and* transplantation, both of which are obviously very exciting and challenging for you."

"True, all true. The most important truth, though, is that the very best part of what I'm doing is having the chance to work with Nick. He's so talented, and I'm learning so much from him, but with each passing day the awkwardness I feel and the conspicuous absence of our

118

relationship becomes all the more obvious." **Elizabeth** paused. Then murmuring softly, almost to herself, she admitted, "It's just very difficult."

I can see how difficult this is for you, Larisa thought. You really care about this ice man, don't you? Oh, Liz, have you fallen in love at long last?

As Larisa's blue eyes left her friend's emerald ones and gazed outside to the dazzling glitter of San Francisco at night, she wondered, Nicholas Chase, whoever you are, how crazy can you be?

Chapter Nine

"You're going to operate?" the surgery resident asked incredulously, regretting his honest, startled question the moment his eyes met Nick's. "I mean . . . it seems . . . don't the lab data we have—the X rays and scans—indicate such massive tissue injury that there's no hope?"

Nick's icy glare relented slightly at the resident's uneasiness. He was an excellent resident, hard-working and careful, and he was also probably absolutely right: there was very little hope, probably none, for the four-year-old boy who only an hour ago had been happily playing in the safe sanctuary of his own front yard. The warm tranquility of the sunny morning—and the promise of the young sunny life—had been irrevocably shattered as a drunk driver had spun his car out of control and into the yard. Because of its reputation for the treatment of pediatric trauma, the badly injured little boy had been rushed to Pacific Heights Medical Center. The driver of the car, almost certainly lethally injured, too, had been taken to San Francisco General.

"You may well be right," Nick admitted to the resident. "You probably are. But I'm going to operate."

Nick hesitated a moment, not debating his decision to

give the small boy every possible chance to live, but debating whether or not to involve Elizabeth in what was virtually destined to be a tragedy without a silver lining. They would almost certainly open the small abdomen and find irreparable harm, far beyond the limits of modern medicine to save. Why involve Elizabeth in that unspeakable sadness and loss? The answer came quickly: Because if there is a chance to save this precious and innocent young life, I need her delicate talented fingers, her calm resolute courage, and the radiant hopefulness of her lovely emerald eyes.

"You don't really need to get involved," Nick told the resident. "Just Doctor Jennings and I will scrub, if she's available. Would you mind paging her for me to see if she's free while I get the consent from Danny's parents?"

Elizabeth was on the pediatric ward when the page from ER came. She was just completing the discharge orders for Molly, who was going home a remarkable seven days after her transplantation surgery. Mary Ann had been discharged four days earlier, although she had been in the hospital almost continually ever since, watching her infant daughter grow stronger and healthier each day. Elizabeth frowned briefly as she dialed the number displayed on her pager. She wasn't on trauma call today.

But Nick was, the resident said when she answered the page. And he wondered if she would be available to operate with him—right away—on a critically injured child. Yes, of course, she told the resident. She would be down in just a few moments.

* * *

As she neared the emergency room, Elizabeth caught sight of Nick. He was in one of the private waiting rooms that had been specifically designed for families of the most critically injured and were a discreet distance from the noise and chaos of the general waiting area. Facing Nick, listening intently to his words, was an obviously anxious and distraught young couple. The little boy's parents, Elizabeth assumed as she quietly joined them in the small room.

Usually when she and Nick operated on a trauma patient, Elizabeth established rapport with the family while Nick saw to the last-minute details. He would always meet the family before the surgery, of course, but usually long after she had. This time it was Nick who was with the family . . . and it was Nick who spoke the honest and extraordinary words that Elizabeth overheard as she neared.

"I don't want to give you any false hope. The chances of saving Danny's life are very small, perhaps even nonexistent. But I want to operate, to be absolutely certain that there is nothing that can be done."

"You'll do the surgery yourself, Doctor Chase?" Danny's father asked with soft hope. He recognized Nick, of course, the famous transplant surgeon who had so recently performed the miraculous life-saving surgery on little Molly.

"Yes." Nick turned to Elizabeth then and added, "And this is Doctor Jennings. She'll be operating with me."

"You operated on Mary Ann and Molly, too, didn't you?" Danny's mother asked, recognizing Elizabeth's name but not her face because the photographic coverage had been only of Nick.

"Yes." Elizabeth smiled warmly, instinctively wanting to reassure but feeling a bit awkward because what Nick had told them was so terribly far from reassuring. But, she thought, there was one point on which she could authentically reassure: with Nicholas Chase as their son's surgeon, Danny was in the best hands on earth.

The best hands. Nick's strong, lean fingers worked with graceful—yet almost frantic—agility to stop the bleeding, and Elizabeth's delicate fingers joined the frenzied dance, moving in perfect wordless harmony with Nick's. But for the first time in all the times that she and Nick had operated together, Elizabeth wondered what they were doing. True, more than once, she had been with Nick when his talented fingers had saved a life that had seemed almost beyond hope. But for Danny there was so obviously no hope at all. There had been far too much destruction to his small body.

Once Elizabeth had overheard Nick talking about the possibility of emergency organ transplantation in cases of severe trauma. It was a thrilling idea, one which she had often wondered about as well, an exciting and innovative concept that she and Nick might have talked about—if they talked. But even if donor organs were available to them, to Danny, right this minute, and even if they decided to try the avant-garde therapy, Elizabeth knew that still this little boy could not be saved.

Nick didn't have any surgical advances to offer Danny. He had only his immense talent and whatever it was deep inside that filled his intense dark blue eyes with such torment and compelled him to fight desperately to save this young life. Nick was a noble warrior valiantly fighting a battle that he could not win. But, Elizabeth knew, Nick would not view his valiant fight as either noble or heroic—only as a devastating defeat. And she could not

123

shake the ominous impression that when Danny died something within Nick would die too.

Why are you doing this, Nick? she wanted to cry. Even you can't save him. And if you can't, no one can. Stop, please, before you destroy yourself!

Elizabeth would never say such words aloud in the operating room. She, like Nick, always operated as if her patients were wide-awake and quite able to hear all words, and sense all emotions and all fears. Elizabeth didn't speak the words, and her skillful delicate hands helped Nick and Danny without faltering.

It was Nick who finally broke the silence. And when he did, his voice was very soft and very calm, so that if somehow Danny could hear, he would feel neither alarm nor fear.

"It's time to close."

Nick spoke the words with reassuring calm, but his blue eyes were filled with excruciating anguish; and as he closed the young skin with such tender care, there was apology, too, in the tormented blue depths.

While the anesthesiologist and scrub nurse were getting Danny ready to be moved to the nearby recovery room, Elizabeth and Nick left the operating suite, as was customary, to give instructions to the nursing staff in recovery in advance of the patient's arrival.

This time there were very special instructions. Nick gave them to Stephanie, a beautiful woman who knew him well—at least intimately.

"Danny isn't going to live much longer, Steph," Nick told her. "I want you to find a quiet and private place for him—not dark, just quiet and private. And I want his parents to be with him if they want to be. I'll talk to them. If it's too difficult for them to be with him when he dies, then I'll be with him. If they do decide they can be here, you need to know that I'll be waiting in the surgery lounge. I'm counting on you to let me know right away when you think they need me."

"Okay, Nick," Stephanie answered solemnly as she gently touched his taut bare forearm. "You can count on me."

"Good. Thank you."

As Elizabeth and Nick walked in silence from recovery to the room where Danny's parents were waiting, she thought about how effortlessly Stephanie had touched him. It hadn't been a gesture of intimacy, just one of understanding and empathy, the kind of warm touch Elizabeth herself might have offered any other man who was so obviously as troubled as Nick. She and Nick *had* touched today, of course, as they always did when they operated, the necessary touches of the intricate surgery they performed together. Usually when their fingers touched, Nick's felt quite warm, symbols of the fiery heat and smoldering sensuality that blazed within him. But today there had been no warmth at all in the long talented fingers with which her own had danced with graceful precision. Today Elizabeth had felt only ice . . . and she sensed such tension in the strong lean body of the warrior who fought so valiantly beside her.

When they reached Danny's parents, it was Nick who spoke. He hadn't given them false hope before the surgery, and now he simply told them more truths.

"Danny is alive still, but he's not going to live much longer," Nick said quietly. And then, even more quietly, he added, "I'm so sorry."

"Can we see him?"

"Of course you can. He won't regain consciousness,

but that doesn't mean he won't be able to hear your words and know that you're with him. So, if you can, don't let him hear your fear, only your love, only your happiness that he's your little boy." Emotion stopped Nick's voice. After a moment he added with exquisite gentleness, "Maybe that's impossible for you to do."

"No," Danny's mother answered. "We can do it. We *will.*"

"Yes," his father agreed. His eyes flooded with tears, but his voice, like his wife's, was resolved to be strong for their son for as long as Danny needed their strength. "We will. And thank you, Doctor Chase. We know that you tried and that you cared."

When Nick had told Stephanie that he would be waiting in the surgery lounge, he had said "I" not "we." But Elizabeth accompanied him to the lounge anyway. True, Danny's parents clearly looked more to Nick than to her, but Danny was her patient too. And, even if Danny's parents didn't need her, Elizabeth wanted to be available for Nick in case he did.

In case Nick *needed* her? The foolishness of the thought became quickly and abundantly clear. Nick was withdrawn, completely lost in his own thoughts, neither knowing nor caring that she was there. As Elizabeth watched the unrelenting torment in his dark blue eyes, she felt helplessness—and anger. Anger was such an unfamiliar emotion for her, and this anger was so unfocused. It was an ache, imprisoned deep inside, in her heart, and it paced with restless power, wanting to scream—and needing to escape. With any other surgeon, even if it was someone she barely knew or liked, after an emotionally devastating surgery such as this, they would have talked.

126

They would have tried to make sense of the senselessness and expressed at the very least their shared anger at the whim of fate that had so swiftly and violently taken a little boy's life.

But not with Nick.

Was that why she was angry? Because Nick was shutting her out? Or was she angry at herself for her own lack of courage in simply reaching out to him? She was angry with both herself and Nick, she decided. And yet, when she finally articulated the anger, the target was neither of them, but instead the tragedy itself and its real perpetrator. The tragedy that had befallen Danny had not, of course, been a whim of fate. It had been the irresponsible act of an adult human being against an innocent little child.

"How can people drink and drive? Hasn't that lesson been learned yet?" she demanded, her voice quiet yet impassioned. She wanted to talk to Nick, to draw him out, but when his blue eyes lifted to hers, Elizabeth trembled at what she saw. The blue was as ice cold as his hands had been and as hard as the taut tension she had sensed in his strong body. Nick was angry. No, she realized, he was *enraged*. Was his rage at the driver who had caused such a senseless tragedy? Or was it at her for her lack of compassion? Her voice trembled as she whispered, "I'm sorry, Nick, I guess that sounds too uncharitable. I know that alcoholism is a disease, a terrible disease——"

"Yes," Nick interjected harshly, his voice as hard and uncompromising as his eyes. "Alcoholism is a terrible disease. But it should be a private one. If you're a drunk, you should spend every second of your life making certain that you give your disease to no one else—especially not to an innocent child. Don't waste any charity on drunks, Elizabeth, it's pure foolishness."

Pure foolishness. Nick's harsh words stabbed like the sharpest of knives. Elizabeth should have gotten even angrier. She should have told him what she thought of him and his condescending arrogance. But her anger vanished as quickly as it had come, taking its courageous energy with it, leaving her feeling empty . . . and a little lost . . . and terribly sad.

I'm so sorry I involved you in this! Nick thought as he gazed at her lovely stricken emerald eyes. I so desperately needed your talent and your courage and your hope. But now I've hurt you with my harshness.

But his harshness had come from the icy truths of his own heart, and if his cruelly honest words made Elizabeth think less of him then that was for the best—at least it was best for *her*.

"You don't need to wait," he said finally. "I'll stay. Thank you for operating with me."

Now he was dismissing her! Elizabeth felt the warm flickers of new anger, but she didn't allow them to burst into flame. What was the point? There was no point. She had wanted to talk to him—and had wanted him to talk to her—but it was obviously, so obviously, impossible.

After a moment, without another word, Elizabeth turned and left . . . as Nick had requested.

I hate you Nicholas Chase. The surprising thought came with such energy that for a startled moment Elizabeth's hasty retreat came to an abrupt halt. Was it true? Did she really hate him? Elizabeth tested the thought and the feeling of tranquility that could come with it. If she hated Nick, if he was deserving of her hatred, her heart could stop defending him and she could stop caring . . . and hurting.

But the tantalizingly peaceful thought of hating Nick

didn't survive even the most superficial scrutiny. Elizabeth knew that what she felt about Nick was very far away from hatred. She didn't hate him, and never could. Which meant that she would simply—oh, not so simply!—have to keep caring . . . and hurting.

Elizabeth had started walking again and when she emerged from her thoughts and noticed where she was, she discovered that her steps had unerringly guided her to the quiet sanctuary of Stephen's research lab. She wouldn't share the sadness of this morning with her good friend, nor would she tell him what had happened with Nick; but just talking to Stephen and feeling the genuine warmth of his gentle dark brown eyes would make her feel better . . .

It was only when she turned the knob of his laboratory door and found it locked that Elizabeth remembered: Stephen was downtown discussing the final details of the Immunology Institute with the building's architect.

Chapter Ten

When the board of directors of the Pacific Heights Medical Center's future Immunology Institute selected architect Peter London's proposal from the many that had been submitted by architectural firms throughout the country, the selection was greeted with a mixture of enthusiasm and worry. Peter London's talent was indisputable, as was the thirty-six-year-old architect's reputation for quality and excellence. But Peter's fame had come from designing homes, hotels, commercial buildings, and resort complexes, not hospitals. And the San Francisco Bay Area already boasted one architecturally beautiful and award-winning hospital that was not quite as functional as it should have been—its corners a little too tight for stretchers to sweep through in one pass, its laboratories a bit too far away from where the specimens were actually obtained.

The board's enthusiasm for a building designed by the man whose trademark was accessible elegance eventually outweighed its worry. Still, to be absolutely certain that the expensive structure would be functional as well as elegant, the institute's future director, Dr. Stephen Sheridan, was given the task of working closely with the celebrated architect—to make sure that Peter understood the idiosyncrasies of a modern state-of-the-art medical facility.

Before meeting Peter, Stephen had been concerned that the famous architect might not be terribly receptive to his suggestions, caring far more for style than for function. But from the very beginning it was reassuringly apparent that Peter London was as committed to quality, excellence, and precision in his work as Stephen was committed to the same in his. With Stephen's technical advice and Peter's unfailing willingness to make changes until everything was exactly right, the end result was an efficient and functional work of art.

The structural blueprints had long since been completed. Now, with the celebration ball at the Fairmont just three weeks away, all that was left were finishing touches, the elegant embellishments and fine detailing that distinguished a Peter London creation from all others. Peter had surprised Stephen by wanting his opinions on those artistically—but not medically—important touches. After all, Peter had reminded him, the institute would be a second home to Stephen's patients. Peter hadn't added, although it was true, that he would never have solicited Stephen's artistic input had it not been very obvious that he and Stephen shared the same taste for understated elegance.

Only a few decisions were left to be made, and the purpose of today's meeting was to finish making them so that the scale model of the institute that would be on display at the ball would be as accurate as possible.

"I've had an eleventh-hour thought about the entrance," Peter said after the other decisions had all been made. "I think I can make it feel even lighter and more welcoming. If you have time, there's a boutique I'd like to

131

show you—just about a block away—with an atrium similar to what I have in mind. What I would do in the institute would be less lavish than what I did at Sydney's, but the concept is essentially the same."

"You designed Sydney's?"

"Yes. Have you been there?"

"No, but I've certainly heard about it. I don't need to get back to the hospital for a while yet, so I'd be happy to go there with you now."

As Peter and Stephen made their way through the bustle of Union Square to Sydney's, Peter explained his relationship to Sydney and Walter Prescott. They were the Prescotts of Napa Valley's renowned Prescott Vineyards, and ten years before they had taken a chance with a bright young architect. The award-winning mansion at Prescott Vineyards had been one of Peter's first creations. Walter and Sydney had been so delighted with the mansion that they had commissioned Peter to design the bed-and-breakfast hotel they also owned in Napa as well as their hilltop home in Tiberon. And when, four years ago, the fashionable and energetic fifty-year-old Sydney Prescott announced that she had had it with traveling to New York and Paris to buy clothes and was going to bring the designs of the world to the women of San Francisco "or bust," she had asked Peter to design her elegant boutique.

Peter's obviously fond recounting of his relationship to the Prescotts finished just as he and Stephen arrived at Sydney's. Within moments of walking through the huge French doors into the rose-fragrant luxury, they were greeted by the glamorous Sydney herself.

"Peter!" Sydney smiled with obvious delight at the surprising yet very welcome appearance of her handsome and famous friend. "Don't tell me you're hand delivering the sketches for my Fifth Avenue boutique two weeks early?"

"No. But you will have them within two weeks," Peter assured. "Sydney, I'd like you to meet Doctor Stephen Sheridan. Stephen, this is Sydney Prescott."

"The Doctor Stephen Sheridan of immunology fame?" Sydney asked. Then, hesitating only a beat, she added knowingly, "Of Madolyn Mitchell fame?"

Stephen wasn't terribly surprised that Sydney had so swiftly and accurately made the connections. He had long since gotten the distinct impression from both Elizabeth and Madolyn that Sydney's was a sorority of sorts, a place where the regulars felt so relaxed and comfortable that they often shared tidbits from their personal lives. He was, apparently, a tidbit that had been shared.

"Guilty on both counts," he admitted, conveying with a warm smile and easy laugh that it didn't bother him that he had been discussed.

"Well, a lot of business has come my way because of both of those counts," Sydney said graciously. "Madolyn does all of her shopping here, and the boutique has become the unofficial supplier of evening gowns for the Immunology Institute ball. I have a feeling that most of San Francisco will be at the Fairmont that night. And why not? A celebration in honor of a building designed by the world's best architect and which will be home to the world's most brilliant immunologist is a pretty tough ticket to pass up."

"Well," Stephen countered with matching graciousness. "The reason everyone in San Francisco is buying their evening gowns here is because of you. Madolyn raves about the boutique, as does Elizabeth Jennings."

"Which must mean they rave about Christine," Sydney said. "I'm sure that Christine would very much like to meet you, Stephen. If you would like to meet her too, why don't I see if she's free?"

"That would be nice. I would indeed like to meet the famous Christine."

"In the meantime, Stephen and I will be wandering through the atrium," Peter said.

"Be my guest." Sydney started to turn to leave to find Christine, but suddenly remembering, she turned back and asked, "How was your trip to New York, Peter? Did you find a model?"

"No." Peter frowned. "Not yet."

"Well, it hardly matters. *Promise* will sell itself." Looking to Stephen for confirmation and seeing only interested surprise, Sydney added, "I guess Peter hasn't mentioned his latest venture to you?"

"I guess not."

"Well. *Promise* is a perfume. The reason why Peter London, architect, is marketing a new perfume is, apparently, a long story—which he has never fully disclosed," Sydney explained, her voice filled with teasing fondness and not a trace of censure at Peter's secrecy. "However, the ending to the long and mysterious story is that *Promise* is sensational." Smiling at Peter she added, "I do hope that model or no model you're still planning to release it next spring."

"I am. Model or no model," Peter affirmed quietly. "So, Syd, we're going to look at the atrium."

"And I'm going to go find Christine."

Sydney and Christine had not appeared by the time Peter and Stephen had finished discussing a modified version of the atrium which, Stephen agreed, would make the insti-

134

tute even more warm and welcoming. Peter had to leave for a marketing meeting for *Promise* in Sausalito, but Stephen decided to wait a little longer—to meet the famous Christine.

But Stephen didn't need to meet the famous Christine. He had met her two years before. She hadn't been the famous Christine then. She had simply been the quietly courageous Mrs. Andrews.

Mrs. Andrews. That was how Stephen had always addressed her. He had called David by his first name, and David had called him Stephen, but there had always been the formality with David's wife—despite the hundreds of times that Mrs. Andrews and Dr. Sheridan had seen each other during that year, and despite the emotional intimacy of the many conversations they had had about her beloved husband's life . . . and death. Stephen had known her first name, of course. David had spoken it often, gently wrapping it in the tenderness of their extraordinary love. But David had never called his wife Christine. She had always been Christie, his lovely and so beloved Christie.

Now Mrs. Andrews . . . Christie . . . Christine was approaching him.

There was no surprise on Christine's face, of course, and there was even a soft smile of greeting in her luminous lavender eyes—but there was something else, too . . . a wariness.

"Hello, Doctor Sheridan. I'm Christine."

"Hello, Christine," Stephen said, understanding then the other message in the remarkable lavender—Christine wanted to conceal their previous acquaintance. He smiled, acknowledging her wish for privacy and his respect for same, and then to the shy and beautiful woman who had always called him Dr. Sheridan, but who now

135

wanted to behave as if they were meeting for the first time, he said, "I'm Stephen."

As Stephen and Christine exchanged smiles, Sydney filled the silence with praises for both of them, as if they both were her prized pupils, Christine, the fashion genius, and Stephen, the miracle worker. Stephen murmured softly that he already knew that Christine was a fashion genius, and her lovely lavender eyes eloquently told him that she already knew that he could work miracles.

Only moments after saying hello, Christine and Stephen said goodbye. Her two o'clock appointment arrived, ten minutes late and breathless, having raced to salvage as much of her appointment as possible because she knew full well that Christine would be booked solid as always for the rest of the day.

As Stephen drove back to the medical center, his mind filled with memories of the first time he had said hello to Christine Andrews . . . and the last time he had said goodbye.

"Hello, Mrs. Andrews."

"Hello, Doctor Sheridan. Can you help my husband live a little longer?" The question had been asked with soft desperation, and it had been a plea neither for a lifetime nor a cure—just a little more precious time with the man she loved so much.

"Yes, Mrs. Andrews, I think I can."

LKC had given David Andrews twelve more months of life and love; eleven months of remarkable energy and health and a final month of deterioration and goodbye. During that year, every time David had received the life-prolonging yet potentially life-threatening infusions, Stephen had been at his bedside. In the beginning, both men had spent the hours in tense and expectant silence. But eventually, even though the risk of fatal anaphylaxis remained an ever-present concern, they had spent those long hours talking.

What David Andrews had talked about, all he had ever wanted to talk about in the final year of his life, was his beloved wife. He told Stephen a little about Christine's life before their love . . . and a great deal about the immense joy that that love had given him.

Christine had been the youngest daughter in a very large family. The fabric of her family had been loosely woven, not tightly knit, and the very shy Christine had been a forgotten thread left to fend for herself. David's voice had filled with bitterness when he had spoken of the family who had neglected Christine as a little girl and forgotten about her entirely—and forever—the day she left for college; but, David had admitted lovingly, his generous Christie had never felt any bitterness whatsoever. As a girl she had found her own quiet joy making beautiful clothes for her hand-me-down dolls and bravely dreaming of the day when she would be a fashion designer.

It was because of shy Christine's bold dream that she and David had met . . . and then there had been the new and wondrous dream of their lifetime of love together. Eventually, Christine had encouraged David to pursue the dream that had lived in his own heart for so long, the dream of becoming an artist. Until Christine, he had been afraid to pursue that dream, afraid to fail, perhaps, or maybe simply reluctant even to struggle. But the shy and beautiful woman twenty years younger than he had made him believe with her quiet confidence and boundless love that all dreams were possible, and eventually he had left the safe cloistered world of academia to pursue his dream.

For a long time they had had very little money, but they had had their wondrous love, and even the leanest years had never felt like a struggle at all. Finally, in the same year that would bring with it the diagnosis of lethal liver cancer, David Andrews had his first one-man show—at the prestigious Gallery in Ghirardelli Square.

David's voice had filled with bitterness when he had spoken of the family who had simply forgotten their shy and lovely daughter, but there had never been bitterness at all when he had talked about his own life-ending disease. And when he had spoken of his fears, there had never been mention of his own fear of dying—only his great fears for the young wife he would leave behind.

At least, David had told Stephen, she wouldn't be burdened with debts from his illness. Yes, the savings account that had just begun to grow would be largely depleted to pay the high deductibles, but they had an excellent health insurance policy and most of the enormous cost of his catastrophic illness would be covered. It had been Christie, David added softly, the always responsible Christie, who had insisted that they buy good health coverage when he left the university, even though the expense had cut sharply into their already modest income.

David had been spared the worry of leaving behind a destitute and indebted wife, but he had worried about her still. He wanted her life after his death to be a happy one, filled with love and laughter and all the dreams as yet unfulfilled . . . her brave girlhood dream of becoming a fashion designer . . . and her more recent and far more important dream of becoming a mother.

Just as David and Christine had decided that it was at last economically possible for them to begin having children, his cancer had been diagnosed. They had tried still, but as the doctors had warned it might, the toxic but necessary chemotherapy had poisoned the fragile sperm. During the final year of his life, they had made love to be as close as they could for as long as they could, but they had long since abandoned the hope that David could leave a part of himself with her. But, during that final year, David had received Stephen's innovative immunotherapy, not the toxic chemotherapy, and two months before his death, Christine had discovered that she was pregnant.

As he had received the last dose of LKC—because the miracle therapy had finally come to the end of its magic— David shared with Stephen the immense joy of Christine's pregnancy. It was a joy, not a sadness, because already the tiny life growing inside her filled Christine with great happiness. There would be some money left in their savings account after all the insurance deductibles had been paid, David explained, and Christine could make whatever additional money that she and the baby would need by working as a seamstress—work she loved and could do at home.

There had been a loving glow in David's dying eyes as he had told Stephen about the baby he would never see. The glow had always been there, of course, for Christine, because of Christine; just as her beautiful lavender eyes had always glowed when she was with David. Christine Andrews never permitted the man she loved so much to see anything but her love, her hope, and her joy. Her lavender eyes had always glowed, and her voice had always been soft and musical, and the delicate hands that had touched David whenever they could had never been frantic nor possessive, just calm, just loving, just wanting to touch.

For David, Christine's loving eyes and voice and hands filled only with joyous hope; but in the private conversations she had with Stephen, the radiant lavender became stormy with anguished tears and the soft voice strained with heart-stopping fear and the delicate courageous hands trembled.

"David wants to die at home, Doctor Sheridan."

"Yes, I know. But how do you feel about that, Mrs. Andrews? I'll arrange for visiting nurses, of course, but still it may be very difficult for you."

"I want what David wants. It won't be difficult for me. And, please, don't arrange for anyone to come by. I won't need any help. We'll be all right, just the two of us."

Yes, but soon, Mrs. Andrews, very soon, David will leave you, and in that moment of his death, when his body is there but he is gone and you are alone . . . Stephen didn't speak that worry aloud to her, but he made her promise that she would call him when David died, no matter the time of day or night.

As he drove from Sydney's to the medical center, Stephen recalled the day that David had died, his frown deepening as he realized that the one-year anniversary of that death had been just a few days before. That Sunday afternoon in August had been quite glorious, the sky a brilliant sapphire, the summer sun a radiant gold, a day for celebrating—not for watching a most beloved husband die.

Stephen had been in his lab on that Sunday afternoon. Christine knew the phone number there, and that he often worked on weekends, but on the day her husband died, she did just what Stephen had told her to do: she dialed the number to his pager so that she wouldn't have to search for him.

Stephen heard a soft apology in the quiet voice at the other end of the phone, as if Christine was sorry to have disturbed him on this splendid Sunday afternoon. But it was *he* who wanted to apologize to *her!* His immunotherapy was a breakthrough, a pioneering effort that might eventually light the way to a cure for cancer. But for David and Christine Andrews, the innovative therapy had not been a cure, only a stay.

Had David's illness simply come too soon? Stephen wondered. Or had his own bright mind simply missed some tiny clue years ago, a clue that might have led him to the revolutionary concept even sooner? Stephen didn't know, but still he thought, I'm so very sorry that I couldn't keep him alive for you forever, Mrs. Andrews.

Stephen's unspoken apology became a silent scream when Christine greeted him at the door of the modest house that she and David rented on Twin Peaks. She was dressed as she always dressed for David, in soft romantic pastels, her golden hair a cascade of glitter that gently framed her lovely face and spilled freely onto her shoulders. She looked beautiful, as she always looked for David, even for his death. Her spun-gold hair glittered, and the pastel dress sent a message of romance and love, but the glow was gone from her lavender eyes, and so was the fear—because what she had always feared most had finally happened. Her eyes were dark, almost gray, and her face was ashen, deathlike, as if she had died with her husband.

All the arrangements had been made in advance. Even before Stephen arrived, Christine had made the necessary call, and shortly after his arrival the two dark-suited men appeared to silently carry out their solemn task. Stephen needed to sign and date the death certificate, which he did, and then David was gone, and Stephen was alone with Christine.

David's parents were dead, Stephen knew, and Christine's family had forgotten her years ago, and no friends had ever visited David in the hospital. The world of David and Christine Andrews had been the very private world of two lovers, a world Stephen had witnessed perhaps more intimately than anyone else ever had. She was very much alone now, and Stephen very much wanted to stay with her, but it was abundantly obvious that she wanted him to leave. She seemed, in fact, almost desperate to have him go. She assured him that she was fine, and that some "very good friends" would come to be with her as soon as she called them. Stephen knew it was a lie and was amazed at how convincingly she spoke it, her gaze steady and unflickering.

There were no friends, Stephen knew: that was a lie. Christine was almost desperate in her wish to have him leave: that was the truth.

Before reluctantly acceding to her wish, Stephen promised, as much to David as to her, that he would call in a day or two to see how she was.

"No," she countered swiftly. Then, as if in apology for the swiftness of her refusal, she added softly, "Thank you."

For a terrifying moment, Stephen wondered if Christine wanted him to leave so that she could take her own life, an impulsive act of desperation, needing to be with David, knowing that she would not survive long without him anyway. How could she, with only half a heart? Stephen knew she would vehemently deny that intent if he asked her, and for a moment he considered simply staying anyway, forcing his unwanted presence on her, holding her, protecting her, comforting her.

But then he remembered. Christine was carrying David's baby. She would do nothing to harm the small precious part of David that lived within her.

So he left. And later that night he called her, even though she had told him not to, because he had been suddenly seized by an ominous and unshakable feeling that she was dying. Had she not answered the call, he would have gone to find her. But she did answer, and with a voice that was flat but clear, she told him that she was fine.

Stephen decided he wouldn't call her again. He was, after all, a grim reminder of David's death. But he did call, five days later, because he was so worried about her still . . . and because, he told himself, David would have wanted him to. Stephen heard a little more energy in her voice then, a little anger perhaps—and still the very clear message to stay away.

After that, he did stay away, never calling her, even though he thought about her often. With time, his worry changed to hope. He envisioned the same comforting image that had allowed David to die with such peace: the image of Christine and her baby. Stephen thought about the new life growing inside her, filling her with love and hope, and five months ago, when he finally figured out why he himself had been feeling so inexplicably happy and hopeful it was, astonishingly, because his subconscious mind had been envisioning Christine Andrews cradling her just-born infant.

But now Stephen had seen Christine again and all the comforting images had been instantly shattered. *There was no baby.* Madolyn had been raving about Christine for the entire six months that Stephen had known her, and she had even wondered, more than once, what she would do if Christine ever got pregnant and took a protracted maternity leave.

143

Had there ever been a baby? Stephen wondered. Or had that simply been a lie of love whispered gently and joyously so that David could die in peace? Yes, Stephen thought, as he remembered how courageously Christine had hidden her own fears from her husband. Yes, she would have given David that gift of love.

As he pulled into his parking space at the medical center, a dark frown crossed Stephen's handsome face. There was something more that Madolyn had said about her worry that Christine might become pregnant and leave, something that had made that possibility seem quite real. Christine worked very long hours, as if she were trying to earn as much money as she could—for a nest egg, Madolyn assumed.

There were other reasons why someone might work long hours at Sydney's, especially someone who was an aspiring fashion designer. The elegant boutique was an excellent place to establish a reputation for fashion and style, and Stephen had learned today that Peter London was designing a new boutique in Manhattan, in the heart of the fashion world . . .

But the woman Stephen had seen in Sydney's today didn't look like someone pursuing an exciting dream. Yes, Christine had been smiling and pleasant, and perhaps to anyone who hadn't known her before, she would have seemed perfectly fine. But Stephen knew how her lavender eyes looked when they were filled with hope and joy and love and dreams; and even though she had looked much better today than the last time he had seen her, Christine still looked to him like someone who had lost all of her dreams . . . not someone who was pursuing new and exciting ones.

Maybe she worked the long hours in the lovely rose-fragrant boutique simply to escape the terrible loneliness of her life without David. That was possible, Stephen thought. In fact, it was a very good reason and a very good place for her to be.

But what if, as Madolyn had presumed, Christine was working so hard because she needed money?

What if there had been other lies of love spoken to David so that he could die in peace?

Chapter Eleven

After thirty troubling yet illuminating minutes with the supervisor in hospital billing, Stephen went to medical records and requested all four volumes of David's medical file. The four thick charts, a compendium of all records from the referring hospital as well as the records kept during his year of care at the center, were in the archives, the basement room in a remote corner of the medical complex where the records of patients who had died were kept, because by law they had to be, but far away because the patients to whom they had once belonged would never again require further care. Medical records prided itself in being able to produce any active file in a matter of minutes; but trips to the archives were rarely made more than once a week, and never urgently.

Yes, Stephen told the surprised clerk, David Andrews was deceased. But, he added pleasantly but firmly, he needed the file right away anyway.

David was, and still is, my patient, Stephen thought. And there is more care that I need to provide for him.

Stephen extracted a promise from the clerk that she would go to the archives herself, as soon as the flurry of finding charts for the walk-in clinic subsided, then he left to wait in his office. As he walked, Stephen thought about the truth he had uncovered and the questions that lingered still. There was no baby. But had that promise of a new life, the great joy that part of David would be with Christine always, been simply a lie of love? Or had she really been pregnant, but so overwhelmed by the enormous debts after David's death that she had . . .

"Stephen?"

"Elizabeth," he answered as he turned in the direction of the familiar voice that had interrupted the deeply disturbing question. "Hi."

"Hi. You were about a million miles away." As she met his obviously troubled brown eyes, she asked softly, "Is something wrong?"

"Do you have time to talk?"

"Sure. In fact, I was on my way to your office to see if you'd returned yet from your meeting with the architect. Was there a problem with that?"

"No, no problem at all. Why don't we pick up a coffee and a tea in the cafeteria and go to my office?"

"Do you remember David Andrews?" Stephen asked when they were in his office and behind closed doors. "He was the patient who had hepatic cancer—"

"Of course I remember."

"Well, I just discovered that the Christine at Sydney's who you and Madolyn have been raving about all this time is his wife."

"Yes."

"*Yes?* You knew?"

"I've only known since Saturday."

"Were you going to tell me?"

Elizabeth stiffened slightly at the sharp demand, then

met his frowning dark eyes directly and admitted quietly, "I honestly don't know, Stephen. I hadn't decided yet. Christine didn't know that you and I were friends—but she knew that we both worked here and she certainly knew about you and Madolyn—and she made the choice not to mention her past association with either you or the center."

"Until last Saturday."

"No. She only mentioned it then because of another coincidence. It's a long story, but as a result of that story, it came up quite naturally. Christine hasn't been trying to be secretive, Stephen. I think she's just very private, not at all the kind of person who would purposefully search for either attention or sympathy. It's been a year since David's death, after all, and she's obviously getting on with her life."

"But she's *not* getting on with it," Stephen countered. "She's spending every minute working as hard as she can to pay the hospital bills that should rightfully have been paid by her insurance company."

"What?" Elizabeth's emerald eyes widened with surprise and concern. "How did that happen?"

"Apparently when David was initially diagnosed, there was a question of whether he was predisposed to developing hepatic cancer because of a family history of hemochromatosis."

"A logical question to consider in anyone presenting with that type of cancer."

"Yes. And, in fact, there was even a cousin who had had what David thought might have been hepatic cancer. As it turned out the cousin had hepatic metastases, not primary liver cancer, and in the meantime all underlying risk factors including hemochromatosis had been categorically excluded anyway. But still, based on the

148

initial suggestion of a possible family history of hemo-chromatosis, the insurance company refused to pay a penny for his care."

"The bills must be staggering," Elizabeth offered quietly. "Hadn't he been treated at another hospital for quite a while before being referred here?"

Stephen nodded solemnly. "He had a year of extremely aggressive—and very appropriate—chemotherapy, during which he had more than his share of catastrophic complications. By the time he was transferred here, his bills were already in excess of three hundred thousand, and once here, he was an inpatient on the oncology service—in the ICU for almost three weeks—before the decision was made to try LKC."

"At which point all his medical expenses were covered by your grant, weren't they?"

"Yes. Which is why I never had to fill out any insurance forms and had no idea of the truth." Stephen sighed softly. *The truth.* "I had no idea—and neither did David. Christine just quietly met with the supervisors in the billing offices here and at the other hospital and promised to pay all the bills in full, no matter how long it took her. David died believing that they had excellent coverage—which in fact they did—although the deductibles on the policy were higher than he had realized."

"But David must have been told that the studies showed that he didn't have hemochromatosis."

"I assume so, although I don't know for sure. That was all very ancient history by the time he was transferred here. My guess is that David did know the diagnosis had been excluded, but that he had no idea how important that knowledge was. He probably never even mentioned it to Christine, because it was a tiny detail that had no impact whatsoever on the outcome of his disease."

149

"But Christine knew the impact of that tiny detail on the insurance coverage, and yet apparently she never asked either David or his doctors about it. I wonder why not."

"Because," Stephen answered with quiet confidence, "she was afraid that David would find out that they didn't have insurance coverage after all. She knew that if he knew that his illness would leave her indebted for the rest of her life he would have refused further treatment."

Elizabeth's emerald eyes became solemn as she thought about the gifts of love David and Christine Andrews had been so willing to give to each other. David would have died to spare his beloved wife financial hardship after his death, and Christine had committed her life to repaying the debts that had enabled her to spend as many precious moments as she could with her husband.

"I wonder why Christine waited this long after David's death before coming to you to confirm the diagnosis."

"Christine didn't come to me, Elizabeth. It turns out that Peter London designed Sydney's and since he wants to use a similar atrium for the institute the two of us stopped by the boutique this afternoon. I saw Christine, and we exchanged a brief hello as if we'd never met before, and after I left I started thinking about how hard Madolyn has always said she works. Madolyn's assumption has always been that the hard work was because she needed money, but I knew from David that she should have been fine financially. I got to worrying and stopped by hospital billing when I returned."

"And the supervisor told you that Christine had met with her and promised to pay all her bills in full."

"That, and that she could have declared bankruptcy, which is what the overwhelming majority of people with far less debt than this usually do." Stephen's voice softened as he added, "But that's not Christine. She's repaying the bills as promised, slowly but surely, sending as much money as she can every month and getting by on very little herself. I really hate the fact that she has struggled all this time . . . and that she was planning to struggle forever."

"Christine works very hard, Stephen, but I do think she enjoys what she does at Sydney's. She and Larisa met briefly in college—which is how this all came up last Saturday—and she had plans then to become a designer. Working at Sydney's isn't a bad stepping-stone for someone with that goal, and once the insurance fiasco is resolved, she can spend fewer hours in the boutique and do some designing, if that's what she wants."

Elizabeth had hoped that her truthful words would begin to reassure the turbulence in her friend's very dark eyes. But in the midst of her gentle reassurance, Stephen's expression grew even darker and more troubled—as if there had been something truly terrible about Christine having spent the past year working so hard at Sydney's.

"What are you thinking, Stephen?" she asked gently. Then, suddenly finding a possible answer to her own question, the gentleness vanished as she demanded, "Have you decided that Christine is a modern-day Cinderella who has spent the past year slaving away, dressing everyone else for the ball? Because, you know, if you have that casts me—and Madolyn, by the way—as the wicked stepsisters."

"Whoa!" Stephen commanded the suddenly flashing emerald. "That wasn't what I was thinking at all." *I was thinking about the baby.* "It probably has been good for Christine to work at Sydney's, to spend time in such a happy upbeat place doing something for which she is obviously so appreciated and respected."

"Okay, well, sorry I bristled." Elizabeth smiled. Then, tilting her dark curls thoughtfully, she added, "Even though it wasn't what you were thinking, in one way, perhaps the most important way of all, Christine actually is a modern-day Cinderella."

"Oh?"

"Yes. She found her Prince Charming, and he found her. I remember your telling me about their relationship, how extraordinary it was, and hearing her talk about David last Saturday made me realize that she had truly lived the wonderful fairy tale about which most people only ever dream. Their love couldn't go on forever, but I imagine the memory of it will be enough to last Christine her entire lifetime."

"Yes," Stephen agreed softly. He had been a witness to the fairy-tale love of David and Christine, and even though David had confided in him his wish that Christine would find another love, it seemed impossible to Stephen that any other man could ever penetrate the wall of magnificent memories that surrounded her loving heart. Christine would never search for a new love, would never want or need to, but she had other dreams—and it was Stephen's hope to free her to follow them. "I've asked medical records to get David's files from the archives. Once I've got the pertinent lab reports in front of me, I'm going to call the insurance company and straighten this out."

"After first speaking with Christine."

"What? No, I hadn't planned to talk to her at all."

"I think you should, Stephen."

"Why? She surely wouldn't have any objection. She didn't choose to spend her life in debt. In fact, even though she and David had very little discretionary income, they made certain that they had good health coverage despite the fact that because they were self-employed the cost was very high. I'm simply correcting an error that was made a long time ago, Elizabeth. Any of David's doctors would have done the same had they known. I don't even particularly want Christine to know that I'm the one involved."

"I absolutely agree that the error should be corrected and that the insurance company should assume the debt. But I still think you should discuss it with Christine in advance. I can't explain why I think this, Stephen. It's just a feeling."

"And your feelings are usually right on target. Which worries me, because it hadn't even occurred to me to speak with her first."

"Well, I'm probably entirely wrong about this," Elizabeth said with a soft shrug. "My instincts about what's right—and wrong—to say have been very far off target today."

"Something with Larisa?"

"No. Something—or rather nothing—with your good friend Nick. As usual." Elizabeth gave a wobbly smile as she waved her slender hand in dismissal of the hopeless topic of Nicholas Chase. The four-hour-ago scene in the surgery lounge was still painfully fresh, but there was absolutely no point in discussing it with Stephen. He would be very annoyed at what Nick had done, as always, and, as always, she would only annoy him further by suddenly leaping to Nick's defense. Quickly finding a safe topic, she said, "Speaking of Larisa, though, she is at this very moment meeting with my brother to talk about her divorce from Julian. Hopefully it can happen soon. I don't think she'll really be better until all ties with Julian have been severed."

* * *

"Hello, Larisa." Mark greeted her warmly when he appeared at the doorway to his inner office only moments after his secretary had buzzed him to announce Larisa's arrival.

There was very little physical resemblance between Elizabeth and her blond-haired blue-eyed older brother. But now as Larisa met the smiling blue eyes, she realized that there were striking similarities between the Jennings siblings nonetheless, deep and important ones: kindness and generosity . . . and great strength of character.

"Hello, Mark."

"Please come in."

"Thank you."

Mark gestured toward a conversation area across his plushly carpeted office. As Larisa led the way, she hoped that her gait looked more graceful and confident than it felt. The stylishly loose-fitting silk harem pants that she wore still, a week after her desperate escape from Manhattan, gave the illusion of graceful elegance. She needed that illusion to cover her wobbliness just as she needed the pants to cover the fading-but-still-apparent bruises. The bruises were slowly fading, and the pain was gradually relenting, and her energy was returning in small unpredictable promises. Today, wanting to appear as strong and confident for Mark as possible, she had conserved her limited energy all day, hoping for a burst when she needed it.

When she reached her destination, Larisa paused in front of the window, her blue eyes smiling appreciatively at the spectacular view of the bridge and the bay. Then, swept by a sudden wave of weakness, she settled onto the

154

nearby sofa and focused on the silver-framed portrait of Mark's two girls that sat on the coffee table.

"They're gorgeous, Mark," she said truthfully. "And so grown up."

"They grow up too quickly," Mark answered softly. "Wendy and I hope that you and Elizabeth will come to dinner sometime soon. We live in Atherton, which means we need to find a time when my little sister feels she can be that far away from the hospital."

"A feeling that has nothing to do with whether she's officially on call or not."

"So you've noticed." Mark smiled.

Larisa returned the smile and said quietly, "Last weekend she wanted to stay close by the hospital—to which she checked in frequently—because of Molly and Mary Ann. She made it sound like a special situation, but I had the distinct impression that there's always some patient she needs to be near."

"Always," Mark confirmed, his voice filling with a mixture of love and pride. "That's why, every so often, she has to be encouraged to leave town."

"I know she's really looking forward to Christmas in London." All the Jennings would be there and Elizabeth had already graciously invited Larisa to join them. "We'll take Harrod's by storm," she had teased. Larisa could think of nothing more wonderful than spending Christmas in England with the Jennings family, but it was a faraway dream. For now all her thoughts and energies had to be focused on trying to heal, trying to be stronger with each new golden sunrise than she had been the sunrise before. During the past five days, her thoughts and energies had had a very specific goal: to be as strong as possible for this all-important meeting with Mark. Mark . . . he seemed so warm, so welcoming. But, Larisa wondered with a shiver, when he learned the truths about her would he approve of his generous little sister's gracious offer that she join their family holiday?

"Christmas in London will be terrific," Mark agreed. "But, Larisa, maybe sometime you could convince Elizabeth to do something really frivolous like a pure vacation—something without family obligations or medical meetings or guest lectureships or cameo appearances in operating rooms."

"I'll give it my best shot," Larisa answered, amazed that this protective older brother who had once worried that she might lead his innocent little sister astray now wanted her help in orchestrating a frivolous adventure for her. It was a flattering request, but a most difficult one, because the once fearless and adventuresome Larisa Locksley who had existed at Berkeley existed no more. "I can't promise results, Mark. The truth is that Elizabeth is very happy working twenty-four hours a day."

"I know." Mark smiled. Then, because they had finished sharing their mutual love and concern for Elizabeth, he suggested quietly, "So, Larisa, tell me."

"Why I want a divorce?"

"You don't need to tell me that if you don't want to," he assured the suddenly worried blue eyes. "And the courts don't need to know anything more specific than irreconcilable differences."

"I guess that's good. Much more private."

"Yes." Mark hesitated briefly before adding, "Ideally, though, you and Julian should both know why the marriage is ending."

"Julian and I both do know, Mark," Larisa answered quietly. "But that doesn't mean that he isn't going to fight this. Julian doesn't like losing anything. He's going to be very angry when he learns that I want a divorce. In fact, I honestly don't think he'll permit it."

"You'll get your divorce, Larisa," Mark said confidently to the woman who had herself once glittered with limitless confidence but who now seemed so uncertain and fragile. "We'll—I'll—weather Julian's anger until he accepts the reality that the divorce will happen. So why don't you and I just discuss the settlement? Do you have a prenuptial agreement?"

"No. We had about a two-second discussion on the topic. I told Julian I wanted our love to last forever, and he said he wanted that too, and so we decided that the whole idea was too unromantic to pursue." Larisa shrugged softly at her own foolishness. "I know that everyone says a prenuptial agreement makes good sense, and everyone was definitely saying that six years ago, but . . . I don't have one."

"Don't be too hard on yourself, Larisa. The fact that you don't have a prenuptial agreement means that instead of getting ten, fifteen, or twenty-five million dollars, you're entitled to half of what Julian has earned or acquired while you were married. From what I know about Julian Chancellor, his empire is rock solid, not a house of cards built on a precarious foundation of volatile junk bonds or grandiose visions."

"That's right. Julian's empire is built on good old-fashioned cash and his instincts have always been pure gold. His empire isn't about to crumble." Larisa's blue eyes met Mark's as she said solemnly, "But I didn't marry Julian for his money and I don't care about it now. All I want is a divorce."

"You are legally entitled to millions, Larisa. In fact, I suppose that half of what Julian has made in the past six years could even entitle you to something in the billions."

157

"I don't care about any of it, Mark, not a penny," Larisa repeated softly. "And I can assure you that Julian will care. He hates to lose. He doesn't even know how to. In the six years I've known him, I know of only one instance in which he didn't get exactly what he wanted . . . and when it happened he was furious, enraged." A shiver of ice swept through her as she remembered that night and she was suddenly aware of the intense pain in her hands as her pale delicate fingers dug mercilessly and ever-deeper into her snow-white palms. Forcing her fingers to uncurl, at least a little, she continued, "No matter how bad our marriage has been, Julian is going to strongly resist the idea of a divorce. Attaching a price tag to that loss, making him part with even the tiniest piece of his empire, will make him only more determined to block the divorce. Really, Mark, just getting him to agree to a divorce would be a monumental triumph."

"Surely we can be more triumphant than that."

"No. All I want is the divorce—no money, no property, just my freedom." For a moment Larisa's eyes lit with a radiant hope, as if the brilliant blue could actually see that distant and wonderful dream. Then she returned to the present, tilted her shimmering firelit golden head thoughtfully and offered quietly, "But that wouldn't make for much of a contingency, would it?"

"Contingency?" Mark echoed, feeling a sudden and powerful rush of anger as he realized that she was referring to his fee, *his* percent of the millions or billions. The surprising strength of the anger was because it came with old memories, reminders of the Larisa he once had known, the dazzling young woman who had so defiantly and contemptuously rejected his willingness to protect her as he had protected Elizabeth—as if Larisa didn't trust him. Her instant mistrust of him had been insulting and infuriating then, and now the implication that he would be disappointed if she didn't try to get as much as possible from Julian was insulting and infuriating once again. Mark struggled with his own emotions, finally subduing them by looking at the fragile woman who was seated across from him. Larisa had obviously been terribly hurt by Julian. Even without knowing the details, it seemed quite clear that she had loved and trusted her husband—and had been betrayed.

When he was calm enough to speak, Mark explained evenly, "I never work on contingency in divorce cases, Larisa. I made no contribution whatsoever to the marriage, so why in the world should I benefit from the divorce?" His voice became more gentle, more normal, as he added, "My fee for handling your divorce will be my usual fee for a family member—a smile, maybe?"

Mark hoped for a smile then, but Larisa's beautiful face remained solemn as she reminded softly, "You don't have a usual fee for family members, Mark. There has never been a divorce in the Jennings family, has there?"

Mark waved a dismissive hand. "If it will make you feel better, I'll keep track of my time and as part of the divorce agreement we'll let Julian pay all legal expenses. So," he continued swiftly, definitively, "I know you've said that you would be happy with just a divorce, but for the sake of argument, let's talk a little more about a financial settlement. You must have entered the marriage with a fair amount of money of your own. You were a top—*the* top?—fashion model when you met him, after all."

"My net worth when we married was about a million dollars. I was very rich by any standard in the world except Julian's—and I simply gave all my money to him. It wasn't a grand gesture, Mark. What I had was just a tiny drop in the vast ocean of Julian's wealth. He handled

159

all our finances. I didn't have credit cards or a separate bank account, and I had no need for either. Julian has standing accounts at all the major boutiques, restaurants, and clubs in Manhattan, so with just my signature I could get whatever I wanted—and there was always cash at the penthouse for incidentals." Larisa shrugged softly at her confession, proof-positive of her own silly romanticism and so very contrary to the conventional wisdom of the eighties which strongly encouraged women to protect themselves financially. That important information had been communicated to the women of America through talk shows and national magazines. How ironic that so often it had been a photograph of supermodel Larisa Locksley that had induced women to buy those magazines. Her beautiful face had become a dazzling symbol of the strong yet feminine, romantic yet independent woman of the eighties; but Larisa herself had ignored all the sage advice and had given everything to Julian—her financial worth . . . and her self-worth. "Pretty foolish, huh?"

"No," Mark replied with quiet reassurance. "Even though I have to give legal advice about sensible strategies to protect oneself in the event that a marriage doesn't survive, I guess I still like to believe . . ."

"In the fairy tale."

"In the fairy tale," Mark echoed. "Yes."

"Well," Larisa said. "So much for happy endings. Where were we?"

"We'd established that you had about a million dollars when you entered the marriage."

"That was a gift freely given from me to Julian. I wouldn't expect to get it back, not that Julian would consider returning it anyway. I think he would view a million dollars as trivial compensation for six years of his life wasted in a failed marriage."

"All right. Tell me a little more about your life-style then. You've already said that your signature could buy anything you wanted."

"Yes. I was a princess living in a world of limitless luxury," Larisa said quietly, her wry, sad smile eloquently conveying the emptiness of that luxurious world. "It wasn't a life-style that I needed then . . . and it's certainly not a life-style I need now. I don't want—or need—support from Julian. Except for the six years of my marriage, I've worked virtually all my life. I'll find a way to support myself again."

"You hardly need to find a way to support yourself, Larisa. You'll go back to modeling, won't you? I got the impression from Elizabeth that you enjoyed it very much."

"I did. I loved it. But I think I'm a little past my prime as a model, don't you?" Larisa didn't pause long enough to allow Mark to answer. She knew his words would be far more gracious and encouraging than truthful. He was a Jennings, after all, and therefore much too kind to agree that yes, in fact, now that he really looked at her, it was obvious that she was past her prime. That truth hardly mattered anyway because . . . "Julian wouldn't permit me to model again anyway."

"Julian will have no say over what you do once you're no longer married, Larisa," Mark said calmly, even though he felt another powerful rush of anger. This time, at least, it was appropriately directed where it belonged: Julian.

"You don't know him, Mark. He has incredible power and influence. If it became known that he didn't like the idea of his ex-wife modeling again, no one would hire me.

I'm not talking about anything criminal, of course. The only force Julian needs is the strength of his wealth. The simple truth is that no one—not the magazine publishers who would run the print ads, nor the fashion designers who might use me as a model, nor even the giant cosmetic companies—would risk Julian's disapproval."

"Okay," Mark agreed, despite his own powerful wish to go into an all-out battle with Julian Chancellor, to make him really pay for so obviously hurting Larisa. Mark subdued his own wish with the memory of the hopefulness in her brilliant blue eyes at just the thought of a divorce. Smiling, he said gently, "So, let me see if I have this right. What you would like is a nice, simple divorce."

"Nice, simple," Larisa echoed. "But impossible. Oh, Mark, I probably shouldn't even get you involved in this."

"Nonsense on both counts. First, it's not the least bit impossible, especially given that you're willing to forgo any settlement at all. And second, you've made me more than a little intrigued about Julian. I like challenges, Larisa. I'm looking forward to speaking with him."

"He can be very persuasive and very charming. He may say terrible things about me, Mark." Larisa frowned and confessed, "I've made mistakes, I don't deny that, but I'm sure that Julian will make them sound like horrendous crimes."

"Of course he will. That comes with the territory. I'm used to it, and, don't forget, I'm on your side." Mark smiled reassuringly and after a moment asked, "Just for the record, are there any mistakes that Julian's made that I should know about? A little ammunition I could use in return if I thought it was useful?"

"Julian knows what he's done," Larisa answered quietly. He knows what I've allowed him to do, she thought. But I can't tell you, Mark. I'm far too ashamed.

"Okay. I'll just weather the volleys, paying no attention to them whatsoever, and eventually Julian will have to talk to me about the divorce."

"I hope so."

"I know so," Mark countered firmly. "I suppose I could get Julian's telephone number from you?"

"Oh, sure."

As Larisa provided the number to the direct line to Julian's office and the name of his private secretary, Mark carefully recorded both on the yellow legal pad that had until that moment been quite untouched. Despite a memory that was almost as photographic as his little sister's, Mark always took comprehensive notes during meetings with clients. But he had taken none with Larisa. Her wish was simple and crystal clear. He wouldn't forget it.

"I'll call Julian first thing tomorrow morning," Mark said when he finished writing.

"Okay." Then, almost urgently, Larisa asked, "Julian doesn't need to know where I am, does he? I really don't want to talk to him . . . or see him . . . ever again."

"No, he doesn't need to know. But don't you think he might guess that you're with Elizabeth?"

"Yes, but as far as I know, he thinks she's still in Dallas."

"Oh. Good. He'll probably make the connection with my last name, though, so I'll plan to be up-front about the fact that I'm Elizabeth's brother and that you contacted me because you two were college roommates." Mark smiled. "I'll keep you posted on all relevant developments."

"All right."

"And remember, Larisa, nice and simple."

"Oh," she answered softly, "I hope so."

After speaking with Christine first. By her own admission Elizabeth's suggestion had been based on vague feelings, not a clear and logical reason. Still, because he respected and trusted her instincts—with the glaring exception of her inexplicable defense of Nicholas Chase—Stephen paused to reconsider her advice before calling the insurance company.

Elizabeth had an uncanny ability to sense the deepest layers of emotion with the minimum of clues. But, Stephen thought, this was a clear-cut issue of red tape, not an issue of deeply layered emotion. The error needed to be corrected, and it was his responsibility as David's doctor, as David's friend, to see that Christine not be encumbered for life by debts which were rightfully not hers to pay. This time, he decided, Elizabeth's instincts were wrong.

Stephen politely but firmly insisted on speaking with the insurance company's most senior available official. He knew that it would take a while to unravel the red tape, but starting at the top would surely make the unraveling process proceed more swiftly. And, as he pointed out when he finally had the right official on the line, surely the company itself, which in fact had an excellent reputation, would want a swift resolution as well. Stephen's approach was calm and collegial, a friend notifying a friend of an unwitting mistake, never implying even for a moment that the error might have been made intentionally to avoid paying the huge claim.

When the official pointed out that the case would need to be carefully and thoroughly investigated, Stephen readily agreed. But he did not allow the conversation to end until a definite time had been set for him to go over David's medical record with the claims adjustor to demonstrate exactly how the error had been made—and then to provide the documents that unequivocally proved that David Andrews's cancer had been simply a tragic whim of fate unrelated to any preexisting condition whatsoever.

Chapter Twelve

"We—Larisa, you and I—all know the truth about what really happened, Mr. Chancellor," Mark said quietly. "The question is, do you want the world to know?"

The silence at the other end of the phone told Mark that there was something, some dark secret truth that Julian had assumed Larisa would never disclose. Larisa *hadn't* disclosed the secret, of course, but Mark decided to try the bluff anyway. It was necessary, he had decided, because in the past five days, Julian hadn't budged at all from his initial position of no divorce. He hadn't budged, but he had been more than willing to talk. Julian wanted his wife . . . and Mark was his only link to her.

Julian was everything Larisa had promised he would be: arrogant, dogmatic, persuasive, confident. With the patient and almost-bored haughtiness of the very wealthy, he had explained over and over again that there *would be no divorce*. To which Mark had replied, over and over again, without haughtiness but with matching patience, that in fact there *would be*. Eventually Julian had taken the tack Larisa had predicted he would—a litany of her crimes. His approach was clever, his voice gentle not vituperative as he spoke of her cocaine abuse, her wanton-

166

ness, her emotional instability. He was very willing to forgive everything, he said, because he loved her so much. And, because he loved her so much, he wanted to see that she got the professional help she so obviously needed. With almost convincing emotion, Julian told Mark that once Larisa got the help she needed and was truly better, he was confident that she would want to return to their wonderful love.

After five days with absolutely no headway, Mark decided to try the bluff, to let Julian believe that he knew the sordid secret and to further let him believe that Larisa was willing to make that secret public. And now, as the bluff was met with a silence that lingered a few beats longer than the carefully measured strategic pauses that had typified the past five days, Mark sensed victory—a first step toward victory—at last.

When Julian finally answered, the contempt in his elegant voice was unconcealed. "Larisa's life with me has always been luxurious, pampered, *perfect*. Whatever fantasy she has told you about any harm she might have suffered because of her marriage to me is purely a lie."

"Well. I was convinced," Mark replied with confident calm, even though he knew he was skating on the thinnest of ice. There was some specific secret, that was obvious now. But he seriously doubted that Larisa, who wouldn't even confess it privately to him, would be willing to reveal it publicly. Still, maybe all that mattered was that Julian believed she would. Mark repeated firmly, "I was convinced. I think most people would be."

"She's manipulating you, Mr. Jennings, just as she manipulated me."

"I don't feel the least bit manipulated, Mr. Chancellor."

In the resigned silence that followed, Mark sensed capitulation. He waited with restless patience, hoping that Julian's next words would be the ones he expected to hear.

The wait was worth it.

"I suppose Larisa is quite capable of manipulating the press." Julian sighed heavily. "All right. Larisa will get her divorce. But be warned. Just because I don't want her lies to become headlines in the scandal sheets doesn't mean that I'm going to roll over and play dead. Tell her for me that there are going to be some ground rules for this divorce."

"He's really willing to give me a divorce?" Larisa whispered with disbelieving joy when Mark called. "I can't believe it."

"We don't know the terms yet, Larisa," Mark reminded. "From now on I'll be dealing with Julian's attorney. Our initial conversation is scheduled for ten tomorrow morning."

"But the terms don't matter, Mark! I told you, I don't want anything from Julian but the divorce."

The terms did matter though, very much, because the first condition stipulated by Julian's attorney was simply impossible for Larisa to accept. Julian wanted them to live together again, for a period of six months, after which time, if it was what she still wanted, she could walk away with half of his fortune.

"I can't do it, Mark. I can't live with him again." She repeated with soft despair, "I just can't."

"I know. I already told his attorney that I doubted you

would agree, but I promised I would discuss it with you anyway."

"The divorce isn't going to happen, is it?"

"Yes, Larisa, it is," Mark insisted with quiet and reassuring calm. He added lightly, "Don't worry. This kind of negotiation is all pretty typical. I'll call you back as soon as we're finished with the next round."

Mark calmly reassured his anxious client, but the truth was that the divorce between Julian and Larisa Chancellor wasn't typical at all. The bargaining chips in most divorces were money, property, and children; but the currency of the Chancellor divorce was quite different: emotion, control, power, and image. Mark had no idea how strong his—Larisa's—position was. There was obviously something quite specific that Julian did not want revealed. His own cocaine use, perhaps, or perhaps something else. But Julian had said from the outset that he wasn't going to roll over and play dead, and Mark sensed that he could be pushed only so far. Not that Mark was pushing. He had still asked for nothing except the divorce.

It was Julian himself who was doing the pushing. It was obvious that he wanted some concession, some proof of his power and control, and Mark feared that if Julian wasn't placated in some way that despite his intense distaste for scandal he would go to war in the arena of public opinion. And in that arena, Mark feared, Julian might well win. Larisa had herself admitted that her life-style had been that of a pampered princess, and surely Julian had many powerful and influential friends who would be very willing to confirm that Larisa Chancellor had been a most adored and treasured wife.

Larisa wanted nothing and Julian wanted something and Mark felt the pressure of time. They needed to come to closure soon, before Larisa's fragile hope became resigned defeat and before Julian's ever-diminishing patience disappeared altogether and he returned resolutely to his initial stance of no divorce.

It seemed like forever, but in fact only eight days had elapsed between Larisa's visit to his office and Mark's Friday afternoon phone call to present her with what he believed was the best he could do.

"Julian absolutely refuses a cash settlement of any kind."

"That's fine, Mark. That's what I expected. And as I told you, it doesn't matter. I don't want any of Julian's money."

"I know, but here's the interesting part: Julian wants to support you, in whatever life-style you choose, even a most lavish and luxurious one. He says that he will pay all of your expenses, every bill you send him, without questions or limits. I didn't ask for this, Larisa, and frankly it surprises me. But it seems to be something that Julian really wants to do."

Of course he wants to do it, Larisa thought. He knows that I couldn't bankrupt him—or even put the smallest dent in his vast wealth—no matter how hard I tried. This is just like when we were married. I had carte blanche, the wonderful illusion of freedom, but I was really always completely under his control. Julian wants that control still, watching me from a distance, knowing everything I do, every dress I buy, every salad I eat, every phone call I make. As if we were still married. . . .

Larisa felt the panicky breathlessness of suffocation as the invisible chains began to slowly tighten around her chest.

"Would I have to sign something requiring me to allow him to support me?" she asked finally, a rush of words that escaped in a gasp.

"No. In fact, Larisa, if you ever need any money, I would be very happy to—"

"Thank you, Mark," she interjected softly. "I'll be fine."

"Okay, well, just don't ever hesitate to ask if you need anything. So, let me tell you the rest of the terms. Julian wants both of you to agree never to disclose the details of the marriage or the divorce to anyone. He's obviously most concerned about revelations to the press—magazine articles, books, movies—but the language of the contract will read 'anyone,' so you need to know that that's what you're agreeing to."

"I agree to it. But the divorce documents will be filed with the courts, so won't they already be in the public domain?"

"No. Since this will be an uncontested divorce, the only documents filed with the court will be the signed dissolution papers proving that you both agree to the divorce. Everything else, the terms we're discussing and the contracts you'll sign agreeing to them, is strictly between you and Julian."

"I see. That's good. More private."

"Which doesn't mean there won't be interest in the divorce. Despite his distaste for publicity, Julian wants to meet it head-on by preparing a statement, preapproved by both of you, that will be released to the press as soon as the papers have been filed."

"Damage control. That's fine with me."

"Larisa," Mark cautioned quietly, "Julian's idea of putting a positive spin on the story is to make it appear as if it's he who is divorcing you. He also wants to give the clear impression that he feels so terrible about having fallen out of love with you that he has been immensely generous with the financial settlement. This really gravels me, but—"

"But I don't have a problem with it, Mark. Pride's an expensive luxury. Julian cares so much about image, and I couldn't care less."

"You're really amazing, you know."

"No. I just know what I want." *What's so very necessary for my survival.* She added softly, hopefully, "And it seems as if this is really going to happen . . . ?"

"There's just one final thing," Mark said very quietly. He wondered if it would be too much, a deal breaker even though they were so close, something she simply could not do. *Courage, Larisa.* "Julian wants a photograph to accompany the press release, a smiling picture of the two of you together once all the papers are signed."

"Oh, Mark," she whispered. "No."

"He wanted dinner in San Francisco, but I rejected that without even speaking to you, and also without revealing whether or not you're living anywhere near here. But, Larisa, I think the idea of getting this photograph is extremely important to Julian."

"Meaning if I say no, it might delay the divorce?"

"I honestly think it might," Mark answered solemnly. "With your permission, I'd like to suggest lunch in New York for the four of us—you, me, Julian, and his attorney."

"You would be there?"

"Every step of the way. I know this would be very difficult for you, but in addition to the fact that it will permit the divorce to progress without delay, I also think that the public interest will be greatly minimized if there's no hint of either scandal or bitterness. Going to New York will also give you—us—a chance to get whatever you left behind in the penthouse."

172

"There isn't anything in the penthouse that I want," Larisa said. "If possible, though, I'd like to have my clothes sent to Second Hand Rose. It's a shop that sells used designer clothes and gives the profits to charity."

"Done. So?"

"So, if we did have lunch in New York, when would we do it?"

"Two weeks from today. All the divorce documents and the press release will have been approved and signed in advance, so it would just be a matter of lunch and the photograph. We would arrive Thursday evening and plan to catch a flight back Friday afternoon."

"Two weeks from today," Larisa echoed. *I will see Julian again two weeks from today.* But how can I? *Because it's the only way you will ever be free.* "Okay."

"Good. And, Larisa, there's one final thing, a good thing, I think. The press release will include a statement from Julian expressing his support for the resumption of your modeling career, if that's what you decide you want to do."

"I can't believe Julian agreed to that." Larisa's grateful disbelief lasted only a few seconds before being harshly swept away by a crashing wave of reality. Julian could afford to be magnanimous about her career, because he knew what she knew: that no one would want her as a model again anyway. She and Julian both knew that truth, and Julian obviously assumed that she would never have the strength or courage or confidence to find something new. He fully believed that she would be dependent on him forever, bound to him by her own weakness, controlled by his immense power, as she had allowed herself to be controlled when they were married. And that was where Julian Chancellor was very wrong. "Did Julian agree to pay your legal fees?"

"You bet. And he will of course pay for our first-class trip to New York."

"How can I ever thank you, Mark?"

"You could give me that smile you owe me. I think I'd like to collect in two weeks. Let's say on our Friday evening flight back to San Francisco."

The thank-you smile for Mark would be easy, but the all-important smile for Julian's scandal-squelching photograph would be almost impossible. How could she smile a radiant, untroubled, convincing smile as she sat beside the man she once had loved and trusted but now hated and feared? Larisa didn't know. She only knew that somehow she had to find a way.

I will be able to smile that smile in two weeks, she promised herself. Somehow, for those necessary moments when the camera's eye winked at her, she would wear a radiant smile.

And, she decided, on that day she would also wear a new outfit, something that she—not Julian—had chosen, a brave symbol of her new life of freedom and choice. The bruises on her skin were almost gone, mere ghostly shadows of violence, and by next week they would have disappeared entirely. She would go to Sydney's then and amid the fragrance of roses and with Christine's talented help, she would find something lovely and hopeful to wear.

Larisa tried to envision her life beyond the lunch with Julian—where she would live, the kind of job she would try to find—but it was impossible. Until that important and terrifying event was behind her, until she had actually survived seeing him again, all thoughts and energies had to be focused on steeling herself for that day.

Still, she realized, she needed something, a small flicker

of light at the end of the dark tunnel, a hopeful glimmer of proof that there would be life after seeing Julian again.

She would be seeing Julian in New York on Friday, and on the following night San Francisco would be celebrating its new Immunology Institute with a lavish black-tie ball at the Fairmont. What could be more hopeful than the celebration of a new building in which many lives would be saved and perhaps even cancer would be cured? Elizabeth had been encouraging her to accompany her to the fabulous ball, and it would be nice to meet Stephen at last, and maybe even the mysterious Nick.

I will go, Larisa decided. And I will wear the romantic, delicately beaded, flowing white silk gown that I wanted to wear on the eve of my marriage, but which Julian would not allow.

Her decision felt brave and triumphant, until she was suddenly swept by thoughts that stole her breath and made her tremble with icy fear. What if Julian had no intention whatsoever of allowing this divorce? What if this was all just a clever trap?

Chapter Thirteen

Perfect, Madolyn mused approvingly as she gazed at the breathtaking reflection of herself. She was standing in front of a full-length mirror in one of the private dressing salons at Sydney's and she was wearing the gown designed by Christine for the Fairmont ball. The sapphire silk demurely yet alluringly draped her beautiful body, and there were tiny buttons, meticulously sewn, which Christine had added to enhance the exquisite detailing, but which privately delighted Madolyn for another reason altogether. She imagined Stephen's talented fingers struggling to undress her, wanting her so much, frustrated by the tiny buttons, and then wanting her all the more. Wanting her enough to ask her to marry him? *Yes.* That was part of her delicious fantasy—no, her plan—for the festive event that was now only eight nights away.

On that night of champagne and celebration, she would tell Stephen that she had decided to accept the network position in New York, and he would ask her to marry him, and for a while theirs would be the modern, sophisticated, bicoastal marriage of the very successful. Madolyn knew that Stephen would feel an obligation to remain in San Francisco until the construction of the institute was complete and a new director had been found. But then he could leave. His research could be done anywhere, after all, whereas she *had* to be in New York, the epicenter of network news.

Madolyn Mitchell had a history of getting exactly what she wanted, she made sure of it, and now she was about to get the two things she wanted most—a dream job in New York and a dream marriage to rich, sexy, brilliant Dr. Stephen Sheridan. Madolyn was quite confident that she didn't *need* the romantic gown Christine had designed for her for that special night. But, she thought with a soft seductive smile, looking this alluring couldn't hurt.

"It's wonderful, Christine," Madolyn gushed finally, remembering at last that Christine was there and had been quietly awaiting her assessment.

"I'm glad you're happy with it, Madolyn."

"I'm *delighted* with it, and Stephen will be too. In fact," she added as her beautiful violet eyes envisioned total triumph, "how would you like to design a wedding gown for me? We haven't set the date yet, and I suppose I should wait until I get Stephen's reaction to this gown. Oh, but I know he'll love it. I'd want you to do the entire wedding, of course—the gown for the rehearsal dinner, the bridesmaids' dresses, and maybe even a few especially romantic items for the honeymoon."

"I'd be very happy to," Christine murmured softly.

Christine was behind Madolyn, kneeling on the salon's plush carpet, making a minor adjustment in a silken fold. As a result, Madolyn didn't see the worry that filled Christine's lavender eyes at the mention of Stephen's name. Ever since their chance meeting two weeks before, Christine had worried that Stephen might have been offended that she had pretended not to recognize him—as if she was dismissing him . . . as if he hadn't mattered to her . . . as if she had somehow forgotten the most extraordinary gift he had given her, a gift no one else on earth could have given, one more year of love with her beloved David. Surely Stephen knew that she had forgotten nothing. Surely he understood that it simply made everything easier, more private, if her clients and coworkers didn't know about her loss . . .

Four hours later, as the city bus huffed and puffed its way from Union Square to the bus stop two blocks from her small rented house on Twin Peaks, Christine was worrying again about Stephen. She was still distracted by that worry when she arrived home and began to glance idly through the day's mail. Her attention became a little more focused, however, as her eyes fell on an envelope from a surprising source: the company from which she had purchased their health insurance. There had been no communications from the company for over three years, not since shortly after David's cancer had been diagnosed and coverage had been denied because of the preexisting condition.

Even though the envelope was marked "personal and confidential," Christine opened it unhurriedly. It was probably a form letter, urging her to renew her lapsed policy.

But the letter was, in fact, quite personal, too personal.

Dear Mrs. Andrews,
    I am writing to inform you that a most regrettable error was made concerning your claim. Heretofore

the expenses incurred during the illness of your husband, David Andrews, have not been covered because of the exclusion clause for preexisting illness. However, on August twenty-second, it was brought to my attention by Dr. Stephen Sheridan that the diagnosis of familial hemochromatosis as a preexisting condition for your husband's malignancy had in fact been ruled out.

Thus, in accord with the terms of your policy, we will assume responsibility for payment of medical expenses incurred in excess of the agreed-upon deductibles. I have contacted the hospitals regarding the payments that you have made to date, and having determined that the total amount remitted by you exceeds the required deductibles by $12,380, I am enclosing a reimbursement check for that amount.

Please be assured that the remainder of your husband's medical expenses will be paid promptly, and please accept my apologies for this error and for any hardship that this misunderstanding may have caused you. I assure you that the matter is being fully investigated . . .

Christine stopped thinking and simply began to act, compelled to action by powerful feelings she could neither define nor control. First the feelings willed her to walk to the kitchen drawer where she had kept the all-important notecard—and where it lay still. Stephen had given it to her the first time they met and on it he had written all of his phone numbers—office, lab, pager, home. The once so familiar numbers were indelibly etched in some quiet corner of her mind, but the powerful feelings that pulsed

179

through her came with their own thunder, making the search for a quiet memory quite impossible.

It was ten-thirty Friday night. During the year in which David had been Stephen's patient, Stephen had often been in his laboratory late at night, even on Fridays. Christine didn't know if Madolyn had been in Stephen's life then, but she did know that Madolyn had a newscast in thirty minutes, which meant that Stephen might logically be working late as well.

As Christine dialed the number to Stephen's lab, she realized that she had no idea why she was calling him, or what she was going to say. It doesn't matter! the powerful feelings thundered with astonishing confidence. *We* know why you're calling. *We* will give you the words to speak when it's time to speak them.

Stephen glanced from his watch to the silent telephone. In a moment, the phone would ring. The caller would be Madolyn, calling from her private dressing room at the station, the copy already written and rehearsed for her newscast, the final makeup check not due for a few minutes. She would be calling because it was Friday night, and she was off for the weekend, and that meant she wanted to see him. Madolyn would make her desires abundantly clear, her voice soft and sultry as she whispered her provocative suggestions . . . and promises.

Promises of passion were the only promises that he and Madolyn ever made to each other. Stephen frowned at the thought, amazed and vaguely troubled that their relationship had endured for this long on so little. But that was the relationship's appeal, of course. Its demands were physical not emotional, and its commitments were those made to pleasure, not to each other.

Stephen had never had a relationship like this. Always before there had been at least the hope of love. But with Madolyn there had never been that hope, not for either of them, not from the very beginning, and that had made it emotionally so very easy—and so very empty. Their relationship would be ending soon. Madolyn would surely get the network position in New York that she so obviously wanted. And that would be that.

It was an end, he realized, that he anticipated with as much relief as regret . . .

Stephen was still frowning when the telephone rang—right on cue.

"Hi," he answered distractedly.

"Doctor Sheridan? This is Christine Andrews."

"Hello, Mrs. Andrews," Stephen replied quietly, no longer distracted but frowning even more deeply as he realized that the informal first-name greetings of two weeks ago at Sydney's were apparently forgotten. They had regressed to their old roles of doctor and patient's wife, but her voice was very different from the soft courageous voice he had heard so often during the last year of David Andrews's life.

"Why did you contact the insurance company?" the new voice demanded, courageous still, but not at all soft.

"Because I believed it was wrong for you to pay for what should rightfully have been covered."

"But it was none of your business!"

"I'm sorry. I thought it was."

"Why?"

"Because David was my patient. I felt a responsibility to him and to his wishes. I knew he wouldn't have wanted you to spend your lifetime repaying his debts."

"But what about what *I* want?" The question came without warning, stunning and confusing, and suddenly

181

the powerful feelings, with all their confident anger and indignation, simply vanished. *Stephen was right.* David had wanted her life after his death to be totally unencumbered, so that she was free to go on to new happiness and new dreams. But she had accepted the insurance company's decision without question, more than accepted— embraced. Why? Because she wanted a life committed to repaying his debts? Because then she would be living every day of her life for David still, feeling needed by him in his death as she had been so needed by him in his life? Because she would be so very safe, living forever in the memories of their love, never venturing beyond those wonderful memories, never being forced to find new dreams?

Because she was so terribly afraid?

"Mrs. Andrews?" Stephen's voice intruded very softly in the lingering silence. And then, even more softly, he asked, "Christine?"

"I have to go now," she whispered. "I'm sorry."

As she quietly replaced the receiver, hot tears began to spill from her stormy lavender eyes and violent sobs shook her slender body. The anguished grief might have flowed from her heart a year ago, the day that David had died, the same day that she had lost his baby. But the grief hadn't flowed then, she hadn't allowed it to, and she had kept David alive by devoting her life to repaying his debts.

But now there were no more debts to repay . . . and Christine cried tears of pure pain as she at last truly faced the irrevocable loss of her beloved David . . . and of his precious unborn child.

* * *

Elizabeth was right, Stephen thought sadly as he slowly replaced the receiver. I should have spoken to Christine before calling the insurance company.

But what was it that had bothered her so terribly? Was it his decision to invade her privacy? Or was it a decision she herself had made, an anguished decision about an unborn baby made because of the erroneous belief that she had a lifetime of debt ahead of her?

Stephen's hand rested on the receiver, reaching to her still. He wanted to go to her, to hold her and comfort her. But how could he? It was he, after all, who had caused her immense sadness.

When the phone rang, he answered it immediately, hoping it would be she . . .

"I tried to call a few minutes ago but your line was busy." Madolyn added with a seductive purr, "Don't tell me there's another woman."

Yes, Stephen thought. There is another woman. A lovely and loving woman whom I have unwittingly hurt. And all I want now is a little privacy in which to think about the unhappiness I have caused her.

Part

Three

Chapter Fourteen

Manhattan
September 1991

Julian, his attorney, and the photographer who would take the picture of the amicably divorcing couple were standing outside Le Cirque when the limousine carrying Larisa and Mark arrived. At the sight of Julian, Larisa's already fluttering heart took flight, and the aching in her stomach became a gnawing pain, and there wasn't nearly enough air.

"Are you okay?" Mark asked as the limousine pulled to a gentle stop.

"No," Larisa confessed. "But I will be . . . in about three hours."

"We'll have a very nice flight home," Mark promised. "So, shall we?"

"I guess we shall."

Then they were standing on the sidewalk and polite introductions were being made and Julian was staring at her. His face wore the identical expression it had worn the first time they met—a charming and compelling blend of tenderness and seduction, desire and respect. Love at first sight, he had told her later, and it had been love at first sight for her too.

And now Julian was staring at her precisely as he had stared at her on that long-ago day, eloquently reminding her of a love that had once seemed so perfect.

Clever! her mind warned as all the pieces of her shattered heart began to tremble and scream with pain. How desperately she had needed to believe in Julian's wonderful love. How joyously and gratefully she had accepted it. You know what he's doing now, don't you? her mind demanded. Yes, of course I know, her heart replied. It's just that he does it so well. Which is why he is so very dangerous—still.

"Hello, Larisa," Julian said with the same soft wonder of their first meeting.

"Julian."

"Shall we go in?" he asked pleasantly, quite undaunted by the coolness of her greeting. "Daniel has prepared your favorite dishes and Sirio has made certain that we have our favorite table."

"Our favorite table?" Larisa echoed weakly. *Their* table was in a secluded corner, a rare place of privacy in the celebrated restaurant where the rich and famous came to see and be seen. Most of Le Cirque's clientele would be annoyed if they were not seated in the center of the room. But Julian was beyond such snobbery, above it. For the past six years, he and Larisa had always been seated at the very remote table for two.

"Have lunch with me, Larisa," Julian urged quietly, his dark eyes sending both a challenge and a plea: a challenge to her courage . . . and a plea to the heart that once had loved him so much that she would have died for him— perhaps had died for him. "Just the two of us, please."

"We agreed that we would all have lunch together,"

Mark reminded with quiet resolve, speaking the words to Julian as his eyes sent a silent message to Larisa, a confident reminder of his promise that he would stay with her.

"And we will, if that's what Larisa wants." Julian smiled tenderly and asked softly, "Larisa?"

"It's all right, Mark," Larisa said finally, bravely accepting the challenge to her courage, but not, not even for a moment, acquiescing to the plea. "I'll have lunch with Julian."

He knew I'd say yes, Larisa realized when they reached the table. The photographer was already there, positioning the flowers just so, and the sommelier hovered, waiting to pour the already chilled Dom Perignon into the crystal champagne flutes. Once seated, the champagne poured, Larisa and Julian raised their glasses, clinking gently and smiling, giving the photographer and the world a dazzling portrait of harmony.

"Aren't you going to drink any?" Julian asked after the photographer had left and Larisa had placed her still full glass of champagne on the pink tablecloth and returned her hands to her lap. "Just a sip to celebrate?"

"No. Thank you." Her mind needed to be alert and wary, and her memory needed to be very clear. "You go ahead."

"But I have nothing to celebrate. No, that's not true. I celebrate your well-deserved freedom from me." Julian's dark, seductive eyes smiled with solemn and wistful sadness. "I'm very serious, Larisa. I'm proud of you for leaving me, and I'm ashamed beyond words for what I did to you, not just that last night but for a long time. I have problems. We both know that. Your leaving me was the jolt I needed to seek professional help. I'm seeing someone now. It's just a beginning, but . . . maybe . . . I'll find some answers. And, maybe, someday you'll be able to forgive me."

"Don't ask me to forgive you, Julian. Not yet. Maybe not ever." Beneath the pink tablecloth, Larisa's tapered fingers dug deep, ever deeper, into her palms. "I am glad that you're getting help."

"So am I, I guess. I've spent a lot of time thinking I don't even deserve the chance to improve." He smiled a self-deprecating smile and confessed quietly, "I've also spent a lot of time thinking that it would have been best if you had just shot me."

Larisa's sharp nails journeyed even deeper. Until that moment, as Julian's words abruptly jarred the terrifying memory, she had completely forgotten that grim detail of the nightmarish night. But now she remembered that at one point in the midst of his brutal rage, she had managed to twist free and had crawled to the nightstand where she kept the small handgun Julian had given her. Julian hadn't tried to stop her frantic quest for the weapon, nor had he lunged for it when her trembling hands had pointed it directly at him. Instead, he had mocked her—just as years before another cruel and violent man had mocked her before raping her—laughing at her false and foolish bravery, taunting her to shoot him, knowing full well that she would never pull the trigger even to protect herself. She was so vulnerable, so desirable in her fragile courage, such a delicious victim.

Larisa had always been far too ashamed to tell Julian about the violent rape that had stolen her trusting innocence years before. He knew nothing about it, and yet, four weeks ago, he had eerily recreated that ancient scene, laughing at her . . . goading her to shoot him . . . brutally punishing her when she could not.

And now he was telling her that she should have shot him.

"I mean it, Larisa. I gave you that gun to protect yourself against anyone who might ever try to harm you. Maybe, even then, I knew that one day it might be me."

"I don't want to talk about this, Julian."

"Just a few more words. I want you to take the gun with you today. My attorney has it and the documents required by the airline in his briefcase. He'll give both to Mark before you go."

"I don't want the gun, Julian."

"Please take it, Larisa, so that I can know that you will be safe." Julian paused, smiled wryly, and added with menacing softness, "And so that I won't use it on myself."

"Julian . . ."

"Not fair, I'm sorry. But, please, just take the gun. And promise that if anyone ever tries to hurt you again, you'll pull the trigger."

"I'll take the gun," she agreed quietly, acceding to his wish, fighting the suffocating feeling in her chest as she did so. "Could we please talk about something else?"

"Sure."

For the remainder of the gourmet meal that was virtually untouched by either of them, Julian smoothly guided the conversation from one topic to the next, recounting amusing anecdotes with his effortless charm. Only over coffee at the end of the meal did he return the conversation to them.

"Where are you living, Larisa?"

"Oh," Larisa breathed, startled by the direct question and not certain that she wanted to answer it. But it was all right now, wasn't it? The divorce papers were already signed and in just a few more minutes she and Julian would part forever. "I'm living in San Francisco for now."

191

"That's good. The Bay Area is your home. I know how much you like it there—far better than the crowded chaos of Manhattan." He gazed at her, his handsome face solemn and thoughtful, and after an intense silence, he asked quietly, "May I call you?"

No! Never! her mind warned instantly. You see what he's doing, don't you? He's told you how despondent he feels, and how hard he's going to work to try to change, and now he's asking for your help—just an occasional transcontinental phone call. He's making it sound like such a small request . . . even though it is an enormous one.

"Julian, I . . ."

"It's too soon, isn't it? I know. I understand. It's too soon, too painful for me, too. But maybe in a month or two? May I call Mark then and ask him for your number, or at least your address? I could write the words I need to say, and you could tear up the letter unopened if you wanted . . ."

Julian seemed so humble, so contrite, so apologetic. But that's not the real Julian, her mind insisted. The *real* Julian is the one who is making you feel guilty for your apparent reluctance to help him. Yes. I know.

But Larisa also knew that the real Julian would persist, at least for a while, and she was very reluctant to put Mark in the middle. He had been there long enough.

"Let's leave Mark out of this, Julian. I'll give you my address and telephone number. But, please . . . it's really far too soon."

"Okay. Thank you." Julian waited in patient silence as Larisa wrote the information on a piece of paper she had withdrawn from her purse. Then, as she handed it to him, and their fingers touched briefly, his warm, hers icy, he

192

asked, "It wasn't all bad, was it? Our love wasn't all bad. Didn't we have some happy times?"

The happiest times of my life, Larisa thought as she quickly withdrew her hand and then stood so abruptly that her untouched coffee splashed over the edge of the china cup. But the happy times were because *I* believed in *your* love. It was my foolish belief, my foolish illusion. You tricked me then, just as, I suppose, you think you're tricking me now. But you're not.

"Mark and I have to go now, Julian. There's going to be Friday afternoon traffic, and—"

"And you need to get away from me." Julian stood too and his dark eyes gazed at her with tender sadness. "I understand. I don't blame you. Goodbye, Larisa."

As the limousine made its way to the airport, Larisa realized that for the past month her focus had been on simple physical survival. Because her body had been so badly wounded she had concentrated all her energies on healing herself physically and had blocked entirely the immense emotional damage that Julian had caused as well.

But now, as her healed body traveled away from him and the deeply wounded heart that had been strangely silent for the past month began to scream its excruciating pain, Larisa wondered if this was a pain that she could survive. Would she ever be able to silence these screams? Or would the shrill and anguished cries be with her forever, relentlessly reminding her of Julian's brutal betrayal of her love . . . and reminding her, too, of her own betrayal of herself?

* * *

As Larisa made her way to the airport, serenaded by the piercing screams of her wounded heart, an elated Julian returned to his penthouse office high above Park Avenue and savored his triumph. One of Julian Chancellor's great talents was his ability to spot his opponent's weakness and prey on it; and that was what he had done today—*always*—with Larisa.

Julian regarded Larisa's willingness to help those who needed rescuing as a weakness, but now he was quite grateful for that weakness which he had always before held in such contempt. He would let Larisa rescue him, or believe that she had, and only when she had returned to him would she realize the truth.

Julian smiled as he remembered how she had looked today, so beautiful, so brave, so wonderfully fearful. She still wanted his love. That was abundantly obvious from the wistfulness he had seen in her beautiful expressive eyes.

Julian's smile faded and his lips tightened menacingly as he thought about what else he had seen in the bright shimmering blue. Somewhere, very deep, he had seen a courage, a strength, that he had never seen before. As if Larisa actually believed that she could simply walk out of his life.

He had been forced to give her the divorce. Not, as she had doubtless assumed, because of the fear that she would cry rape. He didn't give a damn if she told the entire world that he had raped her. Who would believe her word against his? No one. He would have made quite certain of that.

No, it wasn't the threat of the so easily trivialized cry of rape that had forced his hand. It was what else Larisa might have inadvertently said. In recounting the events of the night that had caused her to leave him, she might have mentioned that he had been enraged because of a real estate deal that he had lost . . . and Julian could not, would not, allow Peter London to know his immense anger at having been outsmarted by him.

Some day, when it suited Julian Chancellor, Peter London would pay very dearly for his cleverness; just as, some day, Larisa would pay very dearly for daring to leave him.

As Julian's thoughts shifted from Peter to Larisa, the cruel and dangerous smile returned to his lips. There had been such fragile yet defiant courage in her brilliant blue eyes today. Julian liked that delicate, hopeful bravery very much. It would make his conquest—and her punishment—all the more exciting.

Larisa actually believed that she could leave him.

In time she would learn how terribly mistaken she was.

Chapter Fifteen

"How are things going in there?" Larisa asked through the closed door of Elizabeth's bedroom just before eight Saturday night.

A limousine would be arriving soon to take them to the ball at the Fairmont. It was time now for last-minute inspections. Larisa had already inspected her own looks, briefly, just long enough to be certain that there were no major problems. The entire "look" was a problem, of course. She was dressed as she would have dressed, had Julian allowed it, on the most hopeful and joyous evening of her life. Then, as now, she would have worn her magnificent hair long and flowing, a shimmering cascade of firelit golden silk, and she would have worn the delicately beaded white gown that was so hopeful, so innocent, and so pure.

Who was she kidding?

"This may be as good as it gets," Elizabeth announced when she opened the bedroom door.

"As good as it gets is pretty gorgeous," Larisa said softly. "You look terrific, birthday girl."

"Thanks." Elizabeth's emerald eyes smiled warmly at

her best friend. "Likewise. I'm so glad you decided to come."

"Me too. I can't wait to meet the very nice Stephen Sheridan, not to mention the very infamous Nicholas Chase."

"You may not get to meet Nick."

"Really? From my reading of the admittedly complicated schedule posted by the phone in the kitchen, I'd concluded that the other transplant team is on call tonight and that neither you nor Nick is on call for trauma either."

"That's right. I assume Nick will be at the ball, but there will be so many people there." *And Nick isn't likely to seek me out.* As Elizabeth's thought continued, a wave of uneasiness swept through her. Nick wouldn't cross a crowded ballroom to say good evening to *her*, but he would most certainly make the journey to meet Larisa. Nick would be attracted to Larisa, and Larisa would be attracted to him, and . . .

Interpreting the sudden frown on her friend's face as concern that she might say something outrageous to Nick, Larisa assured quickly, "Don't worry. If I do happen to meet Nick, I will be very well behaved, I promise. I may casually try to spot the fatal flaw, however. I *know* you believe that such a flaw doesn't exist. But it does, Liz, it *must*. Nice men always like you. If Nicholas Chase doesn't, there must be something dreadfully wrong with him."

"What a good friend you are!"

"You're the good friend, Lizzie," Larisa said quietly. "I'm just speaking the truth."

The question of if, when, or how Larisa and Nick would meet was settled within moments of Elizabeth and

Larisa's arrival at the Fairmont. Nick was standing alone in the middle of the elegant lobby, having also just arrived.

"That's Nick," Elizabeth said quietly as she realized the inevitability of the imminent meeting.

Nick had seen them arrive. Politeness demanded that he wait where he was until they reached him. But Nick did something even more polite. Instead of simply waiting, he walked to greet them.

"The iceman cometh," Larisa murmured softly as Nick approached.

Then he was there. He smiled politely as he said good evening to Elizabeth, and smiled still when he shifted his gaze to Larisa as Elizabeth made the introduction.

"Hello, Larisa."

"Hello, Doctor."

As her bright blue eyes met Nick's dark blue ones, Larisa realized that despite the fact that Elizabeth had told her about his reputation with women and his history of passionate yet meaningless affairs, she was still somehow unprepared for his compelling sensuality.

Are you one of those arrogant men whose looks have gotten you everything you have ever wanted, whenever you have wanted it? she wondered as she gazed at the devastatingly sexy black-haired blue-eyed surgeon. Has your pursuit of pleasure always been so easy that you've never had to make any effort whatsoever? Have you only pursued women who dazzle with the most superficial glamour—women like me—and never the truly beautiful ones, like Elizabeth? I suppose your seductive and arrogant dark blue eyes are simply too blind to see Elizabeth's extraordinary beauty. Well, it's your loss, Nicholas Chase. Because for some inexplicable reason, she actually likes you.

Really likes you, Larisa realized as she shifted her gaze from Nick to Elizabeth. Her friend's cheeks gave lovely and eloquent pink testimony to her discomfort in Nick's presence, even though her emerald eyes glowed with a deep shimmering radiance. Oh, Elizabeth, you have fallen in love with this stunningly handsome and stunningly arrogant man, haven't you? That's why you so defiantly defend him, despite his cruel indifference to you. A shiver of ice swept through her as Larisa thought, Oh, Elizabeth, how can you have fallen in love with someone like Julian?

"Well," Elizabeth murmured after the few moments of awkward silence during which Larisa's bright blue eyes had unflickeringly appraised Nick—and his dark blue ones had unflickeringly appraised her in return. "I should probably go find Stephen and Madolyn."

"I'll go with you," Larisa replied swiftly. She cast a final glance at Nick, a look of ice-blue contempt that both startled and intrigued him. "Goodbye, Nick."

"Goodbye, Larisa." Turning from the flashing bright blue to the radiant yet uncertain emerald, he added quietly, "Goodbye, Elizabeth."

What a contrast! Larisa thought moments later when Elizabeth introduced her to Stephen. True, as with Nick, she had been quite unprepared for Stephen's striking handsomeness—because, of course, when Elizabeth described people she described the important things: who they were not how they looked. Like Nick, Stephen was compellingly handsome and sexy, but when *his* sensual dark eyes greeted hers, Larisa felt kindness and warmth, not arrogance and ice.

This is the gorgeous man with whom Elizabeth should

fall in love, she thought. But Stephen and Elizabeth were friends, and it was obvious from the genuinely untroubled smiles they gave to each other that neither was tormented by deep unrequited feelings. The only torment Larisa detected was the unconcealed disapproval in Madolyn Mitchell's indignant violet eyes as her own brilliant blue ones gazed appreciatively at Stephen.

The conversation with Stephen and Madolyn was quite brief, interrupted first by someone who wanted to congratulate Stephen on the directorship of the institute—and to hear all about LKC—and moments later by someone else who wanted to meet the star anchorwoman.

Elizabeth and Larisa drifted away from Stephen and Madolyn, and for a while they tried to mingle together, but it quickly became apparent that it was impractical to do so. Finally, with a soft laugh, Larisa assured her friend that she was perfectly fine wandering by herself. Elizabeth didn't need to feel responsible for her. If she saw someone she wanted to meet, she assured, she would simply introduce herself.

Larisa had no wish to meet anyone. What she wanted was privacy—and champagne. The bubbly honey-colored liquid helped a lot. Larisa had forgotten how much. It was something she had learned during her marriage, a lesson in survival, even though in the past month, she hadn't had a drop to drink. She had needed her mind to be absolutely clear, to concentrate intently on willing her wounded body to heal; and besides, she had felt safe with Elizabeth—so safe so far away from Julian.

But now Julian was with her again, a vicious demon living deep inside her, clawing mercilessly at her wounded heart, relentlessly reminding her of all the betrayals and causing unremitting pain. In the past twenty-four hours, the screams of pain from her shattered heart had only

200

become louder and more strident, wearing her down with their piercing shrillness, draining energy from her barely healed body. She needed escape, just for a little while, just long enough to regain the strength she needed to do battle with the pain.

The champagne worked wonderfully, magically, making her numb . . . and strong . . . and brave.

Privacy was impossible in the crowded ballroom, but Larisa finally found a place where she could stand forever with her back to the sea of rich and famous, turning only when she needed to lift another glass from the silver trays of golden champagne that wove like glittering threads through the colorful tapestry of silk tuxedos and satin gowns.

The private place was in front of the scale model of the soon-to-be-built Immunology Institute. Larisa had seen hundreds of models of grand buildings, pieces of Julian's vast empire. The model of this building might have triggered more unwanted memories of Julian, except that its style was so unlike anything Julian had ever chosen to build that the memories kept still.

Peter London, Architect, Larisa read as her eyes gazed at the engraved gold plaque beneath the model. Peter's name, like his distinctive architectural style, was quite unfamiliar to her. She was very certain that Julian had never commissioned Peter London to design any of his many buildings—even though he should have.

When installed in the lobby of the medical center on Monday morning, the model would surely be encased in clear acrylic. But tonight there was no protective covering over it, nor were velvet ropes draped around it preventing access. Larisa could get as close as she wanted . . . and she wanted to get very close . . . because it was like a wonderful dollhouse she had never had as a little girl. Someone had cared very much about even the most minute details of this dollhouse, just as she would have, had it been hers. Each tiny room was fully equipped with miniature state-of-the-art medical instruments, of course, but each was also painted and papered in the most unhospitallike springtime pastels and floral prints. There were dolls in the dollhouse, health care workers and their patients. Very nineties, Larisa decided, smiling softly at the discovery that about half of the tiny white-coated doctors were women.

As Larisa gazed at the model, she felt a wonderful sense of warmth and welcome. If one had to be sick, this would be a very comforting place to be. Beginning with the elegant white-pillared entrance with its chattering fountains and lush gardens of flowers, the building seemed to extend a most gracious greeting to all who visited it.

Larisa's soft smile faded abruptly as her blue eyes fell on two tiny dolls, a woman and a little girl. They were doubtless supposed to have been mother and daughter, but they weren't walking together. The mother was walking a bit ahead, and in her own weeping heart Larisa felt the little girl's panic as she desperately tried to keep up, so afraid of being left behind, so afraid of everything.

Larisa shifted the empty champagne flute from her right hand to her left and with her delicate fingers moved the little girl doll forward until she was beside her mother, their tiny hands touching. There. That was how it should be: the mother holding her daughter's hand, wanting to touch her, and protect her, and comfort her.

It had never been that way in Larisa's own life.

But that was how it should be.

Peter London stood nearby watching the astonishingly beautiful woman who gazed with such interest at the building he had designed. She was wholly absorbed in her

202

task, and Peter was wholly absorbed in watching her, mesmerized by the play of the soft light of the crystal chandeliers on her fire-kissed golden hair, bewitched by her regal grace, and enchanted by the lovely innocence and purity of the gown she wore.

Peter had been drawn to her by her astonishing beauty; but what had intrigued and captivated him was the extraordinary vulnerability of her brilliant blue eyes and the gentle softness of the smile that touched her lovely lips. He would have been quite content to simply watch her all night, never breaking the magical spell; but when her delicate fingers tenderly moved the small doll beside the larger one, Peter saw such sadness that all he wanted to do was rush to her and hold her until the immense sadness was banished from her sensitive heart forever.

Peter didn't rush, not wanting to startle her, but he did move closer, until he stood beside her facing the model as she did.

"What do you think?" he asked quietly.

Even though the deep voice was quiet, and strangely gentle, it startled Larisa nonetheless. She pulled herself from her faraway thoughts, and somehow remembering the hot mist of tears that blurred her vision, when she answered her words were spoken to the model, just as his had been.

"I think it's wonderful," she said softly. "Very beautiful and welcoming—and yet so functional."

"I take it you work at the medical center?"

It was safe to face him then, the mist had cleared, and when she did Larisa formed an instant and uneasy impression of elegance and power—an impression that came with an icy shiver as she thought, Like Julian.

Not exactly like Julian, she amended swiftly—and with surprising confidence. Perhaps it was the hair, the color of midnight's darkest shadows, beautifully cut but slightly too long for true blue-blood fashion. Or maybe it was the eyes. At first, Larisa had thought that they were the color of shadows, too; but as the light of the chandelier gently caressed them, she saw that they were green, not black, the dark, rich, inviting green of a forest at twilight. Inviting? For Larisa the image of a forest was an inviting one. As a little girl she had spent endless private hours in the wonderful dark green sanctuary of towering pines.

Larisa gazed at the seductive eyes, and for a trembling moment joyfully accepted their dark green invitation for sanctuary from all her pain, wondering if she even saw in them a wisdom as solemn and ancient as the forest itself. But then the beckoning green became even more intense, and demanding—wanting something from her—and her mind warned suddenly, He's just like Julian!

Remembering his still unanswered question, and assuming that his asking meant that he did not work there, Larisa looked at him with proud defiance and said, "Yes, I work at the center. I'm a trauma surgeon."

Larisa didn't know if her lie came from the simple wish to be Elizabeth—and not herself—or if it was a challenge to this handsome and powerful man. I'm not just a beautiful woman, you see, not just a plaything for a man like you. I have my own worth, my own talent, my own power.

As soon as her lie was out, Larisa steeled herself for his reaction. A trauma surgeon? he would echo with obvious disbelief. And then as the seductive forest green suddenly became contemptuous and mocking, he would embellish, Not very likely. Forget the fact that you look frivolous and decorative—not serious and competent. There are other equally revealing clues to your lie. You simply don't seem strong enough emotionally. Your courage, such as it is,

204

seems very fragile and very precarious. I seriously doubt that you could make important life-and-death decisions about your own life, much less about the lives of others.

Larisa waited for the taunting assault. But the dark green flickered with neither surprise nor disbelief. They simply gazed at her invitingly . . . *the woods are lovely, dark and deep.*

"Trauma surgery must be very difficult," he offered finally. "Emotionally as well as technically."

"Yes, it is," Larisa admitted as Elizabeth would have. Then, as her optimistic best friend would have done, she added, "But it is also very rewarding."

"I'm sure that's true." Peter smiled then, a gentle half smile, sexy and seductive. "As a trauma surgeon will you have much reason to go to the Immunology Institute?"

"Not at first. But eventually I will—if, when, emergency organ transplantation becomes standard care in acute trauma."

"That's going to happen?"

"I think so." At least, Larisa added silently, Elizabeth thinks so. "Trauma surgeons operate to control damage and to repair what can be repaired, but if there has been significant injury to a vital organ there's sometimes nothing that can be done."

"Trauma to the heart, for example?"

"Yes," Larisa answered softly, suddenly wondering if it was he who was the trauma surgeon and the dark green had just made the ominous discovery that the trauma to her own heart had been so massive that without a new one she herself would not survive. I will survive, Larisa told herself urgently; and then, with matching urgency, she told herself that she needed to get away from this dark handsome man. The dishonest conversation was suddenly becoming far too honest. She needed to escape before the searching forest green eyes—that so obviously wanted something from her still—discovered the truth. "Well. I really need to go check on a patient. There's an on-call team in the hospital, of course, but . . ."

"It's your patient and you want to be sure."

"Yes. Goodbye."

She vanished quickly, obviously as anxious to get away from him as to check on her patient. As he watched the glittering beacon of firelit hair disappear into the crowd, Peter felt an immense loss, an astonishing emptiness. She was rushing away from him, and all he wanted to do was follow her, and he might have . . . but then he saw her exchange smiles with Stephen Sheridan as she passed, and Peter knew that she wasn't lost to him forever. If he needed to know, if his heart compelled him to find out, he could learn from Stephen the name of the beautiful trauma surgeon whose lovely blue eyes had been filled with such sadness.

Larisa crossed the ballroom, acting out the charade that she was going to the lobby to make a phone call until she was far enough away from the dark green eyes that it was safe to change course toward the silver fountain of champagne beside the dance floor.

When she reached the fountain a soft smile touched her lips. She could stay here for a long time, listening to the romantic songs of love played by the band and marveling at the everchanging reflection of the crystal chandelier in the shimmering golden pond. And whenever she wanted she could get more champagne by simply holding her empty glass beneath one of the splashing waterfalls.

Perfect.

"Haven't you drowned it yet, Larisa?"

This time the invasion of her privacy came from directly behind her, and this time the male voice was familiar—and unwelcome.

"I beg your pardon?" she asked, her soft smile vanishing as she spun toward him.

"Haven't you yet drowned whatever it is you're trying to drown with champagne?" Nick clarified quietly.

"*Excuse* me? Have you been watching me?" *Just like Julian used to watch me?* "Have you been counting the number of glasses I've had?"

"I was counting," Nick calmly told the flashing blue eyes. "It was an interesting diversion for a while. However, quite frankly, I eventually lost both count and interest."

"But now you're suddenly interested again."

"I'm not interested in the amount—I know it's a lot—but yes I am interested in why you're drinking so much."

"I am not drunk, Doctor," Larisa announced coolly, her words clear and unslurred. She wasn't drunk. She was just a little high, high enough to float ever so slightly, unweighted by her pain for a brief wonderful time. Her graceful gait was steady, her words were clear, and her cheeks, until now, had been pale not pink. And the conversation with the forest-eyed stranger in which she had pretended to be Elizabeth? That wasn't a sign of intoxication either. During college, when she rarely ever drank, she had frequently, soberly made up new identities for herself. It had been a game then, a harmless and playful diversion. But tonight it hadn't been a game, Larisa knew. Tonight it had been a wish to be someone else, someone so much better . . . and yes, perhaps, the champagne had allowed that deep wonderful wish to float a little closer to the surface.

"I know you're not drunk," Nick answered solemnly.

"That's the most worrisome part of all. It means that you're so accustomed to consuming large amounts of alcohol that you've become tolerant to the effects."

"I don't know about my tolerance to champagne, but I do know that my tolerance to this conversation is rapidly vanishing. No, let me correct that, it's completely gone." Larisa glared at his arrogant blue eyes and added sarcastically, "Oh, I know what happened. I had an alcohol blackout and someone appointed you my guardian and I just don't remember. Right?"

"I appointed myself. I freely admit that you weren't involved in the decision."

"Well, you're off the case now, Doctor. I'm quite capable of monitoring my own alcohol consumption. Besides," she told the dark blue eyes that had watched her drink the necessary champagne but were far too blind to see her best friend's infinite beauty, "I have Elizabeth."

"Elizabeth?"

"Yes. And she's terrific, in case you hadn't noticed." Larisa paused to try to read the dark blue response to her pronouncement. But Nick's blue eyes would not be read. They were inscrutable as always. But, Larisa realized with surprise, they weren't cold. And were they perhaps even a little interested? When she continued, her voice filled with fondness for her friend, "If I did have a problem with alcohol, which I don't, living with Elizabeth would be like being at the best clinic in the world. In fact, during the past month while I've been staying with her, I haven't had a drop to drink."

"And you're still this tolerant after four weeks of abstinence? That's a very serious relationship with alcohol," Nick murmured quietly, worried about Larisa—and wondering about Elizabeth, what she really knew about alcoholism. Dr. Elizabeth Jennings knew all the medical complications and consequences, of course. But did she have any idea about why people drank? Had anyone ever told her about the desperate need to fill the gnawing emptiness or the frantic desire to silence the screaming pain? "Has Elizabeth actually been helping you?"

"Yes, of course she has."

"How?"

"By being there. By being Elizabeth. By being a wonderful friend."

Nick smiled softly as he thought about Elizabeth. She would help the only way she knew how, by being gentle and compassionate—and forgiving.

"If Elizabeth were really helping you, Larisa, she wouldn't have let you have anything to drink tonight."

"Oh, I see. Tough love, right? Well, that's not Elizabeth's style. She's emotionally very strong, of course, and inspirational and wonderful, but . . ." Larisa stopped abruptly. Why in the world was she trying to convince this arrogant man how wonderful Elizabeth was? Why didn't she just walk away, run away to find Elizabeth and tell her gently but firmly that perhaps her idea of looking for a job elsewhere, as far away from Nicholas Chase as possible, was the best idea she'd ever had? Because, Larisa realized, there *was* something about Nick . . . something that wasn't all cruelty and arrogance . . . something that perhaps, when discovered, would reconcile her own diagnosis of deep flaws with Elizabeth's defiant conviction that he was sensitive—and wonderful. Maybe by talking to him a little longer and with a little less hostility, she might begin to discover what that something was. Smiling beautifully, she said softly, "I appreciate your concern, Nick, I really do. I probably have had too much champagne tonight, but it's just a one-time celebration."

"What are you celebrating?"

I want to talk about you, Nicholas Chase, not about me, Larisa thought. Tilting her golden red head coyly she teasingly countered his question with one of her own, "Have you ever been married, Nick?"

Larisa expected mock horror on the handsome face of the man famous for his midnight liaisons of passion—a mock horror swiftly embellished with an emphatic, "No, of course not!" Then, perhaps, she and Nick would discuss his views on the subject of marriage, and she would learn something more about him.

But there was neither mock horror nor a swift emphatic reply. Instead, the strong handsome face darkened with a troubled frown and there was a sudden storm in the dark blue eyes. When Nick finally answered her question, it was a soft and honest confession.

"Yes, I have been married, Larisa. Once. Very briefly."

"Are you divorced?" Larisa's voice was soft, too, as she suddenly became fearful that something tragic had happened to Nick's wife.

"Yes."

"Well, then maybe you'll understand. I signed my divorce papers yesterday. For me, that's a very good reason to celebrate."

It had been a reason, an excuse, for Nick to celebrate, too. He had done it with a weekend of Scotch.

"I have a great idea, Larisa," Nick said after a moment. "Why don't you try celebrating by dancing with me? It's much better for you than champagne."

"You really think so, Doctor?"

"Why don't we find out?"

Nick took the still full champagne glass from her hand and guided her to the nearby dance floor. There, as they swayed slowly to an evocative melody of love, Larisa made a discovery about Nicholas Chase: he was a wonderful dancer. Just as, she supposed, he was a wonderful lover. Nick had, it seemed, an instinctive understanding of how male and female bodies were supposed to move together.

"Let's talk about your marriage," Larisa suggested with a provocative smile.

"Let's not," Nick replied, smiling, too, the charming and disarming smile for which he was so well known. "Let's talk about yours."

"There's nothing to say about my marriage except that its end is a very good reason to celebrate."

Nick didn't want to talk about his marriage, and Larisa most certainly didn't want to talk about hers, and so they simply danced in slow sensual silence until Larisa spotted Stephen and Elizabeth dancing nearby.

"Stephen Sheridan is a very nice man, don't you think?"

Nick followed Larisa's gaze to Stephen and Elizabeth. After a long moment he answered, "Yes. He is."

"He obviously thinks Elizabeth is pretty terrific."

Nick nodded, his eyes thoughtful but not surprised.

What do *you* think about Elizabeth, Nick? Larisa wanted to ask. Had there been, she wondered, a flicker of dark blue envy when Nick's gaze had first fallen on Elizabeth dancing with Stephen?

Larisa didn't ask, knowing that Nick would never answer, but she reminded him quietly, "Of course, we've already established that Elizabeth *is* pretty terrific." After a brief pause, she suggested boldly, "I have a great idea. I would really like to dance with Stephen. He and I didn't have much of a chance to talk when we met earlier. And, Nick, I don't remember hearing you wish Elizabeth happy birthday."

211

"Today is Elizabeth's birthday?"

"Yes. So young, and yet so accomplished." Encouraged by dark blue eyes that had seemed genuinely interested in discovering that personal detail about Elizabeth, Larisa urged softly, "So . . . why don't I dance with Stephen and you dance with Elizabeth?"

He wants to dance with Elizabeth, Larisa thought. Good.

"No."

"No? Come on, Nick! It's been wonderful dancing with you, really, so much better than champagne, but—"

"I said no, Larisa."

Why not? Larisa wondered. Why would Nick deprive himself of Elizabeth's wonderful warmth and goodness? Three years before, when Larisa herself had withdrawn from Elizabeth's friendship, it had been because of her own shame about what she had become, what she had *allowed* herself to become. She had wanted to shelter her lovely friend from the ugly truths about herself.

Could it possibly be the same for Nick?

Nick wanted to dance with Elizabeth, Larisa was sure of it. But his ice-blue eyes and the sudden steely tension in the lean body that touched hers told her with silent eloquence that he wasn't going to. And very soon, Larisa realized as she sensed his sudden restlessness, he was going to disappear. He wasn't going to spend another dance watching Stephen dance with Elizabeth. Which was fine, best, because for a deeply troubling moment Larisa had seen a flicker of doubt in Elizabeth's emerald eyes at the sight of her dancing with Nick.

Oh, Elizabeth! There's nothing between me and Nick! Yes, of course, he's gorgeous and seductive and sexy. And, yes, I think so little of myself and need so desperately to be touched by a man who doesn't want to own me that

I could imagine spending a few hours learning from him the gentle and beautiful way that male and female bodies were meant to make love together. But don't you know that I never would?

I never would, Larisa vowed confidently. And, with matching confidence, she thought, neither would Nick.

Nick moved his taut body away from Larisa as soon as the music stopped. But he didn't run away. Instead he waited patiently until her blue eyes met his. Then he offered quietly, "Call me, Larisa, if you ever need anything."

"Like a little tough . . ." Larisa stopped abruptly. Tough "love" was presumptuous. Tough "like"? Admittedly, right now, if pressed, Larisa would find herself defending Nicholas Chase against his critics. And yes, right now if pressed, she would confess that she actually liked him. But "like" seemed presumptuous as well. She needed to finish the sentence. Nick was waiting, politely, patiently, despite his restlessness to leave.

Finally, rescuing them both, Nick finished Larisa's sentence for her.

"Like a little tough love," he said quietly, acknowledging the presumptuousness with a gentle and almost uncertain smile. After a moment he added, "I mean it, Larisa. I'm available. I'm even a pretty good listener."

"Thank you, Nick. I mean that too."

Chapter Sixteen

"I have some news, Stephen," Madolyn purred softly when she and Stephen returned to her posh Nob Hill apartment following the Fairmont ball. "I've decided to accept the job in New York. They made me an offer I really couldn't refuse."

"I knew that they would. Congratulations. When do you start?"

"November first. My last day at the station here will be October first, so I'll have a month to find a place, get settled . . ." Plan a Christmas wedding, perhaps? Madolyn walked over to him, rested her perfectly manicured fingers delicately against his chest and looked up at his surprisingly solemn face. Was he worrying about her being so far away? Good, she thought. I'll help him arrive at a wonderful solution. Kissing his lips provocatively as she spoke, she whispered, "What are you thinking, Stephen?"

Stephen wasn't thinking, only feeling; and what he felt was relief that their intimate yet emotionally empty relationship would end so easily, so naturally . . . and so soon.

"Nothing."

"Well. Let's not think, then. Let's just *do*. Why don't

you undress me? There are a hundred tiny buttons that need to be undone by your talented fingers. Of course," Madolyn whispered seductively as her own fingers drifted teasingly lower, "I'll be trying to undress you at the same time. It doesn't matter if you run out of patience, Stephen. Christine will just have to repair whatever damage occurs in the name of passion. I'll simply tell her that it was proof positive of how much you liked the gown."

"Christine?" Stephen asked, pulling away abruptly. *Christine.* It felt so strange to speak aloud the name that had been echoing in his mind and filling his heart ever since she had called him two nights before. "What about Christine?"

"She made this dress for me to wear to the ball. I told her how special tonight would be for you—for us."

"When did she make it?"

"She designed it weeks ago, of course, but she didn't actually finish the final detailing—she's such a perfectionist!—until late last night."

"Last night," Stephen echoed softly, frowning as he envisioned Christine working late into the night to finish this magnificent work of art—for him, to be enjoyed by him, despite the anguish he had caused her.

"Stephen! What's going on? I told Christine to make a gown that you would find absolutely irresistible, and I think she has. I'm not sure why you're resisting now. Stephen?"

Madolyn started to move toward him, to begin the seduction anew, but Stephen held up his hands to stop her.

"Let's not do this, Madolyn," he said quietly. "Let's just have it end with the memory of the last dance. That was very nice, didn't you think?"

"Yes. But it was a beginning, Stephen, not an end."

Stephen sighed. He didn't want a scene. He just wanted privacy to think about the lovely woman who had made Madolyn's beautiful evening gown . . . and he very much wanted to get away from the woman who so obviously regarded Christine as a servant—a Cinderella—after all.

"No, Madolyn. It was an end . . . the end."

"I don't understand what's happening!" Madolyn's violet eyes flashed with indignant anger. "Out of the blue, you've decided to end our relationship because I've taken a job in New York? Is my success so threatening to you, Stephen? Is this your latent sexism coming out of the closet? A wife who dabbled in local news was just fine, but—"

"A wife?" Stephen's mind spun. "We never talked about marriage, Madolyn. In fact, we never talked about us at all."

"Let's talk about us then! I love you, Stephen!"

"No. You don't. Please, Madolyn, let's not do this. Let's not change the rules at the last minute. I'm very sorry, terribly sorry, if I have misled you about my feelings. Until this moment, I honestly had no idea that you expected more than what we've had." *What little we've had.* "Believe what you must, but the truth is that this has nothing to do with your decision to move to New York. I think it's wonderful that you got the job. You've worked very hard and you certainly deserve it."

"But I don't deserve you? Is that it? How dare you patronize me!"

In her fury about the careful plans she had made and which were now destroyed, Madolyn needed something else to destroy. If they hadn't been in her apartment, surrounded by her prized crystal vases and delicate figurines, she might have reached for something to hurl at him. As it was, what Madolyn chose to destroy was the beautiful gown Christine had made for her. The gown was quite valueless to her now, and it had failed miserably in its mission to assist her in enticing a proposal of marriage.

In a frenzied rage, as if the soft satin had suddenly caught fire and was blazing against her fair skin, she tore it off. It happened in a flash, the magnificent sapphire gown shredded beyond repair before Stephen could even move to stop her. As he witnessed the willful and petulant destruction of something so painstakingly created, Stephen felt the immense and ominous power of his own rage . . . and he knew, an almost urgent knowledge, that he needed to get away from Madolyn—*fast*.

Stephen drove to the beach and stood at water's edge, listening to the thunder of crashing waves and staring into the vast darkness of the moonless autumn night.

And there, in the thundering darkness, Stephen thought about love.

He had no firsthand experience with it, of course. But he had had the extraordinary privilege of being an eyewitness to the extraordinary love of David and Christine, marveling at it, respecting its privacy . . . until three weeks ago when he had so unwittingly intruded.

Stephen had wanted to intrude again in the past two days, but he truly believed that it wouldn't help Christine to speak to him. It was he, after all, who had caused the harm. Stephen hadn't tried to speak to her; but he had called Sydney's each day to be very certain that she was there—that she was safe.

And now, in the middle of this moonless night, Stephen felt a powerfully compelling desire to go to her small house on Twin Peaks and intrude once again. He wanted to tell her how sorry he was for everything . . . for unraveling the insurance mix-up without speaking to her first . . . for Madolyn treating her like Cinderella . . . and, most of all, for his own failure to save her beloved David.

Stephen wanted to intrude once again.

But he didn't.

He had intruded far too much already.

A few miles away, Christine lay awake in the darkness of her Twin Peaks home, wondering if David's ghost might suddenly appear. Such a luminous vision would be only an illusion, she knew, its image merely a phantom created by her own fatigued mind, its words only the desperate wishes of her own aching heart.

David's ghost would not appear. It would not be driven by restlessness from the afterworld to speak words in death that David had been unable to speak in life.

Because there were no such unspoken words.

Because of Stephen Sheridan, she and David had had the chance to say all the words of love . . . and all the loving goodbyes. There was no need for David to return to her; but, Christine thought, he might return still, to speak again the words he had spoken with such loving urgency before he had died.

"Don't let the memory of our wonderful love fill the rest of your life with sadness, my Christie. Remember our love, my darling, and always be warmed with joy at that wondrous memory, but go on with your life. Promise me, please, that you will allow yourself to find new love, new happiness, new joy."

Christine had listened to David's impassioned plea and she had made promises to him that she knew she would never keep. She would never find a new love, and her happiness and joy would be remembered only, renewed every day of her life as she worked to pay his bills. She had been so grateful for the enormous debt. It had given her life purpose, a reason to live, the only reason to live after their baby died.

And until two days ago, when the letter from the insurance company arrived, she had been doing just fine, living entirely in past memories, quite oblivious to the present and without any fear of the future. The future, like the present, held no surprises, no demands, and no risks. It would be spent keeping the memories alive, keeping David alive, renewing with every payment she made her own deep gratitude to all those who had worked so tirelessly and compassionately to save him.

And now because of the doctor who had done the very most, but to whom she had never even owed any money, her life was hers again, with no purpose except what she chose to give it . . . and she felt so lost, so adrift, so scared.

Christine didn't know what she was going to do with the new life that had been given her; but she knew that she had to apologize to the man whose brilliance had given her a final year of love with David and whose concern for her had now given her a chance to begin again.

She had to apologize to Stephen . . . and she had to do it in person.

An icy tremble of fear swept through her as she thought about returning to Stephen's laboratory. Once she had gone there often, late at night after David had fallen asleep in his nearby room, and there she had confessed to Stephen all the fears and worries she had kept so carefully hidden from her beloved husband.

It would be very difficult to return to that place of such memories. But she had to—and would.

Christine wished that she had something more than an

apology to give Stephen Sheridan. Well, perhaps she did. She left her bed then, and in the predawn darkness of that moonless September night she began to sketch for Madolyn Mitchell a most beautiful and romantic wedding gown.

The following night, Christine caught the nine-thirty P.M. bus from Union Square to Pacific Heights, arriving at the medical center shortly after ten. It took eight more minutes to follow the once familiar route from the lobby to the research wing. Her footsteps slowed as she neared the corridor that led to the ward and stopped entirely when she reached it. As she stared at the long stretch of shining linoleum, Christine was transported back in time. If she walked down the corridor, beyond the nurses' station to the last room on the left, David would be there, waiting for her, healthy again after an infusion of Stephen's miracle therapy, so happy to see her . . .

Blinking back a sudden hot mist of tears, Christine made herself walk on, past the beckoning corridor to the other familiar one—the one that led to Stephen's laboratory.

The door was ajar, as it always had been, casting a golden beam of light into the shadowy hallway, inviting even the most timid of visitors to enter. How many wives and husbands had come here late at night to talk privately with their spouse's doctor? she wondered. Was that why Stephen worked so late at night and on weekends, to be available to them away from the daylight rush of rounds and conferences and clinic? Stephen did his important research during those quiet times, of course; but there were surely times when the research itself was quiet, when all tissue cultures were incubating and the new miracle therapies were being given a chance to work their magic without intervention. Was Stephen in his lab even during those times, like a teacher who holds office hours whether the students come or not, just in case there is a needy student who at last finds the courage to appear?

Christine had never encountered another anxious spouse on her late-night visits to Stephen's lab. But, she thought, if there's someone here tonight, someone whose loved one is still living—or still dying—I will leave, because it is so much more important for Stephen to talk to them than to me. She slowed her gait as she neared the golden beam and listened for the sound of voices coming from within, but there was only silence. And when she reached the open doorway, she saw him, quite alone, peering intently into his microscope. Looking for cancer? Looking to see if the cancer had vanished, vanquished or at least in retreat because of the therapy he had given it?

"Doctor Sheridan?"

"Mrs. Andrews. Hello." Stephen smiled softly as he stood and walked toward her. His dark brown eyes were as warm and welcoming as the golden beam of light. "Please come in."

"Thank you."

Without even thinking about it, Christine sat in the chair where she had always sat. And, as he always had, Stephen moved his stool until he was sitting directly in front of her. For a moment they were both a little lost in a bittersweet sense of déjà vu. Bittersweet, because there had been nights, especially in the beginning, when he had had such good news to give her. And then, in the end, when there had been only bad news to give, in quiet emotional conversations, the two of them had made the loving plans that would allow David to die the way he wanted to . . . at home with his Christie.

But this was a different time, and returning to the present at the same moment, they whispered in unison, "I'm sorry."

And then, in response to the other's apology, each offered gracious protests.

"It was so nice of you to check on the insurance."

"I should have checked with you first."

"No, you shouldn't have. It's just that . . . I guess it caught me by surprise."

"That's why I should have checked with you first."

"No, really."

"Yes." Stephen smiled and then added gently but firmly, "Really."

Christine's next protest was intercepted by a smile of her own, a soft answer to his, a silent acknowledgment that enough apologies had been given and received.

"Okay."

"Okay. And my name is Stephen, Christine."

"Okay, Stephen." After a moment she said bravely, "I wondered if you and Madolyn would like to have dinner at my house sometime. I know that you're both very busy, so it may not be possible to arrange, but . . ."

"Madolyn and I aren't seeing each other anymore," Stephen said quietly. Then, gazing intently at her surprised lavender eyes, he added, "However, I would very much like to have dinner with you. If that's okay."

"Oh," Christine whispered. "Yes. Of course it is."

"Good." Stephen smiled at the welcoming yet uncertain lavender. He felt uncertain, too; not about having dinner with her, he was *very* certain about that, but about the powerful, exhilarating, and dangerous feelings that suddenly pulsed through him. "Did you have a specific time in mind? I know you're busy, too."

"Well, as of today, I'll be less busy, at least I'll be

222

spending fewer hours at the boutique." Christine shrugged, then confessed to the man to whom she had once confessed her deepest fears, "I decided that I need some time to think about what I'm going to do."

"Because someone, without checking with you first, suddenly changed all the plans you had made."

"In a good way," Christine assured softly. After a moment she repeated bravely, "This is good for me, Stephen. It will just take me a little time to adjust."

"Do you have any idea what you'll do? Designing, maybe? The gown you designed for Madolyn was magnificent, truly a work of art."

"Oh. Thank you. Well, yes, maybe a little designing, or at least a little bit more sewing. Anyway, I told Sydney that I'd like to work only every other weekend for a while."

"Is this weekend on or off?"

"Off."

"I'm off, too."

"Well, then, Saturday at seven?"

"That would be fine."

"Do you remember where I live?"

"Yes." *How could I ever forget?*

Chapter Seventeen

"I gave your name to a number of women at the ball last Saturday," Madolyn told Christine when she arrived for her Thursday afternoon appointment at Sydney's. "I think you'll be getting more requests to design gowns."

"I already have been. Thank you very much for referring them to me."

"Well, the dress *was* a sensation. Stephen loved it, of course. He simply couldn't keep his hands off me! Would you like to hear a sad story, Christine?" Madolyn gave a dramatic sigh. Without waiting for Christine's reply, she elaborated, "I suppose it's the story of the nineties, the inevitable conflict between romance and career. I've just been offered a terrific—and very important—position with the network in New York. However, that great career triumph has had a huge price tag—my relationship with Stephen."

"Oh, Madolyn, I'm so sorry."

"I'm sorry, too, although not as sorry as Stephen is. I'd actually believed that he and I could have a modern, sophisticated marriage. I'd imagined we would simply commute for a while until he could join me in New York. Given his sense of responsibility to the institute that would have been next summer at the very earliest. I could have easily handled such a separation, but, unfortunately, Stephen couldn't. He wanted *much more* of me than that." Madolyn gave another dramatic sigh. "I thought we liberated the men, too, Christine, but it turns out that Stephen is really quite traditional. He showed his true not-so-nineties colors when he pleaded with me to stay here, not just until next summer, but forever."

But that's wonderful! Christine wanted to say. Isn't Stephen's love more important than anything else in the world? And isn't the work he does more important, too? Yes, he could move to New York, once the institute is built and they find a new director. But the move, no matter how smoothly and quickly it is done, would surely interfere with his research, wouldn't it? And mightn't that loss of a month, or a week, or even a day cost a month or a week or even a day in the life of some future patient?

"I'm afraid that what Doctor Stephen Sheridan wants is to have the little woman at home—or at least at the local television station." Madolyn shook her head as if still amazed by the revelation. "Poor Stephen. The truth is I just don't love him enough to sacrifice my career for him. I finally had to admit that to myself—and to him—even though it hurt him terribly. It seemed better, kinder in the long run, to simply make a clean break of it now. When he's recovered, he can go on, hopefully to someone more domesticated and less successful than I." After a moment, she added, "I certainly hope *your* husband is more modern than Stephen, Christine, because it's going to happen to you, too, you know. Someday a top fashion designer is going to discover you and convince you to move to the Big Apple. Frankly I hope it happens very soon, because in a month I'm going to need you in New York." An expression of mock horror touched her beautiful face as she exclaimed, "What am I going to do without you, Christine? Will you move to New York with me? *Please?* I know that Sydney is planning to open a boutique on Fifth Avenue. Maybe you should talk to her about transferring there."

"I'm really very happy in San Francisco, Madolyn." And you should be happy here, too, with Stephen, Christine thought as she felt a rush of emotions—a deep wish for Stephen to be loved and happy, and anger at Madolyn for her selfishness. Christine didn't want Stephen to be unhappy, ever . . . and yet something very powerful prevented her from bravely urging Madolyn to reconsider her decision to move.

"Oh? Well, I guess that means I'll just need to get the most out of your talent before I move. I'll need a whole new wardrobe, of course. I'd like to get started on selecting it as soon as possible. What openings do you have for this Saturday?"

"None, I'm afraid," Christine admitted quietly. "I actually won't be working at all this Saturday."

"Not at all?" Madolyn's disapproving expression clearly conveyed another question: Don't you understand that you are to be available to me *at all times,* Christine?

"No. Not at all." I'll be spending all day Saturday preparing dinner for Stephen. Not very nineties, Christine thought. Or maybe it was. Maybe the nineties would be the decade in which love and family became important again . . . and when the choices people made were choices of love.

"Good evening, Christine."

"Good evening, Stephen," she echoed softly. "Please come in."

226

"Thank you."

Stephen steeled his heart as he entered the small house. He had been here only once before, on the afternoon David died, and the somber memory of that death and its anguish had somehow forever shrouded the house in darkness. It would be even darker this evening, more dreary, because the scowling clouds that had hovered all day now wept cold soggy tears.

But Christine's house wasn't dreary at all. Not now, and, Stephen suddenly realized, not on the day of David's death either. How could it have been dreary? Christine had spent her marriage filling her husband's life with happiness and joy, and their home had always been a bright cheery symbol of that joyfulness.

The house smiled, and so did Christine, her beautiful face softly framed by the spun-gold silk that had been freed from its sedate chignon and now floated gently over her shoulders. Her smile was warm and welcoming, shy and brave, and there was something more in the lovely smiling lavender eyes.

What was it? Stephen wondered as she turned to hang his raincoat in the nearby closet. It looked almost like sympathy. For him? Was it actually possible that she might believe he was mourning the loss of Madolyn? Had Christine somehow imagined his relationship with Madolyn as comparable to hers with David? The thought was astonishing. And yet, perhaps, the shy and innocent girl who had fallen in love once and forever at age eighteen had grown into a woman who knew nothing at all about relationships that began without love and faltered for the same reason.

Stephen wanted to tell her not to worry—that his very intimate relationship with Madolyn had meant *nothing*— but he had no wish to shatter her lovely innocence. He didn't tell her in words not to worry about him or his heart; but the untroubled smile that greeted her when she turned back to him surely assured her that he was fine.

"Do I hear a crackling fire?" he asked.

"Yes you do. In the living room. If you'd like to wait in there, I'll bring you something to drink. I had thought white wine, because of what we're having for dinner, but I do have other options."

"White wine would be nice. Shall I help you?"

"No. Thank you."

The living room seemed completely unchanged from the day David had died, nothing moved, nothing added . . .

And nothing taken away, Stephen realized with relief as his gaze fell on the magnificent portrait above the mantel. He had feared that it might be gone, sold to help pay the bills, but it was still there, where it belonged, where David had always wanted it to be.

Stephen had barely glanced at the portrait on the day of David's death. His own tears on that day had been far too close to the surface to risk it. But now he stood before the painting, admiring the talent and marveling anew at the extraordinary love. The portrait was of Christine, and it was stunning proof of David's artistic gift; but mostly it was stunning proof of their wondrous love. The painting was, remarkably, a portrait of love as seen through the eyes of *both* lovers: the gifted artist who had painted his beloved wife's beautiful face with such exquisite tenderness . . . and the lovely woman whose glowing lavender eyes spoke so eloquently of her immense love for him.

"I couldn't sell it," Christine said quietly when she returned.

"David wouldn't have wanted you to."

"No," she agreed softly. "He wanted me to have something, some part of him, always."

"Yes," Stephen said with matching softness. He vividly remembered David's great happiness that he would be able to finish the portrait before he died. A gift of love that Christine would have forever, he had said. Stephen also remembered how that great happiness had paled in comparison to David's joy at the news of Christine's pregnancy. After a moment Stephen turned from the glowing lavender eyes in the portrait to the solemn ones beside him and admitted quietly, "I know he did. He told me."

"Oh." Christine's eyes widened briefly with surprise, then became very thoughtful, as if she were debating saying something else, something that suddenly filled the crystal-clear lavender with clouds as dark and stormy as the ones outside.

"Christine?"

She answered with a soft shake of her golden head; and, as if banished by the silky sunshine, when her eyes met his again the clouds were gone and the lavender was clear again and smiling.

"It seemed like such a blustery, soup kind of day, that I thought we'd begin the meal with French onion soup," she explained as she finally handed him his wine. "That's why I decided white wine beforehand seemed reasonable."

"This is wonderful wine," Stephen said after he took a sip.

"Oh, good." She tilted her head and asked, "Do you like French onion soup? Not everyone does. I suppose I should have checked with you first."

"I love French onion soup," Stephen assured truthfully. "And I think it's awfully nice—and brave—of you to have made it. Admittedly, I don't cook much, but my limited experience with slicing onions has always been pretty disastrous from the standpoint of watery eyes."

"The trick is to keep your mouth closed while you're slicing."

"Really? That easy?"

"That easy."

Christine smiled a beautiful and untroubled smile, but still Stephen's mind filled with troubling images. This afternoon, as she had sliced the onions for the soup, Christine's lovely mouth had surely been closed, because she had been quite alone, without anyone to talk to or laugh with as she sliced. She had been alone, without companionship or laughter.

Had she been terribly lonely? he wondered. Had tears spilled from the beautiful lavender anyway?

Stop this, Stephen told himself. She's smiling now. She's not alone now . . .

Stephen had worried that he and Christine might have difficulty finding things to talk about. During the year that her husband had been his patient, they had, of course, spent many hours in quiet conversation; but those conversations had always been entirely focused on David.

But, Stephen discovered with relief, because of the honesty and emotions they had already shared, because they had already talked to each other about love and loss and joy and fear, they could talk about anything.

And they did, in a conversation that flowed like the gentlest of rivers, always in motion and yet unhurried, not rushing to its final destination because there were so many discoveries to be made along the way, a new one around every winding bend. Sometimes the discoveries were joyful, a cascade of soft laughter embellished by sparkling lavender eyes, and sometimes they were very solemn . . .

"What is it, Christine?" Stephen asked gently when the dark clouds that had been there earlier returned to her expressive eyes.

"Did David tell you that I was pregnant?"

"Yes."

"I lost the baby, Stephen," she said with quiet despair. "I miscarried."

As Stephen looked at the lovely lavender, gray now and so very empty, he realized that that was how it had looked the day David died. Her eyes had been gray then, and her face had been taut and ashen . . . and she had been almost desperate to have him leave.

"Oh, Christine," he whispered. "You lost the baby the day David died, didn't you?"

"Yes." She shook her golden head in soft disbelief still, after all this time. "The pain started just after he died, as if the baby had been destined to live only long enough to give him joy and peace at the time of his death." A smile of love touched her lips as she added, "And he did die peacefully."

Yes he did, Stephen thought as he looked at the extraordinary woman whose great love had protected her husband from truths that would have worried him and who even now, as she talked about a day when she herself had lost both that man and his unborn baby, was still focused on David, on his happiness and peace.

"But what about you, Christine?" he asked very gently.

"I suppose it was destiny for me not to know on the day my husband and my baby died that the insurance company's refusal to pay David's bills was simply a mix-up," she admitted quietly. "Having the bills to pay gave my life a purpose. I needed that purpose then, Stephen."

"And now that I've caused that purpose to be taken away?"

"Now I have to find something new." Christine smiled then, a brave smile intended to assure him that it was all right, that she was ready now to begin the courageous journey toward new dreams. "Actually, the something new is finding me. This week I agreed to design six more gowns . . ."

Stephen left the cheerful house on Twin Peaks shortly after three A.M. He hadn't wanted to leave, but he had early rounds and even though this was her weekend off Christine was meeting with a client to discuss the sketches she had done for a silver and gold silk chiffon evening gown.

Stephen hadn't wanted to leave Christine at three, or ever; and as he drove away he had to fight the powerful urge to simply turn the car around and return to her.

The urge was very powerful, and very wonderful, but so was the weapon Stephen had with which to fight it: the truth.

The hopeful truth . . . Christine is beginning her new life. The delicate butterfly is courageously emerging from her cocoon and in time she will soar gracefully to her dreams.

And the bitter truth . . . she is married.

Chapter Eighteen

Sausalito, California
September 1991

BEAUTY AND THE BILLIONAIRE—The Fairy Tale Ends. It wasn't the headline on the cover of *People* magazine that caught the attention of Peter London's dark green eyes as he stood in the checkout line of Sausalito's Marina Grocery. It was the accompanying photograph of Julian and Larisa Chancellor, crystal champagne flutes raised in toast to their amicable divorce.

Peter reached for a copy of the magazine. Then, realizing that with the magazine he now had eleven items to purchase—not the ten that was the upper limit for the express lane in which he was standing—he moved to the end of another, much longer line. The wait didn't matter. After reading the brief article about Julian and Larisa, Peter was quite lost in thoughts and memories—thoughts of Larisa, who had bewitched him nine nights ago at the Fairmont ball . . . and memories of Julian, who was his most bitter enemy.

* * *

Peter never knew his mother, she died at his birth, but he knew and deeply loved his father. Thomas London was fifty-five-years-old when his son was born. He had been a carpenter for over forty of those fifty-five years, and he had been illiterate for all of them.

His father had dyslexia, Peter realized when he himself was older and well educated. And even though Thomas was a truly gifted artisan, his inability to read or write had always been a source of great frustration and shame, a bewildering and unconquerable flaw that had driven him from school at age twelve and had compelled him—until his marriage at age fifty—to live a mostly solitary life.

Peter sensed his father's shame and even as a young boy tried to teach Thomas to read. But it was impossible. The dyslexia was far too severe. Peter couldn't teach his father to read, but Thomas taught Peter about carpentry, sharing with his beloved son his love for his craft—and sharing too with Peter the dreams that he had for him. Thomas wanted Peter to have the luxury of choice that had never been his, a life whose opportunities and dreams were limited only by talent and desire, what one could do; not, as it had always been for Thomas, by what he couldn't.

"I'm going to be an architect, Pop," Peter announced at the beginning of his senior year in high school. It was Peter's own dream, what he truly wanted for his life, but it also was what Thomas would have been had he been able to read. "I'm going to go to Harvard and I'm going to become an architect."

Peter wanted to go to Harvard because of its academic excellence, of course, but mostly because it would keep him near the aging father he loved so much. Their home was in Concord, where Thomas had spent much of his life lovingly restoring the historic buildings of the Revolutionary War. Their life had been humble, and there had been times when they had truly struggled, but there was such happiness in their life, such a richness of spirit and a wealth of love that Peter had never felt the least bit deprived.

Father and son were a family of two, and Thomas was both father and grandfather, far older than the fathers of Peter's classmates, and magical, and wise. Despite his age, until he was stricken by arthritis, Thomas had had more energy than any of the other fathers. His mind remained lively, even after his art had been crippled, and on his seventy-third birthday, he joyfully celebrated Peter's acceptance to Harvard.

Peter arrived at Harvard as a young man eager to pursue his dreams—and to share that pursuit with his father. He knew college would offer new friendships and experiences, but still he had not anticipated a friendship with someone like Julian Chancellor. Peter had never known anyone like wealthy and privileged Julian, and he was surprised—and, yes, flattered—that Julian wanted the friendship. Peter didn't realize until much later, too late, that what Julian really wanted was his academic excellence.

Peter was both impressed and a little overwhelmed by his charming and confident new friend. Which was why, in the beginning, Peter chose to forgive the troubling things he noticed about Julian.

Julian Chancellor could buy anything he wanted. But he stole—no, Peter amended swiftly, he took. The clothes and books and albums and even money were always taken on the pretext of borrowing, but Julian never had any intention of returning them, nor was he ever apologetic when he didn't, as if his immense wealth and the privileges of his blue blood entitled him to whatever he wanted.

Carelessness, Peter decided. His wealthy friend was simply so accustomed to having everything without any effort at all that he just didn't understand the value of possessions that had been acquired through hard work. Peter justified and forgave Julian's carelessness, and he did the same for the laziness he saw. There was no doubt that Julian was very bright. But he couldn't be bothered to concentrate his intellect on his schoolwork. Always charmingly apologetic, having spent his days and nights partying instead of studying, Julian would appear on the eve of an exam to look at Peter's meticulous class notes.

Julian's carelessness and laziness were understandable, forgivable consequences of the effortlessness of his golden life. But Peter could neither understand nor forgive the way Julian treated Marcy. Marcy was Julian's girlfriend, and there were times when Julian seemed almost cruel to her, openly criticizing her, embarrassing her in front of others. Such unkindness was as foreign to Peter London as was the pampered life Julian Chancellor had lived; and as time went by Peter searched for a diplomatic way to discuss his deep concern with his friend.

Julian invited a small group of friends, including Peter, to spend the last weekend in April at a beach house at Cape Cod. They arrived at the twelve-room "bungalow" belonging to one of Julian's father's business associates late Friday evening, and on Saturday afternoon Julian insisted that they all accompany him to a twenty-five-acre estate located nearby.

"This is Innis Arden," Julian said as he drove his Mercedes through the massive stone pillars that marked the entrance. Then he drove in silence for a while, allowing his friends to marvel at the magnificence of the location, a secluded yet commanding site high above Nantucket Sound. Finally, when he was certain that they understood the significance and value of the breathtaking estate, he announced, "And it is rightfully mine."

"Yours?" one of the young men asked, not doubting, because he had learned never to doubt Julian, but amazed nonetheless.

"*Rightfully* mine," Julian repeated. "At the moment it's on loan to the people of Cape Cod, a gift from my mother's mother. It had been in her family for generations and when the dotty old bird died five years ago, she stipulated in her will that it would be open to the public for twenty years after her death. Which," Julian added as he scowled at an oncoming car, "as you can see, it is."

"And at the end of twenty years you inherit it?"

"No," Julian answered with obvious disgust, not at the question but at the grandmother who had chosen not to will the estate directly to her heirs. "I have to buy it when it goes on the auction block fifteen years from this August. The sale will be by a sealed bid, but I will be the highest bidder."

"How do you know?"

Julian arched a surprised eyebrow. "There are ways of knowing—and I'll know. And then, Innis Arden will be mine, as it should be, and I'll transform it into one of the world's most exclusive resorts. It will take a lot of work, of course, and a lot of money. The existing mansion will have to be completely demolished to make room for a luxury hotel, and there will be separate private bungalows over there where the meadow is now . . ."

* * *

Julian decided to begin the tour of the estate that would one day be his with the secluded cove—which, he assured his friends, would eventually rival the marina in Monte Carlo as a home for the greatest yachts of the world. The path to the cove was through the meadow.

And that was as far as Peter got. As the others continued on, he remained in the meadow, a most willing captive to the enchantment of color and fragrance that surrounded him.

The meadow was an extraordinary community of flowers—some cultivated, some wild—all crowded together and yet blooming in magnificent harmony, sharing the nurturing rays of the golden sun as if in mutual respect for the splendor of the other. Bright blue forget-me-nots delicately graced the elegant stalks of snowqueen irises; and lilies and lupines bloomed in a brilliant mosaic of sapphire, apricot, scarlet, and flame; and daffodils and daisies smiled their dazzling golden smiles at the dazzling golden sun.

The flowers bloomed in a magnificent harmony of color. And, Peter realized as he inhaled, there was a magnificent harmony of fragrance, too. Even the strongest of perfumes didn't overpower the delicate one of its neighbor. Lavender, and jasmine, and lilac, and violet all blended together, an intoxicating tapestry of fragrance into which were also gently woven the vibrant scents of forest and sea.

As Peter gazed at the astonishing beauty of the meadow and inhaled the flower-kissed air, he was swept with emotions that were at once powerful and empowering. Everything seemed possible here. All dreams . . . all hopes . . . all promises.

And Julian was going to destroy this paradise?
No!

Peter's impulsive "No!" became a solemn promise of love an hour later when he wandered through the mansion. Luxuriantly cloaked in lavender wisteria, the mansion was grand and elegant, lovingly built and impeccably maintained, a triumph of graciousness and style. The original structure was almost two centuries old, but there had been a more recent embellishment—a music room overlooking the enchanted meadow.

This was his father's work. Peter was certain of it. The obvious love of the wood—the joyful blending of different grains, the artistic use of knots and swirls to add texture, the meticulous detailing, the grace and majesty—were unmistakable.

"Hi, Pop."

"Peter!" A broad grin lit Thomas's unshaven face. Then, as he rubbed his arthritic hands over the stubble, his expression became a little sheepish, a silent confession that he no longer shaved every day, it was far too difficult. He shaved only when he expected to see his son, which was every other weekend. "I . . . I wasn't expecting you. I would've shaved if I'd known you were coming."

"It doesn't matter, Pop!" Peter exclaimed, keeping hidden from his loving voice the sudden rush of emotion, of sadness, he felt.

"I thought you were planning to spend this weekend at the Cape."

"I was there last night, but . . . Pop, did you ever work at Innis Arden? I was there this afternoon and to me the music room looked like something you would have created."

"It was." Thomas gave a slight shake of his head as the old memories swept through him. "My, my, it was over fifty years ago that I worked there. How did you happen to be in the mansion, Peter?"

"Innis Arden is open to the public now. We visited there because it used to belong to Julian's maternal grandmother."

"Ginny," Thomas said softly. "One of her daughters married a Chancellor, eh?"

"Yes, I guess. *Ginny?*"

"Virginia Alcott Forrester. She was the reason I got the job. She'd seen an alcove I had done in a house on Beacon Hill and trusted me to work on her beautiful home. Innis Arden was hers even then, a wedding present from her grandparents. Her husband was a financier who didn't like the remoteness of the Cape, so the estate became Ginny's private retreat when her husband was traveling and her children were off at the exclusive boarding schools they attended."

"It sounds as though you knew her quite well."

"She was forty and I was twenty, and she was wealthy and well educated and I was illiterate and poor. But she was very lonely, trapped in an unhappy marriage, and I could help her just by listening, and it didn't make my illiteracy seem so shameful. The only other woman I ever met who was as kind and as courageous as Ginny Forrester was your mother," Thomas said quietly. Then reading the silent question in his son's forest green eyes— Had his father had an affair with Julian's grandmother?— he smiled lovingly and elaborated, "Ginny and I felt a great fondness for each other—and yes, perhaps it was

240

love—but we were worlds apart. Nothing ever happened between us, Peter."

"Did you maintain your friendship after you finished the music room?"

"No. That would have been very awkward for her. Impossible really. Shortly after your mother and I were married I heard on the radio that her husband had died. I remember thinking that she was free of him at last and I hoped that she would be able to live the rest of her life in peace at Innis Arden."

"I think that's exactly what she did, Pop." And, Peter thought, I bet she never became the dotty old bird her grandson described with such contempt. "She died about five years ago. In her will she stipulated that for twenty years following her death Innis Arden would belong to the people of Cape Cod."

"For weddings and picnics, I imagine," Thomas embellished with quiet confidence. "Ginny always believed that Innis Arden was a magical place that should be shared. She wanted to share its magic with her own family, but I don't think that either her husband or her children really ever appreciated it."

"They still don't. At least, her grandson doesn't. In fifteen years, when the estate is sold, Julian plans to buy it and convert it into a luxury resort. But, Pop, I think I'll buy it instead. I think it would be a very nice place for us to live, don't you?"

"A very nice place indeed, Peter," Thomas agreed lovingly. Thomas knew that he wouldn't be alive in fifteen years, but his eyes filled with hope as he imagined a future scene of joy. "A very nice place for my grandchildren to frolic."

Peter smiled at his father's allusion to grandchildren. Peter wanted his own family, some day, but that was a faraway dream. There were much more urgent dreams to pursue first. After a moment, he suggested, "Why don't we visit Innis Arden next weekend? Wouldn't you like to see it again?"

"Yes, Peter, I would. I would like that very much."

Ten days after Peter's first visit to Innis Arden, he discovered that Julian had paid another student to steal a copy of an exam that he was scheduled to take. Julian didn't attempt to conceal what he had done, nor did he express even a flicker of shame. He was Julian Chancellor after all, wealthy and privileged and fully entitled to have advantages over everyone else.

Peter knew it was time to confront his friend. At first, he earnestly implored Julian not to cheat simply because it was wrong to do so. And then, when it was obvious that Julian had no intention of altering his plans, Peter quietly warned that should Julian cheat, he would inform the administration of his flagrant violation of the honor code.

For several silent moments, the haughty dark eyes of the privileged heir met the solemn forest green ones of the carpenter's son. Finally, with an easy laugh, Julian relented, eventually even thanking Peter for showing him the error of his ways.

But even as he was expressing his heartfelt gratitude, Julian was plotting the destruction of the presumptuous Peter London. And Julian knew exactly how to get to Peter: through Marcy. It had been obvious for a while that Peter liked her. In fact, Julian thought with delight, whenever *he* was cruel to Marcy, it was *Peter* who seemed to suffer the most.

* * *

"I had to get away from Julian," Marcy whispered with soft despair when Peter opened his door to her timid knock at midnight. As the springtime moonlight illuminated her beautiful tear-glistening eyes, she cried, "I hate him, Peter! He's so cruel, so selfish, so . . . unlike you."

Marcy was lovely and sad and needy, and Peter was young and kind and gentle. He made love to her with tender passion, and afterward they fell asleep in each other's arms. When Peter awakened at dawn, Marcy was already dressed and getting ready to leave. She softened her abrupt goodbye with a lingering kiss and a promise to return again that night.

Within an hour of Marcy's departure, school officials hammered on Peter's door. They had received an anonymous "tip" that Peter had stolen copies of exams hidden in his room. The exams were found in his desk drawer; and there was money, too, far more than his academic scholarship had ever provided, tucked between the mattresses on the side of the bed where Marcy had slept.

Disciplinary committees were convened. They heard the testimony of Marcy, who resolutely denied the midnight visit during which she had planted the exams and money in Peter's room. And they heard Julian's testimony, his solemn admission that he had known about Peter's plan to cheat and had tried unsuccessfully to get him to change his mind; and his additional damning confession that yes, he had had a great deal of money stolen during the school year and had assumed that the thief had been Peter; and then his heartfelt wish that he had done more to help his poor troubled friend.

Two weeks before the completion of his freshman year at Harvard, Peter London was expelled.

* * *

"I'm still going to be an architect, Pop," Peter whispered hoarsely when he returned to Concord and was hugged tightly and lovingly by his father's crippled arms. "You'll see. It's too soon to try to get into another college yet. But I promise you, someday I will. I'll simply tell the truth, explain exactly what happened, and eventually I will find someone who believes me and is willing to give me another chance. In the meantime, Pop, I'm going to find work as a carpenter."

Thomas London knew that his son was neither a cheat nor a thief. But still, despite all Peter's hard work, his honesty and his talent, his dream had been stolen from him. And even though Peter promised to recapture his dream, their dream, the glow that had always lighted Thomas's aging eyes when he envisioned his son's bright future was gone . . . and almost overnight, his health began to fail.

Thomas lived less than a year after Peter's expulsion from Harvard, long enough to make many trips to Innis Arden with his son, but not long enough to see even the beginning of Peter's immense success.

Peter returned to Innis Arden three days after his father's death. It was late April, almost precisely a year since his first visit. The extraordinary meadow was in bountiful and fragrant bloom, having somehow triumphantly survived the icy cruelty of a most harsh winter. The delicate flowers had survived against all odds, defiant and brave in the face of all hardships, and now they reached joyfully for the golden sun.

In the enchanted meadow where all things were possible—all dreams, all promises, all hope—Peter inhaled the perfume of a thousand valiant flowers and whispered, "I will become an architect, Pop, and I will buy this magical place. I will never allow Julian to destroy this heaven. He has already destroyed so much." A rush of white hot rage swept through him, blurring the vivid colors of the meadow; but the shimmering heat did not blur in the least his determined vision of the future. "I promise, Pop. I *promise.*"

It took several years and countless rejections but finally Peter was able to convince a small midwestern college to give him another chance. Within five years of his graduation, he was regarded as one of his alma mater's most distinguished graduates. From the very beginning of his career in architecture, Peter worked alone, selecting only projects in which his taste, his style, and his vision would not be compromised. Peter's uncompromising vision brought him fame—and wealth, more than enough to ensure that when the time came he would be able to make a most generous offer for the estate.

Over the years, Peter traveled to Innis Arden often, one of the estate's many springtime visitors, and with each journey he became more restless for the time when it would be his—to protect and treasure always.

But what if despite his own substantial wealth the magnificent estate went to Julian? Peter might still be able to save the mansion, or at least his father's music room. The wooden structure could easily be moved to another location. But what about the meadow? Its intoxicating fragrance was a rare gift of nature, an exquisite harmony of the scented whispers of flowers and forest and sea that was absolutely unique to that magical place.

If Innis Arden became Julian's, the extraordinary fragrance would be lost forever.

I won't let that happen, Peter vowed four years before the estate was to be sold. He found the best *parfumiers* in the world and sent them to the meadow in late April with all the other visitors. There they spent days inhaling the remarkable fragrance, memorizing its many layers and delicate nuances, finally returning to their laboratories to try to reproduce the evocative blend.

After three years, the scent was finally—and perfectly—recreated.

And Peter named the magical new perfume *Promise*.

Several months before the date in August when all sealed bids for Innis Arden would be opened, Peter had his own attorney contact the attorneys who would be handling the sale. He was delighted, but not surprised, to learn that the attorneys also represented the beneficiaries of the sale—Virginia Alcott Forrester's four grandchildren, Julian Chancellor and his three cousins. Julian would surely be able to "convince" one of his attorneys to "preview" the other sealed bids so that the bid he himself submitted would win—assuming Julian even cared about Innis Arden any longer.

It didn't matter to Peter whether or not Julian still cared about owning the estate. Peter's own reason for wanting the magnificent property had everything to do with dreams and promises . . . and nothing whatsoever to do with revenge.

Peter submitted a sealed bid in June. The amount he offered was well above the appraised value, much higher, he guessed, than any other interested parties, except Julian, would be willing to go. According to the rules of the auction, all sealed bids were to be received in the Manhattan office of the estate attorneys by noon on Wednesday, August fourteenth. At eleven-forty-five on that August morning, Peter and his attorney personally

246

delivered a new bid—an offer two hundred thousand dollars higher than Peter's previous one—and they remained in the office while all the bids were opened.

Peter's new bid was the highest. The next closest belonged to Julian and was an offer just ten thousand dollars above Peter's original bid. Proof positive, Peter decided, that Julian had cheated—or at least had tried to. Peter's own clever yet honest tactics had tricked Julian's dishonest ones—and honesty and Peter had triumphed.

Innis Arden was his. Peter celebrated the fulfillment of the solemn vow he had made by spending the hot August afternoon looking through photographs at both the Eileen Ford and Elite Modeling agencies. He was hoping to find a model for *Promise*. She had to be as extraordinary as the fragrance itself, delicate yet courageous, fragile yet valiant, hopeful against all odds. Peter knew that he might never find such a woman. He was resigned to that possibility and was fully prepared to market the perfume simply with the beautiful photographs of the meadow which he had had taken over the past four years.

At one A.M. on the humid August night that Innis Arden became his, Peter stood on the balcony of his suite at the Plaza remembering his first visit to the estate. "Innis Arden will be mine," Julian had confidently announced on that long-ago day.

What was Julian's reaction to his loss today? Peter wondered. He had bid on the property, and had even cheated to win, but Julian Chancellor had a vast real estate empire now. Did he really care whether Innis Arden was part of it? Or was the businessman in him quite content with his share of the profit from the sale?

Julian's reaction didn't matter, Peter reminded himself. It was just idle curiosity on his part.

But the truth was that had Peter known Julian's reaction and its consequences, it would have mattered to him very much. Because at the precise moment when Peter was idly wondering about that reaction, just a few blocks away his ancient enemy was savagely venting his immense rage at Peter's victory on his bewildered and terrified wife.

Julian's wife . . .

From the moment he had first seen the lovely woman with fire-caressed golden hair and vulnerable bright blue eyes, Peter's heart had raced with a sense of discovery. And when her delicate fingers had moved the tiny doll of the daughter to be beside her mother, he had known with absolute certainty that at last the extraordinary woman for whom he had been searching had been found. She knew about the promises of love. She would understand the meaning of *Promise*, the valiant hopefulness of flowers that survived the bleakest of winters to reach for the golden springtime sun . . . and the courage of human hearts to dream even when all the dreams had been shattered.

Peter had flown to Tokyo the morning after the Fairmont ball. During the past nine days, he had eagerly anticipated his return to San Francisco and the call he would make to Stephen Sheridan to learn the name of the lovely trauma surgeon. Now he had just returned, and hadn't yet called Stephen, and in the checkout line at the Marina Grocery in Sausalito he had learned her name himself: *Larisa Chancellor*.

According to *People*, Larisa would soon be the very wealthy ex-wife of the man who had once shattered Peter's dreams. But, the article asserted, despite the fortune that would be hers—a generous parting gift from the husband who no longer wanted her—Larisa had thoughts of perhaps resuming her modeling career.

Peter wanted the woman he had met at the Fairmont to be the model for *Promise*. But she was Larisa Chancellor. And, his mind warned, once before Julian had sent a beautiful and vulnerable woman to destroy his dreams.

It seemed impossible that Larisa had been at the ball to meet him. And yet, why had she been there? And why had she lied about who she was when she had known full well that in a matter of days the truth would appear on the cover of *People?* Had it all been a devious game orchestrated by Julian to bewitch, to intrigue, to seduce . . . and ultimately to destroy?

It seemed impossible.

And Peter needed her for *Promise*.

Which meant he would simply have to find out.

Chapter Nineteen

Larisa stood at the living-room window of Elizabeth's apartment and gazed at the splendor of the autumn twilight. The brilliant blue sky had faded to pale pink, a soft pastel backdrop for a herd of plump lazy clouds that were bright white against the pale pink and haloed by a shimmering gold farewell kiss from the departing sun.

So beautiful, Larisa thought. And so peaceful.

Even as she was reflecting on the peacefulness, the tranquility was disrupted by the shrill wail of a nearby ambulance. Others might have heard the sirens as harbingers of tragedy, but neither Larisa's soft smile nor her sense of peace wavered at the strident sound. In the past few weeks, the frequent sirens had become symbols of safety and protection, comforting reminders that there were people out there, very close by, who were ready at all times to do battle with trauma and dedicated to doing whatever was humanly possible to conquer it. To Larisa the sirens had become symbols of Elizabeth . . . and like Elizabeth they were friends.

The sirens stopped abruptly, a silent signal that the ambulance had reached the medical center's emergency room. Almost immediately, a new strident sound filled the living room: the ringing telephone. Had she not just heard the siren, Larisa would have assumed that the caller would be Elizabeth.

It will be Elizabeth anyway, she decided as she walked toward the phone. Not all sirens signaled trauma, after all. Some signaled joy. Perhaps this ambulance had carried a soon-to-be new mother . . .

But the caller wasn't Elizabeth, and when Larisa heard his voice there was no more peace.

"Hello, Larisa."

No! her mind screamed, its silent scream more shrill and forboding than a thousand sirens, but in its silence totally futile. No trauma experts would be summoned to rescue her. She would be forced to endure this trauma alone. *You promised that if I gave you my phone number you wouldn't call for at least a month. It's only been ten days!*

"Julian," she answered finally.

"I know I said I wouldn't call for a while, but I haven't received any bills from you and I wanted to be certain that you understand that I expect to pay all your expenses."

"I do understand that."

"I know you took almost forty-four hundred dollars with you, but I would imagine that by now you're running a little low."

Almost forty-four hundred dollars. Did Julian know the exact amount she had taken? He had always acted so casual about the money in the penthouse, such a trivial amount for a man with his wealth. But, Larisa realized with an icy shiver, he had probably always known exactly how much she had taken—and when.

Julian's voice had shattered her fragile peace, and now his words sent the harsh and unnecessary reminder that she had almost depleted the money she had taken. The motel at JFK, the last-minute full-fare plane ticket to San

Francisco, the bottles of iron and vitamins, the lovely dress she and Christine had selected for the lunch and photograph in New York . . . Soon, very soon, she would either have to accept Julian's support or find a way to support herself. Not that there was a choice: she would find a way to support herself. She had already decided that next week, when someone else's face was on the cover of *People,* she would begin the search. She had even thought about approaching Sydney regarding a job—as an assistant to Christine, perhaps?

"Don't you need money, Larisa?"

"No."

"All right," Julian said softly. "I understand. You want nothing from me, nothing to do with me. How can I blame you? But, darling, I want you to know this: I miss you and our love, and I'm spending every second of my life trying to face my flaws and correct them. Do you miss me at all, Larisa? Not the monster I became, but the man who fell in love with you?"

Are those really two different men, Julian? she wondered. Didn't the monster simply clothe himself in gentleness to seduce me into betraying every promise I had ever made to myself?

"Larisa?"

"I have to go, Julian."

"Okay," Julian agreed quietly, forcing subdued resignation in his voice despite the elation he felt at the fear he heard in hers. She was still very afraid of him and the power he had over her. Good, he thought. *Wonderful.* He added gently, "I understand. I'm sorry. I love you, Larisa. Goodbye."

* * *

252

What an illusion it had been to have believed she was actually getting stronger! What folly to have marveled at the peaceful sunset and imagined that such peace could ever be hers! Julian's voice had opened the floodgates of her pain, mercilessly drowning her foolish illusions in the brutal truth. She had not been loved. She had been only possessed and conquered and betrayed.

Larisa struggled to fight the gushing river of pain that flowed from her heart, to will it away with the magnificent sunset and memories of comforting sirens and promises she had made to herself about how much better everything would be tomorrow. But the sun was gone now. The pink and gold had faded to gray and the once plump and happy white clouds had been stretched into gaunt black lines, shredded like cotton candy torn apart by too greedy fingers.

The clouds were gone, and the comforting sirens were silent, and as the river of pain threatened to drown her, Larisa could not even imagine a tomorrow.

She needed to subdue the ever-rising waters, just a little, please. But she simply wasn't strong enough. She needed help. An army of trauma specialists, or . . .

A little alcohol? Yes, that would do nicely. If she could just escape for a while, just float far above the gushing river like a fleecy cloud. Larisa knew the eventual fate of that cloud, of course, but she needed to float now anyway, to bask for a moment in sun-kissed gold.

As she walked into the kitchen, it suddenly occurred to her that there might be no alcohol in Elizabeth's apartment. Oh, but surely there was! *There had to be.* A small supply for guests at least.

As her frantic search took her from one cupboard to the next without results, Larisa realized that she might actually have to leave the apartment to find a drink. Thanks to *People* and all the tabloids she would very likely be recognized. Well, she could smile, couldn't she, somehow, and say something clever about celebrating? Maybe, if she really had to—but was there really no alcohol here? Was this tough love from Elizabeth after all?

Just one drink, Lizzie, please. I promise I'll sip it very slowly.

Then, at last, in a cupboard above the refrigerator, Larisa found the treasure she had been so desperately seeking. The bottle of Courvoisier she had given Elizabeth for her twenty-first birthday was there, scarcely touched, as were almost full bottles of bourbon, Scotch, and gin. Her slender fingers trembled as she hastily filled a glass with bourbon, and then the glass trembled as she raised it to her lips and took a large swallow.

And then another.

Magic, she thought, as she felt the wonderful warmth begin to fill her, a brave and able warrior in her battle against pain. The bourbon was softening the knife-sharp stabs to her badly wounded heart, blunting the effects of their violence, and in a few moments they would be all but forgotten. A smile began to curl her lips, but it stopped abruptly when she turned and looked at the kitchen. It looked like a disaster area, its drawers open and its cupboards ajar, gaping in silent and horrified testimony to her desperation.

She had been so desperate . . . in such pain . . . because of Julian. Because of Julian? a voice deep inside asked. Are you going to permit him to control you still? Are you going to betray yourself once again because of him?

But . . . you don't understand! her wounded heart cried. The pain is so great, too great. I'm not strong enough, not now, not yet.

But you have to be strong, and the strength has to begin

right this minute. If you allow yourself to escape this way, even just for tonight, then Julian has won, hasn't he? *Hasn't he?*

There was no point in arguing with this voice. Larisa knew it spoke the truth. Of course, with another swallow of bourbon, or another glass, it might be muffled into silence. Or perhaps not. The voice was very strong and very determined. Did it truly come from within her? she wondered. From a tough loving place in her heart that believed in her still and trusted her still despite her own betrayals? Or was it a voice from the outside, the voice of a recent memory, a voice with dark blue eyes that seemed to understand.

What does Nicholas Chase know? the part of her that wanted to take another swallow of bourbon petulantly demanded.

"He knows a lot," Larisa whispered softly. He knows a lot about me, about things I don't want to face—but must.

Call me anytime, Larisa, Nick had said.

Larisa looked at the surgery call schedule posted on the corkboard beside the phone. Nick wasn't officially on call tonight, but would his pager be on anyway as Elizabeth's always was? From what Elizabeth said about him, Larisa guessed that it would be. And if not, she *could* dial the number penciled in beside his name, the unlisted home number given to Elizabeth but never used because it was too great—too bold—an invasion of Nick's privacy.

Larisa decided that she would page, but not call. If Nick didn't answer the page, then she would intrude no further.

"Daphne, the magical dragon, flew bravely toward the shimmering rainbow," Nick read quietly to his almost asleep son. Justin was on his lap, his small sleepy body curled close, Nick's lips gently caressing silky strands of golden hair as he read the bedtime story.

When Nick's pager sounded, Justin's blue eyes fluttered open, not with alarm but with interest.

"Oh, oh, Daddy. The hospital needs you."

"I guess so." Nick reached for the pager, but before looking at the lighted display himself, he showed it to his now wide-awake, very bright son. It was a fun game they always played. Justin would read his father's pager and then tell Nick who was paging him. It was far more than a game, of course. It was Nick's way of sharing with his son the hours of their lives when they were apart. Nick had never taken Justin to the hospital—his son was far too young and their life was far too private—but Nick had described it to him in great detail, and in Justin's imagination it was a happy place for his father to be. "Who needs me, Jussie?"

Justin knew by heart the telephone numbers of the places in the hospital to which Nick was most frequently paged. But the seven-digit sequence flashing on the pager now was quite unfamiliar to him.

"I don't know, Daddy," he said. "Who?"

"Well, let's see." It was a number that Nick recognized immediately, but one that Justin would never have seen. Pages to Elizabeth's home phone always came late at night, long after Justin was asleep. She would be on first call, and he would be on second, and she would page him because she had just been notified about an incoming patient who would need them both. "It's Elizabeth."

"The nice lady doctor who works with you?"

"Yes. The nice lady doctor who works with me," Nick answered with an untroubled smile despite the fact that he was, in fact, a little concerned about the page. He had always told Elizabeth, and everyone else, to feel free to page him even when he was officially "off." Everyone else *had* always felt free—and paged him often—but Elizabeth never had . . . until now. "I'd better go call her. So, why don't I tuck you in, sleepy one?"

"Okay."

"Okay," Nick echoed softly as he lifted Justin from his lap and into the bed where Mr. Bear lay waiting. Nick tucked the billowy quilt around both boy and bear, lightly kissed Justin's cheek, and turned out the light before crossing the hallway to his own bedroom to answer Elizabeth's page.

"Larisa? This is Nick Chase. I'm answering Elizabeth's page."

"It wasn't Elizabeth's page, Nick, it was mine," Larisa confessed. "You made the mistake of telling me that if I ever needed to talk . . . but maybe this isn't a good time—"

"It wasn't a mistake, Larisa, and this is a good time," Nick assured. Then, very gently, he encouraged, "Tell me what's happening."

Larisa couldn't answer right away. She was suddenly swept with emotion, an overwhelming rush of gratitude and relief.

"Larisa?"

"Yes, I'm here." She took a soft breath. "What happened is that Julian called, and what's happening right this minute is that I'm staring at a few bottles of alcohol. So far, I've had a little bourbon, but I'm thinking about drinking all of it."

"But you don't want to. You believe that you need to, but you don't want to."

"Yes. That's right," Larisa answered quietly. "I need to, but I don't want to. I guess what I don't want most of all is to allow Julian to do this to me."

"Julian is forcing you to drink?"

"No," she admitted solemnly. "This isn't Julian's fault." *It's my fault for allowing him to do what he did, for trusting him more than I trusted myself, for being so blinded by my need to be loved that I betrayed myself in the process.* "I'm responsible. I'm to blame. Is that what I'm supposed to say?"

"Not if it isn't true."

"Well, it is true. It *is* my fault. I guess it's up to me to find a way out, huh?"

"Has the way out always been alcohol?"

"No! In fact, I rarely drank—really, almost never— before my marriage. It was always so important to me to be in control. Isn't that strange? I used to avoid alcohol for fear of losing control and now I'm turning to it." With soft bewilderment she asked, "Why am I doing that?"

"Because drinking is a kind of control. Because when you drink you can finally control the pain."

"You really do know, don't you, Nick?"

"What I know, Larisa, is that you're going to be okay."

"Really?" she countered sharply, upset that he had so swiftly rebuffed her question about him, her attempt to reach out to him as he was reaching out to her, but mostly terribly disappointed—and terribly afraid—that he had so quickly lost interest and was dismissing her by pronouncing her imminently curable when what she felt was mortally wounded. "That sounds awfully facile, Doctor. Awfully easy."

"It won't be easy, Larisa. I'm not implying that it will," Nick replied calmly. "But the truth is that you have a lot going for you. You don't have a lifetime pattern of drinking. You understand why you're drinking now. And, most importantly, you understand why you don't want to. Isn't that right?"

"Yes. But I hurt, Nick, I *hurt*. And what I want most of all is for the hurt to go away. How do I make that happen?"

"By trying to understand why you hurt."

"And that will magically make it go away?"

"There's no magic, Larisa. But understanding why you hurt will return to you some of the control that you've lost. It will allow you to make choices about your life. You know this. You've already told me as much. If you let the pain control you, then you will always be its victim. I seriously doubt that you are solely responsible for the pain you are feeling now, but you are—you can be—entirely responsible for how you choose to deal with it."

"Right now I want to deal with it by escaping from it. I want that desperately," she added quietly as she frowned at the gaping cupboards. "I don't want to feel this desperate . . . but I do. I can't think, or analyze, or try to understand when I feel like this. Something very powerful inside me is urging me to escape. How do I stop myself from succumbing to that urge, Nick? What do you do?"

Larisa regretted her second question the moment she asked it. This was about her, not him, and yet it was so obvious that what Nick knew—the secrets that she so desperately needed him to share with her—came from his own personal battles. For whatever reason, Nick had once been where she was now, and he had found a way to do what to her at this moment seemed quite impossible.

Larisa needed Nick's help, his expertise, his experience. But he had made it abundantly clear that he didn't want to talk about himself. And besides, she realized, she already knew how Nick found escape. Somewhere along the line, the gorgeous blue-eyed doctor had discovered

259

that he could drown his own pain not in alcohol but in pleasure.

Nick hesitated before answering. His own situation had been so different from Larisa's. And, he thought, he had never himself followed the advice he had just given her. Oh, yes, he had explored the reasons for his own pain, and understood them perfectly, but despite that insight he had still chosen to drink. And it had been his choice to make because then he had been responsible to no one but himself.

Nick drank for himself, because he didn't care enough about himself not to, and when he had stopped drinking it had been because of the precious, wounded little boy who had needed everything he had to give. It had been so easy to stop drinking for Justin, an effortless decision of love; but it had been hard, too, because the tormenting pain hadn't abated, nor had the compelling and powerful wish to escape from it disappeared.

"I run, Larisa," he answered finally. "I run as fast as I can for as long as I can—and then a few miles farther, until I'm too exhausted to think or feel or even breathe. I'm not sure it would work for you, and I'm not recommending that you run through the streets of San Francisco in the middle of the night, but . . ."

"I think it might work for me." Larisa's voice held a delicate whisper of hope. "I used to exercise all the time when I was modeling. After the most strenuous workouts, I remember feeling an almost blissful calm. That's a very helpful suggestion, Nick. Thank—what was that? Your pager?"

"Yes." It was a number Justin would have recognized instantly: the ICU. "I'd better answer it and call you back."

"You don't need to call me back, Nick," Larisa said bravely. "It's time for me to get to work."

"Are you sure?"

"Yes. As soon as we say goodbye, I'm going to run in place until I drop."

"Okay." Nick laughed softly, then said solemnly, "Call me anytime, Larisa."

"Thank you, Nick. You've really helped."

It sounded so easy when she was talking to Nick. His words were so wise and the calmness of his voice was so comforting. But now the lifeline was severed and she was alone in the kitchen where the open cupboards reminded her of her desperation and the bottles of liquor still stood defiantly on the counter beckoning to her. Fighting sudden panic, Larisa slowly and deliberately closed all the cupboards. Then, with a deep breath, she returned the bottles to their hiding place above the refrigerator.

There, she thought triumphantly as she washed the glass she had used. *Triumph*—except that the pain was back now in full force, screaming for relief and reminding her how terribly fragile she was. Larisa hastily dried the glass then abruptly left the kitchen for the spacious living room to exercise to exhaustion—and beyond.

She would exercise to music, she decided, as she pulled the curtains and crossed to Elizabeth's compact disk player. Although Elizabeth had made the modern transition from stereo to CD, she had not abandoned her—*their*—favorites from the past. All the oldies but goodies were there on the small shiny silver disks: the Beach Boys's sunny songs of summer, the songs of love by Streisand, the Beatles, and Patsy Cline, and the primal and energetic music of the Rolling Stones.

The Stones, Larisa decided. She selected a disk from the two-disk "Hot Rocks" collection, set the volume thoughtfully low, then moved to the center of the room and began to dance.

Dancing had always been a favorite form of exercise, but it had been a very long time since she had danced like this—or even exercised at all. The model thinness she had maintained throughout her marriage hadn't been the sleek healthy fitness of her modeling days. Instead, it had been an anxious thinness, the result of very little food and almost constant nervousness. Once her perfect body had been in perfect shape, and now? Now, quickly, so quickly, her lungs and muscles gasped with pain.

But that was good, she realized as she moved even faster. Because, just as Nick had promised, this new physical pain seemed to muffle the screams of her heart.

The phone rang midway through "Jumpin' Jack Flash." As she turned down the volume before answering, Larisa wondered if the caller would be a neighbor concerned about the noise. No, she told herself, the music wasn't loud to begin with and the apartment building was very well built.

The caller would be Elizabeth, or maybe Nick. It would *not* be Julian.

Whoever it was, she had to answer, because if it was Elizabeth and she didn't answer her friend would worry.

"Hello?"

"Larisa? It's Stephen."

"Oh . . . hi . . . Stephen."

"Hi. Are you all right? You sound a little out of breath."

"Out of shape to be exact." Larisa exhaled the words in a rush then gasped for more necessary air. "I've been exercising." Another necessary pause. "Elizabeth isn't here."

"I know. It's actually you I need to talk to. So why don't I do the talking while you listen and catch your breath? How does that sound?"

"Good!"

"Okay. Well, I just got a call from Peter London, the architect who designed the institute. He's planning to market a new perfume this spring and is looking for a model."

"An architect . . . marketing a perfume?"

"He says it's a long story, and I haven't heard it, but I can assure you from having worked closely with him on the design for the institute, Peter will have done his homework. He will have hired the best people to help him and will have insisted on quality and excellence at every turn."

Recalling the uncompromising impression of quality that had been obvious even in the scale model of the institute, Larisa offered, "Without compromise?"

"That would be my guess. So, anyway, he's looking for a model to represent the new fragrance and read in *People* that you might be resuming your career. Apparently he saw you at the ball, and noticed you and me exchanging smiles, so he called to see if I knew how to reach you. I wasn't sure you'd want me to give him your number, but I did tell him that I'd call you and have you call him if you're interested. If not, I can call him back and tell him that."

"Interested? In what?"

"In being the model for his perfume."

Larisa's breathing was calm now, as was her voice as she countered, "I can't believe that that's what he wants, Stephen. I'm sure he just wants to know if I know of someone who would be good."

"No. I'm very certain that who he wants is you."

And I'm very certain that he doesn't, she thought. He can't. He *won't*. Still, suddenly a little breathless again, she asked, "I get the impression that you like him?"

"Very much. So, shall I give you his number?"

"Okay. Yes. Thank you."

Before dialing Peter's number, Larisa thought about the architect who was so successful that he had the money to invest in launching a new perfume, an enterprise that she knew was both terribly expensive and terribly risky. She knew the reason for Peter London's success—she had seen the model for the institute after all—but she wondered if it was truly wise for him to take time away from his sketches to devote it to a project such as this. Did the world really need a new fragrance? Had Peter somehow discovered something so unique and so special that women would abandon their own signature scents to try it? Or would it simply go the way of most new perfumes, a flurry of energy and money and then nothing because the fragrance was ultimately so forgettable that it vanished into thin air?

Well, that was Peter London's problem. And it paled in comparison to her own. Peter had apparently seen her from a distance at the Fairmont, her face softly illuminated by the gentle light of crystal chandeliers, his own vision perhaps a little blurred by champagne. And he had seen the dazzling photographs of her in *People*, a collage of her most famous magazine covers and the photograph taken at Le Cirque in which she had managed to look almost radiant.

Once Larisa Locksley had been a talented actress. Once she had been able to light her brilliant blue eyes with shimmering optimism, as if she truly believed the world was filled with endless and wonderful possibilities. But not now. True, her perfect body was model thin, and she could still curl her magnificent lips into a provocative smile, but she could no longer force a look of glowing hopefulness into her blue eyes. It had taken her two weeks to prepare herself for the all-important photograph at Le Cirque, a command performance that had taken every ounce of energy and will, and it was an effort she could neither repeat nor sustain.

Peter London would see her haunted, vulnerable blue eyes, and he would be disappointed. But, because the famous architect was a man who could make a hospital a warm and welcoming place for its sick and needy visitors, he would conceal his disappointment and tell her with gentle tact that her "look," although sensational, wasn't quite right for his fragrance after all.

Unless . . . what if Julian was behind this? Peter was a gifted architect and Julian owned an empire of buildings. Larisa had never heard Julian mention Peter's name, nor if the new institute was any indication had Peter ever designed anything for Julian. But surely they knew each other.

Julian Chancellor had never commissioned Peter London to design a building, but had he hired him now to approach Larisa with the tantalizing possibility of a wonderful job? She wouldn't get the job, of course. On Julian's instruction, Peter would tactfully—or not so tactfully—reject her; and it would be Julian who was mocking her foolishness for even thinking about modeling again, shattering what little was left of her confidence in hopes of manipulating her into accepting his support after all.

Was Peter London friend or foe? Larisa wondered. Stephen obviously liked and respected Peter, which was an endorsement as strong as an endorsement from Elizabeth would have been, but . . .

Larisa sighed softly and promised herself that as soon as the call was over, no matter the outcome, she would dance again to exhaustion—and beyond.

"Mr. London? This is Larisa Locksley." Locksley, not Chancellor. She gave her maiden name advisedly. If Peter were in Julian's employ, it might cause a few beats of guilty silence.

"Hello, Larisa," Peter replied swiftly, without even the slightest pause, his voice as warm and welcoming as the hospital he designed had been. "It's Peter and thank you for returning my call. Did Stephen explain why I wanted to speak to you?"

"Something about a new perfume that you're planning to market."

"That's right. I'm looking for a model and read in this week's *People* that you might be resuming your modeling career. I wondered if we could meet to discuss the possibility of your appearing in the ads for the perfume."

"All right," she agreed cautiously.

"Good. When would be convenient for you?"

"I'm really quite free." Free? The word twisted and twirled in Larisa's mind. Free? Isn't the truth that you are completely trapped in a prison of memory and pain? She repeated quietly, "Quite free."

"Well, then, how about tomorrow? My architectural offices are in Union Square, but everything having to do with the fragrance is in my condominium in Sausalito."

Your condominium? Larisa echoed silently. An architect launching a new perfume was implausible enough, but to orchestrate that multimillion-dollar endeavor from a condominium? Still . . . Peter had Stephen's endorsement, and tomorrow would be a glorious day to drive across the bridge, and she had always loved Sausalito.

"Why don't we meet in Sausalito?" she suggested.

"Great. Shall I send a limousine for you and plan to have lunch here?"

"No . . . thank you . . . to both. I'll drive myself and there's really no need for you to feed me . . ."

After the conversation ended, Peter smiled softly as he thought about her. He had heard in her voice tonight the intriguing blend of courage and vulnerability that had enchanted him at the ball, the extraordinary combination of delicacy and strength that reminded him of the proud defiant flowers in the meadow at Innis Arden. Peter's smile faded as he thought about the trap he had laid for her by not telling her that they had already met. But it was necessary. He needed to know if she was genuinely surprised to see him . . . or if the surprise was feigned, because she had known who he was all along—because she had been sent by Julian to destroy his dreams.

Peter hoped, how he hoped, that Larisa would be genuinely surprised that it was he.

After the conversation ended, Larisa smiled softly as she allowed herself to indulge in the wonderful fantasy of modeling again. The fantasy was brief, as was the smile. Even if Peter London's interest in her was completely legitimate, he would be disappointed when he saw her and her tell-tale blue eyes at close range. And if Peter was working for Julian? The outcome would be the same. He would tell her that she wasn't right after all. At least she would be able to escape quickly, without lingering over an awkward lunch.

267

But what if it was a trap? What if Julian was waiting in the condominium for her?

The terrifying questions transported Larisa's mind instantly to the beckoning bottles of alcohol in the kitchen, and for three impulsive footsteps, her trembling body followed. But somehow she willed her mutinous feet to stop, and then to turn toward the disk player . . . and in moments she was dancing a breathless dance to "Satisfaction."

Chapter Twenty

"Doctor Chase just called," Elizabeth's secretary announced when she returned to her office from the clinic. "I told him that I expected you back any minute."

"He wants me to call him?"

"Actually, he wants to see you. He'll be in his office for the next hour."

"Okay. I guess I'll go there now then."

"He said he could come here."

"No. That's all right. I'll go there."

Walking the one flight of stairs and three long corridors of linoleum that separated her office from Nick's was far better than anxiously waiting in her office for him to arrive. The walk gave her something to do, a chance to try to release a little of the nervous energy that pulsed through her. "Actually, he wants to see you," her secretary had said. Why would Nick need to *see* her? What couldn't simply be discussed over the phone?

Elizabeth knew at least one possible answer to that question—what had happened between them in the surgery lounge the day Danny had died. She had imagined their discussion about that morning a hundred times, a thousand. As she had rehearsed what she would say to him, Elizabeth had made the uneasy discovery that her own script changed with each rehearsal, sometimes indignant, sometimes apologetic. And as the days had become weeks, and it had become increasingly obvious she and Nick weren't ever going to discuss that morning at all, Elizabeth decided it was for the best.

Five weeks had passed, and in those weeks there had been other lives that she and Nick had fought to save— and some they could and some they could not; and they had operated in perfect wordless harmony as always; and as always Nick had been very polite yet very distant.

But now, after all this time, had Nick decided that they needed to discuss that morning after all? Would that discussion be a preamble to a discussion of what was so painfully apparent, that they simply didn't click and never would? Would he ask her if she had ever thought of finding a position elsewhere? Or would he be more subtle, casually mentioning a wonderful job he had just heard about and even graciously offering to call and recommend her?

"Hi."

"Oh, Elizabeth," Nick answered, standing up from his desk. "Hi."

"Jane said you wanted to see me?"

"Yes." Nick frowned. "I told her I could come to you."

"I know. I felt like walking." *I still feel like walking . . . running . . . because oh how I don't want to hear you politely suggest that I leave.*

Elizabeth didn't run. She simply stiffened, steeling herself as Nick left his desk and walked toward her, a neatly typed letter held in his hand. Was it from a colleague, somewhere on the East Coast, desperately seeking a surgeon uniquely trained in both trauma and transplantation?

Nick stopped in front of her, a polite distance away, and into the all-important space between them he extended the strong, lean, talented hand that held the letter. Elizabeth took the letter, but she didn't even glance at it. Instead her proud emerald eyes bravely sent a defiant message to his dark blue ones, *You tell me what it says, Nick.*

What's wrong, Elizabeth? he wondered as he gazed at her magnificent, yet almost fearful, green eyes. Whatever it was, the lingering silence seemed only to aggravate it, so he spoke.

"That arrived yesterday afternoon. It's an invitation to the International Congress on Transplantation Surgery that will be held in Paris in February. The planning committee for the congress wants the keynote address to be on living donor liver transplantation, and they also would like state-of-the-art presentations on both immunotherapy and renal transplantation. They asked me to give the keynote, and Stephen has agreed to do the immunotherapy talk, but I wondered if you would like to give the presentation on renal transplantation?" Nick stopped, was stopped, by the sudden and wonderful transformation in the lovely emerald. The fear was gone, replaced by soft surprise and luminous joy, and for a wonderful moment he was lost in the glowing emerald—lost, with no desire ever to be found. But, he reminded himself firmly, he had no right whatsoever to linger in the emerald loveliness, even though it sparkled with such warmth and welcome. "You would need to review the literature, of course, as well as our experience here. It's a lot of work, but probably fairly interesting, and I think the congress itself is worth attending. They'll pay all expenses plus honorarium, of course."

271

Nick stopped speaking, and now it was her turn, but all that swirled in Elizabeth's swirling mind were completely unaskable questions. *You really want me to do this, Nick? You're really comfortable having me represent you and your transplant program at this prestigious meeting?*

Those questions were very important, and quite unaskable, but they paled by comparison to the question that made concentration almost impossible: *What were you thinking, Nick, when you paused to look at me? There was such softness in your eyes . . . it looked like tenderness . . . and for a wonderful moment I thought I saw longing too . . . and even dark blue desire.*

The look was gone now, the blue cool and polite as always as Nick waited patiently for her to speak.

"You said the meeting is in February?" she murmured finally.

"Yes. It begins with the keynote address on the evening of the sixteenth. That's a Sunday. The meeting itself will run until noon on Thursday the twentieth. I plan to return as soon as the meeting is over, but if you would like to spend additional time in Europe, I'd be happy to cover the service. Stephen is hoping to stay longer, to visit some of the major immunology centers, and I thought I overheard you say that your parents are on sabbatical in England."

"They are. I'll be visiting with them at Christmas, but it would be very nice to have a chance to see them again in February."

"Does that mean that you'd like to go to Paris? You don't need to give me an answer right now, of course, but I probably should let the planning committee know by early next week."

"I can give you my answer now, Nick." *I can easily give*

you the answer to your question . . . but how I wish I could know your answers to mine. "I'd love to go to Paris. Thank you."

It was a glorious autumn day. Larisa wanted to feel the warm caresses of the breeze off the bay, so before beginning the drive across the Golden Gate Bridge to Sausalito, she rolled down all the windows of Elizabeth's car. She would repair her hair when she reached Sausalito, or maybe she would simply leave the magnificent golden red mane tangled and wind-tossed. That was the California girl look, after all, fresh and natural. Perhaps it was just the right look for what she assumed would be Peter London's fresh and breezy new fragrance.

The instructions Peter had given her guided her unerringly to a condominium building adjacent to the marina. After she parked, Larisa stood for a moment and simply admired the extraordinarily beautiful building. Obviously a Peter London creation, she decided—a triumph of grace and elegance and quality and style.

Everything she wasn't.

Peter's unit was the penthouse. Before entering the private elevator that would carry her there, Larisa looked at her reflection in one of the foyer's many mirrors. Her slender body and the wind-swirled golden red silk looked good, maybe even alluring. Perhaps, for his California girl fragrance, Peter London could be convinced to permit her to wear sunglasses to conceal her haunted and vulnerable blue eyes?

Wishful thinking!

Larisa sighed, pressed the button for the private elevator, and when it opened to more mirrors in the penthouse foyer, she walked to the door and rang the doorbell without so much as glancing at her reflection.

273

"Hello, Larisa."

"Oh," she whispered as her eyes greeted the familiar forest green ones. They were as seductive and inviting in the bright light of day as they had been in the soft glow of a crystal chandelier, and the very handsome man with hair the color of midnight shadows was as compellingly seductive and elegant dressed casually as he had been in a silk tuxedo. "You."

"Me," Peter confessed, immensely relieved to see surprise that was so obviously genuine. The bright blue surprise lasted only a few seconds. Then it was replaced not with indignation, as it might well have been, but with sudden apprehension.

"I guess I shouldn't have pretended to be a trauma surgeon," Larisa offered quietly. "It wasn't a very plausible disguise, was it?"

"Yes, it was," Peter assured swiftly. "I was completely convinced. You certainly seemed to know what you were talking about."

"Well, my best friend is the real trauma surgeon."

"I see." Peter smiled his gentle and sexy half smile. "So, please come in. It's cluttered but . . . there's method in the madness."

Peter's penthouse was cluttered, but it was the energetic clutter of creative passion, not the careless consequence of indifferent laziness. Sketches were strewn everywhere, hastily scribbled memos of sudden inspiration, beautiful designs that one day might be given elegant and graceful life; and there were stacks and stacks of blueprints; and small models of buildings in progress; and framed and yet-to-be framed portraits of works of art that had already been built.

Peter's spectacular bay-view penthouse was so very different from the spectacular Fifth Avenue penthouse where Larisa and Julian Chancellor had lived. Julian had always been absolutely intolerant of clutter. Their impeccably designed surroundings had been lavish and luxurious, but nothing was ever moved even a millimeter from where it had been placed by the interior designer, and there was never any dust, not even a speck.

The stylish and inflexible sterility that Julian had insisted on in their home—in their life—was another reason that Larisa had stopped mourning her own sterility. How tolerant would Julian have been of the playful clutter of children? Not tolerant at all.

Unlike Peter, Larisa found herself thinking, quite unaware of the soft smile that touched her lips at the thought. For now it was obvious that Peter's buildings were his children, but it was somehow both very easy and very wonderful to imagine him with real little lives. He would so joyfully welcome their exuberant clutter. And, she decided with absolute confidence, he would proudly and lovingly display every finger painting and crayon drawing their small hands ever created.

"What are you thinking?" Peter asked gently, wanting very much to know what invisible image had touched her lips with such lovely happiness and had lighted her luminous blue eyes with a glow from very deep within.

"What? Oh," she murmured, "I guess I was thinking that I like the clutter."

"So do I."

The living room where they stood was brightly lighted by the golden autumn sunshine that smiled from outside. After a moment, Larisa looked directly at him, bravely raising her eyes to his, providing the beckoning dark green with the disappointing blue proof of too much unhappiness and too much betrayal. Larisa let her eyes be fully exposed, hiding nothing, not even trying to—because suddenly she wanted to get it over with. She wanted to put an end to the teasing fantasy that she could be even a tiny part of the wonderful creativity and passion that surrounded her.

Peter answered her direct gaze with a welcoming smile. Finally he said, "I really hope you're going to want to be the model for *Promise.*"

"*Promise?*" Larisa echoed.

He teased gently, "You were expecting something more like California Dreamin' or Glitter Baby or Star?"

"I guess I was. But I like *Promise.*" *I like the way your voice and eyes soften when you say it.*

Peter had planned to simply talk to her for a while, to make certain that his memory of her hadn't been playing tricks, but he already knew that it hadn't and he was very anxious to learn the answers to the all-important questions. Would Larisa like the fragrance? Would she understand it and believe in it as he did?

"Shall we see if you really do like *Promise?*" he asked as he removed a small glass vial from his shirt pocket and handed it to her.

Larisa's delicate fingers fumbled slightly with the glass stopper, but in moments she had it out and touched it to her wrists.

"Oh," she whispered as she inhaled the remarkable fragrance. "Oh, Peter, it's lovely."

Lovely and romantic and hopeful, she thought. *Wonderful things that have nothing to do with me. I will buy this extraordinary perfume, and I will feel more hopeful just by wearing it, but I would be very wrong as its model. So very wrong,* she thought as she lifted her eyes to meet the dark green that didn't seem to share that knowledge—and should have, unless . . .

How much is Julian paying you, Peter? she wondered

with a silent scream of pain. How many resorts has he promised you to look this wonderfully—and so convincingly—happy that I love *Promise?*

"Julian is behind this, isn't he?" she demanded accusingly.

"Julian?" Peter seemed genuinely startled by her accusation, startled not guilty, but there was something else in the surprised green, a deep dark shadow that Larisa couldn't interpret. "No. He is not."

"But you do know him."

"I knew him very briefly, fifteen years ago, when we were both freshmen at Harvard." Peter watched her reaction as intently as she watched his. Either she was a sensational actress or she knew absolutely nothing about the past history of Julian Chancellor and Peter London. Not that Julian should have shared that history with his wife. From Julian's standpoint it had all been quite trivial, another enemy conquered and forgotten. It had not been Julian's dreams, after all, that had been so cruelly destroyed. "I haven't spoken to Julian since college. And I assure you, Larisa, he had nothing to do with my decision to ask you to be the model for *Promise.*"

"Then I don't understand why you want me," she murmured almost to herself. Then, as she found another possible reason, a thoughtful frown touched her lovely face. "Julian may not be behind it, but it's because of him, isn't it? Because I was his wife and that would attract attention?"

"No." *The fact that you were Julian's wife was a huge deterrent.* "Ever since the ball, I've been planning to call you to see if I could lure you from the OR long enough for a few photo sessions. The reason I want you to be the model for *Promise,* Larisa, is because of you."

277

"Old and withered *moi?*" she asked softly, disbelieving despite his smiling yet so serious green eyes.

"Old and withered you, yes. You're mature, Larisa, and that's important, because this is a mature fragrance, don't you think? To me, *Promise* isn't wide-eyed and naive. It's a little wiser than that, fully aware of life's struggles and setbacks yet optimistic and hopeful still."

"Yes," Larisa agreed, that was *Promise*. But that wasn't her. Oh yes, she was very aware of life's struggles and setbacks. But couldn't Peter see that she was filled only with hopelessness and fear?

"I think you like the fragrance," Peter said gently to the confused and beautiful blue eyes. "But you seem uncertain about something."

"You really think I'm the right model for *Promise?*"

"I know that you are."

She gave a bewildered shake of the golden silk that was kissed always by its own dazzling red fire but now glittered too with the fiery caresses of the autumn sun.

"I *know* that you are," Peter repeated with soft urgency, needing her for *Promise*, but needing even more that she not vanish from his life. "Do you have an agent I should call?"

"No."

"Well, then, shall we just talk about the terms of the contract right here and now?"

Larisa wanted so much to believe in whatever it was that the seductive dark green eyes saw in her, and she wanted so much, too, to accept the wonderful invitation to share with him the passion he obviously felt for his extraordinary fragrance.

"All right," she answered bravely, disbelieving still but unable—no, unwilling—to say no to either Peter or *Promise*.

278

"Good." Gesturing to a nearby chair, Peter suggested, "Why don't you make yourself comfortable and tell me what terms are important to you?"

"Okay." After they were both seated, she began haltingly, "Well . . . I'd like to be Larisa Locksley—not Larisa Chancellor."

"Done. I told you: I want you for you. So, Larisa Locksley, what else would you like?"

"Stephen said that you're planning to release *Promise* sometime next spring?"

"The last week of April."

"So, you will begin to run the print ads when?"

"That week." Peter guessed gently, "You'd like as much time as possible to elapse between the cover of *People* and your next appearance in a national magazine?"

"If you don't mind."

"I don't mind at all. At the risk of repeating myself, I want you for you. I'm quite happy to keep your participation entirely under wraps until that week if that's what you'd like."

"Yes." *Because if Julian doesn't know, then he can't interfere.* "Please."

"You got it." Peter smiled. "What else?"

"Well . . ." There was just one more issue, one that Peter probably hadn't even thought would be of much concern to her. Based on the *People* article, he undoubtedly believed that she had just signed divorce papers that would make her one of the richest women in America. Did that mean he thought she would be willing to model for free? No, Larisa assured herself, of course not. Smiling a beautiful untroubled smile, as if the question was merely idle curiosity, she asked lightly, "Were you planning to pay me, Mr. London?"

"Indeed I was, Ms. Locksley. Let's see. From the research that I've done, it's my understanding that top models get about ten thousand dollars a day."

"Yes," Larisa agreed bravely, even as she steeled her heart for the next words he would surely say: "Of course, you're not exactly a top model these days." She knew that somehow Peter London would find a gentle way to say the words; but she knew, too, that they had to be said. The truth was the truth, after all, and business was business.

"Is that okay?" Peter asked finally. "Is ten thousand a day all right with you?"

As Larisa realized that Peter wasn't going to say that of course she was no longer a top model, her carefully steeled heart began to race with disbelieving gratitude.

"Larisa?"

"Yes, that's fine," she answered finally, her voice astonishingly calm even though her mind now raced as rapidly as her heart. How many days would she need to work to free herself from Julian forever? "How many days of work did you have in mind, Peter?"

"I'm really not certain. All that I have lined up so far are the photo sessions for the print ads. They're scheduled for the third week in February." In response to Larisa's obvious surprise that the sessions had been scheduled so far in advance, Peter explained, "Even though I wasn't sure I'd ever find a model who was right for *Promise*, I knew that if I did I would want the photographs to be taken by Emily Rousseau Adamson. She's very eager to do them, but since she's expecting her first baby soon, we agreed on the dates in February—at her home in Los Angeles."

"Emily Rousseau Adamson?" Larisa knew the famous name, of course. She had seen the stunning celebrity portraits Emily had taken over the years, including most recently an extraordinary one of the beautiful and intriguing Princess of Wales. "She's really the best."

"That's my plan for *Promise,* Larisa, only the best," Peter said quietly. Her cheeks flushed a beautiful pink at his obvious inclusion of her in that category—happy to be included, yet uncomfortable too. Rescuing her quickly, Peter returned to the issue they had been discussing. "Anyway, there will be at least five days of photo sessions for the print ads, more if we need them, and I may decide to do some television spots as well. So I guess that means somewhere between fifteen and twenty-five days of work."

"Would it be possible to agree on no less than twenty full days?"

"Sure. Does that mean that I could put you to work helping me brainstorm about marketing ideas if I can't keep you busy modeling for all twenty?"

"You can." After a moment of obvious uncertainty Larisa offered bravely, "I'd be happy to help you with the marketing ideas anyway, Peter."

"Terrific," he swiftly assured the brave yet uncertain blue. Smiling gently he added, "I will hold you to that, Larisa. In fact, if you have time today after we've finished our negotiating I could show you what we have so far."

"I'd like that."

"Good. So, let's finish our negotiating. Was there anything else you wanted to discuss?"

"No. That's it."

"Okay. Well, then, I have just one final detail. I'd like you to sign an exclusive agreement with me."

"What does that mean?" Larisa knew the answer of course: it meant that as nice and as wonderful as Peter London was, as different as he seemed from the men she had always attracted, he wanted to own her—as all men always had.

"It means that you would agree not to model for anyone else for the term of the contract," Peter answered, surprised by the question but mostly surprised and concerned by the sudden sharpness of her voice and the wariness of her flashing blue eyes. "I'd like to begin with a one-year agreement with an option to renew."

"Does it also mean that you have approval of my wardrobe for the entire year? And that I couldn't cut my hair or gain one single ounce?"

"No! It doesn't mean any of that. I'd like us to decide together the clothes for the ads, but what you wear the rest of the time is completely up to you. And it's your hair, and whatever length or style you prefer is fine with me, and given that you refused lunch today, I'd probably be in the position of wanting to force-feed you rather than the opposite." Peter paused, smiled gently, and said, "Here comes an understatement, Larisa: something bothers you about this. Please tell me what it is."

"It's the idea of being owned."

"Believe me, I hate the idea of being owned, too. I assure you that that is not my intention. I guess it's just that I feel that *Promise* is so unique that I want as its model someone who is uniquely associated with it." Peter paused, made the very difficult decision very quickly—because it wasn't so difficult after all—and then said, "But if it's important to you not to sign an exclusive deal, then we'll just do without it."

"No," Larisa said, having made her own difficult yet-not-so-difficult decision almost as quickly as he. "I would be very proud to be uniquely associated with *Promise*. I'd be happy to sign an exclusive contract."

"Are you sure?"

"I'm absolutely positive."

"Thank you," he said softly. "So, I'll have my attorney draw up a contract in which you will agree to model exclusively for *Promise* for a term of one year with an option to renew. It turns out that 1992 will be a leap year, so if we do a calendar year—something like October first to October first—the amount for the year would be three point six-six instead of three point six-five. Okay?"

"Three point six-six?"

"Three hundred sixty-six days at ten thousand dollars a day."

Three point six-six was three million six hundred sixty thousand dollars. He was going to pay her for every day of the year whether she worked or not. It was the kind of exclusive deal that top models signed, but . . .

"Larisa?"

"Yes, that's okay," she murmured finally. "That's fine."

"Do you have an attorney to whom I should send the contract?"

"Yes. His name is Mark Jennings. I think I may even have one of his cards in my purse. Peter, could you have your attorney put something in the contract stipulating in irrevocably etched-in-stone legalese that Mark gets ten percent of the total amount?"

"Sure." Then it was done. Larisa was going to be the model for *Promise*. "Would you like to see the marketing ideas now, Larisa? We can count this toward one of your twenty days, if you like."

"Oh, no, Peter, this one is on me. And I'd love to."

Chapter Twenty-one

The room in Peter's penthouse that housed the creative energy and passion that had been lavished on *Promise* was as large as the living room—and as cluttered. There was an invisible organization to the clutter, and Peter could have guided her on a very logical tour from concepts for marketing to sketches for the perfume bottle to backdrop photographs for the print ads; but as soon as Larisa walked into the room, she began to explore on her own, and Peter was quite willing to simply watch her make her own discoveries.

Willing . . . and anxious. Would she recognize the meadow at Innis Arden the moment she saw the photographs? he wondered. Had Julian ever shown her the magical place that he had once hoped to destroy? If he had, Larisa would surely recognize it, and then they would have to talk about Julian again, and Peter didn't want to—not yet. There had been such haunted vulnerability in her blue eyes when she had spoken Julian's name. Someday, Peter vowed, he would tell her his truths about Julian; and someday, he hoped, Larisa would share her own truths with him. But Peter hoped that it would not be today. He sensed that it was far too soon—and far too painful—for Larisa to talk yet about the husband who no longer wanted her.

Peter would know very soon whether or not Larisa recognized the meadow, because even though the photographs were on a table in the farthest corner of the room, that was where her graceful strides were taking her. She had seen the poster-sized blowups propped against the wall, and she wanted to get closer to that beauty. Peter followed, and almost immediately his worry was allayed, and he was left with the quiet joy of watching her gaze upon the magical meadow for the first time.

At first she simply looked, her blue eyes filling with astonished wonder. As she leaned down to get a closer look, a long strand of firelit golden silk fell across her beautiful face, veiling her eyes and obscuring her view. With a flicker of impatience, one slender hand captured the misbehaving strand while the other found its twin, and with deft graceful motions she knotted the two silken ropes together at the nape of her neck. Then, her eyes uncurtained once again and her hands free, her delicate fingers reached for the photograph to touch the beckoning flowers, gently, tenderly, with the trembling softness of whispered kisses.

It wasn't enough, Peter knew. Larisa wanted, needed, to get even closer to the meadow. And he wanted and needed to take her there. It was an astonishing realization because with it came a willingness to trust as he hadn't trusted for years, not since Julian; and with it came a willingness to *en*trust, to place the most important parts of himself—his heart, his secrets, and his dreams—in someone else's care.

I am very willing, Larisa, Peter thought. I am so ready and so willing. But I can see that you are wounded now, fragile and wary; and I know that it will be a while before you can allow yourself to trust again. But you can trust me, Larisa. I would never hurt you. *Trust me* . . .

Larisa turned toward him then, as if in response to the silent call of his heart, and for a wondrous moment her brilliant blue eyes seemed to answer, I do trust you, Peter.

Then the shimmering blue suddenly filled with confusion and she looked away from him, down at the photograph she held.

"Is this where *Promise* comes from?"

"Yes. It's a meadow on an estate in Cape Cod. It won't be in full bloom again until late April, so we'll use these photographs as backdrops for the pictures that will be taken of you."

"You don't need me," Larisa said quietly, her eyes still downcast, gazing at the meadow.

"Yes, I do." *Yes I do.* "Larisa?" *Look at me.*

"Yes?" she asked, finally looking up.

"Yes, I do need you."

There was another wondrous moment as the astonishing messages of his heart glimmered without shadows in his eyes—and the brilliant blue seemed to understand and to welcome the dark green invitation to share its desires and its dreams.

Then, in just a flutter of long beautiful lashes, the moment changed dramatically, the lovely blue inexplicably losing its welcoming wonder and filling with sudden wariness and fear. *I do need you.* Peter's words had been spoken with such gentleness, and they had been eloquently embellished by dark green desire, but nonetheless the words themselves had triggered in her memories of the cruel man whose need for her had been a controlling and destructive obsession.

As Peter gazed at the suddenly haunted and so fearful blue eyes, and sensed that in another moment she might

286

simply turn and flee, his heart sent a powerful command. Don't leave, Larisa. Stay and share *Promise* with me. Stay and share all the promises and all the dreams.

Forcing reassuring calm into his voice, Peter said to the very wary blue eyes, "Right now, Larisa, what I need are your thoughts about a designer for your wardrobe for the ads. I have a list of names—reputedly all top designers—but I'm not really sufficiently familiar with their styles to make an informed choice about who would be best for our needs. I imagine you've worked with all of them. Larisa?"

The worried gentleness registered first, and then the words, and as she met the gentle and worried green eyes, the reminder came: Peter London and Julian Chancellor are very different men. For whatever reason Peter believed that he needed her for *Promise,* and now he was asking for her opinion about a designer . . . and the green eyes told her quite clearly that he needed—and valued—that opinion.

"Actually, Peter, I do know someone who I think would be wonderful. Her name is Christine Andrews. She works in the city at a boutique called . . ." Larisa's mind filled with the warm, welcoming, fragrant images of Sydney's. "You designed Sydney's, didn't you?"

"Yes. That's where Christine works?"

"Yes, although she's going to be spending less time there and more time at her home designing and sewing. She's really very talented."

"So I should talk to her to see if she's interested," Peter said. Then, wanting Larisa to be as involved as possible, he asked, "Or would you like to ask her?"

"Yes," she answered with a soft smile. "I would like to very much."

"What?" Peter asked gently, wanting to know what had triggered the lovely smile.

"I actually met Christine years ago, in college. We shared the dream then that one day I would model dresses that she had designed. We talked about it when we saw each other again six weeks ago, but by then the dream seemed impossible."

"But now it's going to come true."

"Yes," Larisa answered softly. She looked at Peter for a thoughtful moment, and then, because the dark green was so very welcoming, she asked even more softly, "But that's what *Promise* is all about, isn't it? Impossible dreams becoming possible after all?"

"I hope so, Larisa." Peter wanted to say much more, but he had to be so careful with this lovely and wary woman. Finally he simply said, "Now that you've so easily solved the dress designer dilemma, how would you like to give me your opinion on the design for the perfume bottle? I've gotten as far as deciding to carve a single kind of flower in the crystal with its leaf as the stopper. Doing clusters of flowers didn't work—the detailing got lost— but since it is a meadow and the fragrance is a blend of many flowers, one possibility would be to have a number of different bottle designs. I guess that's what I'll do if I—you—can't decide that one flower is clearly the best." Peter gestured to a nearby overstuffed couch. "You'd better have a seat. There are sketches of every flower in the meadow, so this may take a little time."

Before Peter handed Larisa the sketches, she told herself that she would look through the entire stack once fairly quickly, for an overview and first impressions, and then she would carefully study them one by one.

But only five sketches into the first pass, she said, "Oh, dear. I'm afraid I'm going to have to disqualify myself as

288

a judge. I should have known this was coming. I saw them in the photographs of course."

"Them?"

"The forget-me-nots."

"I assume this thing you have about forget-me-nots is a good thing?"

"I love them. They're so delicate and hopeful."

Larisa looked up then and Peter realized that the extraordinary bright blue of her eyes was the same extraordinary bright blue of the flowers that she loved so much. Peter sensed that Larisa herself had never made the connection—and, of course, the true bond between the lovely woman and the delicate and hopeful wildflowers was so much deeper than the magnificent color they shared. It was a communion of spirit, a valiant courage to survive, to reach bravely for the golden sunshine despite the harshest of winters and against all odds.

"So, you're hopelessly prejudiced," Peter said softly to the beautiful forget-me-not.

"Hopelessly."

"What about the sketch itself? Do you think it's good of the flowers?"

"I think it's very good. Would they look like this etched into crystal?"

"Exactly like that." They *will* look exactly like that, Peter amended silently. The decision had been made. Forget-me-nots it would be.

When Elizabeth returned to her apartment at eleven that evening, she was greeted by a radiant Larisa and a glass-stoppered vial of perfume.

"Oh, Larisa," she whispered as soon as she inhaled the fragrance. "This is wonderful."

"Isn't it? It's called *Promise*, and for some completely unknown reason, Peter wants me to be its model—its spokesmodel, actually, because there may be television commercials in addition to the print ads."

"I can't imagine why he would want you," Elizabeth teased gently, then added with solemn candor, "I think you'll be wonderful, Lara."

"I hope so."

"I know so," Elizabeth said emphatically, her confident emerald eyes holding the not-so-confident blue ones until Larisa answered with a soft brave smile.

"Thanks. Well, anyway, we'll know in April, when *Promise*—and the ads—are revealed." She tilted her golden red head thoughtfully and added quietly, "Peter has agreed to keep my role under wraps until then."

"Because of Julian."

"Yes, although I didn't specifically tell Peter that that was the reason. But it is, of course. If Julian doesn't know, then he can't interfere." Larisa shrugged. "Maybe it's not fair to think that he would interfere, but—"

"But this is yours, Lara, not Julian's," Elizabeth interjected firmly. "What you do is no longer any of his concern. So, tell me more."

"Well . . . I'm pretty sure that Christine is going to design the dresses that I'll wear in the ads. I called her earlier this evening and we're having lunch together tomorrow to talk it over." Larisa hesitated briefly, then added, "After which, I'm going to start looking for an apartment and a car."

"Whoa! You already have an apartment and a car. The drive you made to Sausalito today was the first real exercise—not counting short trips to Sydney's—that my car has had in weeks." Elizabeth's emerald eyes sparkled merrily as she embellished, "I really feel quite guilty that I don't let it out more often—to stretch its little wheels. And, speaking of guilt, I feel even guiltier about the second bedroom. Until you arrived, it had been ignored completely."

"But, Liz, don't you think I've imposed long enough?"

"If it had been an imposition to have you here, then I suppose it would have been long enough. But I love having you here, Lara. Please don't move out because of me. Move out because you want to, because you need more privacy or fewer sirens—you don't need to give me a reason—just don't move out because you think it's what I want."

Larisa didn't want to move out. The sirens had become her friends, and as for privacy . . . because of Elizabeth's busy schedule she really had more than enough privacy in which to wage her desperate battle against the painful memories. Absolute solitude would be an even greater test of her emotional strength, of course, but why test something she already knew was so fragile and precarious? It would be so wonderful to stay here, in the bedroom she would decorate with the photographs Peter had given her of the meadow, her own small safe world filled with *Promise*.

"But what about your privacy, Lizzie?"

"I promise I'll let you know if it begins to feel even the least bit invaded."

"Well, then, I'd love to stay—assuming you'll let me pay my half of everything."

"Whatever!"

"Okay."

"Okay."

It was more than okay with both of them, and they told each other that with smiling eyes.

"I do think I'll buy a car though," Larisa said finally.

"Exercise is one thing, but miles are another, and I may be doing a lot of driving back and forth to Sausalito. Peter says he would like me to attend the marketing meetings."

"I know Stephen likes Peter very much," Elizabeth said. "It sounds as though you do, too?"

"Yes. He's very nice." Nice, she mused with silent amazement. Nice men had always been attracted to Elizabeth, not to her. *Wait a minute! You think that the very nice, and very sexy, and very talented, and very wonderful Peter London is actually attracted to you?* a skeptical voice demanded. Well, no, I mean, he wants me to model for his fragrance. *For some unknown reason.* Yes, but, I thought, I wondered, it seemed to me that when he looked at me there was something more in his forest green eyes. *An invitation to join him in the lovely dark woods?* the voice taunted. *Dream on!*

"Speaking of nice," Elizabeth began.

"Yes?" Larisa encouraged swiftly, relieved to extricate herself from her own uncomfortable internal dialogue. "Speaking of nice?"

"Well, today that basically nice—not deeply flawed—Nicholas Chase asked me to give an important scientific presentation at a very prestigious meeting in Paris in February." Elizabeth shrugged softly. "I'm interpreting it as a vote of confidence."

"I'm sure that's the right interpretation, Liz." Just like I'm sure, too, that Nicholas Chase *is* nice—and deeply flawed. Not that even Nick's deepest flaws would deter lovely and generous Elizabeth. "Will Nick be going to romantic Paris, too?"

"He's giving the keynote address." Elizabeth smiled at her friend and admonished fondly, "Let's not get carried away, Lara."

* * *

292

As she lay in the darkness in the bedroom in which tomorrow she would hang the photographs of the magical meadow, Larisa thought about the three young women who had all been freshmen at Berkeley twelve years before. As her thoughts drifted to that distant time and its limitless dreams, Larisa felt whispers of hopefulness trying to find a home amid the raw wounds of her heart. There was a place there already for the girl whose emerald eyes had envisioned a wonderful dream of becoming a doctor—and of falling in love; and there was a place there too for the lavender-eyed girl who had shyly confessed her dream of becoming a designer.

Larisa felt great hope for the dreams of Elizabeth and Christine.

And what about for herself? Was there any hope for a happy ending to her own loveless and lonely life?

Maybe, Larisa thought bravely. Because, after all, making impossible dreams become possible was what *Promise* was all about.

Part

Four

Chapter Twenty-two

San Francisco
December 1991

"Here are the sketches I've done so far."

"Oh, Christine," Larisa whispered. "These are wonderful, so hopeful and romantic. I think they're just perfect and I know Peter will think so, too. In fact, why don't we show them to him right now? I'm pretty sure he's at his Union Square office all day today."

"You go, Larisa." Christine smiled. "As you can see from the stacks of fabric and sketches strewn all over the house, I have a few projects to do."

Christine's lavender eyes smiled, and she seemed so much more happy and serene than she had when Larisa had first seen her again in August, but still Larisa asked, "Is it all right that you're doing the dresses for *Promise*, Christine? You're not already overburdened, are you?"

"I'm fine! Overcommitted perhaps, but certainly not overburdened." Christine gestured to a stack of red and green felt, quite out of place amid the silks and satins that would eventually be transformed into elegant evening gowns. "I still have a few dresses to finish before the

Christmas balls but at the moment my most pressing—and most important—deadline is the Christmas pageant at my local elementary school."

"How did that come about?"

"I saw a flyer for the school's Thanksgiving assembly, open to the public, and on an impulse I decided to go. I really enjoyed the assembly—the children were all so lively and excited!—but I couldn't help noticing their costumes. Pilgrims and Indians alike were all very ragged and missing such key items as hats and headdresses. The following week I met with the school principal—to offer to repair the costumes for next year—and she told me that the Christmas pageant costumes were even more worn."

"So you're recostuming the entire school?" Larisa asked with a gentle tease as she looked at the large stack of felt, the rolls of silver and gold rickrack, and the small plastic tubes filled with sequins and glitter.

"I guess it's fair to say that I'm the team leader, but I have lots of help from both mothers and teachers." Christine frowned slightly as she gazed at the unmade costumes. "Anyway, the pageant is on the twenty-first, a week from this Saturday, but the dress rehearsal is scheduled for the eighteenth. So, as you can see, I have my work cut out for me. You take the sketches to show Peter, Larisa, and I'll stay here and get to work on outfitting Santa's helpers . . ."

Christine Andrews was much better than she had been on that day in August. And, Larisa thought as she drove her car from Twin Peaks to Union Square, so am I. So much better—because of Julian . . . and Nick . . . and Peter.

Julian's role had been passive since his phone call in

September. She hadn't heard a word from him at all in the almost three months since that night, and Larisa was very grateful. Not that she needed Julian's voice to trigger memories of betrayal and pain. Those memories came anyway, sweeping through her without warning, contemptuous voices of thunder that drowned out the brave and delicate whispers of hope that came now, too, also without warning. At the most fragile moments, as she teetered on the edge of what felt almost like happiness, the memories would come crashing down on her like unwelcome waves on a sand castle, flooding her with pain—and urging her to seek escape.

But Larisa hadn't had one drop of alcohol since the night of Julian's call. She had battled the compelling urges with exercise, as Nick had suggested, and she had also found her own powerful weapon: *Promise*. At the times when she was the most raw, when every cell within her screamed for numbness and escape, she would go to her bedroom and gaze at the photographs of the magical meadow and breathe the remarkable fragrance—and the gentle and hopeful emotions evoked by the perfume would conquer the harsh and anguished ones. *Promise* was a magical potion, an invisible armor crafted by courageous flowers.

For the first few weeks following her frantic call, Nick had called quite often, always late at night, and always, Larisa realized, when he knew that Elizabeth was at the hospital. But as he had become increasingly convinced that she truly was better, not to mention very fit thanks to hours and hours of exhausting exercise, he called less often. Now it had been almost two weeks since Nick's last call, and perhaps she wouldn't hear from him again, and perhaps, Larisa thought, that was for the best. She sensed that he, like she, felt uncomfortable about the late-night conversations that took place in Elizabeth's apartment on Elizabeth's telephone . . . but so conspicuously and carefully without Elizabeth's knowledge. By unspoken agreement they had kept their "relationship" secret from Elizabeth; it was, after all, a relationship based on secrets. Larisa was strong enough now to want to share with Elizabeth her own secrets, her almost desperate need to drink and Nick's all-important role in helping her identify the problem and in dealing with it. But telling Elizabeth her story necessarily involved telling her what little she had learned about Nick—his never-discussed-again marriage and his never-discussed-at-all but obviously significant relationship with alcohol. Larisa knew that knowing Nick's secrets wouldn't change Elizabeth's feelings about him, not at all; but still, revealing them to Elizabeth would be a betrayal of Nick's trust—and Larisa owed him so much.

Larisa was better because Julian hadn't called . . . and because Nick had . . . but most of all, she was better because of Peter—and *Promise*, she amended swiftly, linking the two and firmly reminding herself that Peter's involvement with her was only because of *Promise*.

True, Peter had been wonderfully generous with her, allowing her to share his creativity and passion for the extraordinary fragrance; and he had seemed to truly value her opinions, calling her often to brainstorm about new ideas for the ad campaign, inviting her to the marketing meetings, encouraging her to call him anytime with her own ideas, or even to drop by his offices in Union Square if she happened to be at Sydney's.

Business, Larisa reminded herself as she rode the elevator to the penthouse offices of Peter London, Architect. *Promise* is very important to Peter, and I am the model for that very important project. It doesn't mean that I am important to Peter . . . even though sometimes, when his seductive dark green eyes gaze at me, he seems to be searching not for an angle or expression he wants to be sure to capture in the ads, but for something more, something deeper.

I know what's deeper, Peter, she thought. It was a grim thought, and surely one that would calm the heart that raced as always in anticipation of seeing him. I know what's deeper, Peter, and it's nothing that you would want to find.

"Larisa."

"Hi. You said I should drop by sometime." She shrugged softly and took a breath to provide oxygen to the heart that had been calmed briefly by her own sobering thoughts but now fluttered again in joyful response to the dark green eyes that were so welcoming, so happy to see her even before she had given him her reason for being here. "Christine has finished the sketches, and they're so wonderful that I thought you would want to see them right away."

Peter and Larisa studied the sketches together, giving each work of art its full due, and when they had agreed that what Christine had created was all that they had hoped for and more, Peter said, "We need to celebrate, Larisa."

"We do? Because of the dresses?"

"Among other things. We never officially celebrated your willingness to be the model for *Promise*, nor the decision about etching forget-me-nots on the bottle, nor any of the other major decisions you've helped me make—any of which would have been reason enough for celebration. And now there's yet another reason. This weekend the

301

meadow in Cape Cod becomes mine." Ours, he amended silently. "I signed the purchase agreement a few months ago, but it's taken this long to get all the paperwork resolved. The title officially transfers to me at midnight Saturday. So, Larisa, will you celebrate with me then?"

"Yes," she answered with quiet joy as her racing heart embellished, Of course I will.

Peter smiled his happiness at the forget-me-not blue eyes that seemed so happy, too, at the invitation, and after a thoughtful moment he suggested quietly, "I have a house at Lake Tahoe. Would you like to go there with me for the weekend?"

"Lake Tahoe?"

Peter's heart ached as he watched the glowing happiness fade from her lovely eyes, suddenly replaced by the fearful wariness he had seen in the beginning but which had recently been in hiding. He had so hoped that the wariness was gone forever, but now it was back—because, encouraged by the bright blue radiance, he had broken his solemn vow to be so very careful with her . . . to move so very slowly.

"Oh, Larisa," he said softly. "It can't be a surprise to you to hear that I'm very attracted to you. But I honestly wasn't suggesting anything more than having a chance to spend some time together, to take walks in the snow, and read by roaring fires, and talk about ideas for *Promise* without being interrupted. I know it's too soon for you for anything more."

No, Peter, it's not too soon! her heart cried. But, as she thought about Tahoe and all the ghosts that haunted her still, her mind embellished sadly, It's not too soon . . . but it may be far too late.

"Let's forget about Tahoe," Peter said very gently to the troubled blue eyes. "But, Larisa, please know that no matter where we are, at noon in my office or alone at a lakeside house in Tahoe at midnight, you can always trust me. You never have a reason to be afraid of me."

I'm not afraid of you, Peter! *I'm afraid of Tahoe.*

"I do trust you, Peter," she said softly. Then, bravely fighting her fear, she added, even more softly, "And I would love to go to Tahoe with you this weekend."

Stephen stared thoughtfully at the two theater tickets that he had just removed from the desk in his lab. He hadn't needed to remove them. He knew by heart all the information that was printed on them: *Nutcracker,* Union Square Theatre, December 21st, Eight P.M. The seat numbers engraved on the cobalt blue tickets were for the boxes at stage left, the same seats Stephen had had for the past five theater seasons.

Stephen hadn't been to any of the theater's performances since September. He had had absolutely no interest in finding a date to accompany him; and although he had no qualms about going alone, he decided that his solitude was far better spent in his lab trying to find answers—trying not to miss a tiny clue that might one day save someone's life . . . someone's husband's life.

Stephen's valuable season tickets hadn't been wasted. Elizabeth and Larisa had raved about the productions of *Cats, Phantom of the Opera,* and *Les Miserables* that they had seen in his stead. Elizabeth and Larisa wouldn't be able to use the tickets for the *Nutcracker* on the twenty-first—that was the Saturday evening that they were flying to England to spend the holidays in London with Elizabeth's family—and Stephen had another plan for that night anyway, a decision of the heart made long before it had become a

303

conscious thought. And now the twenty-first was ten days away . . . and it was time to call her.

But, Stephen wondered, should he call, or should he simply leave her alone? He knew from Elizabeth that she was very busy designing beautiful gowns for the women of San Francisco as well as romantic dresses for Larisa to wear in the ads for *Promise*. And although Elizabeth herself didn't see Christine very often, Larisa did—and reported that she seemed quite happy pursuing her dream of becoming a designer.

Was Christine happy? Stephen hoped so. It was a hope that was with him constantly, just as lovely images of lavender and gold were with him too, always, drifting gently through his mind even when he was working. Now he was planning once again to intrude into Christine's life.

And if it was an unwelcome intrusion?

The lavender eyes that had always been able to tell him the most honest and important truths would let him know. He would make it very easy for her . . .

Christine shook her golden head slightly as she stared at the tiny drop of red blood that was forming at the tip of her index finger. She had pricked herself again, because again her thoughts had drifted while she sewed. At least this time the drift of her thoughts had been logical, wandering quite naturally from the elf costume on which she was sewing little bells to the Christmas pageant itself—and the invitation she had been thinking about making. But there had been other accidental needle pricks, lots of them, as her mind had filled with other not-so-logical questions. Was he pleased with the progress on the institute? Was he getting over the unhappiness caused by his breakup with Madolyn Mitchell? Had he found someone else, or did he spend every moment in his lab searching for ways to save others' lives and others' loves?

Christine hoped that Stephen was happy, and that the holiday season would be a joyous one for him, and she wondered if he might like to . . . that was when she had pricked herself, at the point when she was wondering if Stephen might like to go to the Christmas pageant. She would be backstage, of course, helping the excited children with their costume changes so that their proud and admiring parents could be in the audience. But Stephen could sit in the audience too, and it would all be very festive and happy, and it seemed like something that Stephen might enjoy.

But was she really going to find the courage to ask him? Or was she simply going to use her fingers as pin cushions for the next ten days?

"I was just thinking about you," she confessed when the phone rang five minutes later—and it was Stephen.

"You were?"

"Yes," she answered, so pleased that he seemed pleased. "I . . . Hi."

"Hi." Stephen drew a steadying breath, then simply told her why he had called, "I have tickets for the *Nutcracker* for the twenty-first—a week from Saturday—and I wondered if you would like to go with me?"

"Yes," she answered swiftly, then added softly, "And no. I'd like to go with you very much, Stephen, but I'm afraid I can't. There's a Christmas pageant at my local elementary school that night and I've made some of the costumes and have offered to help backstage during the performance. That's what I was thinking about when you called."

"And it had something to do with me?"

"Yes. I thought . . . I mean, it's an elementary school pageant, a far cry from the *Nutcracker*, but it will be festive and fun and . . ."

"And far better than the *Nutcracker*. So, if that was an invitation, I accept." After a slight pause, he asked, "Was it an invitation, Christine?"

"Yes, it was."

"Good." Stephen smiled in response to the lovely smile that somehow so eloquently and beautifully traveled through the phone lines. "I'm on call that night, but the holidays tend to be quiet."

Chapter Twenty-three

Lake Tahoe
December 1991

From the moment Peter and Larisa left her Pacific Heights apartment at noon Friday until they were within a few miles of Lake Tahoe, their conversation flowed easily and comfortably, punctuated occasionally with silences that were equally comfortable. But as they neared their destination, ascending into the snow-caressed world of the mountains—where the majestic evergreens were dressed in their laciest winter best and the streams had frozen into icicles that glittered like diamonds in the winter sun—the silence became tense; and the brilliant blue eyes that should have smiled at the splendor of the winter wonderland became fearful and apprehensive. Larisa sat very still, her taut slender body pressed against the seat, as if trying to push herself as far away as possible from whatever it was, yet knowing with a quiet fearful despair that it still wasn't far enough—she couldn't escape.

What was it? Peter wondered. What invisible monster has filled her with such dread? He wanted to help. But Larisa was somewhere far away, in a terrifying place where, perhaps, she even needed to be. So he simply drove in sympathetic silence, offering gentle smiles of reassurance to her unseeing blue eyes.

Larisa gazed straight ahead, her eyes fixed on an invisible image, the wariness in the forget-me-not blue increasing with each passing mile. Then, when they reached the outskirts of South Lake Tahoe, she turned her head, just a little, just enough to look at a motel, an unmenacing cluster of cheerful green and white cottages surrounded by an asphalt parking lot.

Peter had sensed that Larisa was going to turn her head even before it happened. He had felt her struggle, an increase in her already steely tension, as if she was trying to stop herself from looking, but knew full well that the struggle was ultimately useless. She had to look. She was compelled to by an unwelcome yet unconquerable magnet.

Then the motel was behind them.

Eventually her fists released the isometric clench that had imprisoned them for miles. But she was still very far away. Her gaze was no longer straight ahead but down, her firelit head bent by an immense invisible weight, her blue eyes veiled by a shimmering curtain of golden red silk.

"Here we are," Peter said quietly six minutes later when he brought his car to a gentle stop in the driveway of his lakeside house.

Larisa looked up at the sound of Peter's voice, startled by the voice itself, despite its gentleness, and even more startled to see that the image of the motel—the cottage— had been replaced by a magnificent creation of wood and stone.

308

"It's beautiful," she murmured.

If there had been such elegant lakeside houses here when she was a little girl, Larisa had never seen them. And she would have seen them, during one of her many joyous journeys along the shoreline. How she had loved the majesty of the lake, and how well she had come to know its many faces and moods. There had been days like this day, when the unrippled water was a perfect mirror of snow-kissed mountains and sapphire skies; and there had been other winter days, when the heavens glowered and the wind hissed and the lake roared with a vengeance of waves and spray. And there had been the days of autumn, when the mountain air was crisp and the leaves were red and gold; and the days of spring, when everything was so fresh and new; and the days of summer, when the gently lapping tranquility was disrupted by the noisy play of swimmers.

How she had loved this lake. How important it had been for her to be able to come here, along the trails in the woods known only to herself and the deer, and to stand at its shores. How important. How necessary . . .

"I think I'd like to go for a walk," she said impulsively. "If you don't mind. I won't be long."

"Of course I don't mind, Larisa," Peter said gently. "But please, first let me get you something warmer to wear."

With that, Peter got out of the car and went into the house. When he returned moments later—with an assortment of parkas, gloves, ski caps, and boots—Larisa was standing beside the car, gazing at the lake.

"It's a very long walk back to the motel, Larisa," he offered quietly. "And it's too dangerous to begin walking here now. Twilight will fall within the hour, and a storm front is supposed to be moving in by early evening. So, if

309

you're planning to go there, why don't you take the car? Or let me drive you."

"I'd really just planned to walk along the lake." Even as she spoke Larisa realized that her steps might have taken her into the woods and along the trails she once had known so well, shortcuts from the lake back to town. She asked softly, "Was my reaction to the motel so obvious?"

Yes . . . to someone who loves you. "I just got the impression that it held memories—not very happy memories."

"No, not very happy memories at all."

Whatever the unhappy memories, Peter thought, they weren't memories of Julian. Had Larisa and Julian Chancellor ever been to Lake Tahoe together, they would have stayed in a penthouse suite at one of the grand hotels on the strip, not in the unprepossessing little motel on the outskirts of town.

A gust of wind swept off the lake, an icy whisper that promised soon, very soon, delicate snow-white crystals would begin to fall.

"Are the unhappy memories something you could think about right here? In front of a roaring fire?" Peter's dark green eyes were gentle and inviting. "With a mug of hot chocolate, maybe? The motel will still be there tomorrow morning, Larisa."

"I suppose I had hoped it wouldn't be there at all." She shrugged softly as she realized the futility of that hope. Even if the motel had been destroyed, completely leveled to make way for a high-rise hotel and casino, the memories would not have been demolished with it.

"How long has it been?"

"Since I was last here? Twelve years. But before that, for the first eighteen years of my life, this was home." Home? No, that was a wonderful word that held lovely meanings that Larisa had never known. Tahoe was simply where she had lived . . . and where so much of her had died.

Larisa shivered. From the icy wind that swirled her red and golden hair? Or from the icy ghosts that danced and swirled inside her?

"Let's go in the house," Peter urged gently. He wanted to urge so much more. Tell me, Larisa. *Trust me.*

"I called in an order to one of the local groceries before we left San Francisco," Peter explained when she found him in the kitchen unloading the cardboard boxes of just-delivered food.

It had been forty-five minutes since he had shown her to her bedroom—a wonderful second-floor room whose pine-framed windows overlooked the lake—then left to give her privacy to get settled. He had been worrying, and he saw from her blue eyes that he had been right to worry; but now, at least, she was here.

Peter might have said more about the groceries, a casual allusion to the effect of the wonderful mountain air on the robustness of appetites. But Larisa had spent eighteen years of her life in this exhilarating air. And she was thin. And sometime in the past few months she had confessed to him that she had never eaten very much—not even, he realized now, during the years in which she had lived in this beautiful place that he loved . . . and she so obviously feared.

"Are you a gourmet cook, Peter?"

"Not gourmet," he answered, smiling as he gestured to a bag of spaghetti, proof positive of the truth of his statement. "I cook simple things."

"But good things," Larisa offered as she peered into the contents of the boxes.

311

"I hope so. Actually, I think so. That's not immodesty, because none of the recipes is actually mine. I'm simply a technician."

"Whose recipes are they?"

"My father's. My mother died when I was born, so it was just the two of us. For years he cooked and I watched. Then, when I was a teenager, he became quite crippled with arthritis and I became the cook for the family. But they were still his recipes. They still are."

Larisa smiled at the fondness she heard in Peter's voice as he spoke of his father; and then, because they were in Tahoe, in this place filled with so many of her own memories, her expression became thoughtful . . . and finally sad.

"Larisa?"

"I never learned how to cook at all."

It wasn't, Peter knew, the haughty pronouncement of an heiress whose meals had always been prepared by servants and who would have never wanted it any other way. It was, he decided, the wistful sadness of someone who had wanted to learn—and who most of all sensed how much she had missed by not having someone who had cared enough to take the time to teach her.

Oh, Larisa, please tell me.

"I promised you a roaring fire and a mug of hot chocolate," he said finally. "Or would you prefer something stronger?"

"No. Hot chocolate would be nice."

"Okay. Why don't I finish putting the groceries away and then I'll bring it to you? The fire is waiting for you in the living room, which is a straight shot through that door, and it should already be roaring."

* * *

312

The moment the kitchen door swung closed behind her, Larisa heard the beckoning sounds from the living room, the cheerful crackles of Peter's roaring fire; and when she reached the room she was greeted by a wonderfully welcoming red-orange glow. The fire provided enough light, and enough shadows, and Larisa needed the shadows, because she had decided to tell Peter about the icy ghosts that lived in Tahoe.

Larisa needed the shadows for her eyes—and for his . . . because she didn't want to see the wondrous dark green desire fade to disappointed disgust.

She was sitting on an antique wooden chair beside the fireplace when Peter joined her. It was a solitary place to sit, and although the collector's piece was eminently sturdy and functional, it was so much less comfortable than the overstuffed armchairs or the huge plush sofa. But Larisa had obviously chosen the hard and isolated chair by design—a stark lonely island in the red-orange sea.

"Shall I leave you?" Peter asked gently but reluctantly as he handed her a mug of hot chocolate.

"No, please," she answered, meeting his questioning green eyes briefly, then returning her gaze to the crackles and flames. "I'd like to tell you about the motel."

"Okay." *Good.*

Peter sat opposite her, on the other side of the huge stone fireplace. It felt far away, but at least he could see her profile in the shadows, and if she chose to look at him, he would be able to see her face.

"I guess I should just begin at the beginning. I was born here. My mother was a showgirl. I don't know who my father was. I don't think she knew either. I'm not sure why she had me. She told me often enough that having a

313

baby—having me—was the greatest mistake of her life."

"A mistake that I for one am very glad she made."

Larisa looked at him, compelled by the unconcealed desire in his voice and compelled, too, by her own heart to send a silent warning. *You won't want me, Peter. Not when you know everything.*

Returning her gaze to the fire, she continued, "Anyway, because her pregnancy stole her body from her, she couldn't find work as a showgirl again. She became a cocktail waitress instead and later a blackjack dealer. There were always men, and I think some of them paid her with money or with drugs, but I'm sure she never considered herself a prostitute. Until I was eight, we never lived in the same place for more than a year. Sometimes we moved in with her boyfriends, and sometimes we lived with groups of people. It was the sixties, and even in Lake Tahoe there were communes and flower children." She stopped abruptly, suddenly flooded by emotions that preceded the conscious memory but which made her whisper, "And peace rallies."

"Tell me what happened at the peace rallies."

"I'd forgotten until just now." But now the memory had caught up with the emotions. "I was six. It was summertime. There were rock bands and sunshine and free love—and psychedelic paint. My mother's boyfriend made me take off my shirt and painted the slogan MAKE LOVE, NOT WAR on the front of my bare chest and a peace sign on the back. He wouldn't let me put my shirt back on, and neither would my mother. They paraded me around like that all day." Fire caressed fire as she gave a soft bewildered shake of her glimmering golden red head. "My first modeling experience. How strange. I loved modeling. I never felt at all compromised or embarrassed when I modeled. But I hated that day. I still hate it."

Oh, my darling, and I hate it for you. Peter hated that day . . . and all the days of her young innocent life when she should have been loved and so obviously hadn't been. Fighting his own anger, he reminded her gently, "You never let yourself be embarrassed or compromised during your career as a model, Larisa."

No, Larisa thought. I never did. Not in my career. But she had allowed embarrassment and compromise in her marriage. Julian had wanted her to wear provocative clothes, to display his magnificent prize to his friends, and she had acceded to his wish . . . and in private there had been even more humiliation.

"Until you were eight, you never lived in the same place for more than a year," Peter said finally. Larisa had withdrawn, her head bent in shame, her blue eyes veiled and hidden, and he was suddenly fearful that her story had ended, its retelling suddenly too painful, the anguished secrets of her lovely heart destined to live in shadows forever. Peter couldn't, wouldn't, let that happen. The episode at the peace rally was horrid, detestable, but Larisa had forgotten it altogether until now. It was a trivial memory of pain compared to the memories that lived in the motel. She needed to tell him about those memories. "Was that when you moved to the motel, Larisa?"

Peter held his breath and sent silent messages from his heart . . . and finally she lifted her head and bravely faced the dancing flames.

"Yes. My mother knew the manager and had learned from him that there was one cottage that was impossible to rent even during ski season. I suppose it was intended to be just a storage shack, not one of the rental units, because it was separate from all the others, located at the far end of the parking lot beside the trash cans. It's still

315

there—I saw it today—but I couldn't tell if anyone was in it. Anyway, we were able to have it for almost nothing—no rent, just utilities and my help in cleaning the other cottages after school and on weekends."

"You were *eight?*"

"I didn't mind working, Peter," she said, turning to him, grateful for the indignation in his voice but wanting to reassure him that it wasn't necessary. "I've never minded working. And I liked the little cottage. It was so private compared to the other places we had lived and beyond the parking lot were the woods. I spent a lot of time there, wandering through the forest, finding trails that led to the lake. Sometimes I found small wounded animals in the woods and brought them back with me and took care of them until they were healed."

Peter saw the flickers of happiness in her eyes as she described the cottage from the viewpoint of the eight-year-old little girl who had so desperately needed privacy and had finally found it. But he remembered, too, her dread earlier when she had seen it again.

"So, for a while you were happy at the motel."

"For a while, yes, I was very happy there."

"And then?"

And then . . .

"I was twelve," she said softly, returning her gaze to the fire. "One Saturday night a man came to the door. It was about midnight. I was asleep on my cot in the living room, and my mother was still at work at the casino. Her shift didn't end until two, but he told me that it was she who had sent him, so I let him in to wait for her. That wasn't unusual. There had always been men arriving at all hours, and as always I told him that there was beer in the refrigerator and a television in her bedroom."

Larisa stopped speaking then, and the room was silent

316

except for the chatter of the fire, and when a smoldering ember suddenly burst into flames, adding its white light to the others, her lovely face was brightly illuminated.

And Peter saw such bewildered hopelessness.

He wanted to go to her, as he had been wanting to do from the very beginning. But she was on the stark lonely island where she wanted to be. So he reached out to her, the only way he could for now . . . with his heart.

"Larisa," he whispered with exquisite tenderness. "Please tell me."

"I was a very naive twelve-year-old. I guess I had begun to look less girlish and more womanly. I hadn't really noticed . . . but my mother had." Larisa drew a soft breath and when she spoke again it was a whisper of despair. "He had come for me, Peter, not for her. But she had sent him. She had given me to him in exchange for something— drugs or money or a debt that she owed."

"Let me hold you," he pleaded softly, and there was despair, too, in his gentle voice.

Larisa didn't turn toward him, but she frowned at the gentleness of his voice, a lovely frown of disbelief and hope. Then she shook her head decisively. *I have to tell you everything, Peter.*

"He told me he was a cop. I don't know if he was or not. He wasn't wearing a uniform." She added very quietly, "But he had a gun."

"I hope you killed him." Peter wanted to kill the man himself, wanted so desperately to travel back through time to that night of horror and prevent it from ever happening to her.

"No, I didn't kill him. He must have known that I wouldn't, couldn't, because when he saw me look at the gun he had put on the table, he let me escape from him to get it. I was so young, so foolish, so brave. The gun was very heavy and it wobbled as I aimed it at him. He laughed at me, goading me to pull the trigger, knowing that I wouldn't. When he raped me, he taunted me still, telling me that the reason I hadn't pulled the trigger was because I obviously wanted it . . . him." Larisa paused, then said in a faraway voice, "I've always wondered what my life would have been like if I'd had the courage to pull the trigger."

"It would have been a different kind of hell," Peter gently told the lovely woman who once had been a lovely little girl who had rescued animals, but hadn't rescued herself. And if she had pulled the trigger? She would have lived a lifetime of guilt. Either way, as a raped innocent or an innocent murderess, she was a victim of the most horrendous of crimes. "May I hold you, Larisa?"

"Peter . . ." She turned to him then, and Peter saw a brave flicker of hope drowned swiftly in a sea of sadness. "There's more."

"I know." Peter smiled tenderly and repeated softly, "May I hold you while you tell me?"

"No, Peter . . . I need to tell you everything . . . first."

"Okay." Then, guessing that the rest of the story had to do with revenge against the mother who had broken every promise a parent should make, he asked, "Did you call the police?"

"No. I told no one. I've never told anyone until now."

Even as his heart raced that she had trusted him and him alone with this anguished secret of betrayal, it cried, too, for all her lonely years of silent pain. "And your mother?"

"We never talked about it, but I think she understood what she had done, that she had gone too far. There must have been something in my eyes."

"Something that you saw as well."

"No. I never saw it. After that night, and for the next few years, whenever I looked in a mirror, all I saw was a shadowy blur. I had no idea what I looked like, except that with each passing year more people stared at me and wanted to be with me. The first time I saw a photograph of myself, really saw it, I was sixteen. I could tell that the girl in the photograph was quite beautiful, but I had no sense that she was me."

And you still don't, Peter thought. The article in *People* had described supermodel Larisa Locksley's remarkable ability to adapt her stunning beauty to whatever she was modeling. Whether the product was lipstick by Max Factor, or a gown by Scaasi, or jewels by Castille, she somehow sent the powerful and persuasive message that her extraordinary beauty was because of the rich color that adorned her lips, or the silk and satin that clung to her perfect body, or the rainbow of gemstones that encircled her graceful neck. She was a chameleon, ever-changing, always adapting.

Peter had read about Larisa's remarkable ability—and willingness—to lose herself in the product she was endorsing; and because of *Promise* he had witnessed it firsthand. Every discussion about the ads—the dresses she would wear or how she would wear her hair—had been entirely focused on what would be best for the fragrance, not on what would make her the most beautiful. And now Peter understood: Larisa had no sense of her own identity.

"But the beautiful girl in the photograph was you," he offered gently.

"Well, no, not really. She was just the coat of armor, the magnificent disguise that would enable me to go wherever I wanted to go. Where I wanted to go most of all then was away from here. I left the day I graduated from high school and never came back. My mother had already left

Tahoe by then, five months before, to go to Las Vegas with a man she had met. I haven't heard from her since. I've thought that she's probably no longer alive, but if she is and has stayed away despite the allure of all the money I've had, then maybe she has a shred of decency in her after all."

"May I ask you a question? Now, when you look in the mirror, what do you see?"

"I don't spend a lot of time looking in the mirror."

"Well, you should. If you did, you would see a woman who is very lovely and very courageous. A woman I would very much like to hold."

"Oh, Peter," she whispered, wanting so much to be held by him. "There's more I need to tell you." *The most important truth of all.*

"All right." Peter steeled himself to hear about Julian, about Larisa's great love for the man he hated and her great anguish that Julian no longer wanted her.

But her quiet words weren't about Julian at all.

"Within a few days of the rape, I became quite ill. It was a pelvic infection, I know that now, but at the time I believed that I was being punished—and that I was going to die. Which was fine with me, I wanted to die, I waited for it. Eventually I realized that the pain and fever weren't going to be lethal and I started treating myself. My mother was a smoker so she had a medicine cabinet full of antibiotics that had been prescribed for attacks of bronchitis. She got a new prescription every time, three or four times a year, even though she never took the full course that was prescribed. I learned later, in health classes in high school, that the antibiotics I had taken—ampicillin, tetracycline and erythromycin—were the right ones for what I must have had. But I'd been sick for several months before taking anything, so even though the infec-

320

tion was eventually cured, the damage had already been done."

Larisa looked at the man who was gazing at her so tenderly, who had heard her painful secrets and had not turned away, whose dark green eyes told her that he wanted her still . . . the man whose home was now filled with the creative clutter of his genius but which one day would, should, be filled with the exuberant clutter of his children. She drew a steadying breath and then admitted to that man, "I'm not able to have children, Peter. There are new sophisticated techniques that might be tried, but the damage is so extensive . . ."

"You may not be able to give birth, Larisa, but you can have children. There are orphaned and abandoned children who desperately need mothers." Peter waited until her lovely blue eyes met his and then added very softly, "And you would be a wonderful mother, Larisa. I know because I was watching when you moved the figurine of the daughter to be beside her mother."

"You saw that?"

"Yes." *That was the moment I fell in love with you.* "May I hold you now? Please?"

Her answer came to him in the most hopeful color of forget-me-nots, and as he began to walk to her, she left her stark lonely island to meet him halfway.

And then she was in his arms, where she was supposed to be, and Peter simply held her.

Simply . . . it was an extraordinary joy. Until he sensed her sudden restlessness and felt her pulling away.

"Larisa?"

"Thank you for holding me, Peter," she answered quietly, with grateful disbelief, as if no one had ever really just held her before—and now she had pulled away because the wondrous comfort of being held had already lasted far longer than she deserved.

"I think we have a communication problem here," Peter said. "And it's my fault. When I asked if I could hold you I guess I should have made my intentions clear. I want to hold you, Larisa, just hold you—forever."

He drew her back into the gentle haven of his loving arms, and eventually they moved to the huge couch, and she lay against him, so safe and secure, her head resting on his chest as she listened to the strong and steady beat of his heart. She had never been held like this, by a man who wanted nothing from her, who wanted only to give her comfort, not to take from her perfect body the pleasures it could provide for him.

Larisa had never been held with the unselfish tenderness of love, and never before had it been she who made the first move for even more closeness—more intimacy—because always before such intimacy had led to the man's triumphant pleasure and her own humiliating conquest. But now the delicate whispers of desire that lived within her, but which never before had been allowed to speak, became very courageous. And when she bravely lifted her fire-caressed golden head and saw the tender desire in Peter's dark green eyes, the delicate whispers trembled with joyous hope.

Peter would have simply held her forever, marveling in that extraordinary joy and controlling with love his own immense desire for more of her, all of her. But now she was offering her lovely lips to him, wanting his kiss, and as his lips greeted hers and he discovered a kiss that he had never known before, never even imagined, the part of his swirling mind that was still tethered to thought sent a silent wish, If I could just kiss her like this forever . . .

There was such innocence to the kiss, such wonder at

the magnificent discoveries they made together, such pure joy at the sharing of that magnificence. The kiss was innocent but so very intimate . . . and it was hungry but not possessive . . . and it was powerful but not conquering . . . and it was gentle and tender and filled with soft astonished sighs of desire.

And finally, when they both wanted more, when they wanted to share everything and give to each other all the gifts they had to give, it was Larisa who whispered the request of joy that she had never in her life whispered before.

"Make love to me, Peter. Please make love to me."

They made love in the four-postered bed in her bedroom overlooking the lake. Outside the snow danced, a wondrous swirl of delicate flakes illuminated by the porchlight below.

And inside there was such wondrous delicacy, too, as Peter's gentle lips and tender hands and caressing eyes lovingly nurtured her brave and hopeful desires. Somehow he heard their soft whispers, and he listened to their passionate secrets, and with infinite patience and exquisite care he encouraged them to speak, to blossom with unashamed beauty and courageous joy.

And when they both needed all of each other, when it was time to be as close as they could possibly be and to share all that could possibly be shared, his dark green eyes caressed her shimmering blue ones for a long moment that was beyond all words, and then their lips kissed again, and then their bodies did . . . but the most intimate caresses of all came from their hearts.

* * *

And after, he held her as unashamed tears spilled from her forget-me-not blue eyes, nourishing tears, like the gentle spring rain that enabled the delicate and hopeful roots of just-born flowers to find firm footing in the warm rich earth. Peter kissed the raindrops that spilled without shame from her beautiful blue eyes; and his kisses were as gentle and as nourishing as the tears; and both tears and kisses enabled the delicate roots of hope and love to find firm, courageous footing in the lovely warmth of her lovely heart.

When her tears finally stopped, Larisa's brilliant blue eyes glistened with radiance, and she wanted him to make love to her again. And this time, astonishingly, their loving was even more intimate, and more confident. And this time, after, there were no more tears, only gentle nourishing kisses until she drifted off to a deep and peaceful sleep.

As Larisa slept peacefully in his arms, Peter's not so peaceful thoughts drifted to Julian. His ancient enemy had been in his mind all evening, of course, in the unasked questions that had taunted and swirled as Larisa had told him about her childhood. She had never told anyone about the rape, which meant that she had not ever shared that very important truth with the man she had loved enough to marry.

Why not? Peter wondered. Because she loved Julian so much that she didn't want to disappoint him? Because she knew that his reaction would have been disdainful contempt for the sordidness, not compassion for the innocent girl who had been so brutally betrayed? Because, in her own shame, she feared that Julian might even have blamed her for seducing her own destruction?

And what about Larisa's inability to have children? Had that been an issue—the issue—that had ended her marriage? Peter couldn't imagine the Julian Chancellor he had known ever caring about children—ever caring about anyone but Julian. There were other Chancellors who could pass on the wealthy and privileged blue blood, after all, and as far as immortality, Julian's vast empire of buildings had already indelibly etched his signature for generations to come.

But what if Julian had wanted children? What if he and Larisa had tried without success to have them for the six years of their marriage? The Julian Chancellor who Peter had known would have doubtless blamed his wife for that failure; and since Larisa had never told him the truth about the rape or its consequences, he might have further blamed her infertility on the wild and wanton promiscuity of her modeling days. Peter knew that there had never been such days. Their loving tonight had been so wondrously innocent and so joyously pure that there never could have been.

But what if Julian had accused her of wanton promiscuity nonetheless? Peter already knew that Larisa hadn't offered in her defense the truth about the rape. Had she instead simply accepted Julian's condemnation and ultimately the loss of his love?

Larisa had been very deeply hurt by Julian. That had been obvious in the wary and vulnerable blue eyes from the very beginning. Julian's cruelty to Larisa would have made Peter hate his bitter enemy even more—except that Larisa was here now, in his loving arms, where she belonged.

Where she belonged. It was such an astonishingly confident joy that Peter felt as if she had lived in his heart far longer than just the few months that it had been. Had their hearts, in fact, called to each other long before the night of the ball? Twelve years ago, when he had just been discovering Lake Tahoe, had Larisa, on that same glorious June day, been fleeing her own terrifying memories and vowing never to return? Had they passed on the winding mountain road? And had he felt an inexplicable rush of joy as she had passed, an enchanting yet undecipherable message as her fragile heart had sent a desperate call to his?

Perhaps, Peter thought. Perhaps.

Larisa was with him now, where she belonged, and he was going to spend his life making her happy, loving her as she always should have been loved. Peter knew that he had to be very careful still not to overwhelm her with his confidence in them—and in her. He was so very confident of her, her loveliness and worthiness, but Larisa needed to learn to love herself. She needed to know that it was safe to look in a mirror . . . and to smile with gentle joy at the image she saw.

For now, my lovely Larisa, I will be your mirror, he thought, his lips gently caressing the love-tangled fire-gold silk as she slept so peacefully in his arms. For now, I will reflect back to you with my loving eyes all the wonderful things about you that I know to be true. And someday you will believe those truths. And someday, my lovely forget-me-not, the children who we will find to love will frolic in the meadow at Innis Arden.

Chapter Twenty-four

Larisa and Peter awakened to a fairyland, a world that was dressed in pristine white and caressed by a golden sun that smiled gloriously from a brilliant sapphire sky.

Peter taught Larisa how to make pancakes, and she made one plump happy cloud for herself, and two such clouds and one snowman and a small forest of trees for Peter. And then they went for a walk. The snow was light, soft and fleecy, welcoming their footfalls as they walked along the lakeshore. After a mile, Larisa turned toward the forest, and following a trail that only she and the deer could see, she led the way toward town . . . and the motel.

Larisa wasn't certain how close she wanted to get to the tiny cottage, but as they neared the motel, Peter's dark green eyes journeyed solemnly to the place that had been her home, and her nightmare, and said quietly, "We could ask the manager if the cottage is vacant and maybe take a look inside." After a moment he added very gently, "We could spend the night there tonight, Larisa, if you would like to."

Larisa had spent six years of nights in the cottage after the rape, six years of remembered terror and imprisonment, and since leaving she had never imagined choosing to spend another night there. But with Peter, safe in Peter's arms, maybe it would be possible.

As Larisa was thinking about Peter's suggestion, the door to the tiny cottage opened—and suddenly all thoughts were forgotten and she and Peter simply stared, stunned by what, who, they saw emerge. The man was a police officer, in uniform and with a holstered gun, and the golden-haired girl was about the age Larisa had been when an evil man claiming to be a cop had knocked on the cottage door at midnight.

"Morning," the officer said when he and the girl reached Peter and Larisa. The officer was smiling, and the girl smiled too, her blue eyes as clear and untroubled as the sapphire sky and her smile as golden as the caressing sun. "Can I help you?"

"Has something happened, officer?" Peter asked.

"What? Oh, no. I live here. I'm in uniform now because I'm on my way to work. My wife and I manage the motel—actually she does—and my daughter and I were adjusting the television in one of the cottages."

"It works fine now," the girl added triumphantly.

"Shall we go find my wife? My name is Craig, and this is my daughter Melanie." Then, smiling warmly at the pretty blond woman who was now approaching them, he said, "I see that Darleen has found us."

After first-name introductions were made, Peter explained, "Larisa lived here when she was growing up. By 'here' I mean more than Tahoe, I mean the motel itself. In fact," he added, turning from Darleen to Craig, "she lived in the cottage from which you just appeared—which is why we were both staring at you."

"And now I'm the one who's doing the staring," Darleen said. "You're Larisa Locksley, aren't you? You and I were in high school together. We didn't actually know

328

each other, but I recognize you, of course. I followed your career. We all did. I'd forgotten that you had lived here, at the motel. Maybe I never even knew it. Is this a sentimental journey?"

"I guess so," Larisa replied. It was a partial truth: this was a journey, although it was very far from a sentimental one. "I was wondering if it would be possible for Peter and me to take a look in the cottage?"

"You bet. We have people coming in later this morning—it's our only vacant unit—but you're more than welcome to take a look at it now."

At that moment, the amplified sound of a ringing telephone from the office called to Darleen, who was on desk duty, and Craig said that he really had to get to work. So it was Melanie who enthusiastically, and so fearlessly, led the way to the cottage that held such great fear for Larisa.

"This isn't our best cottage," Melanie explained with youthful candor. "I guess you know that. But Mom has completely redecorated it and Dad put in another window. Personally, I like it a lot. In fact, I think it should become my room the day I turn thirteen. That won't be for almost a year, but I'm already beginning to plant the idea."

The cottage was brighter and cheerier than Larisa had remembered—and so much smaller. She had lived in this tiny place until she was eighteen, but somehow her memory of its size had been the one made when she had first seen it, when she was only eight and it had seemed so spacious compared to the other places she had lived.

Melanie chattered happily about the cheerful new floral wallpaper and the new window that had already been added, and about the window boxes that *could* be added and the flowers that *could* be planted in them—all of which would help, she said, and all of which she would do when the cottage was hers. The happy chatter of a twelve-year-old girl who obviously loved and not feared the tiny cottage was definitely comforting.

But neither the happy chatter, nor the cottage's cheerful facelift, could truly exorcise the ghosts. They were still here. Larisa felt their sinister presence, dancing invisibly in the now brightly lighted corners and lurking beneath the pretty new wallpaper. The ghosts were still here. But, like the cottage itself, they seemed smaller than she had remembered, less monstrous and less menacing.

Why was that? she wondered.

Because of what you yourself have so bravely accomplished over the past few months, a voice answered. It was the same gentle, yet determined voice that had guided her away from Julian in August . . . and had compelled her to call Nick for help a month later . . . and which had, in the past few months, spoken soft encouragement as she had helped herself by facing her own pain, conquering it through understanding and resisting the powerful impulses that urged her to escape its merciless grip by floating far away.

The ghosts were smaller now because of her courageous journey into her own wounded heart. But the ghosts were still there. Because, Larisa knew, there was more gentle exploration still to be done. She needed to keep exploring and discovering until one day she could look into a mirror and see the woman she wanted to be—the woman who, inexplicably but so tenderly, Peter told her that he already saw.

"I'd better get going," Melanie announced with obvious reluctance. Brightening, she explained, "My friends and I are going skiing today."

"Thank you very much for showing us your cottage," Larisa said before Melanie dashed off to spend this glorious Saturday playing with her friends, not cleaning cottages.

"Our cottage. Mom used to show me your pictures on the covers of magazines." Melanie's fresh young cheeks flushed a lovely pink and she added, "I think it's really neat that you lived here when you were my age!"

"Shall I open some champagne? Admittedly the title doesn't officially transfer for another hour and a half, but we could toast things other than the meadow for a while."

Peter's dark green eyes told Larisa with tender desire that the "other things" he wanted to celebrate was them. Larisa wanted to celebrate that wondrous joy, too. But her heart already was celebrating, and the soaring giddiness she had felt in the past twenty-four hours was far beyond any place that alcohol had ever taken her. It would be safe to have a glass of champagne with Peter, but Larisa didn't need its euphoric effects—and she most certainly had no desire to float away from the magical feelings she felt so naturally just being with him.

"Would it be all right if I toasted . . . everything . . . with something soft?"

"Of course it would. Hot chocolate for two?"

They were already awake when the phone rang at six Sunday morning. They had made love and slept, and awakened and made love again, and now they were holding each other and talking.

"My answering service," Peter explained as he gently, and with obvious reluctance, uncurled himself from her and reached for the ringing telephone. "I always leave a number when I have projects under construction."

331

Peter's voice was calm, but Larisa saw the slight frown that touched his face as he spoke. He had projects under construction, yes, and problems routinely arose with such projects—but a call early Sunday morning was far from routine.

Peter's frown deepened and his handsome face grew darkly troubled as he listened in silence to the words of the caller. When he finally spoke, it was a question, "Was there damage to the music room?" The answer to that question caused a brief flicker of relief amid the worry, then there was pure worry again and finally a few succinct commands, "I want around-the-clock guards. I'm leaving tomorrow morning for Chicago and will plan to arrive in Boston on Thursday evening. Call me as soon as you learn anything about the cause."

Peter's hand lingered on the receiver for a solemn moment after he replaced it in its cradle. Then he turned to the lovely concerned blue eyes and quietly explained.

"That was my attorney in Boston, the one who handled the purchase of the estate on Cape Cod. Last night, shortly after midnight, there was a fire in the mansion."

"Oh, Peter."

"Fortunately, two teenagers were somewhere on the property at the time—young lovers who shouldn't have been there, and shouldn't have been doing what they were doing, but who nonetheless had the courage to do more than simply flee when they saw the blaze. They reported the fire immediately, and because of that most of the mansion was saved. If they hadn't called for help when they did, the wooden building would have been completely destroyed."

"I guess love makes one do courageous things," Larisa murmured softly.

"I guess so," Peter answered with matching softness.

For a moment the fire was forgotten, and they were lost in the silent hopes and promises of love, but eventually the shadows of worry flickered again in the dark green depths and it was time to return to that troubling topic.

"Was there something about the music room, Peter? I heard you ask if it had been damaged."

"Until my father was crippled with the arthritis, he was a carpenter. The music room was one of his first creations—built over sixty-five years ago." Peter added with quiet gratitude, "Thanks to those teenagers, it escaped the blaze entirely."

"I'm glad." The mansion had been saved, and the room created by the hands of the father he so obviously loved had been undamaged, but there was still such dark worry in his eyes. "What is it, Peter? What were you thinking?"

"I was wondering if it was arson."

"Arson?" Larisa echoed with surprise. "Do you think that's likely?"

"I don't know. Probably not." *I hope not*, Peter amended silently as he pulled Larisa back into his arms, nestled so close that she could no longer see his troubled face. She had seen and wondered about the dark worry in his eyes as he had been thinking about the question of arson. But there was an even darker worry that he did not want her to see. If the fire had been intentionally set, just moments after Innis Arden had become his, then there was only one person on earth who would have ordered that wanton destruction: Julian Chancellor, the destroyer of dreams. Peter had hoped that his enmity with Julian was past history, long since forgotten by Julian. But what if it was alive still, as hot and blazing as the flames that had engulfed the mansion?

Not once in this weekend of intimacies of the heart had

Larisa mentioned Julian—or even alluded to her marriage or her divorce—and Peter hadn't pushed. He was in no hurry to hear about her great love for the man he hated. One day, when their own wonderful love had history and confidence, Larisa would tell him about her marriage, and he would tell her his own truths about Julian. But if the fire at Innis Arden had been arson, Peter knew that that day would come very soon. And if the inferno had been merely an accident?

Then Peter would tell Larisa everything in April, when they traveled together to the fragrant and enchanted meadow of *Promise*.

The beautiful bouquet of bright blue forget-me-nots arrived Tuesday evening. Peter had told her the evening before, when he had called from Chicago and they had talked for hours, that tonight he had a dinner meeting with clients and probably would be unable to call her. And so he had sent this lovely bouquet instead.

Larisa set the bouquet on the coffee table in the living room and for a very long time simply looked at it, marveling at the exquisite beauty of the delicate and hopeful little flowers. Finally, smiling softly in anticipation of reading his message, she reached for the small ivory card.

I will never forget you, Larisa. Forget me not. Julian.

No! her mind cried in swift silent protest. Julian had once known of her love of forget-me-nots, of course. In a grand romantic gesture, he had even permitted her to depart from tradition and carry a bouquet of them at their fairy-tale wedding. But since that day, he had apparently forgotten—or remembered but no longer needed the pretense of romance *because she was his*—and when he had given her flowers they had always been something else. Until now.

Now Julian had sent her the flowers she had always loved. But the message that accompanied the bouquet wasn't a message of love at all. It was, instead, a most ominous warning. She was not forgotten, Julian was telling her, and she never would be. And, even more ominously, she was *never* to forget him either.

Larisa had been so grateful that Julian had respected her wishes and hadn't called. She had even been hoping that he would never call again, that he had lost interest in her, that she was forgotten. But now she knew the foolishness of that hope, and now she trembled as she wondered, What if Julian has been having me watched? What if the forget-me-not bouquet is his sinister way of telling me that he knows all about *Promise,* including the closely guarded secret that the delicate flower I love so much will be etched on the crystal perfume bottles?

Larisa willed her swirling mind to focus on what it could mean if Julian knew that she was going to be the model for *Promise.* The answer was so simple, and so horrible: it meant that Julian could wield his immense power and influence to sabotage Peter's wonderful gift to the world. Because of her, *Promise* could be destroyed.

Larisa couldn't let that happen.

I need to speak with Julian, she told herself. I need to find out if he knows. And if he does know? Then I will have to say goodbye to *Promise* . . . and to Peter.

* * *

335

Oh, how her heart did not want her to dial the number to the penthouse on Fifth Avenue!

But it was that same loving heart that finally compelled her trembling fingers into action—for Peter, because of Peter.

"It's Larisa," she said quietly when Julian answered.

"I guess the flowers arrived. Are they all right?" he asked, his voice low and gentle. "The florist said it would take some doing to find forget-me-nots, but he assured me that they would be of top quality."

"They are." *The best that money can buy.*

"Good. I remembered how much you love them."

"Is that why you sent them?"

"What other reason could there be? Except, of course, the obvious one: that I hoped you would call." Julian added with loving concern, "I've been very worried about you, Larisa. You still haven't sent me any bills. You really must be almost out of money."

"I've found a way to replenish the money, Julian," she said as casually as possible. "I've found a job."

"A job? What job?"

Julian's voice lost its gentleness, and in its unconcealed harshness it unmasked all his apologies and promises for the lies that Larisa had always known them to be. But it wasn't the proof that she had been right not to trust the contrite and apologetic Julian that made Larisa's heart race with joyous relief. It was that he was genuinely surprised that she had found a job. She was *sure* of it.

But, she told herself, Julian is also very angry at the revelation. Which means I have to be very careful—and very convincing.

"I suppose it could be called free-lance fashion consulting. I give advice to women about clothes, accessories, hair, and makeup. Don't worry, Julian, everyone believes

336

that I'm an immensely wealthy woman and that I'm doing this as a diversion, a lark."

"But you're getting paid for it."

"Of course I'm getting paid for it. In fact, I'm getting paid a lot. If my fees weren't high, my advice wouldn't be nearly as valued as it is." Larisa paused, and then bravely taunted the man who had so often and with such cruelty taunted her, "You taught me that, didn't you, Julian? The more people pay for something the more highly they value it?"

"What about other diversions, Larisa?" he demanded. "Are there other men in your life?"

"The answer is no," she replied evenly. Then, to further convince him, she added with icy indignation, "*Not* that that is any of your business. Our marriage is over, Julian. We aren't part of each other's lives any longer."

"You will always be part of my life, Larisa."

The words might have been a romantic promise of forever love, but from Julian's lips they were simply a warning. He was trying to terrify her, to control her again, to manipulate her with fear as he had always done.

But I'm stronger now, Julian, Larisa thought. There are no more invisible chains. I've cast them off. I am free of you at last.

"Leave me alone, Julian," she said with quiet calm. "It's over. Goodbye."

Oh no, my sweet, it is not over, Julian vowed with silent rage as she softly yet defiantly ended their conversation. It will never be over. But I still find this new courage of yours rather thrilling. I will leave you alone for a while longer, Larisa, just long enough for you to truly believe that I will permit you to live your life away from me. And then, my love, I will remind you, how I will remind you, of the only truth: that you are mine—and always will be.

Chapter Twenty-five

San Francisco
December 1991

On Saturday, December twenty-first, while Peter met with the fire inspector in Cape Cod, and Larisa and Elizabeth finished packing for their trip to England, and Christine ironed the small felt costumes that had gotten rumpled during the pageant's dress rehearsal, and Stephen tried to concentrate on his work but was distracted by images of golden hair and lavender eyes, Nicholas and Justin Chase joined the throngs of last-minute Christmas shoppers in Union Square.

Nick was on call for the transplant service, but it was very quiet. All the patients that could go home for the holidays were already there, and morning rounds on the ones who remained were finished by noon, and now they were shopping for Margaret's Christmas present from Justin. Nick's generous four-year-old son had "lots and lots" of ideas about presents for Margaret and he loved being in the midst of the holiday festivity of Union Square. He hummed happily to the carols that played in every store and paused frequently to gaze at the elaborately decorated windows. It was Justin not Nick who set the pace for the afternoon of shopping and singing and gazing; and Nick was infinitely patient, seeing through his son's shining blue eyes a joyful vision of Christmas that he himself had never seen as a child.

As they crossed Geary to get a closer look at the glittering tree in the center of the square, Nick heard the sound of rapidly approaching footsteps. At the sound, a quiver of anxiety rippled through him, followed swiftly by a powerful rush of adrenaline that sent his body on alert, ready to spring into action, like a soldier trained for battle. Nick's reflexive preparedness had been learned in the hospital, not on a battlefield, but like a soldier, he was instantly prepared for the worst—because people only ran in hospitals when it was a matter of life and death: the trauma team rushing to the ER to help an accident victim, the Code Blue team dashing to the ward in hopes of saving the life of a patient who had had a cardiac arrest. Nick's years of experience in hospitals had trained him to hear the sound of running footsteps as a signal of urgency.

But not here, his brain reminded his racing heart and suddenly taut body. Here, on this festive afternoon in Union Square, running footsteps surely only signaled frolicking excited children making a mad dash to see Santa Claus.

Except, his still tense body answered, these weren't the light footsteps of galloping children. These footfalls were heavy and purposeful—and getting closer. And, as Nick turned toward the sound, he saw at once that as in the hospital these racing steps carried ominous warnings.

There were two men, chasing each other, their faces filled with fierceness, their hands waving guns. Suddenly one of the guns was fired. And then, in the final moments of his life, the lethally wounded man went wild, firing his

339

own weapon in a random rage. It all happened in a matter of seconds. Most of the crowd, although stunned and panicked by the gunfire, had been blissfully unaware of the danger as it had been unfolding. Like most of the crowd, Justin had been quite unaware. And even when the bullets began to fly, *and even when the dying man's gun was suddenly pointed directly at him,* Justin was confused by the commotion, but he saw neither the man nor the gun—and he felt no fear. All the fear belonged to Nick, who saw everything and who swooped down in front of Justin, shielding his beloved son's eyes from the horror and shielding Justin's small precious body with his own.

Nick prevented Justin from witnessing the terror, from being plagued by nightmares of it forever. All that Justin knew was that for some reason the father he loved and trusted suddenly pulled him close and tight against him—to a place that Justin was always quite willing to be. Nick shielded his son completely, his eyes, his body, the future memories of his young mind.

But neither Nick's lean strong body nor all of his love were impenetrable to the violence of a bullet.

Justin felt a soft surprising thud, not a piercing pain, as the bullet struck him, its velocity and impact blunted by its passage first through his father's chest. Then his father was lifting him and holding him even tighter than he had before—and that hurt, just a little—and then his father was running with him, away from the crowd that had formed a wall around the carnage.

Nick had no intention of waiting for the police or paramedics to arrive to methodically analyze what had happened. He knew all too well what had happened. He had felt the bullet strike his own chest, cracking his ribs and puncturing his lung as it traveled through him—and into his son's abdomen. Nick prayed a frantic useless prayer that the sudden hot blood in the place where their bodies touched—his left chest and Justin's right upper abdomen—was only his. But Dr. Nicholas Chase knew with instant, expert, and excruciating clarity that much of the blood was Justin's . . . and he knew, too, that Justin's wound was far more grave than his own.

As the crowd rushed toward the site of the shooting, Nick carried Justin away from the crush. In less than a block, he was able to flag down one of the many police cars that was converging on the scene and asked the surprised officer to drive them to Pacific Heights Medical Center.

"Why don't I call a medic unit?"

"My son needs far more than a medic unit can provide, and it will be much faster if you just drive us there. Please," Nick whispered with trembling emotion. "Please help us."

The police car traversed the streets between Union Square and Pacific Heights "Code Three"—light flashing, siren blaring, clearing traffic and ignoring stoplights. As he drove, the officer radioed dispatch, who in turn would notify the center's trauma team of their imminent arrival. "I have a four-year-old boy with a GSW to the abdomen. His dad's here, too. Apparently he's a doc at the med center—Doctor Nick Chase. He says to tell the trauma team that the boy is in shock, unconscious but breathing, and that he'll need immediate exploratory surgery. He says he thinks the bullet entered the boy's liver . . ."

Within moments of the police car's arrival at the ER, Justin was in the trauma room. The trauma service chief Dr. Ed Moore examined him while other members of the highly trained trauma team inserted the necessary large bore intravenous lines into his small collapsed veins, placed the endotracheal tube in his throat, and drew the necessary tubes of blood.

Whenever a trauma patient, especially one with intra-abdominal trauma, *could* be stabilized, it was desirable to get scans and X rays to assess organ damage in advance of going to the OR. But Justin's blood pressure was very precarious even with the aggressive fluid replacement and pressor therapy that had begun the moment the first line was in. It was abundantly, terrifyingly apparent that he was still bleeding—*briskly*—and even though everyone knew that the preop studies would have been desirable, they also knew that in this case there was simply no time. The age-old surgical adage applied: it was better to look and see than wait and see.

Perhaps it was already too late. The thought echoed silently in the minds of all those who worked on the small pale body. From the entry and exit wounds, it was obvious that the bullet had entered the liver and traveled through it. The liver was such a vascular organ, so easily shattered and so terribly difficult to repair.

"Okay. We're going to the OR in one minute," Ed said with quiet resolve less than five minutes after Justin arrived.

Ed spoke the words as an announcement to the entire team, so that they could all ready themselves for the next important step, but as he spoke, he looked at Nick. Ed and Nick were the same age, and both gifted surgeons, and they had spent hundreds of hours together—in the OR and at the executive meetings they attended as chiefs of their respective services. And since it was literally impossible for anyone to spend any time with Ed Moore without hearing about his own young son, Ed knew that Nick

342

knew that he had a son. But Ed hadn't known until this tragic moment that Nick, like he, was a father—a father who was about to lose his son.

Do you want to be in the OR? Ed asked in solemn silence as his eyes met Nick's. Ed had no idea how he himself would have answered such an impossible question. Would it be better to be in the OR, to know without a doubt that everything had been done, even though everything wasn't enough? Or would it be best, in those moments, to simply be a father, waiting far away from the reality of the OR and praying for a miracle?

As Ed waited for Nick's answer to the impossible, his eyes left the tormented dark blue ones briefly, *they had to;* and in that emotional moment Ed's gaze fell from Nick's anguished face to his bloodied and still bleeding chest. And the impossible question became moot. Nick could not be in the OR. Ed had already learned from the tormented blue eyes that Nick's gravest injury, the one from which he might never recover, was the one to his heart; but he learned now, as his trained gaze quickly understood the solemn meaning of the rapid shallow breaths, that Nick's very survival was in jeopardy.

"We'll do our best, Nick," Ed promised quietly. Then, turning to his chief resident, he instructed, "Take care of Doctor Chase."

Nick was quite unaware of the small army of medical professionals who were working with swift, efficient competence to save his life; and he didn't feel the needles being put into him, nor the chest tube that was inserted between his shattered ribs, nor even the searing flames that ignited as each breath he took was an angry confrontation between his raw chest and his wounded lung. Nick

343

was far away—in the OR with his son . . . and in Union Square, reliving those life-changing moments of terror.

He should have thrown Justin to the ground.

He should have thrown his son to the ground and then fallen on top of him. Yes, that would have hurt and stunned the little boy he had vowed never to hurt again, but it would have taken Justin completely out of harm's way. In those terrifying moments when he had realized that the gun was pointed at Justin, Nick had acted not by thought but by instinct, the deep instinct to protect his son even at the expense of his own life. Perhaps if he had ever been in the military and had been trained for war, he would have known to throw Justin to the ground, not just to shield the small body with his own. But the only war in which Nick had ever fought was an emotional one, doing battle with invisible phantoms and ghostly nightmares, and he had learned many things from his personal war—but not the right things—and now because his own experiences hadn't trained him to make the lifesaving move, his beloved son lay in the operating room with a wound that Nick knew to be lethal.

No! Nick's heart cried with silent despair. Justin will be all right. The trajectory of the bullet will have been away from his liver, not into it. He will have been very lucky. Doesn't my precious boy deserve a little luck? Hasn't his young life been unlucky enough already?

But there was to be no luck for Justin Chase.

"We were able to control the bleeding and he's stable now, but there was very little viable liver that we could save." Ed added with quiet emotion, "I'm so sorry, Nick."

Nick didn't seem to hear. Or perhaps, Ed thought, it was simply too painful to. As he waited, he watched the

344

clouded faraway dark blue eyes become clear and focused.

"Were there other injuries, Ed?"

"No, none. Just the liver. With your permission, Nick, I would like to put Justin's name in the national transplant registry as soon as possible."

"That won't be necessary." *His precious son was lucky after all.* "You said Justin is stable now, Ed?"

"Yes." It was the truth, but both men knew it was a truth that would be short-lived. Justin would be stable for a while, deceptively normal, and then his body would realize that its liver was missing and he would begin to die. "We were able to stop all the bleeding and his pressure is fine off pressors. We're recovering him in the pediatric ICU. When I left him he was still asleep."

"I need to have you find Elizabeth for me, Ed. Please tell her that I'm sorry, I know she's supposed to leave in a few hours for England, but that I need her help."

"All right."

"Will you let me know as soon as you reach her?"

"Sure. Anything else?"

"I need to write some things down."

Ed answered by removing a pen and several unused note cards from the breast pocket of his white coat and handing them to Nick. "Here you go."

"Thanks."

As soon as Ed left to find Elizabeth, Nick felt the flood of hot tears in his eyes, tears that flowed from his weeping heart on a rushing river of pain and fear. For many moments he simply allowed the anguished tears to flow. Allowed? No, there was no way he could have held them back.

Finally he found control, such necessary control, and

345

made his mind focus on what needed to be done. He began making the all important list.

At the top, in capital letters, he wrote the most important item of all: ELIZABETH.

"This is going to be such fun," Larisa enthused. She was sitting on Elizabeth's bed, watching her friend finish packing for their trip. Such fun, she thought, and a chance for us to talk, really talk.

"Lots of fun," Elizabeth agreed. She was about to embellish—a soft tease about taking Harrod's or Buckingham Palace or both by storm—when the phone started to ring. She smiled and predicted softly, "Peter."

"I hope so," Larisa answered as she moved to the phone. Yes, she assured herself. It will be Peter. He will be calling to let me know what the fire inspector said about the cause of the fire, and to wish me a good flight, and to promise to call me in London, and to remind me that we are spending New Year's Eve together. It will be Peter. It *won't* be Julian calling to tell me that even though *I* have told him that it's over, *he* won't allow it to be. "Hello?"

"This is Doctor Ed Moore calling for Doctor Jennings."

"Just a moment, please." Larisa covered the receiver. "It's a Doctor Moore. You didn't forget to sign out, did you?"

"No. I wonder what he wants." Elizabeth frowned briefly as she reached for the phone. "Hi, Ed."

Larisa couldn't see Elizabeth's face because as her friend listened to whatever it was Ed Moore had called to say, she walked to the window facing the medical center and stood there, very still, staring out.

"Please tell him that I will be there right away," she said finally, her voice as still and taut as her body. Then she replaced the receiver and when she turned Larisa saw the heart-stoppingly stricken emerald.

"What is it, Liz?"

"Nick has been shot," she answered quietly, and, even more quietly, she whispered, "And so has his son."

"His *son?*"

"He's four years old and badly injured. That's all I know, Lara. I have to go."

"I'm going with you."

Chapter Twenty-six

"Ed?" Elizabeth asked as she and Larisa came up behind him in the nurses' station in the ER.

"Oh, good. That was fast."

"We ran," Larisa said. "Please tell us what happened."

"This is my friend Larisa, Ed," Elizabeth explained. "She absolutely refuses to wait in the waiting room."

Ed heard the fondness amid the worry in Elizabeth's voice, and saw in her deeply troubled emerald eyes that she wanted her friend with her, and decided without a ripple of uncertainty that he wasn't going to get hung up on the ethics of discussing confidential medical details in front of Larisa. Besides, he knew, very soon the news media would have the story and all of San Francisco would know about the senseless Christmas tragedy involving the gorgeous and heroic doctor who had saved little Molly only months before—and yet had been unable to save his own beloved son.

"According to the police, what happened was that two armed men were chasing each other in Union Square—a drug deal gone sour apparently. One man shot the other and before the second one died he began firing random shots into a crowd which included Nick and his son Justin.

And then what happened, what must have happened given their injuries, is that Nick moved between Justin and the gun, using his own body as a shield to protect his son." Ed felt a sudden rush of emotion as he imagined, *felt,* Nick's terror when he had realized that his son's life was in jeopardy. Unable to speak for a moment, Ed turned toward the nearby X-ray viewing box. When his voice was steady again, he gestured to the chest X rays that were illuminated on the box and said, "These are Nick's X rays. The gun was obviously very powerful. As you can see it shattered his ribs."

"What about his heart, Ed?" Elizabeth asked when she saw the massive trauma that had been done to Nick's left rib cage.

"Amazingly, the bullet missed his heart entirely." *Which doesn't mean that Nick's heart is going to survive what happened to his son.* "The bullet traveled through Nick's chest and into Justin's liver. There's a very small pedicle of viable liver left. It was all we could save, and it's not nearly enough to sustain life."

"Where is Nick now?"

"Still down here, in trauma room three. Justin is in the pediatric ICU, and Nick wants to be with him, but when I told him you were on your way he said he'd wait for you here. I'm not sure why he wanted me to find you, Elizabeth. He's been making a list of some sort, probably names of people who need to be notified. I assume he plans to give that list to you, and as soon as he does I hope that you'll convince him to accept some pain medication."

"He hasn't had anything yet?" Elizabeth asked, alarmed. She didn't look back at the chest X rays, she didn't need to. Her highly trained eyes had needed only a quick glance to assess the enormity of the injury and to imagine the pain.

"Not a thing. Maybe he wants to be clear for Justin." *So he can be awake and focused while he lovingly holds and comforts his son as he dies.* Ed sighed heavily. "But he's going to exhaust himself trying to fight the pain."

Elizabeth nodded solemnly. "I'll see what I can do."

"I'll be waiting right here for you, Liz," Larisa said. Then, looking up at Ed, she added, "If that's okay."

"Sure, Larisa. It's okay by me."

Elizabeth and Nick had been together in Trauma Room Three many, many times.

But never like this. Never with him lying motionless on a stretcher, his handsome face so pale and anguished, his damaged body so taut and still. Nick's dark blue eyes were closed, but the long black lashes glistened with the dampness of recent tears.

Oh, Nick. Elizabeth's heart wept for his immense sadness, and so did her emerald eyes. After a moment, she vanquished the tears, the ones that could be seen, and said very softly, "Nick?"

The dark blue eyes that suddenly opened held deep pain; but there was something else in the anguished blue, something that looked almost like hope.

"Thank you for coming, Elizabeth. I know you're supposed to be leaving for England tonight."

"It doesn't matter, Nick," she assured gently. Nothing matters but you—and whatever I can do to help you survive this immense loss. But what could she do? What could anyone do? "As of this moment, I'm officially on call for the holidays. That's a very small thing, Nick,

350

nothing really. Please tell me if there's **something** else I can do to help you."

"I hadn't even thought about the service. That isn't why I need you, Elizabeth."

I need you, Elizabeth. In the midst of his anguish, as he spoke those four words, Nick's voice softened and his blue eyes filled with exquisite tenderness.

"No?" she asked softly.

"No," he gently told the lovely emerald. "The reason I need you, Elizabeth, is to have you perform a living donor transplantation on my son—from me to my son."

"Nick . . ." *No.*

"I know you have a copy of the protocol in your office, but I've been writing it down anyway, point by point. I suppose mostly to keep my mind focused," he confessed, the emotional confession of a grieving father. It was a moment before he spoke again, but when he did his tone had shifted from personal to professional, from the emotional voice of a father to the calmly analytical one of gifted surgeon. "I think it's possible to get all the tests done and assemble the team and be in the operating room within six hours. Even though this surgery has never been done on an emergency basis before, I've always believed that emergency transplantation would someday have a major role in the acute management of trauma."

"I've always believed that, too," Elizabeth said to the gifted surgeon; and then, to that surgeon whose judgment had been so obviously blurred because he was also a father with a dying son, she reminded gently, "But, Nick, Justin is four years old."

Elizabeth didn't need to elaborate on her statement. The world's leading expert knew perfectly well that the extraordinary surgery he was proposing had only been done on infants. Elizabeth didn't need to tell Nick that, nor did she need to remind him why it was so: because there was only so much liver that could be safely donated from a living donor, enough for an infant's tiny liver but not nearly enough for a four-year-old who had lost virtually all of his own.

"Justin is an ideal candidate for transplantation, Elizabeth. He's a very healthy little boy." Nick's voice broke then, and he was a father, remembering the little boy who had only a short time ago been so happily humming Christmas carols, his bright blue eyes wide and laughing. So healthy, so happy. After a moment, Nick forced the emotion away and became the surgeon again, continuing firmly, "His excellent health makes him a better candidate than recipients who are transplanted because of severe underlying hepatic disorders. Justin's own liver is completely normal—it just needs time to regenerate. The transplantation will give it that necessary time."

"Yes, but . . ." But what about you, Nick? What about your survival? To give Justin enough tissue to sustain his life until his own liver could regenerate would mean taking . . .

"He can have all of my liver if he needs it, Elizabeth," Nick said in quiet reply to her unspoken worry. "I mean it."

The solemn dark blue eyes told Elizabeth with exquisite eloquence that Nick did mean it. Nicholas Chase had already proven once today his willingness to give his own life to save the life of his son. But that had been a moment of instinct, the reflexive action of a parent protecting his child. This gift, and Nick's willingness to give it, was far more calculated, but it was driven by the same instinct of limitless and immeasurable love.

"I can't do this, Nick." I can't let *you* do this.

"Of course you can. You're the best surgeon I've ever

known." Nick saw a flicker of surprise in her emerald eyes and asked softly, "Didn't you know that?"

"No. But it doesn't matter." Not now, Elizabeth thought. Nothing mattered now except somehow convincing the resolute blue eyes that what he was proposing was impossible—and somehow helping him accept the inevitable death of his precious son. She offered another gentle reminder, "You're very badly injured yourself, Nick."

It was the truth. His compromised respiratory status and extensive tissue trauma would make most surgeons quite reluctant to take him to the OR for even the most trivial of procedures.

"I have a few rib fractures," Nick answered dismissively. Then he searched her worried emerald eyes for clues to the other serious medical concern about his own suitability as a liver donor. He had hoped that Larisa hadn't revealed his secrets to her friend; and, he decided as he gazed at Elizabeth, it was quite obvious that she hadn't. But now Nick had to reveal them himself. "Until three and a half years ago, I drank very heavily. I haven't had anything to drink since then, and as far as I know I've never had any hepatic damage as a result of my alcoholism, but you still need to know about it."

Elizabeth did need to know about it. The history of heavy alcohol consumption was very pertinent to her preparation for surgery. But, Elizabeth wondered, was Nick telling her so that she could prepare for the surgery? Or so that she could prepare for his death? So that I won't blame myself if you die, Nick? So that I can blame your death on you and your drinking?

On the morning when another four-year-old boy had died so tragically, and Nick wouldn't share with her the pain they were both feeling, an extraordinary thought had come to her as she had rushed away from him: I hate you, Nick. It hadn't been true then, of course. But as she felt the storm of emotions that swirled inside her, Elizabeth wondered if it was true now.

I hate you, Nick, for not ever trusting me before—*and now trusting me with everything.*

I hate you, Nick, for asking this of me—*and giving me no choice.*

She had no choice, because she saw so clearly in his dark blue eyes that if his son died most of Nick would die with him. She had to operate for Nick, because of Nick, even though in trying to save the life of the son, Elizabeth might cause the death of the father.

The father. A man she hated?

Oh, no, her heart answered. A man she loved. The only man she had ever loved.

"Will you do the surgery, Elizabeth?"

"Yes," she whispered softly to the searching and hopeful blue eyes. "I will do it, Nick." *I will try to save your son—because that's what you so desperately want . . . and because I love you.* Then it was time for Elizabeth to focus, the doctor preparing for the surgery of her lifetime, and when she spoke again her voice was calmly professional. "May I see what you've written down?"

Elizabeth's expression remained calm, doctorlike, but her heart stumbled at the first word at the top of Nick's list: her own name in capital letters, traced and retraced by Nick as he had waited anxiously to see if Ed had been able to reach her. *Her,* the best surgeon Nick had ever known. Doctorlike, Elizabeth moved on, reading the rest of what Nick had written, discovering that it was a verbatim replica of the detailed protocol—until the end, where, as at the beginning, there was a woman's name.

"Margaret?" Elizabeth asked.

"She needs to know," Nick answered almost to himself. "She needs to be told in person. After I see Jussie, I'll need to go tell her."

"Go? Where?"

"To my house."

"You don't seem to understand how badly injured you are, Nick."

"I'm okay . . . and the house is very close by."

"No," Nick's doctor said firmly. After a moment, she added gently, "I won't be able to leave until all the arrangements for the surgery are in the works, but maybe Ed could go, or Stephen, or . . . my friend Larisa is here, Nick. She's very gentle when someone is in need."

"Yes," Nick replied with surprising swiftness. "If Larisa is willing, would you ask her to tell Margaret?"

"I'm sure she'll be willing." Elizabeth paused. Nick had a hidden son. Did he have a hidden wife, too? Someone who had endured his notorious late-night liaisons of passion? She asked quietly, "Is Margaret Justin's mother?"

"No."

As Nick spoke, and a deep fear suddenly filled his blue eyes, Elizabeth felt waves of fear wash through her, too. Sometimes a patient had an ominous sense of doom, an uncanny anticipation of some impending physical catastrophe just before it struck. Was Nick sensing such a catastrophe now? Was his spleen sending a warning that it had been hit after all and was now on the verge of a swiftly lethal rupture? Or was the message from his heart, grazed by the bullet and just about to convulse into a rapidly fatal rhythm?

"Nick, what is it?"

"I was just thinking about Justin's mother," he answered distractedly. Then, focusing quickly, he said decisively, "We're divorced, but I'm going to need to talk to

355

an attorney about what will happen to Justin in the event of my death."

"You're not going to die!"

Nick smiled gently at the beautiful emerald eyes and said softly, "Well, I need to talk to someone just in case. I need to be very sure that she doesn't get custody of him. There's always a lawyer on call for the hospital, isn't there?"

"Yes, for medically related legal issues, but . . . I'm going to call my brother. His specialty is divorce and I know he's in his office downtown this afternoon." Elizabeth saw both the hesitation and the hope in his dark blue eyes—and smilingly dismissed the hesitation. "It's no imposition, Nick. He's only minutes away, and he and his family aren't scheduled to leave for England until tomorrow evening."

"Thank you."

"You're welcome. So, I'd better go get things started. I guess I need your address to give to Larisa."

"Okay." When Nick finished giving it to her, he said, "In the top desk drawer in my study there's a large envelope with Justin's name on it. It contains the legal documents that your brother will need to see and also the immunologic studies that were done on both of us when Justin was born. The match is really quite extraordinary, Elizabeth. Stephen will be very pleased."

"Good. I'll make sure that Larisa brings the envelope back with her." Elizabeth would have left then, but she sensed that there was something more, something that came from the father, not the surgeon. "What, Nick?"

"Could you also have Larisa ask Margaret to bring Mr. Bear?" he whispered finally. *My little boy will need his Mr. Bear.*

Ed and Larisa hadn't moved very far from where Elizabeth had left them in the nurses' station.

"Nick wants me to transplant part of his liver to Justin," Elizabeth told them with quiet calm when she reached them.

"It can't be done, Elizabeth," Ed said firmly. "Justin has virtually no liver left, and even if he did, he's four years old. I'm not telling you anything you don't know, but maybe I didn't explain Justin's injury clearly enough to Nick. I guess I didn't see much point in going into great detail."

"Nick understands perfectly. He understands that Justin will die without the transplantation—and he understands the risks involved to himself."

"He understands that he could die? That, in fact, it's very *likely?*"

"Yes. Nick understands that." Her emerald eyes met his skeptical ones with unflickering resolve. "I'm going to do the surgery, Ed. It will probably take about six hours to get all the tests and assemble the teams. Does Justin have that much time?"

"Six hours? Yes, I think so. But not a lot longer than that. Elizabeth . . ."

"This is possible, Ed. It's never been done but it *is* possible. Justin's own liver will regenerate, so I just need to give him enough of Nick's to buy him the necessary time. With the three-dimensional scans and Bill's expertise, I should know before I enter the OR exactly how much he needs."

"Who is Bill?" Larisa asked.

"Bill Barnes, the pediatric hepatologist."

"And will there be an adult hepatologist to tell you how much liver Nick needs to keep?"

"Yes. Her name is Rebecca Lansing." And, Elizabeth thought, Bill will tell me how much donated liver Justin will need, and Rebecca will tell me that it's far more than Nick can safely give . . . and somehow I will have to find a perfect balance—so that both father and son will survive.

Ed Moore knew that it was futile to argue further with the resolute emerald eyes, and he was a father with a young son of his own, so finally he simply said, "I'm here, Elizabeth. Hell, everyone on staff who hasn't already left town for the holidays will be here. There shouldn't be any problem assembling the two teams. In fact, if you like, I'll get working on that right away."

"That would be a big help, Ed. Thank you."

After Ed left, Elizabeth started to ask Larisa if she would be willing to go to Nick's house; but, because of the suddenly deeply troubled expression she saw on her friend's beautiful face, she asked instead, "What is it, Lara?"

"Did Nick tell you that he used to be an alcoholic?"

For a very long moment Elizabeth simply stared. Finally she answered quietly, "Yes. He did."

"Well, doesn't that make this all the more dangerous for him?"

"Yes." Elizabeth hesitated, not wanting to ask, not wanting to know, and yet needing to. "How did you know that about Nick?"

"On the night of the ball in September, I drank a lot of champagne, glasses and glasses with very little effect. Nick noticed and had a fairly blunt conversation with me about my obvious tolerance to alcohol and my potential for using it to escape from my problems. He offered to help me and I took him up on the offer ten nights later when Julian called."

"Nick came to the apartment?"

"No. In fact I haven't actually seen him since the night at the Fairmont. We've just talked on the phone a few times." Larisa gazed at the emerald eyes that had always been so generous with her—and now looked so betrayed—and assured, "There's absolutely nothing between me and Nick, Elizabeth."

"But you didn't tell me about this."

"I wanted to, but I sensed—although he never specifically said so—that Nick didn't want you to know about his drinking. But you need to know now because of the surgery, don't you? Even though I'm quite sure he doesn't drink anymore."

"Did you know about Justin?"

"No. I knew that Nick had been married briefly, and I got the impression that the marriage had been a disaster, but I had no idea until today that he had a son."

"Do you know who Margaret is?"

"Margaret? No."

"Do you know where Nick lives?"

"Liz, *Lizzie*, I know nothing!" Larisa pleaded with soft urgency to the still-so-betrayed emerald eyes. "Nick and I talked about me, not about him. He didn't want to talk about himself, not to me anyway. You were right about Nick, Elizabeth. He is sensitive and compassionate and kind. He helped me a lot and now I want to do whatever I can to help him—and you. Please?"

Elizabeth gave a bewildered shake of her luxuriant dark brown curls. "I'm sorry, Lara. There's just so much going on, so many revelations."

"And you can't even stop to think about any of them now because of what you have to do. I know, Liz. But please don't worry at all about this revelation. And please let me do whatever. I can to help. Let me be the good friend to you that you've always been to me."

"You are a good friend, Lara," Elizabeth said softly. "And I do need your help. Nick wants Margaret, whoever she is, to be told in person about what happened to him and Justin. Would you be willing to go to his house and tell her?"

"Yes, of course I would."

Mark Jennings already knew about the violence that had happened many floors below his Union Square office. He had been drawn to his window by the screams of sirens and had seen from above the bloody aftermath. When his little sister called asking for his help for Nick, Mark told her without hesitation that he would be there soon.

Elizabeth's next call was to Stephen. As she dialed, she realized how glad she was that he was the immunologist on call today. Not, of course, that his partner wasn't fully capable; but it had been Stephen who had managed the intricacies of the immunosuppression for little Molly in August.

"Nick says that the tissue match between himself and Justin is astonishingly good," Elizabeth elaborated to the stunned silence that had fallen the moment she finished explaining why she was calling and what she was planning to do. "We're sending blood for emergency tissue typing anyway, of course, but Larisa is getting a copy of the apparently very extensive immunologic studies that were done when Justin was born."

"It's not the immunologic match that I'm worried about, Elizabeth. It's the surgeon."

"You don't think I can do this?"

"You know perfectly well that I'm not questioning your skill. But there's a limit to how much liver can be transplanted, and you just finished telling me that almost all of Justin's liver was destroyed."

"Yes, but apparently there's a viable broad-based pedicle onto which we can graft the donor tissue. And maybe when we get the scans, we'll find that Justin has more tissue mass left than Ed thought. You know how revealing the scans can be."

"What if the scans reveal that Justin has even less viable tissue than Ed thought? What then, Elizabeth?"

"I'm going to do this, Stephen, and I need your help." She paused, then added quietly, "And I need your support."

"You know you have that, Elizabeth. I'll be there soon."

"Oh, no," Christine's voice filled with sympathy and concern when Stephen called her moments later to explain why he wouldn't be able to go to the pageant with her after all. "How difficult for Elizabeth. Will you let me know what happens?"

"Of course. In fact, why don't you have me paged as soon as you're home from the pageant? The surgery will probably still be going on then, but I may have some news . . ."

Chapter Twenty-seven

"Elizabeth, this is Margaret."

"Hello, Margaret," Elizabeth said, smiling warmly at the attractive white-haired woman who appeared in the ER nurses' station with Larisa. Deep worry was abundantly apparent in Margaret's pale blue eyes and her slightly gnarled fingers tightly clutched the much-loved Mr. Bear.

"Hello, Elizabeth. I'm so relieved that you're here and I know how relieved Nick must be, too." Then, confident that father and son would be together, she asked, "Where are they?"

"In the pediatric ICU. It's on the sixth floor. I'd walk up with you but I'm waiting for my brother to arrive."

"Why don't I wait for Mark?" Larisa suggested. "You two go on up and we'll find you when he arrives."

Nicholas Chase should have been lying down in his hospital bed on 8 South, heavily medicated with Demerol, gathering strength for the assault on his already badly injured body that would begin again in just a few hours. But instead he sat bolt upright and drug-free in a chair that was positioned as close to Justin's ICU bed as possible. Nick's face was that of a loving father, except that it was terribly pale and the rippling muscles in his taut jaw sent silent signals of the physical pain that was compounding the emotional one. Nick wasn't dressed the way another father visiting his son would have been dressed, either. He wore a hospital gown and robe and a bracelet that identified him as a patient, not a visitor; and there were plastic tubes attached to his body—an intravenous line in his right arm and a much larger tube draining bloody fluid from the left side of his chest.

Nick gazed at his sleeping son, not wanting to awaken him because Justin's rest was so important, and needing more time himself anyway to find exactly the right words to say when he did. Nick wanted to say words to his beloved son that would endure beyond his own death, a comforting promise of love that would be with Justin forever; but he was so afraid of frightening Justin with his loving goodbye. Justin slept, and Nick ignored the crescendoing screams of pain from his own ever-weakening body and simply marveled at his son's wonderfully peaceful slumber, memorizing the moment, making a precious memory that would last for eternity.

Oh, my Justin, my beloved Jussie, how I love you.

Nick sensed movement behind him and turned to smile a silent greeting to Margaret and Elizabeth as they entered the small room.

"Daddy?"

"Hi, my little man," Nick whispered as he turned back to Justin. Then, extinguishing with love the sudden fire in his chest, he leaned forward and kissed his son gently on his cheek. "I'll bet your tummy hurts, doesn't it? You and I were in an accident together, and now we're at the hospital. Margaret is here, and Mr. Bear, and, Jussie, this is Elizabeth. Remember me telling you about Elizabeth?"

Justin nodded at Nick and then focused his clear blue eyes beyond his father and smiled his happy little boy smile at Margaret and Elizabeth and Mr. Bear.

"Remember the surgery that Elizabeth and I did last summer on Molly and Mary Ann? Well, Elizabeth is going to do that exact same surgery on you and me. She's going to put part of me inside you. And you need to remember, Jussie, that that part of me will be with you always, inside you, loving you." Nick stopped abruptly, stopped by his own shaky emotions and by the sudden flicker of worry in his son's blue eyes. "Anyway, we're very lucky that Elizabeth is here today because she's the best."

"I'll need to examine you a little later on, Justin," Elizabeth said quietly, sensing Nick's shakiness and rescuing him by distracting for a moment his son's blue eyes. "Will that be okay with you?"

"Yes."

"Good. Right now, though," she added, looking back at Nick, "according to what the nurse said when Margaret and I arrived, they're ready for Justin in radiology."

"They need to take a picture of your liver," Nick explained gently to his son's trusting blue eyes. "They'll be taking one of mine, too, so that Elizabeth can know all about the size and shape before the surgery. It's just a picture, nothing more, nothing that will hurt."

While Margaret accompanied Justin to radiology, Nick was officially signed in as a patient on 8 South. He needed to lie down, it was obvious even to him, although he still refused pain medication. His mind had to be clear and alert for his meeting with Elizabeth's brother.

364

Nick was lying flat in his hospital bed when Elizabeth and Mark arrived, but as they entered his room, he quickly sat up straight. The sudden movement triggered a burst of flames in his chest and a whirling in his head, and it took him a few moments to recover. He was so helpless. There was so much to be done—and he was *so helpless.*

"Thank you very much for coming, Mark."

"It's no problem at all, Nick. Elizabeth said that you have some concerns about the custody of your son?"

"Yes."

"I'll be in the ER, Mark," Elizabeth said as she started to leave to give them privacy.

"Will you stay, Elizabeth?" Nick asked. "You'll be caring for Justin so you need to know the truth." And, he thought, I also want you to know all the truths about me before I die. It will make my death easier for you.

I'll be caring for *both* of you, Elizabeth amended silently as she answered, "All right."

"Thank you." Nick returned his gaze to Mark and began his story. "Five years ago I became involved with a woman named Glenna Parker. We weren't in love, far from it, but nonetheless she wanted to make our relationship permanent and as a result intentionally became pregnant. We married, but it was obvious long before Justin was born that the marriage was a disaster and we agreed to a divorce that would become final after his birth. Glenna wanted sole custody of Justin—and a great deal of money for his support—and I gave both to her quite willingly. You need to know this, Mark, because if she charges that there was once a time when I chose to have nothing to do with my son, it is absolutely true."

"Okay," Mark said. "Was there a reason?"

"Yes. I was—I am—an alcoholic. Because of that, and

other things that I had come to realize about myself, I believed that it was best for Justin if I never even tried to be a father to him." The soft breath Nick took caused a fire of pain, but it was trivial, so trivial, compared to the pain of the memory of his decision to let Justin live with Glenna. "When he was six months old, Glenna decided that she no longer wanted to care for him—not that she had ever really cared for him. She had obviously totally neglected him. He was terribly fearful and very quiet and withdrawn. He didn't seem to know anything about being safe or loved. You need to understand how Glenna treated Jussie when he was with her, Mark. You need to understand that he *cannot* be returned to her."

"And you think she'll try to claim him? Has she ever tried before?"

"I haven't heard a word from her in three and a half years. But if I die, and she'll know about my death because the news media is going to be very interested in this surgery, it will occur to her that Justin has no parent and a great deal of money. Money has always been very important to Glenna, and Justin will inherit far more even than the substantial earnings I've made over the past few years. I carry a two million dollar life insurance policy of which Justin is the sole beneficiary, and Margaret has put most of her own personal wealth into a trust fund for him as well." Nick gestured to the large envelope that Larisa had brought from his house and which now lay on the nightstand. "I have a will, of course. It's in here, along with the divorce and custody papers. In it I've named Margaret as Justin's legal guardian."

"Excuse me, Nick," Mark interrupted. "But who is Margaret?"

"Margaret Reilly," Nick clarified. Then, as he clarified further, his voice filled with gentle fondness. "To Justin, to Justin's heart, Margaret is a combination mother and grandmother. But," he continued, the fondness giving way to concern, "she's not actually related to him. Margaret is the wife—the widow—of the surgeon who was my mentor during my residency. When Glenna brought Justin to me, I asked Margaret for help, and we've been a family ever since. Justin loves her and trusts her, and in the event of my death he should be with her. That's my will, and that's what's written down, but my fear is that the courts, not knowing the truth about Glenna, might give her custody, as Justin's biologic mother, rather than giving custody to a seventy-four-year-old woman who isn't a relative at all." Nick frowned, looked at Mark's solemn face, and asked, "Is that a legitimate fear?"

"I think so," Mark admitted with quiet candor. Then, smiling reassuringly, he added, "So, let's see how we can make absolutely sure that it won't happen. What does Justin know about Glenna?"

"Probably because of Margaret, he hasn't been terribly curious or concerned about Glenna's absence. When we have talked about her, I've told him that she and I weren't good enough friends to live together, and that I was very lucky to have been the one who got to live with him. He'll want to know more as he gets older, of course, and I've always planned to tell him everything when he was ready to hear it." The silent echo of his own words—*I've always planned*—stirred the immense sadness that Nick was fighting so hard to control. He wouldn't be the one to tell his son about his mother after all. Someone else would tell Justin. Margaret would tell him.

"May I look at the documents?" Mark asked.

"Of course."

During the silence in which Mark studied the divorce papers, the subsequent custody agreement, and Nick's will, Nick looked at Elizabeth for the first time since his story began.

Now you know all about me, Elizabeth, the apologetic dark blue eyes told the lovely emerald ones. Now you know the kind of man I really am. Now you must understand why I have stayed so very far away from you.

Nick hoped he would simply see comprehension—Yes, Nick, I do understand, and you were very right to stay away from me. But he steeled his heart for condemnation—You abandoned your baby? You chose alcohol over your son?

There *was* a message in the beautiful eyes that met his, but it was very pure, and very clear, and without any reservations whatsoever. *I love you, Nick.* The radiant emerald bravely told him that truth, and then lovingly encouraged him to reveal his own still-hidden truth, the most important one of all. And he did, he couldn't help it, because it was swept from his heart to his dark blue eyes on a joyous and powerful river of love. *I love you too, Elizabeth.*

For a few magnificent moments, Elizabeth and Nick were somewhere else, far away in a distant dream in an imaginary place where there were no dying fathers or dying sons ever, and where all the sins of the past were forgotten, and where even the deepest and most painful wounds were magically healed—a place where all things were possible . . . and where even their impossible love could flourish.

"This is interesting." Mark's voice broke the enchanted spell, returning them swiftly from the magnificence of the imaginary to the harsh truths of the real. "In addition to granting you sole custody of Justin, Glenna also signed papers that would enable your future wife to legally adopt

368

Justin should you remarry. That's a little unusual, a little more final than the simple assignment of custody."

"So that should be helpful, shouldn't it, Mark?" Elizabeth asked. "Isn't that more proof that Glenna didn't want her son ever?"

"Yes, but . . ."

"But it's not really that helpful since I haven't remarried," Nick added quietly, correctly interpreting Mark's concern. Nick looked at Elizabeth then, and even though they were no longer in that wondrous imaginary place, and never could be, and even though the question was for Justin, and not for him, there was such soft hopefulness in Nick's voice as he gazed at the lovely emerald and asked, "Will you marry me, Elizabeth?"

"No."

The swift, harsh answer came from Mark, not from Elizabeth. Nick never saw Elizabeth's answer to his proposal because he looked so quickly to Mark, startled by the vehemence of his protest, yet quite unoffended by Mark's instinctive protectiveness of his little sister. Nick felt protective of Elizabeth, too. He had, after all, so very carefully protected her from his own love.

"The marriage could be annulled if I lived, Mark," Nick said quietly. "But if I died, Justin would legally have a mother, and that would effectively preempt any claim Glenna might make. From a practical standpoint, Justin would still live with Margaret."

"First of all, Glenna's lawyers would very easily establish that Elizabeth had no long-standing relationship with Justin." Mark drew a breath, trying to calm himself, then added as evenly as possible, "And second of all, Nick, I'm already concerned enough about the surgery that you're asking my sister to do."

"What do you mean?"

"I mean, I'm already worried that should you die, some self-appointed advocacy group will decide that what Elizabeth did was unethical and perhaps even bring criminal charges against her. If she were in any way a beneficiary of your death, I have no doubt that charges would be filed instantly."

"I'm not asking Elizabeth to do anything unethical, Mark. I'm asking her to use her incredible talent to save the life of an innocent little boy." Nick looked back at Elizabeth then, and with the same softness with which he had asked her to marry him, he asked, "Am I asking too much of you, Elizabeth?"

She hadn't even had a chance to answer, or recover from, Nick's question about marriage—and now there was this new one. But Elizabeth knew her answer to both questions, and it was the same for both: Yes.

Yes, Nick, I will marry you. Of course I will.

And . . . Yes, Nick, you are asking too much of me. You are asking me to watch you die.

But what Nicholas Chase was asking of Elizabeth Jennings was so very much less than what Nick was asking of himself. Nick was willing to die to save the life of his son, and he had not even for a moment questioned that immense decision of love.

And now Elizabeth didn't question the decision that she, too, had made for love.

"No, it's not too much, Nick," she softly told the dark blue eyes which, despite all he had to worry about, were now obviously concerned about her. Then, turning to her brother, she said, "It's not unethical, Mark. Just a little avant-garde."

"Nonetheless, you cannot appear to be a potential beneficiary. Legally, the best approach anyway is to have an affidavit taken today in which Nick openly admits to the charges that Glenna might use against him, and details her disinterest in Justin both while he was in her custody and over the intervening years, and then underscores that it is his will to have Margaret become Justin's legal guardian."

"That can be done now, today, before the surgery?"

"Sure. I can arrange that without any difficulty." Mark saw the gratitude in Nick's eyes and relented a little on his personal stance about the man who he knew had caused his little sister such uncertainty ever since his arrival at the medical center. Whatever else Nick was, he was a loving father, as Mark himself was. "I promise you, Nick, I won't let Justin be given to Glenna. I'll keep the case tied up in legal red tape until he's fully grown, if necessary, and I won't touch a penny of his inheritance doing it."

After Mark left to make the arrangements for the affidavit, Elizabeth remained in Nick's room to update him on the progress of the impending surgery.

"We're scheduled to begin at eight and so far that seems a realistic time frame. Ed has agreed to first assist me in both rooms."

"Good."

"And . . ." Elizabeth told him by name every member of both teams. It was a reassuring list, the very best and most experienced, some of whom had not been officially on call on this holiday weekend but had been more than willing to come in.

"I should probably examine you now."

"Okay."

"Is there any additional history that I need to know?"

With a patient who wasn't a physician, Elizabeth would have gone through the comprehensive review of systems, the long list of questions designed to cover every aspect of the patient's past medical history, even the remote, long-forgotten childhood illnesses that could nonetheless be pertinent. But she didn't need to go through such a list with Nick, because he could tell her without prompting all the pertinent things she needed to know before taking him to the OR.

"I told you that I stopped drinking three and a half years ago, the day Glenna brought Justin to me, but I didn't tell you that I began drinking when I was eleven and that I drank very heavily, essentially daily, until the clinical years of medical school. After that I only drank when I could—whenever I could—when I wasn't in the hospital or on call." Nick paused for a moment to be certain that she, who was so dedicated to medicine and so responsible to her patients, had heard and understood that he had never violated that solemn trust either. Elizabeth's emerald eyes told Nick that she had heard; and the lovely green told him more: that it didn't surprise her. "As I mentioned earlier, as far as I know, I have never had any hepatic damage from the alcohol."

Elizabeth acknowledged his words with a thoughtful nod and then asked, "Is there any family history that I should know about?"

"I don't know much about my mother. She killed herself when I was three. I suppose it's possible, likely even, that she drank, too. My father was definitely an alcoholic, and also a very successful and highly respected trial attorney. He died six years ago from a combination of alcohol and barbituates that the coroner judged to have been an accidental overdose." Nick saw the sudden sympathy in her eyes and said softly, "His death wasn't a tragedy for me, Elizabeth. He was never a father."

No, she thought sadly. The tragedy was that you never had either a father or a mother.

"I think that's all the pertinent history on me. As far as Justin is concerned, he's had all the usual childhood illnesses. Margaret can give you the dates. There's been nothing else, no previous hospitalizations. He's very healthy." Nick heard in his own determined voice what he had heard so often in frantic parents whose children had become innocent victims of senseless twists of fate. But he's so healthy! Just a few hours ago he was laughing and playing! Just a few precious hours ago, Justin had been frolicking in Union Square, his eyes gleaming with joy at all the festivity, his beautiful smile wide and bright as he talked excitedly about presents for Margaret. He will smile and frolic again, Nick told himself. I won't be there to see it, but my little boy will have a lifetime of happiness.

"I guess that's all the history. Can you think of anything else?"

Yes! When we looked at each other, while Mark was reading the documents, I saw love in your eyes, didn't I? And when you asked me to marry you, even though it was to protect Justin from Glenna, there was much more, wasn't there?

Elizabeth knew that it wasn't the right time to ask such emotional questions. Later, when Nick and Justin were safe and well, then would be the time. Right now, she was a surgeon examining her patient for the most important operation of her lifetime—and his.

"No, I think that's all," she answered finally, removing her stethoscope from her white coat in silent signal that she was about to begin the physical examination.

Nick had been carefully examined in the ER, of course. The obvious trauma from the gunshot wound had been well documented and there had been compulsive and repetitive searches for other consequences of that injury—occult bleeding due to a splinter of bone that had punctured the spleen or arrhythmias from glancing trauma to the heart. Elizabeth needed to repeat the examination again, to be certain nothing had changed and to search for anything that might have been missed.

As Elizabeth's delicate fingers touched his skin, she felt icy coolness at the surface . . . but just beneath that there was heat, the fire she had felt before . . . and beneath that was his lean strength, steely taut now because of all his pain.

He's a patient, Elizabeth told herself as her slender hands traveled with expert and necessary boldness over his injured body. Just like any other patient.

But he wasn't just like any other patient.

He was Nick.

And he was a doctor, which meant that Elizabeth could examine him without words or instruction, in the same way that they always operated together, in perfect silent harmony. Elizabeth didn't need to tell Nick to stare at a place beyond her shoulder when she looked into the fundus of his dark blue eyes, or to take a breath each time her stethoscope touched his chest in a new spot. No words were necessary, and none were spoken at all until Elizabeth was midway through her examination of his heart. It was then, as she listened intently for soft rubs or whispered murmurs that might have been missed in the chaos of the ER, that Nick spoke.

"Elizabeth?"

"Yes?" she answered as she removed the stethoscope and looked at him.

There was so much more he could have said to her before he died. But all Nick said was, "Thank you."

And all that Elizabeth said, as she made a silent promise to her heart to tell him so much more when he and Justin were both safe and well, was, "You're very welcome."

Chapter Twenty-eight

All of San Francisco should have been holding its breath. All of its vibrant activity should have come to a shuddering and solemn halt.

But despite the tragedy that had befallen Nicholas and Justin Chase, the world continued to spin, and on that Saturday before Christmas, the staff of Pacific Heights Medical Center was kept exceptionally busy with a never-ending stream of new patients requiring care. Which meant that there was no one else available to do what Larisa was able to do, no one else without conflicting responsibilities. Larisa had only one responsibility: to do whatever she could do to help.

And in the six hours before the historic surgery began, Larisa had never felt more useful—or more trusted. She hadn't been given life or death tasks, of course; but still, during those important and frantic hours, she had been relied upon by Elizabeth, and by all the other doctors and nurses who had at first wondered how this beautiful woman was involved but eventually stopped questioning and simply relied upon her, too. Larisa kept a constant supply of fresh food and hot coffee in the first-floor conference room where the two teams assembled to discuss the minute details of the intricate surgery that they were about to perform; and she placed pages with the hospital operators and when the return calls came, relayed the important messages herself; and she made very certain that Elizabeth, Stephen, and the two hepatologists knew each bit of lab data the moment it became available.

The six hours passed with astonishing speed. It felt as if so much had been accomplished, but in fact it had simply been the compulsive and necessary preamble to the all-important task that lay ahead in the OR.

All-important, and impossible? Larisa had wondered as she had overheard the many conversations of the afternoon, some eager, some skeptical, and some, in whispers far away from Elizabeth, filled with the worry that neither father *nor* son would survive. Larisa had heard the conversations and she had seen the liver scans—Justin's, which showed in three dimensions just exactly how very little liver he had left, and Nick's, completely normal in size and without even a hint of the scarring that would indicate occult cirrhosis. And Larisa had been there, standing beside Elizabeth, when Bill Barnes had handed her a piece of cardboard that was his best estimate of the minimum amount of donated tissue that Justin would need to survive; and Larisa had seen, and surely Elizabeth had seen too, the grave expression of concern on Rebecca Lansing's face when that piece of cardboard was laid on top of Nick's scan. It was too much, Rebecca's expression said. *Far* too much.

Now the six hours were over. The two operating teams and their two patients were en route to the OR. There was nothing left for Larisa to do now but wait with Stephen and Margaret in the secluded waiting room. Larisa and Margaret and Stephen would wait there, and Mark would wait at his home in Atherton with his wife and

377

daughters, and six thousand miles away, Elizabeth's parents waited, too.

Just as Larisa was sitting down beside Margaret to begin their vigil, she heard her own name on the overhead paging system.

"It's probably the head of personnel wanting to hire you on the spot," Stephen said with a warm smile that told her again—even though he and the others had told her more than once before—how valuable she had been.

"It's probably the press," Larisa countered with a frown. Early on the head nurse in the ER had given her a white coat to wear, a pristine camouflage that made more easy and unquestioned her wanderings from radiology to ICU to clinical labs; but still, some of the many journalists assembled to cover the dramatic story had recognized her as the once-famous model and now even more famous ex-wife of Julian Chancellor. "Where's the nearest phone?"

"Halfway down the hall on your left. Have the page operator get a name first, Larisa," Stephen suggested. "If it's not someone you recognize, don't take the call."

But it was a name she recognized. She hadn't known where to reach him in Boston, and she wouldn't have had the time to try anyway. But now, exactly now, when she had time and she needed him so much, he was calling.

"Peter."

"Hi. I just turned on the eleven o'clock news and heard. The newscast said they've just gone to the operating room?"

"Yes, just."

"How does it look?"

"I don't know, Peter. I don't know. Elizabeth is so

378

skilled, so talented, but there's a limit to what's possible."

"How are you?"

"I'm okay. Worried, but okay. I'm so proud of Elizabeth, and of Nick, but I guess I'm very afraid for both of them."

"Is anyone with you?"

"Yes. Stephen and a very lovely woman named Margaret."

"Good. I'll be there as soon as I can. It may be a while because it's snowing here and there are delays at Logan."

"You're coming back tonight?"

"Of course I am."

The tenderness in Peter's voice as he spoke the words enveloped her as if he were with her already, holding her in his strong and gentle arms. He was coming back to be with her and she wasn't even going to offer the slightest protest. Suddenly remembering why he was where he was, Larisa asked, "What did they decide about the fire?"

"There wasn't anything that specifically pointed to arson, so they're officially calling it accidental."

"Isn't that good, better, than if it had been intentionally set?"

"Yes, but the problem is that they aren't sure. There's nothing to point to arson, but they can't absolutely exclude it either."

"You sound discouraged, Peter," she said softly.

"I guess I am. I had hoped to have a definitive answer, and now I know I never will."

He lay before her, so pale, so still, and so totally powerless. He had relinquished his mind and his strength and his will to the anesthetic, and he had given the control of his heart and of his life to her.

We should have said more to each other, Nick! The thought came with a rush of panic as Elizabeth gazed at him and struggled against the heart-stopping impression that here, in this sterile room with its glaring lights, his pale motionless body looked almost dead. We should have said much more than "Thank you" and "You're very welcome." *I should have told you that I love you.* I should have said the words instead of simply hoping that you saw them in my eyes. I thought it wasn't the right time, I guess we both thought that, but . . . but what if it was the only time we were ever going to have?

We didn't say goodbye, Elizabeth reminded herself, calming herself with the memory. Nick and I didn't say goodbye—because we will see each other again and again.

"Are you ready, Elizabeth?" Ed asked, startling her.

But she needed to be startled out of her thoughts about the past and the future. She needed to focus all the concentration of her brilliant mind and all the gifts of her talented hands solely on the present.

Which is what she did.

"Yes. I'm ready, Ed."

She drew a soft breath, then made a straight and steady incision into Nick's abdominal wall. The strong, tautly disciplined muscles were relaxed now, paralyzed by the anesthetic, and the scalpel cut through them with deceptive ease.

Nick's liver appeared entirely normal, just as the high-tech scan had promised it would. That scan and Justin's smaller one were displayed on the view box a few feet away, and the autoclaved cardboard facsimile of the tissue that needed to be removed was lying on the sterile blue-green towels that draped Nick's badly wounded chest. The cardboard had been sterilized so that Elizabeth could

380

safely touch it—but she had no need to. Her fingers already knew its size and shape, and in the past few hours, as her hands had memorized those two dimensions, her mind had imagined how she would make those two dimensions become three.

The piece of cardboard was a pattern, like the ones created by Christine to transform her magnificent two-dimensional sketches into flowing works of art. But there was a very critical difference. Even when the silken gowns caressed the bodies for which they had been expressly designed, adjustments could still be made, a tuck here, a seam easement there. But once Elizabeth had cut her piece from the extraordinary fabric of living tissue, there could be no adjustments, no fabric added or returned, no tucks, no easements, no embellishments—no matter how gifted a seamstress she was.

The incision Elizabeth would make could save two lives . . . or only one small one . . . or none at all.

She—they—had one chance and one chance only.

Elizabeth made the all-important incision with surprising confidence. She had known that she would be able to will her skilled fingers not to tremble, of course, but she hadn't expected the sudden inner confidence, the amazing certainty that had come just as she made the incision. But the confident certainty had come, a gift from somewhere, from Nick, perhaps, or from an even greater . . .

"He's in shock, Elizabeth," the anesthesiologist announced, his voice calm despite both the urgency and the disbelief that he felt. His brain and hands worked as he talked, increasing the rate of fluids in the intravenous lines from slow drops to wide open with quick flicks of his fingers, then reaching for the already prepared syringe of dopamine to chemically raise the blood pressure that had so mysteriously and precipitously vanished. "He was absolutely rock steady. There was no warning whatsoever, not even a trace of tachycardia, and now his heart rate's one-seventy and his pressure is sixty-palp. Something catastrophic has happened. He must be bleeding."

Had they missed an occult injury to the spleen after all? Or a tiny nick to the aorta, a pinprick from a splinter of shattered rib that had now caused the great artery to simply explode? Either of those catastrophes would have filled Nick's abdomen with blood, bright red and churning as his heart pumped frantically to try to counteract the sudden hypotension. But Nick wasn't bleeding, at least not in his abdomen. The ruptured vessel, if there was one, had to be in his chest; or perhaps the shock was an idiosyncratic reaction to the anesthetic; or perhaps she had taken too much tissue from him and all the cells in his body, sensing their imminent death, had just surrendered to the inevitable, collapsing all at once in astonished defeat.

Elizabeth didn't have time to either think about what had happened or to try to solve it. The rest of the team would have to find the answers that would save Nick. Right now, *right now,* she and Ed had to take the precious tissue that she had just so confidently removed to the little boy who lay motionless and pale in the adjacent operating room. Perhaps she had taken too many cells from Nick, maybe even only one too many, but the one cell that might have cost Nick his life could be the same one that would save the life of his son.

Elizabeth left, not knowing whether Nick would live or die and forcing herself not to think about it. Her mind and hands and heart had to be entirely focused on the delicate stitches that would embroider the precious tissue from the dying father to his dying son.

"Christine." Stephen stood as she walked into the surgery waiting room shortly after ten.

"Hi. I started to call you after the pageant, but I called a cab instead." After a hesitant moment, she confessed, "I guess I just wanted to be here."

"I'm very glad," Stephen said, his dark brown eyes warmly welcoming the uncertain lavender ones.

"I'm very glad, too," Larisa added as she joined them. "Peter is on his way back from Boston. Oh, Christine, this is Margaret."

Larisa didn't explain relationships. It simply wasn't necessary. They were all here because they cared, and that was all that mattered.

Two hours later, just after midnight, Elizabeth walked into the waiting room. Her emerald eyes were exhausted, but beneath the fatigue glowed a soft light of hope.

"They're okay," Larisa breathed.

"Well, they both survived the surgery. Justin sailed through it, without any complications whatsoever."

"And Nick?"

Frowning, Elizabeth said quietly, "Nick went into shock just after I removed the piece of liver."

"Anesthetic reaction," Stephen suggested swiftly, seeing at once her worry that it was the incision she had made that had caused the shock.

"I don't know. Maybe. That or the incision itself. No other reason was found."

"Is his pressure back up now?"

"Yes, and it's maintaining well off pressors. Both Nick and Justin are being transferred upstairs right now. Nick will be in the surgery ICU on the eighth floor and Justin will be back in the pediatric ICU on six. He's already awake, Margaret, awake but groggy, but he'll know that you're there."

"And Nick? Is he awake yet?"

"No," Elizabeth answered softly. "Nick's not awake yet. He was still quite deep when I left the OR to come here . . ."

Chapter Twenty-nine

"Daddy's sleeping," Justin was told every time he asked about his father. The words were spoken by the nurses and Margaret and Elizabeth, all of whom spoke them with the most gentle of reassurance. Margaret had shared with those who needed to know what had happened in August, when Justin had been ill and had regressed to the fearful and withdrawn silence of the first six months of his life. Margaret wasn't sure how they could prevent such a regression now, especially as one day became two and then three.

But Justin's recovering body needed long hours of sleep, and that made him quite unaware of how much time had actually passed, and it made perfect sense to him anyway that his daddy was as sleepy as he . . . but it made no sense at all to the many medical experts who examined Nick in his ICU bed. He should have long since awakened. *But he hadn't*. Nicholas Chase was in a coma as mysterious and inexplicable as the shock that had developed so suddenly in the OR.

By the evening of the twenty-third, forty-eight hours after the historic surgery, Nick was no longer Elizabeth's patient. He didn't need to be. From a surgical standpoint, he was absolutely stable. Not a drop of blood had been lost from the hepatic incision site, and the perfectly straight abdominal wound that Elizabeth's scalpel had created was healing beautifully. Nick's care was transferred to a neurologist, who tried to make sense of his coma; and to a pulmonary specialist, who managed the chest tube and fractured ribs; and to Dr. Rebecca Lansing, who had been there from the beginning and was now monitoring Nick's lab values very carefully to determine if the amount of liver Elizabeth had left was enough to sustain his life until new tissue could grow.

Nick was no longer Elizabeth's patient, but she had other patients in the hospital now—including two new renal transplant recipients, patients for whom Nick would have performed the surgeries on the twenty-second and twenty-third, while she and Larisa had been taking Harrod's by storm, if only . . .

"Peter and I thought it would be nice for all of us to have Christmas Eve dinner together," Larisa said. "All of us" was Larisa and Peter and Stephen and Christine and Margaret and Elizabeth, and all except Elizabeth were in the ICU waiting room when Larisa made the suggestion.

"I think that's a wonderful idea, Larisa," Christine said.

"Oh, good, I'm glad." Larisa smiled at Christine and then turned to Margaret. "The apartment where Elizabeth and I live is very close, and I hoped that if we planned dinner for eight, when Justin is asleep, that you would come too."

"Well, I suppose, if Justin is asleep . . ."

"We'll hold dinner until he is."

"All right, Larisa," Margaret agreed. "Thank you."

"Would you like help with the meal?" Christine asked.

"Sure! We haven't planned much further than turkey and stuffing, which Peter's going to make from a recipe his father taught him. Any other specialties are more than welcome."

Christine's lavender eyes cast a tentative glance toward Stephen just as he shifted his gaze to find hers. Their eyes met, and in answer to the silent question in his dark brown eyes she gave a slight nod and a beautiful smile.

"I happen to know that Christine makes sensational French onion soup."

"Really? Would you like to for tomorrow, Christine? You could prepare it right at the apartment if that would be easiest."

"I guess that would be easiest, and yes, I'd be very happy to." Tilting her golden head she said to Stephen, "Maybe I could show you how I slice the onions."

"I'll be there," Stephen promised. Then, reluctantly taking his eyes from the smiling lavender ones he suggested to Larisa, "Why don't I plan to pick up something from Just Desserts?"

"Wonderful." Larisa's expression changed from smiling to solemn as she added, "But, Stephen, there's something else I had hoped you would be responsible for bringing tomorrow."

"Okay. What's that?"

"Elizabeth," Larisa said quietly. Elizabeth, my dear friend who is working far too hard and being far too strong. Elizabeth, who needs to talk about her fears but won't . . . and who most of all needs to speak aloud her unspoken worry that it is she who caused Nick's shock and Nick's coma.

* * *

"I have to stop for a minute!" Christine exclaimed softly.

She turned to him then, lavender eyes glistening, cheeks flushed pink, a lovely smile on her lips. The tears in her eyes were sparkles of happiness, not raindrops of grief. As she had been slicing the onions for the soup, she had been talking almost breathlessly to Stephen, as if for the past three months she had been saving up things just to tell *him*—and now the words tumbled out in a rush, eager to be free and quite unwilling to hold back because of something as trivial as the imprudence of slicing onions and talking at the same time.

"Too much talking," she murmured.

Not enough talking, Stephen thought, his smiling dark brown eyes not wavering even when he felt a twisting ache deep inside as she delicately dabbed away the tears with her left hand—her wedding ring hand. The slender band glittered at him, a solid gold reminder of the truth, the warning: Christine is married. She will always be married to David. She is going on with her life—her dream of becoming a designer—and David would be so happy for her. This is what he had hoped for his beloved Christie.

They had been talking about her designs just before she had turned from the onions to him, and now, wanting to keep the conversation focused still on the dream that made her lavender eyes sparkle, Stephen said, "You clearly have the talent to design anything you want, but do you have favorites, dresses or outfits that you enjoy designing the most?"

"Oh." Christine's already flushed cheeks became a little rosier at his compliment, and then her beautiful face grew thoughtful as she considered his question. "I'd never really thought about it before. Making the costumes for the pageant and working with the children was wonder-

388

ful, and designing Larisa's dresses for the *Promise* ad campaign has been very exciting. But, I suppose, if I had to limit myself, I would design dresses for romantic occasions—prom dresses and wedding dresses, something like that."

"Did you design your own?"

"Prom dress and wedding dress? No, neither. I didn't go to the prom, and David and I were married by a justice of the peace, just us and the two required witnesses, at the town hall in Berkeley." She hesitated a moment. Then, encouraged by his welcoming smile, she said, "As I was helping dress the girls in their costumes Saturday night, I was very tempted to make an offer then and there to sew their prom dresses for them when the time came, and their wedding dresses too, if they wanted me to."

"Like the man in New York who promised to pay for the college education of any and all the children in a certain elementary school class who graduated from high school?"

"Well, my offer isn't quite as significant as that."

"Oh, I don't know," Stephen quietly told the lovely lavender. "I think romance is probably pretty significant."

Christine answered with a smile of soft surprise, and, after a moment of slight confusion, turned back to the onions that still needed to be sliced.

Stephen watched in silence as she sliced, not prompting her with questions, because the questions that swirled in his mind now were ones that he had absolutely no right to ask.

What about romance in your life, Christine?

What about making prom dresses and wedding dresses for your own daughters?

Margaret arrived promptly at eight. Justin was asleep, she told them, and Nick was unchanged. By eight-fifteen, when Elizabeth had neither called nor appeared despite the promise exacted from her by both Larisa and Stephen that she *would* be there, Stephen quietly announced that he was going to the hospital to get her.

Stephen knew Elizabeth's patients very well. He was managing their immunosuppression after all. The patients who were officially in Elizabeth's care were completely stable. She wouldn't be with them, Stephen knew. She would be with a patient for whom she had already given everything she had to give. Stephen found her in the surgery ICU, standing outside Nick's room, staring at him through the plate glass.

"Time for dinner."

"Oh." She turned, obviously startled from a faraway thought. "Stephen. Is it time? I had no idea it was that late."

"Well it is, and I've come to personally escort you to the gourmet feast."

"I'll be there soon, Stephen, I promise. Please tell the others that I've gotten delayed and ask them to start without me. I'll be there, I will, but there's something I have to do first."

"Okay," Stephen agreed, relenting without an argument because the fatigued emerald eyes that met his were so very resolute.

Something I have to do first. Words I have to say to Nick. Elizabeth had talked to Nick often in the past few days, every time she visited. She had gazed at the handsome face that even in this deepest of sleeps seemed so very tormented; and she had told him how well Justin was doing; and she had pleaded softly with him to awaken, and sometimes she had even commanded him to. Elizabeth had spoken gentle words of reassurance, but there were other words, other truths, that remained unspoken.

Because he is going to wake up, she kept telling herself. And when he does we will both speak aloud the silent messages that were in our eyes before surgery.

But what if Nicholas Chase never woke up? Then she would never hear the secrets of his heart.

Maybe I will never hear the secrets of Nick's heart, Elizabeth thought as she entered the room and moved very close to him, to the bed where he lay. But at least, perhaps, *please,* he will hear the most important truths of mine.

"Hi, Nick. It's me, Elizabeth. I've just seen Jussie. He's fine, sleeping now, better and stronger with each passing minute, and very eager to see his daddy." Elizabeth's voice began to falter as she thought about the beloved little boy. Justin didn't know it was Christmas Eve, and they had decided not to tell him, to delay Christmas altogether until a time when he could celebrate with his father. *Let him hear your love, not your fear.* The words Nick had spoken to Danny's parents on that tragic day in August came back to her now, giving her strength as she confessed softly, "I love you, Nicholas Chase. I think you already know this. I suppose it's been obvious from the very beginning. And, Nick, I think that you love me, too. Maybe you thought I wouldn't love you if I knew about your drinking, or that once you believed it was best for Justin not to live with you. But I know both those things now, and I love you so much, Nick, *so much.*"

Elizabeth had to stop then. Her voice was too shaky

and tears filled her emerald eyes. She turned from Nick's bed and gazed out the window into the winter darkness. Nick had been given the room with the best view. Below was the courtyard, twinkling with cheerful white Christmas lights, and in the foreground lay the city, glittering like a crown of brilliant jewels in the clear winter air, and somewhere beyond, in the vast darkness, was the bay. Elizabeth didn't see the glittering lights, nor did she hear the Christmas carols that played softly in the distance. She saw only the vast darkness—and she shivered as she imagined its endless iciness and its endless silence.

"Elizabeth?"

For a moment she didn't believe the sound. It was a horrid hallucination—Nick's voice calling to her from the vast icy blackness.

But then she turned and saw his dark blue eyes. They were gazing at her, a wondrous expression of disbelief and hope, like someone who knew he must surely be dreaming . . . but was hopeful, so very hopeful, that the magnificent dream might possibly be real.

"Nick," she whispered as fresh tears filled her emerald eyes. Her tears caused sudden fear on his face, but swiftly and so joyously she reassured, "Justin is fine, Nick."

"He is?" *Justin is fine and I'm alive?*

"Yes. In every way. The grafted tissue is already functioning very well, and emotionally, even though he keeps asking about you, he hasn't become withdrawn or fearful."

"How long has it been?"

"Three days, almost to the minute. It's eight-thirty, and it's Christmas Eve." After a moment she admitted to the surprised blue eyes, "Your surgery was a little more complicated than Justin's, Nick. Within seconds after I did the resection from your liver, you went into shock."

"Not because of the resection."

"Well, it was either because of that or because of the anesthetic. We don't have another explanation. Nor do we really have an explanation for why it took you so long to wake up."

"Maybe both were due to my alcohol use," Nick said quietly, solemnly reminding her of his deep flaws, gently shifting the responsibility from her, where it didn't belong, to him, where it did. Then he smiled, and reminding her of the astonishing truth for which she *was* responsible, he said very softly, "But I'm awake now, and Jussie is fine."

"And he's going to be so happy to see you."

"Not as happy as I will be to see him."

Elizabeth wanted that happiness now, as soon as possible, for both of them.

"Neither of you is officially my patient anymore, so before I start arranging father-son reunions, I'd better make some phone calls. I'll go do that right now. In the meantime, there's a phone call you could make."

"Oh?"

"Yes. There's a Christmas Eve dinner going on at my apartment. Larisa insisted on it and scheduled it for a time when she knew that Justin would be sleeping so Margaret could be there." Elizabeth's emerald eyes sparkled. "I think I can say with extreme confidence that a phone call from you would really make Larisa's party."

"Okay," Nick agreed, smiling gently. After a moment the gentle smile faded from his dark blue eyes and they grew very solemn. "Elizabeth?"

"Yes?"

"Thank you."

"You're very welcome."

Those were the words they had spoken to each other before the surgery—those words, and not goodbye . . .

and not, either, the silent messages that had been in their eyes. And now the surgery was over, and both father and son had miraculously survived, and it would be safe at last to allow those silent joyous messages to return, and even to speak them aloud.

But there were no joyous messages of love in Nick's eyes now. The dark blue was only solemn—and troubled.

"What, Nick?"

It took a moment for him to answer, and when he did his voice was dangerously soft, and his words were a quiet warning. "Please don't care about me, Elizabeth. I have very little to offer, far too little."

It was amazing to Elizabeth how quickly—and with what clarity—she understood the devastating meaning of those quiet words. Perhaps he had heard her confession of love, or perhaps he was merely remembering the silent messages his own eyes had sent when he had believed he was going to die. But either way, Nicholas Chase wanted to set the record straight as soon as possible.

His exquisitely gentle and eloquent gazes of love had been his farewell gift to her, so that she could believe forever that her so-obvious love for him had been reciprocated after all. It was a most generous gift, but not a terribly risky one since he had fully believed that he was going to die.

But now Nick knew that he wasn't going to die after all, and now it was time for the real truth: *I know you love me, Elizabeth, but I don't really love you.* Nick didn't say it that way, of course. He was far too polite—and far too experienced in extricating himself from women who loved him—to be so brutally blunt. Instead he gallantly cast himself as the villain of the piece, placing responsibility for the love that couldn't be directly on himself, blaming himself just as he blamed himself and his alcohol use for every adverse event that had happened in the OR.

But Elizabeth knew the truth. It wasn't that Nick had far too little to offer. It was simply that he didn't want to offer what he had to *her*. His words and their meaning were as crystal clear as the cool winter night, and the emptiness she felt was as black and icy as the vastness beyond.

But somehow she smiled.

And somehow she spoke.

"I understand, Nick. And now I really want to get going on those phone calls."

When the phone rang at the apartment, Larisa assumed it would be Elizabeth, calling to say that she wasn't going to make the Christmas Eve dinner after all . . . so Larisa simply began issuing her gentle yet exasperated command the moment she lifted the receiver, "Elizabeth Jennings, you get over here right now! There's absolutely no reason for you to be there, and it's not even good for you to be. You have to let it go, Elizabeth, just for a little while."

"That sounds like some pretty tough love to me, Larisa."

"Nick?" she whispered. *"Nick."*

Part

Five

Chapter Thirty

San Francisco
February 1992

The nightmares were worse than all the ones that had come before. He dreamed about Justin, of course, relentlessly reliving the day of terror in Union Square, and he dreamed about Elizabeth. There were guns aimed at her, too, and he couldn't stop the bullets, even though he tried to so desperately. "I love you, Nick," Elizabeth called to him from the infinite abyss as she fell and fell and fell. He stood on the very edge of the abyss, watching her endless fall, and in answer to her dying pledge of love, he whispered a harsh warning of ice, "Don't care about me, Elizabeth!" And his words were more lethal than all her bloody wounds. He saw the hurt, the death in her emerald eyes, just before she vanished into the darkness forever.

The nightmares came every night, awakening him drenched and gasping after only a few moments of sleep. And even though his terribly weak body needed sleep so badly, Nick would leave his bed then and cross the hallway to Justin's room. There, he would try to calm himself by gazing at the very peaceful sleep of his very healthy son.

Six weeks had passed since the day in Union Square, and it had been almost five weeks since he and Justin had been discharged from the hospital. Justin was virtually well. The donated liver was functioning magnificently, and by now even if it was suddenly rejected, Justin's own liver had already regenerated enough to sustain him. Physically, his son was almost whole again, and emotionally, Justin was remarkably unscathed. He had neither nightmares about the day in Union Square, nor troubling memories of the events that had followed in the hospital. His only memory of the day in the square was a memory of love, the loving arms of his father curled tightly around him protecting him from a harm he never even saw; and his memories of the hospital were foggy, but not frightening. His daddy had been there, sleeping too, and Margaret and Elizabeth and Mr. Bear had been with him, and he had felt safe and loved.

Justin slept peacefully, as he always had, and Nick's sleep was more tormented than it had ever been before. Before . . . when his body had been strong and fit and he had been able to run in the midnight darkness until his exhaustion blurred the nightmares and muffled the screams of pain. Nick could have safely gone out into the darkness now, because Justin would not awaken, frightened, from his deep and peaceful sleep; but his once strong body was far too weak to run even a block much less the miles and miles he would need to run to vanquish the pain. He would need to run farther and faster than ever before, because the anguished cries of his heart, like his terrifying nightmares, were so very much worse than they had ever been; because, as with the nightmares, Nick's emotional pain now involved Elizabeth, loving her so much . . . and knowing that she loved him too . . . and knowing that their love was impossible . . . and remembering the hurt in her eyes when he had told her not to care about him. The emerald hurt had lasted only a flicker, but the memory of the immense pain that he had caused the woman he loved was indelibly etched in his waking mind and relived every night in his nightmares.

Nick had neither seen nor spoken to Elizabeth since the day that he and Justin were discharged. They had talked on that day, a painfully formal discussion of the plans for the transplant service while he was away. He would be on leave until the first of June, the minimum convalescence time that Rebecca Lansing would allow. During his five-month absence the two two-membered transplant teams would become one three-membered one, and Elizabeth would become acting service chief.

Nick hadn't seen her since that day. He might have seen her by accident had he kept his appointments in the hepatology clinic; but Nick couldn't risk seeing Elizabeth by accident, nor could he permit anyone to report to her how he looked. So he stayed away from the hospital entirely. Margaret drew the necessary weekly blood tests on him at home, and he and Rebecca discussed the results over the phone. The lab tests simply confirmed what Nick already knew from the oppressive weakness he lived with every second of every day: he wasn't getting any better. His liver wasn't regenerating the way it should have been by now.

His survival wasn't in jeopardy. He could live forever like this. This—being alive and having the extraordinary joy of watching his happy and healthy son grow up—was so much more than he had ever dared to hope. Justin's survival had been all that mattered. That had been gift enough, miracle enough, but he had been given even more—his own life—because of the talent and courage of the woman he loved so much . . . and had hurt so deeply.

Nick knew the sadness it would cause Elizabeth to see him this weak, as if she had failed, as if it was her fault that his liver wasn't regenerating—even though it was because of her that he was alive . . . and because of his own deep flaws, his past history of alcohol use, that he wasn't recovering as he should have been.

Nick couldn't let Elizabeth see him like this, and it was already February third, and in a few hours he would make the phone call he should have made weeks ago, but had kept putting off, hoping to be certain that he would be well enough to see her again by the fifteenth.

He was no better on this dark winter dawn, but he was going to make the call today anyway . . . and somehow, in the next twelve days, he was going to become well *for her*.

Elizabeth took a steadying breath before pressing the flashing button on her telephone which her secretary had just told her was a call from Nick.

"Hello, Nick. How are you?"

"Fine. Far better than my lab data might suggest," he said firmly. He didn't know if Elizabeth had been following his discouraging lab tests, but as a result of this phone call he knew that she soon would be. His voice softened, "I'm just fine, Elizabeth, and I have a very healthy little boy. How are you?"

"Everything's fine here, too," she said, answering his question as if it had been asked about the transplant service and not about her. "There are really no problems at all."

"I'm not surprised, but that's not why I'm calling."

"No?"

"No. I wondered if you would be willing to give the keynote address at the International Congress."

"You're not going to Paris after all?"

"Yes, I am going." *And somehow I will be well.* "But I thought that for the keynote address I would make an appearance as a specimen rather than as a speaker. A review of the world's experience with living donor liver transplantation would obviously be incomplete without a detailed account of what you did in December—and that's your surgery. I've already done a complete review of everything before then, and can get that information to you to use and restructure however you like, but the review is merely a preamble to what you did on Justin and me. That needs to be presented in great detail, Elizabeth. It was a very important surgery." Emotion touched his deep rich voice as he added, "I only know the stunning results—I'm living them—but I have no idea how you worked the magic."

As Elizabeth listened to Nick's words, and heard the surprised and gentle gratitude in his voice, she realized anew that he had had no expectation whatsoever that he would survive the surgery. He had convinced her to operate on him, fully believing that the incision she would make would be lethal. She felt a deep and powerful anger beginning to swell within her; but she subdued it, tranquilized it, with the icy memory of what Nick had said to her on Christmas Eve. *He doesn't want you to care about him—so don't!* Elizabeth subdued the anger with that memory, and then calmed it further by reminding herself of the most—the only—important truth: Nicholas Chase was alive. That was what mattered, all that mattered. The other wishes of her heart, that he could love her as she loved him, were quite trivial in comparison.

"Will you give the address, Elizabeth?" Nick asked into the lingering silence. "I realize that this is a last-minute request, and I would be happy to do the renal transplantation presentation if that would free some time for you to prepare the keynote."

"That talk is basically done. I can just give you all my notes."

"No. If you've already done the work, why don't you present it? Why don't you present them both?"

"All right," she agreed quietly, fighting the memory of her happiness the day that Nick had asked her to give just one of the presentations. A vote of confidence, she had decided joyfully. It had been wonderful, *enough;* but since then Nick had given her the greatest vote of confidence possible. He had entrusted to her care the life of his precious son—not to mention his own life. And after that she had wanted even more, something that wasn't hers to have: Nick's love. Nicholas Chase is alive, she reminded herself. That's all that matters. "Did you want to meet before we go to Paris, to go over what I'm planning to say?"

"It's not necessary. This is your show, Elizabeth."

Stephen smiled at the embellishment his secretary had playfully made on his appointment calendar at the top of today's date: a smiling red heart, complete with a feathery arrow.

Stephen needed no bright red reminders that today was Valentine's Day. He knew, and his own heart smiled as he thought about the evening that lay ahead. He and Christine were dining at the Top of the Mark, high above the glitter of the city, amid roses and candlelight and romantic music. Ever since Christmas they had seen each other

404

often, usually making plans only from one date to the next. But candlelight dinner at the Top of the Mark on February fourteenth required advanced reservations; so he had invited her in advance, weeks ago, and she had accepted immediately, and they had decided together that they would dress formally for the special occasion.

Stephen smiled as he anticipated the evening ahead, but the smile faded a little as he thought about the sixteen days that would follow. Three months ago, when he had scheduled the visits to the major European centers of immunologic research, the itinerary he had been able to arrange had been quite thrilling. It still was—from a scientific standpoint. After attending the first two days of the congress in Paris, he would spend the following two weeks in Vienna, Edinburgh, Geneva, and Stockholm, learning, teaching, and sharing ideas with his colleagues. Three months ago, being away sixteen days had been a concern only from a professional standpoint—arranging coverage for his patients and making certain that his research was at a phase that could be ably managed by his research associates.

But now sixteen days away meant sixteen days away from Christine.

Stephen couldn't cancel the commitments he had made to his overseas colleagues, and it was a unique opportunity, but he hated the thought of being away from her for so long. He had even considered asking Christine to join him. She couldn't the first week, he knew. She and Peter and Larisa would be in Los Angeles, at the Bel Air home of Emily Rousseau Adamson, for the photo sessions for *Promise*. Larisa wanted Christine to be at the sessions, to make certain that the graceful folds of silk and the delicate whispers of lace on the magnificent dresses she had designed fell just so. And the second week? Christine would be busy, as always, designing the beautiful gowns that were in ever-increasing demand throughout the Bay Area.

But there was another reason Stephen had decided not to ask Christine to join him in Europe. He didn't want to overwhelm her. An entire week together would be a vast leap from what they had done since Christmas—evenings, many evenings; dinner, or dinner and the theater; and yes, more than once, talking until almost dawn. But that was all.

All? Stephen knew what those wonderful evenings of gentle laughter and quiet conversation and lovely lavender eyes meant to him—and what he wanted them to mean: the beginning of a lifetime together. And if that was an impossible wish? If Christine was married forever to David?

Then Stephen wanted to live his own magnificent delusion for as long as possible . . .

"I made myself a prom dress," Christine said, as she greeted him with a shy shrug and cheeks that flushed the same pale pink as the very romantic—yet demure and elegant—silk chiffon dress that she wore. It was a dress for a woman, but Christine had never gone to a prom, and even though the dress was womanly, her lavender eyes glowed with the hopeful innocence of a teenaged girl.

"It's beautiful." Stephen added softly, "You're beautiful."

"Oh!" The radiant lavender bravely met his appreciative gaze. "Thank you."

"You're welcome. I brought you some roses."

As Christine took the fragrant bouquet of exquisite

cream-colored rosebuds from his hand, Stephen's heart nearly stopped.

She wasn't wearing her wedding ring.

Christine's eyes followed his eyes to the band of skin on her left ring finger that was even more pale than her delicate fairness. Then, lifting her beautiful face to his, she said quietly, "I decided it was time for me to take it off."

They caressed with soft smiles and gentle gazes across the flickering flames of pale pink candles; and they touched lightly but wondrously as they danced slowly to the most romantic songs of love; and when they stopped dancing their hands intertwined still . . . his right hand, which so carefully had administered to David the miraculous life-prolonging therapy . . . and her left hand, ringless now, its delicate fingertips tender from the needle pricks that had unceremoniously pulled her back from the astonishing, and terrifying, and sometimes terribly sad thoughts that had swirled in her mind since Christmas.

At midnight, when they stood on the secluded porch of her small house, quite hidden from all eyes but their own, Stephen kissed her. And Christine kissed him back.

It was a gentle hello greeted by a tender welcome . . . the joyous beginning of magnificent discoveries, of passionate warmth, and silent promises, and soft sighs of crescendoing desire. It was a shared and wondrous joy— until Christine pulled away.

Stephen saw desire still in the lovely lavender, but even as he watched, the shimmering desire was replaced by bewildered confusion.

"Christine?"

"Thank you for the lovely evening, Stephen."

"You're welcome," he said softly, wanting so much to

help her but seeing so clearly in the confused lavender eyes that what she wanted was privacy.

Had his kiss overwhelmed her? Had its gentle but unconcealed passion somehow even frightened her? No, Stephen decided. Christine was confused, and troubled by her confusion, but she was not frightened. For a hopeful moment, he even thought that she was going to say something more, to try to articulate to him her bewildering emotions.

But then her eyes left his, and she fumbled to find the keys in her purse, and after she opened the door, she turned back to him very briefly and whispered, "Good night."

"Good night," Stephen echoed gently as she disappeared.

He didn't try to stop her. Her sudden wish for privacy was so obvious, and so compelling. But as he drove away, Stephen knew that he would speak with her in the morning, before he left for Paris—and the sixteen days that would be spent so very far away from her.

The tears began to spill the moment Christine pulled the door closed behind her, and as she walked even deeper into her house, *their* house, her vision became blurred with the hot dampness. But Christine didn't need her lavender eyes to see where she was going. Her footsteps were unerringly guided by her weeping heart.

And then she was there, standing before the magnificent portrait he had painted of her, and she whispered softly, "Oh, David. Oh, *David.*"

Stephen waited until eight A.M. to call her. But there was no answer then, or at eight-fifteen, or at eight-thirty. Worried, he drove to her house.

Christine didn't answer his knock, but the porch light that had illuminated her glowing and then confused lavender eyes was off, and the flag on the mailbox was up—reassuring signals, Stephen decided, that she had long since awakened and left. Today was probably one of the rare Saturdays that she still worked at Sydney's, a long day dedicated to helping the many clients whose wardrobes depended still on her gift for fashion and style. This was obviously going to be such a day, and Christine had gone in early to prepare.

Sydney's didn't officially open its doors until ten, so Stephen returned to his apartment, put his luggage in his car, and arrived at the boutique just as the elegant French doors were being swung open.

Sydney herself greeted him.

"Stephen!"

"Hello, Sydney," he answered, a little surprised by the warmth of her welcome. He and Sydney had seen each other only twice before, in August when he had come to look at the atrium with Peter and a few weeks later at the Fairmont ball. Perhaps, he thought hopefully, Sydney's memory of him had been kept evergreen, and obviously warm, because of something Christine had said. "I'm looking for Christine."

"She's not here today, Stephen. I imagine that at this very moment she's having a power breakfast with Colin Gallagher."

"Colin Gallagher?"

"He just happens to be New York's hottest fashion designer."

"Yes, I know," Stephen said quietly. Christine had told him all about Colin Gallagher, how talented he was, how innovative and visionary. She had told Stephen about Colin Gallagher weeks ago, but she hadn't said a word

409

about him last night. Stephen heard the disbelief in his own voice as he asked, "Christine is with Colin Gallagher this morning?"

"I assume so. I know she was with him all yesterday afternoon, and presumably they had a candlelight dinner together somewhere last night. He's wooing her, you see, trying to get her to move to New York to work with him." This was exciting news, but Sydney stopped abruptly when she saw that Stephen obviously didn't share her excitement. "All of which means that Christine isn't here this morning. Sheila is available, though, and I'm sure she'd be happy to help you."

"No, thank you, Sydney." Stephen forced a smile. "I just stopped by on impulse, and I actually have a plane to catch."

As he drove to the airport, Stephen realized that Sydney obviously knew nothing about his relationship with Christine. Why would she? he chided himself. *What* relationship?

Despite Christine's sudden confusion during their kiss, so very understandable given her immense love for David, last night had felt to Stephen like a joyous beginning, a brave and wonderful step toward happily ever after.

But, he wondered, had the evening that had felt to him like such a wondrous hello been in truth the gentlest of goodbyes? Even before their candlelit dinner, had Prince Charming already placed on Cinderella's delicate foot the glass slipper with which she would courageously journey ever closer to her own fairy-tale dreams?

* * *

As she walked to her preassigned seat in the first-class cabin, Elizabeth wondered if instructions had been given to the travel agency in Paris regarding who should sit next to whom. She already knew that she and Stephen had been assigned to sit together. And Nick? As she saw him take a window seat on the opposite side of the jet's expansive cabin, she decided, yes, such instructions had been given.

She and Nick had already spoken, of course, a brief polite greeting in the boarding area. Elizabeth would have walked on, but Margaret and Justin were there, and as she talked to them Nick had silently watched their animated conversation.

Elizabeth and Nick had scarcely spoken, but she had been so aware of him, how terribly pale he was, how dark circled his blue eyes, how uncertain his smile. Elizabeth saw the uncertainty and pallor and fatigue, but she sensed, as always, the taut strength and smoldering fire in his lean and powerful body. The noble warrior had been badly wounded, but he was proud still, and strong, and disciplined.

Had it been sheer pride that had finally and so dramatically caused his lab tests to improve? she wondered. The improvement had begun six days ago, and it was so dramatic that Rebecca, hopeful yet disbelieving, had asked Margaret to draw additional blood samples yesterday— and the repeat blood work was even better still.

Had the incredibly disciplined Nick simply willed his own improvement because he had known that for the next five days he would be on display? Elizabeth herself had no intention of displaying him, of course, neither having him stand where he sat in the audience nor join her on the stage—surely he knew that; but most of the other surgeons attending the congress already knew what

411

the famous Nicholas Chase looked like, and they would be looking at him now with renewed interest and curiosity.

Proud, and strong, and disciplined. The same adjectives could easily have been applied to her. She, too, looked very pale, and her emerald eyes were dark circled, too, from far too little sleep. The weeks between Christmas Eve and Valentine's Day had been frantically busy, handling the administrative responsibilities for the transplant service in Nick's absence and, at her insistence, taking call for both transplant and trauma as always. Elizabeth had kept herself very busy; but all the while, like Nick, she had been preparing herself to be on display— not for hundreds of eyes, as Nick would be, but just for the dark blue ones that didn't love her.

Elizabeth had hoped that the passing of time would make her better. But when it hadn't, she had done with her broken heart just what Nick had done with his broken body, simply willing it to heal—enough, at least, to send a proud and strong message to the sensuous dark blue: I'm fine, Nick. I'm just fine without you.

During the hectic weeks since Christmas, Elizabeth hadn't had one midnight chat, or even one late afternoon cup of tea, with Stephen. We can talk now, she thought as she settled into the seat beside the friend she had barely seen. We can talk from here to Paris, a nice, private conversation, muffled by the noise of the engines and thankfully very far away from Nick.

But from the moment she sat down, Elizabeth realized that Stephen, too, was very far away. She didn't intrude, not for miles and miles, but finally, when she could stand the sadness in his brooding dark eyes no longer, she asked softly, "What's wrong, Stephen?"

412

"Have you ever heard of Colin Gallagher?"

"Yes, of course. Why?"

"Did you know that Christine has a chance to work with him?"

Elizabeth stiffened at his almost accusatory tone, as if she had known and had intentionally withheld the information from him. It was a tone, Elizabeth realized, that she had heard once before—when Stephen had sharply demanded if she had been planning to share with him her discovery that Sydney's famous Christine was also Mrs. David Andrews. Both times the issue had been Christine; but this time Elizabeth had no hidden knowledge.

"No."

"He's in San Francisco, trying to convince her to move to New York even as we speak."

"I honestly didn't know, Stephen. I haven't even seen Christine since Christmas Eve. She and Larisa see each other quite frequently, but if Christine told Larisa about Colin Gallagher, Larisa didn't tell me." Elizabeth hesitated, then added gently, "I guess I also didn't know about you and Christine."

"Christine probably didn't mention that to Larisa, either. But why would she? There was obviously nothing to tell."

"We've talked before about how private Christine is, Stephen."

"Oh, yes, she's very private," he agreed bitterly. "She spent yesterday afternoon with Colin Gallagher and last evening with me, and she didn't say a word about the fact that he was in town."

"There could be *non*sinister reasons for that."

"Really? I've been trying for hours to come up with one, just one, and so far I've come up empty."

"Well," Elizabeth began, but faltered quickly, at a loss,

413

too, for a silver lining. "You'll just have to call Christine from Paris and find out."

Stephen had been thinking about calling her, of course, but it wasn't a conversation to have over the phone, and he had been thinking about taking the first flight out of Paris back to San Francisco, but . . .

"Aren't you going to call her, Stephen? Won't she be expecting you to?"

"I don't know if she expects me to call, Elizabeth, and I don't know if I'm going to. What's the point in confronting her with something she obviously didn't want me to know? I think she should accept the job with Gallagher, of course. I guess I had hoped it would have been something she would discuss with me."

"Because you would follow her to New York if she wanted you to, wouldn't you?"

"Yes, I would, Elizabeth. In a minute."

Chapter Thirty-one

Paris
February 1992

The plane touched the tarmac at Charles de Gaulle at eight A.M. Paris time. The February morning was overcast, a gray cloudiness that matched the fogginess they all felt as they deplaned after the long flight through many time zones. Elizabeth, Stephen, and Nick shared a taxi to the Ritz; and then, because their lavish suites were all located on the same floor, they shared an elevator, too. Then they parted, to try to get some sleep in the ten hours that remained before Elizabeth's keynote address.

Elizabeth stood at the window of her elegant suite and gazed at the Tuilerie Gardens below, and the Seine beyond, and in the distance the Eiffel Tower. As tired as she was, she felt the invisible and almost irresistible pull of Paris beckoning to her, inviting her to discover its alluring mysteries.

I will, she promised herself. After I get a little sleep.

The keynote address was scheduled for eight P.M. in the hotel's grand ballroom. Elizabeth set her alarm for five, just in case, but she awakened refreshed and eager at one and spent the rest of the Sunday afternoon wandering through Paris, mentally rehearsing her talk as she battled the ever-crescendoing anxiety she felt because of it.

How many lectures have I given? she demanded of herself and her churning stomach as she walked briskly along the Champs-Elysees. The answer was simple: many. All had been compulsively prepared in advance, as this one had been; in fact, her meticulous preparation for the keynote far exceeded all the compulsiveness that had come before. She had written and memorized a precise outline of what she was going to say, in the order that she was going to say it; but, as always, she hadn't planned in advance the exact words she would use. She had learned from experience that finding the words just before she spoke them gave her presentations energy and spontaneity.

I always feel anxious before a lecture, she reminded her racing heart when she stood beneath the massive Arc de Triomphe. And often, the first few sentences of the lecture teetered precariously on a high wire of tightly strung nerves. But eventually the nerves relaxed and the butterflies flew away, and then she would actually enjoy herself—just as her audience enjoyed listening. She captivated her audiences with her energetic vivaciousness, and she intrigued them with her technique of presenting scientific information as if she were telling an interesting story, not simply reciting hard, dry data.

Nick has never heard me give a lecture! She realized with a rush of panic when she reached the charming Bagatelle in the Bois de Boulogne. Dr. Nicholas Chase probably wouldn't approve of her story-telling technique. But that was what she was planning to do tonight when she told the audience of distinguished surgeons the history of living donor liver transplantation. She was going to begin at the very beginning, when the technique was just an extraordinary concept to the visionaries, including Nick himself, and then she was going to reveal how the story unfolded, the triumphs and the failures, including the most recent chapter, written by her over Christmas weekend. It was the only interesting and coherent way to present the information.

But Nick might not agree, she thought as she wandered along rue de Longchamp toward the Grande Cascade. He might think she should have had more slides filled with data and fewer photographs of the people who had been involved. "It's your show," he had said. But still, he might not approve.

Which doesn't matter, remember? she asked herself as her emerald eyes gazed at the tumbling waterfall. Nick's approval doesn't matter anymore.

Long before the chairman officially convened the congress, every seat in the grand ballroom was already taken, and the adjacent meeting rooms, where the keynote address could be viewed over closed-circuit televisions, were already filled, too. As the chairman made his welcoming remarks and began his gracious introduction of the evening's special guest speaker, the butterflies that had been fluttering softly all day in Elizabeth's stomach suddenly became frantic.

Relax, she told herself. Almost without motion, she clenched her fists into tight balls, hoping to trap some of the nervous energy there, in the strong isometric contraction, and then letting it dissipate when she released. It was a technique that worked, Elizabeth knew, a most useful technique that she had learned from Stephen. He sat beside her now, sensing her tension, understanding it and smiling at her with reassuring calm. It helped that Stephen was beside her, and it helped, too, that Nick was far away, at the opposite end of the very long front row.

The sound of applause signaled the end of the chairman's introduction. On cue, Elizabeth rose, walked up the seven steps to the massive stage, positioned herself in front of the wooden podium and gazed at a distant place where the faces in the crowd were indistinct and blurred.

"It is a great pleasure for me to be here tonight," she began. They were rote words, mechanically uttered by all anxious speakers to test how much the nervous energy had affected their voices and to give some of the butterflies a chance to escape. She continued with more mechanical words, "If I may have the lights off and the first slide on, please."

The grand ballroom's glittering crystal chandeliers were dimmed in response to her request, shadowing the faces in the front row and casting all those beyond in total darkness. Elizabeth turned to the screen behind her to be certain that the slide that had been projected was the correct one and that it was right side up.

It was, and it was then that the keynote address really began, and after the first few sentences the butterflies flew away, and she was able to relax and simply share with the enraptured audience the fascinating story. Since the story did not involve Elizabeth until its very final chapter, she was able to recount the evolution of the extraordinary technique with reverence and awe, praising the talent and courage of those like Nick whose story it had truly been.

Elizabeth told that story for thirty effortless and enjoyable minutes, and then it was time for her own chapter, beginning with what happened on the festive December afternoon in Union Square.

Suddenly, with no warning whatsoever, all the emotions of that day came back, in powerful waves, flooding her emerald eyes with a hot mist and filling her mind with a swirling torrent of memories that made her completely lose track of what it was she was supposed to say next. Not that she could speak anyway.

No! a coherent thought defiantly protested in the midst of the sudden chaos. This cannot be happening!

Elizabeth had always known how emotional—and sentimental and romantic—she was. There were television commercials that could make her cry, after all, not to mention weddings and novels and movies. And she had always cried for her patients, happy tears and sad ones. But she had always been able to control her emotions when they needed to be controlled—in the hospital, in the operating room, and, not that it had ever happened before, most assuredly during a scientific presentation.

This is a scientific presentation! she silently pleaded with the mind that swirled with images of Justin and Mr. Bear and the courageous and loving man who had been so willing to give his own life to save his son.

Finally an image—a memory—surfaced that enabled her to regain control. It was an image of troubled dark blue eyes and a memory of icy devastation. *Don't care about me, Elizabeth.*

Don't care, don't care . . . the shattering words echoed in her mind, a calming mantra of ice, and at last Elizabeth knew that she would be able to go on.

At last. How long had it been? To Elizabeth, the moments of silent emotion felt like an eternity. But in fact the pause had been quite brief, and to her rapt audience the moment of quiet reverence for the inexplicable tragedy that had befallen the happy four-year-old boy on that holiday afternoon had seemed quite appropriate. Most of the surgeons in the distinguished audience didn't know

419

Elizabeth well enough to catch the sudden break in her voice, and they were too far away to see the slight tremble of her talented hands or the delicate misting of her suddenly confused emerald eyes.

Stephen knew what had happened. In her bewildering moments of helplessness, Elizabeth had looked to him and she had seen in the shadows his concern, but mostly his support, the reassuring smile that was a proud and confident reminder that she could do anything. Stephen knew what had happened, and what about the other man in the front row, the one who on that emotional day had seen in her eyes the deepest truths and secrets of her own loving heart? Nick was much farther away from the podium than Stephen. But still, if he had been looking, he would have been able to see her spotlighted face quite clearly, and if he had been listening, he would have heard the emotion in her voice.

Elizabeth didn't look at Nick during the eternity of emotion. She didn't dare. But when she finally spoke again, having calmed her voice and calmed, *iced,* her heart with the mantra of his devastating words, she cast a look of proud defiance at the shadowy place where she knew he sat—but into which she could not see. And later, as she described with dispassionate calm his alcohol abuse, his inexplicable shock and coma, and the markedly delayed recovery of his liver function, her proud green eyes traveled repeatedly to the shadows where he was hidden.

Elizabeth had filled her heart with ice not emotion, but to the admiring and enraptured audience her voice still held warmth and energy, and the final twenty minutes of the keynote address seemed as smoothly delivered and as compelling as the thirty minutes that had come before. Still, to Elizabeth, every second of those final twenty minutes was an ordeal—trying to concentrate on the speech, yet so wary of the heart that had betrayed her once already and without warning.

But there were no more betrayals, and at the conclusion of the speech, the entire audience stood and applauded until the chairman of the congress finally intervened and formally adjourned the evening's stunningly successful session. After that, the stage where Elizabeth still stood became crowded with doctors who wanted to both compliment her and ask her specific questions.

Normally, feeling relieved that a talk was over and a little euphoric that it had gone well, Elizabeth would have enjoyed the opportunity for informal dialogue with her colleagues. But now, even though this speech had been a success, she felt exhausted—and precarious. She needed privacy. And somehow she needed to get off the crowded stage and to the much-needed private place without encountering Nick. That was going to be difficult. Nick stood between her and escape, surrounded as she was by a wall of interested surgeons, but even across the distance that separated them, Elizabeth sensed the intense heat of the dark blue eyes that kept drifting to her, searching and demanding.

It was Stephen who rescued her.

"I'm sorry, Elizabeth, but we do have dinner reservations. We really should go now."

"Oh! We are late, aren't we?" she asked as she glanced at her watch. Then, smiling warmly but apologetically, she said truthfully to those who still had questions, "I'll be at the sessions for the next four days. We'll have more time to talk then."

Nick was still surrounded. Elizabeth felt his eyes follow her as she and Stephen whisked by, but she didn't turn to meet them.

* * *

They didn't have dinner reservations, of course, and Elizabeth could have perfectly well forgone food altogether and simply escaped to her suite or taken a long solitary walk through Paris. But Stephen insisted both on food and on his own nonthreatening and nonintrusive companionship.

"Your talk was wonderful," he said when they were seated in a cafe on Boulevard St. Germain in the Latin Quarter.

"If you choose to forget those unprofessional moments of pure emotion."

"Which most people didn't even know were happening, but which, if they did know, could only enhance their respect for you. Any surgeon who didn't understand the extraordinary emotion of that day—and who wouldn't have felt it too—shouldn't be practicing medicine."

"Spoken like a true internist. But you know surgeons, Stephen. I've probably set women, especially women surgeons, back two thousand years."

"At least two thousand," Stephen agreed with a smile.

"Do you think Nick realized what happened?"

"I don't know. I was looking at you, not at him."

"I know," Elizabeth answered softly, her voice filling with gratitude for his support. "Nick probably did realize what happened, and he's probably furious about it."

"Furious?"

"It was his keynote address, which he gave to me to give, and even though you and I believe that emotion is an acceptable ingredient for a doctor, the fact is that this was a very important scientific presentation."

"You think Nick could have talked about the gunshot wound to his son without a flicker of emotion?" Stephen asked. "You know I've never been Nick's greatest fan, Elizabeth, but I was there on that day in December and I don't for a second doubt his love for his son."

"No," Elizabeth admitted. "I don't think Nick could have talked with cool scientific detachment about that day. But he obviously knew that, Stephen. That, in addition to the fact that I was the one who had done the surgery, may have been why he asked me to give the speech." She sighed. "Well, anyway, what happened happened."

"What happened, Doctor Jennings, was a sensational keynote address."

The message light was blinking on the wall of her suite when Elizabeth returned from dinner with Stephen.

"Doctor Chase requests that you call him," the operator told her. "Extension seven sixteen. Shall I connect you?"

"No," Elizabeth replied swiftly. "No, *merci*."

She didn't want to talk to Nick no matter why he was calling—not if he was calling because he liked her talk, and most certainly not if he was calling to express his disappointment in her lack of professionalism.

"I think I'll take a nice long shower and go to bed," she announced to the hotel's elegant notepaper on which, as the operator had given her the message she had written, "Nick" and "716" and "No!"

"I love you, Justin."

"I love you, too, Daddy."

"I'll talk to you tomorrow, okay?"

"Okay."

"Good. May I speak to Margaret again for a minute?"

"Sure. 'Bye, Daddy."

" 'Bye, Jussie." A moment later, when Margaret was on the line again, Nick said, "He sounds fine."

"He is, Nick," Margaret assured. "We're doing just fine. Couldn't you tell?"

"Yes," Nick admitted. He had talked to his son for almost thirty minutes, a conversation in which Justin had excitedly told him the events of his day and during which Nick had detected no undue worry that he was far away. In the weeks before the trip, Nick had told Justin all about Paris, and they had found it on the map, and just as with the hospital and all the other cities to which Nick had needed to travel in the past few years, he had shared Paris with his son, making it seem close and familiar, not far away and unknown.

"How was Elizabeth's keynote address?"

Nick frowned as he remembered but answered truthfully, "It was wonderful."

"I'm not surprised." Margaret wanted to embellish— "Elizabeth is wonderful"—but she knew that that was nothing Nick didn't already know; and she knew also not to intrude on the very private decisions that he had made. "Well, you have a hungry son, so he and I are going to make something for dinner. Please give my best to Elizabeth."

Give my best to Elizabeth. Margaret's words echoed in Nick's mind after the call ended. He himself had given his best to Elizabeth: the gentle warning to her not to care about him.

That was the greatest gift he could give her, distance from him, so that she could find someone far better and far more whole to love, but this evening Nick had learned that Elizabeth hadn't heeded his gentle warning. And worse, she hadn't truly understood it. He had seen the hurt in her bewildered emerald eyes as she had struggled with her emotions. It was the same hurt that he had seen on Christmas Eve . . . and the same hurt he saw night after night in his nightmares—the anguished emerald belief that he didn't really love her.

Nick frowned at his watch. It was almost midnight. No blinking light signaled that Elizabeth had tried to return his call while he was talking to Justin. Perhaps she and Stephen were still strolling the streets of Paris. Needing to know, Nick dialed the operator. *Non, monsieur,* no messages for you, he was told. Ah, *mais oui, mademoiselle le docteur* did receive your message about an hour ago.

After her shower, Elizabeth dressed in her nightgown and robe, sat in a plush chair by the window, and gazed at the sparkling glitter of the City of Light as she thought about the evening—and about Nick's call. Her speech had, on balance, been very good. Stephen had convinced her of that and she herself knew that it was true. The turmoil had been inside her, hidden from everyone except Stephen, who knew her best. Nick probably hadn't even noticed. He was probably calling, as her boss, to tell her that she had done well.

Fine, Elizabeth thought, nonetheless pressing herself even deeper into the plush chair. Whatever it was, criticism or praise, Nick could tell her tomorrow morning. There would be many different scientific sessions running concurrently, but Elizabeth guessed that she and Nick would very likely attend the same ones, those most relevant to their shared areas of research and expertise.

Tomorrow she would run into Nick, and he would tell her, in the midst of a crush of surgeons, why he had called.

The ringing phone shattered Elizabeth's plan.

"It's Nick, Elizabeth. Did I waken you?" Dr. Nicholas Chase had awakened Dr. Elizabeth Jennings many times during the past year, when he and his patient needed her immense talent, and not once in all those late-night calls had he apologized for disturbing her. But those calls had been professional, and this call was personal, so now his voice held a soft note of apology for the intrusion.

"No. I'm awake."

"May I come see you?"

"Now?"

"Yes. I know it's late." Nick stopped abruptly, then continued, "And you're not alone. I'm very sorry to have—"

"I'm alone, Nick."

"Then, may I? We need to talk, Elizabeth."

His words sounded ominous . . . but his voice was so very gentle.

"All right."

"Thank you. I'm on my way."

Wait, I'm not dressed! The thought came after they had hung up and Nick was already on his way the short distance from his suite to hers. But this bulky bathrobe is far more modest than the pajamalike surgical scrubs he has seen me in so often. And the shower-damp dark curls and freshly scrubbed makeup-free face? It doesn't matter what I look like! Nick has seen me look as good as I possibly can look, and he has seen me after exhausting hours of grueling surgery and no sleep.

And, besides, it doesn't matter, remember?

Chapter Thirty-two

Elizabeth's luxurious suite had plush chairs and cozy conversation areas. But still, after opening the door to her midnight visitor and silently leading the way to the elegant living room, she didn't even offer a chair to him. Instead, she just stopped in the center of the room and turned to face him, her slender body stiff and wary beneath her bulky robe, her emerald eyes proud and defiant.

Nick stood a few feet away, a polite and careful distance, his body stiff and wary, too; but his troubled dark blue eyes were neither defiant nor proud . . . they were only very gentle.

"We need to talk about what happened tonight during your address, and about what happened on Christmas Eve."

"Christmas Eve?"

"When I told you not to care about me. You told me then that you understood why you shouldn't care—but, Elizabeth, I don't think that you do."

"Because you don't care about me," she whispered softly, bravely to the gentle blue eyes.

"But I do care about you."

427

"Because you don't love me," she said even more softly, and more bravely.

"Oh, but I do love you, Elizabeth."

I do love you, Elizabeth. The wondrous truth of his words was eloquently conveyed by the exquisite gentleness of his voice . . . and it was embellished even further by the tenderness in his loving blue eyes. Elizabeth's heart raced with pure joy as she whispered, "You really do love me."

"Yes," Nick told the shimmering emerald. "I really do love you. I have loved you for a very long time."

"And from very far away," she said quietly to the man who loved her, and had loved her for a very long time, but who had always kept such a careful distance from her—and who was keeping that distance still. "Why, Nick?"

"Because I knew that our love was impossible."

The tenderly spoken words were as devastating now as his troubled warning not to care about him had been on Christmas Eve. On that night, Elizabeth had quickly drawn her own shattering conclusion about the reason for his warning—that he didn't really love her—and had escaped swiftly from him. Tonight she would let Nick tell her the reason for his devastating words.

But she was trembling now, and she couldn't bare to watch his gentle yet so resolute dark blue eyes tell her why their love could not be—so she turned away from him, and, increasing the distance between them even more, she stood in the alcove where she had been sitting when he had called.

"Is it because of Justin?" she asked finally as she stared out into the glittering winter night.

"Because of Justin?" Nick echoed. Had Elizabeth been looking at him she would have seen his surprise—and his absolute confidence that she would have been a wonderful mother for the little boy who already loved her. "No,

Elizabeth, not because of Justin. Because of me. I think you've somehow forgotten what you know about me, about my drinking . . . and that I once abandoned my son."

"I know that you used to drink, Nick," she countered softly. "And I know that you love Justin more than life itself."

Nick hadn't followed her into the shadows until then, but now he did, standing behind her, keeping a safe distance still, but one across which his words could be quiet and gentle.

"The alcoholism doesn't go away, Elizabeth, even if the alcohol does. I drank to escape from a pain and emptiness deep inside me. I'm not drinking anymore, but the pain and emptiness are there still."

"Because of your childhood."

"Yes. It's not a mystery. I don't know if I was ever loved as a child. If so, I have no memory of it. What I do know is that my mother slashed her wrists when I was three—and my demanding, perfectionistic, alcoholic father blamed me for her suicide."

She wanted to turn to him, to hold him and love him, but Elizabeth forced herself to gaze still at the winter sky. "But you couldn't have believed that, Nick!"

"I was three years old, Elizabeth, and he was my father. I spent my entire childhood being unloved and being told that I was undeserving of love—with my mother's suicide as vivid proof. I know now, of course, as an adult and a parent myself, that I was not to blame for her death. And I know that my father was a monster. But all the knowledge and insight in the world doesn't mean that I can change how that time was lived, or what happened because of it. The wounds will always be there . . . as will the emptiness. I didn't even know about the emptiness until

Justin—and you—but now I understand what's been missing inside me for all these years."

"What's that, Nick?" Elizabeth spoke softly to the winter sky, even though her gentle question was really for Nick's deeply wounded heart. She knew he would have an answer to her question. It was obvious that what he was revealing to her now had been discovered by the bright mind which, in search of the truth about his own pain, had forced itself to make repeated journeys into those deep and anguished wounds. "What's missing?"

"A feeling of joyfulness," Nick answered with quiet and solemn confidence. "An inner core of happiness. You have it, Elizabeth, and somehow, despite the first six months of his life, Justin has it too. It had been almost lost when he came to me, but the ember was still there and with love and nurturing he became happy and hopeful. I suppose I was born with an innocent joyfulness, the potential for it anyway, but it was never nurtured—and now it's simply not there."

"But I see such joy and happiness when you're with Justin, Nick." *And, when you've permitted it, I've seen joy and happiness in your eyes with me.*

"It's *his* joy and *his* happiness, Elizabeth. It all comes from him, but it spills over to me, filling the emptiness inside." *Just as, my beautiful Elizabeth, when I'm with you my emptiness is filled—overflowing.* "I have no joy or happiness of my own to give back. I have nothing to give—except unhappiness."

Like the moon, Elizabeth thought as she gazed at the golden-white ball in the winter sky. It looked like glittering fire, but it was all reflected light, its golden glow a brilliant kiss from the sparkling sun, its black scars and empty craters brightly lighted by the fiery star. Nick believed that he was like the moon, icy and black without the sun's reflected brilliance, but he was so very wrong!

"Justin isn't unhappy, Nick. You have given him so much love . . . and you would have given him your life."

"I've known what to give Justin—all the things that were missing from my childhood. He would be better off with another father, but he doesn't have that choice, and he's been very lucky to have had Margaret."

"He's been very lucky to have had you."

"Justin would be better off with someone else," Nick repeated softly. And then, even more softly, he said, "And, Elizabeth, so would you. That's what I came here to tell you tonight, to make sure that you understand."

"I do understand," she answered, turning at last, because at last she truly did understand. She gazed at the loving blue eyes of the man who had made painful journeys into his own heart and knew a great deal about its wounds and its scars—but so very little else about the rest of it—and said bravely, "I understand that you love me . . . and that I love you . . . and that that's all that matters."

"No, Elizabeth," he whispered to the glowing emerald. "That's not all that matters."

"It's all that matters now, Nick. Right now, in this private place, it's all that matters."

Nick knew that he should have left. But how could he? He had wanted her so much for so long, and now her radiant emerald eyes told him that she had wanted him too, so much for so long. And they had almost lost each other once, almost lost the chance to ever share the truths of their hearts . . . and now they could show each other those joyful truths, sharing with each other all that they could share.

"Oh, Elizabeth." His hands touched her flushed cheeks then, and then tenderly, and with such loving wonder, cradled her beautiful face. "Do you know how much I have wanted to touch you, to feel your lovely softness, your wonderful warmth?"

"Nick," she whispered shakily, trembling from his words, from his touch, and from her own wondrous desires.

Her delicate trembling fingers reached for him then, touching his handsome face with the gentle caress of a whispered kiss, feeling even with that gossamer-gentle touch the strength that lay deep within him—and the fire. As she gazed at the dark blue eyes that smoldered with such passion and such desire—and such love—Elizabeth's heart sent a brave promise to his, *The ember of joyfulness, the deep golden glow of love* is *inside you, Nick. I can see it and feel it. It's there, and through our wonderful love you will discover it and believe in it too. I know you will.*

Long before this night of love, their talented fingers had danced together with graceful beauty. Now that magnificent dance of grace and beauty was joyously joined by their hearts and their bodies and their souls. And if the sensuous blue-eyed surgeon had an expert technique for making love, he didn't use it for loving Elizabeth. Theirs was a loving created just for each other, never rehearsed nor practiced before, created together from every gift each had to give, all joyful trust, all brave desire, all unashamed passion.

And when it was time for them to become one, the intense dark blue eyes held the gaze of the shimmering emerald ones as she welcomed him . . . and for a wondrous and astonishing moment neither of them could speak, or breathe, or move . . . and then, just before their crescendoing desires urgently commanded them to resume again their magnificent dance of love, they whispered, together, "I love you."

Elizabeth didn't want to sleep. She wanted to lie forever in his arms, feeling his heart beat against hers. But she needed to sleep, they both did, so finally she succumbed to the wonder of falling asleep in his strong and gentle arms.

Nick didn't want to sleep, even after he felt the change in her breathing that signaled she was asleep, perhaps even dreaming. Nick didn't want to leave this joyous wide-awake dream of holding her, not ever, and he most assuredly didn't want to leave it for the nightmares that he knew awaited him once his conscious mind relinquished its control to the slumbering demons that lived within.

But finally Nick fell asleep too, and on that night, after he had made love to Elizabeth and while he held her in his arms as together they slept, Nicholas Chase had no nightmares.

Elizabeth awakened first, and for a while she simply gazed at his beloved face. She saw such peace, a peace that hadn't been there before, not even when he had been in the deepest sleep of coma. The bedside clock told her that it was almost seven-thirty. She needed to get up, to gently and carefully free herself from his loving arms . . .

"Good morning," he whispered, his just-opened dark blue eyes already filled with love.

"Good morning," she echoed softly. "I was trying not to wake you. Stephen's talk is in an hour and I told him I would be there. He's leaving right afterward for Vienna."

"I'd like to hear his talk, too," Nick said, gently touch-

433

ing her cheek, a caress of wonder—and disbelief. He had awakened from a sleep without nightmares . . . and now once again he was living this magnificent dream. "I'll go shower and change and meet you downstairs."

Elizabeth arrived at the lecture hall before Nick, put her sweater on one chair and her notebook on the one beside it, then walked to the front of the hall to speak to Stephen.

"Hi. All set?"

"All set. Slides in order, podium lights figured out." Stephen stopped, stared at her, and asked, "What happened to you?"

"Happened?"

"You look . . ." As Stephen paused to search for the right description—radiantly beautiful, sparklingly joyous—he watched the radiant and sparkling emerald travel to Nick who had just entered the room. And then Stephen saw what perhaps no one in the world—except Elizabeth—had ever seen before: what pure happiness looked like on the handsome face of Nicholas Chase. Nick's progress toward them was stopped by a colleague from the Pasteur Institute who wanted to speak to him, so Stephen said quietly, "I guess I know what happened."

"Don't look so worried!"

"Just be careful, Elizabeth."

"I'm not afraid of Nick, Stephen. I never have been."

"I know. It's just that you—one—can be so easily fooled about love, misreading the other's feelings because you want so desperately to have them reflect your own." Remembering the pure happiness in Nick's dark blue eyes, Stephen admitted, "I'm obviously talking about myself, Elizabeth, not you. You know that I want this to work out for you."

"I know."

"Just be careful."

"I will," she promised, even though she knew it wasn't true.

It was far too late to be careful.

For the next three days and nights Elizabeth and Nick were together, sitting beside each other at all the scientific meetings, touching gently as they listened and took careful notes; and they wandered through Paris, discovering its romance and enchantment together; and Nick made his nightly calls to Justin from her suite; and then they went to bed, loving each other more and more every time.

Nick had willed himself to be just well enough—to *look* just well enough—to make an appearance at the congress in Paris. But in Paris, in love with Elizabeth, his strength truly and wondrously returned. His wounded body was finally healed and even his soul seemed stronger, because with her in his arms neither his nightmares nor the screams of pain that haunted him by day dared to intrude.

Nick was basking in the radiant glow of Elizabeth's sunshine, enveloped by the warm golden aura that shimmered around her. And the fountain of joy that danced deep within her overflowed to him, magically filling all the empty places in his heart with happiness, and there were even times when he felt surprising rushes that almost seemed to come from within *him,* as if a tiny ember of innocent joyfulness had defiantly survived the darkness of his childhood after all. But Nick knew that no such ember truly existed within him. It was just Elizabeth, *her* contagious happiness, *her* pervasive optimism and hope. She was giving, and he was taking, and . . .

On Thursday morning, a few hours before he would

board the flight to San Francisco and she would make the brief over the channel voyage to spend a few days with her parents in London, Nick made love to Elizabeth for the last time. And she sensed in his fierce tenderness and the exquisiteness of his passion that it was a goodbye that was far more desperate and far-reaching than the brief separation that was about to begin. And when he whispered a final "I love you" before reluctantly separating himself from her, Elizabeth felt as if her heart had been torn in two.

She watched in silence as he dressed. When he was buttoning his shirt, and she feared he was about to leave, she sat up, clutching the covers to her, concealing the nakedness that had been so unashamed and so joyous for the wondrous days and nights of their loving.

"Nick?"

"I love you with all my heart . . . such as it is," he said quietly, not turning to face her as he spoke. "But I know it's not enough."

"But it is!" she cried with soft despair. And then, even more softly and with even more despair, she asked, "Or have you decided in the past three days that you don't really love me, after all?"

Nick turned to her then, and when her eyes met his he solemnly told the lovely emerald, "Don't ever think that, Elizabeth."

"What else can I think, Nick?"

"What I told you on Christmas Eve and again on Sunday night—that I have nothing but unhappiness to give you." He gazed at eyes that were so unhappy now— proof of his words!—and yet seemed so defiantly disbelieving. After a moment he added quietly, "And what I told you the day Danny died—that alcoholism is a disease you don't give to anyone else. You keep it to yourself, where it belongs." The unhappy emerald was defiant, disbelieving, still. "Oh, Elizabeth, I thought you understood. It's too risky, too dangerous . . ."

"I do understand. I understand the danger and I'm willing to take the risk."

"But I'm not willing to let you take that risk."

The love and joy and desire that had filled the dark blue eyes for the past three days and nights of love were gone now, replaced by the once-so-familiar cool and distant politeness. Cool, distant, polite . . . and so resolute.

Nicholas Chase had made his decision.

"So what are we going to do, Nick?" Elizabeth asked, her words flowing on a sudden raging river of anger. "Operate together forever? Spend a few midnight hours of passion together once in a while?"

"I'm not going to return to the medical center," he answered quietly. "I'm going to find a position somewhere else."

"*No,*" Elizabeth countered swiftly. "If one of us is going to leave, I want it to be me. It's something I've been thinking about for quite a while anyway—because of you; and thanks to the historic surgery that you manipulated me into doing—because you knew how much I loved you—I'm really in great demand. It would be difficult for me to work in a place haunted by memories of you, but I imagine it wouldn't be the least bit difficult for you. You're the expert at sealing off your emotions and burying them deep beside all your other scars."

"Elizabeth . . ."

"I want to be the one who leaves, Nick," she said with sudden calm. Then, calm still, as if they were simply discussing the details of the on-call schedule, she asked, "Do you still anticipate that you'll be able to return to work on June first?"

437

"Yes."

"All right. Well, then, May thirty-first will be my last day." The calm evaporated then. It had been only an illusion, the deceptively tranquil eye of a raging storm. The anger was back, but now it dressed her voice in an unfamiliar cloak of flippancy and sarcasm. "This was *nice*, Nick! You're a terrific lover, just like everyone always said you were. Maybe we can do it again sometime. Our paths are bound to cross again and again at meetings. Of course, perhaps one day you will appear with a wife, having discovered that you aren't fatally flawed after all, that your famous dark side is just a shadowy illusion, easily vanquished by love. Or maybe I'll be the one who marries. Surely there's a man out there for me somewhere, someone with no secrets, no torments, no pain whatsoever. That's what you want for me, don't you? A teetotaler with rose-colored glasses, a cockeyed optimist just like me?"

"I want you to be happy, Elizabeth," Nick answered with quiet despair, loving her so much and so enraged with himself for hurting her. "You deserve happiness."

"Because I had a happy childhood? I'm not to blame for the luxury and privilege of having had a safe and loving childhood—just as you aren't to blame that yours was unspeakably awful." Elizabeth gave her head a soft bewildered shake and when she spoke again her voice was sad and thoughtful. "Because of your love, Justin's childhood will be as happy as mine was. In twenty or thirty years, when he falls in love with a woman who is troubled from something she didn't cause and can't change are you going to tell him to simply forget about her? To find someone who, through sheer luck, had a happy childhood too? I don't think that's the way love works, Nick." She paused, and then said very quietly, "It's certainly not the advice I plan to give our child."

"Our child?"

Elizabeth hadn't been careful, not with her heart or with her body, not with Nick; and Nick, who had always been so compulsive about birth control, hadn't been careful either, not with Elizabeth.

And now Elizabeth spoke the cruel words to hurt him, because he had hurt her so terribly, but when she saw the anguish in his tormented blue eyes, she assured quickly, and truthfully, "We haven't been using any protection, Nick, but I won't have gotten pregnant. My period is due to begin tomorrow and it will, I can already feel it."

As Nick stared at her, Elizabeth saw the full dark blue measure of the pain he had always hidden as carefully as he had hidden the love. She wanted to rush to him, to hold him and love him, but the icy blue warned her away.

"I'm sorry, Elizabeth," he whispered finally, his voice hoarse with emotion. "I'm so very sorry."

Then Nick was gone, and Elizabeth didn't know whether he was sorry that they couldn't live their love forever . . . or that they had had even these few magical days and nights of love . . . or that she wouldn't be having his child.

Elizabeth didn't know very much when Nick left her. But the next evening in England, when she began to bleed right on cue, she knew that she was not carrying Nick's baby; and as she visited her own loving parents, she knew that she would try very hard to convince her broken heart that what Nick had done had been a noble gift of love, that he loved her deeply and truly believed it was best for her to live without him.

But with each passing moment, Elizabeth knew that

her weeping heart would not be convinced. How could it be convinced of the gentle lie when it knew so clearly the painful truth? Nick simply had neither loved her enough, nor trusted her love enough, to have even wanted to try.

Elizabeth knew with certainty that her shattered heart would not be convinced . . . but she had no idea how it was going to survive the agonizing truth.

Part

Six

Chapter Thirty-three

San Francisco
February 1992

Stephen drove directly from the airport to Christine's house on Twin Peaks. She wasn't expecting him, of course. He hadn't spoken to her in two weeks, not since their good-night kiss on Valentine's Day. Now it was the last Friday in February, and as far as she knew he wasn't due back from Europe until late Sunday. But from the moment of his arrival in Paris, Stephen had begun consolidating his schedule of commitments, fulfilling them all in two days less than originally planned.

Now he was back in San Francisco, and soon he would be gazing at the lovely lavender eyes as Christine told him the truth—whatever it was; and even though in the past two weeks he had been unable to find even one hopeful explanation for why she had hidden Colin Gallagher from him, Stephen's heart set a new pace in anticipation of seeing her again. But when he reached Twin Peaks and turned the final familiar corner onto City View Drive, his heart almost stopped.

In front of Christine's house was a large truck. He

watched in stunned sadness as two men loaded Christine's bed—Christine and David's bed—into the van to join the rest of her furniture. Christine was leaving. Now. Today. If he had returned as scheduled on Sunday, she would have been long gone.

She's probably already gone, Stephen thought as the loaded van sputtered away. Still, he parked his car a short distance from the house and gazed at it through the mist of raindrops that now wept from the gray February sky. The front door of the house was closed, and even though the stormy afternoon had been quite dark before the rain began, there were no lights on inside.

Then he saw it—a glitter of gold in the shadowy darkness. Christine was there still. A final check of doors and windows, Stephen supposed, and the final closing of suitcases. And perhaps, a final goodbye to the house where she and David had lived the love that had been enough to last a lifetime . . .

Even though tears blurred Christine's vision as she wandered slowly through the small house for the last time, the memories she saw in each room were very clear. She lingered for a long time in each room, embracing the wonderful memories of love before bidding them a gentle farewell. And even though her journey was slow and lingering, eventually there was only one room left . . . the bedroom . . . where they had shared their hearts and their souls . . . and where they had created the precious new life . . . and where David had died . . . and where just a few hours later that precious new life had died, too, following David to his death as Christine herself had wanted so desperately to do. She had wanted to follow, but she had had debts to pay—and promises to keep. It was in the

444

bedroom where David had held her tenderly before his death and made her promise to go on with her life, to find new happiness, new dreams, and new love. Christine had promised, gentle lies of love, but now, unbelievably, she was keeping those promises.

Christine finally bid farewell to the bedroom, and when she reached the front door, before opening and closing it for the last time, she whispered softly through her tears, "Goodbye, David. Goodbye, my love."

Then Christine Andrews left the protective cloak of memories and walked outside to begin her new life. A life, she discovered, that was going to begin in a torrential downpour. Had it been any other day, Christine would have dashed the two blocks to the sheltered bus stop, or simply gone back inside the house to wait for the cloudburst to pass. But today she could not return to the sanctuary of the place to which she had already said her loving goodbye, nor could she run away from it.

So she walked, slow deliberate steps, not a hasty retreat, amid raindrops and tears.

Stephen watched as Christine walked away from her house, her slender body straight and proud, her golden hair a bright glittering beacon in the storm-dark gray. She wore a raincoat, but carried only a purse and no luggage. The rest of her clothes and luggage were already elsewhere, Stephen assumed. The airport, probably, at the hotel where she would stay until her flight to New York.

Christine hadn't noticed his car, and now she was bravely and proudly walking away from him—and toward her dreams. But Stephen couldn't let her go without talking to her. Getting out of his car and into the rainstorm, his long graceful strides quickly brought him close enough to her to call to her.

"Christine?"

"Stephen," she whispered as she turned to him, startled, and then hopeful, and then aching. The thoughts from which his voice had pulled her had been thoughts about the courageous and hopeful choices she had made . . . and when she had turned she was suddenly face to face with the most courageous hope of all . . . and what she saw made her heart ache. Stephen was back two days early, but his dark eyes didn't send the joyous message that his early return had been because he had missed her.

"Let me drive you wherever you're going, Christine," he said quietly. "I'd like to talk to you."

They didn't talk at all during the three-mile drive from Twin Peaks to the destination Christine had given him—the corner of Lincoln and Twenty-first, across the street from Golden Gate Park. The Friday afternoon traffic was already heavy, and, because of the slick streets and pelting rain, it was also treacherous. Stephen needed to concentrate on his driving, and he forced himself to, even though he was so very aware of her tense body and the tense, awkward silence that traveled with them.

"It's that building there," Christine said, quietly breaking the silence as she gestured to a four-story red-brick apartment. "We can talk inside, if you like."

Stephen was able to park quite close to the building's entrance, but nonetheless their already damp hair got an extra layer of raindrops; and when they were inside the third-floor apartment to which Christine had a key and she reached to take his rain-drenched coat, she asked, "Would you like a towel for your hair?"

"Yes, I guess so. Thank you." He was only vaguely aware of the cold drops that spilled from his own rain-damp hair, but he was very aware of the ones that fell from the glistening spun gold onto her sad and lovely face, caressing it like dewdrops on roses.

Roses. As Christine disappeared to get the towels, Stephen looked at the unfamiliar surroundings—the white wicker furniture, the delicate porcelain lamps, the cheerful pastel pillows. Everything was unfamiliar *except* the bouquet of cream-colored roses on the white wicker coffee table. They were the rosebuds he had given her on Valentine's Day, fully opened now and beautiful still.

The roses he had given her were all that was familiar. The roses . . . and then Christine's shy smile, offered in hopeful response to the very gentle smile that greeted her when she returned with the two plush towels.

"Where are we, Christine?" he asked softly.

"In my new apartment. Well, it's not really new, and it's not really mine. I only have it as a sublet until the first week of May, but that will give me time to find someplace else."

"A place in New York."

"In New York? No . . ."

"You're not moving to New York to work with Colin Gallagher?"

"No." She tilted her damp golden head. "How did you know about that?"

"I stopped by the boutique the morning I left for Paris. Sydney told me. I've spent the past two weeks wondering why you didn't mention it to me." *Wondering, worrying, unable to find an explanation that wouldn't shatter my dreams.* Stephen looked gently at the lavender eyes that were going to save his wonderful dream after all and asked, "Why didn't you mention the job to me?"

"Because I knew I wasn't going to accept it. I told Colin that when he first called, but he insisted on flying out to try to get me to change my mind anyway."

"But he couldn't? It sounded like an extraordinary opportunity."

"Yes, but this," she said, gesturing gracefully to the new apartment, "is as much of a move as I want to make now." She looked up to his gentle brown eyes and asked bravely, "Why did you come to Sydney's that morning?"

"Because I wanted to see you again before I left. I wanted to talk to you about our kiss."

"Our kiss?"

"I wanted you to know that I understood your confusion and that there was no hurry."

"But you didn't regret kissing me?"

"Oh, no, Christine, I didn't regret kissing you. In fact, I've spent the past two weeks worrying that I would never get to kiss you again."

"And I've been worrying that you wouldn't want to."

"I want to. I will always want to," he added softly, searching for alarm in the lovely lavender and seeing only happiness—and raindrops.

He took the plush towels that she still held and gently dried her beautiful rain-damp face and glistening golden hair. And then, as he cradled her face in his hands, his dark eyes grew very solemn with desire, and he kissed her . . . and she kissed him back . . . and the kiss held all the wondrous promise of their first kiss, but it was warmer and hungrier and deeper than before, and more confident, and not at all confused.

Until Christine pulled away. In the startled instant before Stephen's eyes found hers, he felt a tremor of ice.

But the lavender that greeted him glowed with pure and shimmering joy.

"Come to the bedroom, Stephen."

The bed was new, as were the quilted mauve comforter and lacy ivory pillows. There was nothing old or familiar in Christine's bedroom. Nothing at all, Stephen thought, realizing then that he hadn't seen it in the living room and in his subconscious mind had concluded that it would be in here.

But it wasn't.

"Where's the portrait?" he asked quietly.

Christine let go of his hand then and moved away from him, just a little, before answering.

"I gave it to the art museum. They were thrilled, of course, and I know their enthusiasm would have pleased David very much." A thoughtful frown touched her lovely face as she added softly, almost to herself, "And I think he would have understood."

"Understood?" Stephen echoed gently. He saw a flicker of confusion then, as if this wasn't something she had planned to discuss with him, as if she didn't think it had a place in their love. But it did. "I want to make love to you, Christine, you must know how much I want that. But we need to talk first. You've made some very important decisions—and changes—in the past two weeks."

"Yes. But they weren't impulsive decisions, Stephen, and I don't regret any of them." She looked bravely into his loving dark eyes. "I wanted us to have a place without memories, a place where we could make our own memories."

Oh, Christine. Stephen's heart wanted him to go to her now, to hold her and love her and begin to make their

449

own wonderful memories—but his mind wouldn't allow it, not yet.

"But the memories are inside you," he said, wondering what was compelling him to force an issue for which there was no simple resolution. He didn't want Christine to forget David, of course, or to in any way diminish that extraordinary love. And yet . . . he was about to give her all of his heart—no, she already had it—and perhaps he needed to know how great a risk he was taking. "The memories of David will always be inside you."

"Yes," she agreed. Then, as she looked at his loving dark eyes, she asked with soft surprise, "Are you afraid of my memories of David?"

"I guess I am."

"I'm afraid, too, but not of my memories." It was a small confession compared to the one she made next. "I'm afraid of losing you, Stephen, not of loving you."

"Oh, Christine." He couldn't promise that a tragedy wouldn't some day steal him from her, they both knew that, but there was one promise of love that Stephen could make. "I love you, Christine. I will always love you."

"And I will always love you, too, Stephen." And then, as he was about to begin a tender kiss that would take them to her romantic quilted bed and she saw a flicker of worry that told her he knew that she had never been with any man but David, Christine reminded him softly, "I'm not afraid of loving you."

There was no fear in their loving, only joy and tenderness and desire and love, and afterward Stephen held her lovely nakedness against him, his lips caressing her passion-tangled golden hair as he spoke.

450

"Did you say no to Colin Gallagher because you didn't think I would want to move to New York?"

"I knew from Madolyn that you had wanted her to stay here."

"What?"

"She told me that you loved her and—"

"I never loved Madolyn, Christine. I've never loved anyone but you." His lips found hers, and he told her again, showed her again, warmly, deeply, lingering far longer than he had intended to . . . because there were more words, important words, that needed to be said. Finally, reluctantly, he stopped the kiss and suggested, "Why don't you call Colin and tell him yes?"

"I want to stay here, Stephen. I don't care about being famous and I like having the freedom to design only the kind of dresses I want to design."

"Romantic dresses."

"Yes."

"Well," Stephen began softly, moving a golden strand from her eyes so that he could see the lovely lavender as he spoke. "The prom dress you made was wonderful, but I would very much like to see what you could do with a wedding dress."

"You would?"

"Only if you were the bride. Will you, Christine?" he asked gently of the eyes that had already given him their joyous answer. "Will you design a wedding dress and wear it at our wedding?"

"Oh, yes, Stephen. Of course I will."

Chapter Thirty-four

San Francisco
April 1992

"Nick, it's Larisa. I need to see you."

"Okay," Nick answered, surprised that she was calling but detecting a note of urgency in her voice that made him agree to her request without questioning it. "When?"

"Now, if possible."

Now was ten P.M. on Wednesday, April twenty-second. Justin was asleep and Margaret was reading and Nick had been just about to leave for a run. He could run again now, and in the two months since he had left Elizabeth his need to run had increased with each passing moment.

"Now is fine, Larisa. Where?"

"Can you come here?"

"To your apartment?" *To Elizabeth's apartment?*

"Yes. We'll be alone. Elizabeth just got called in for a major trauma. I guess you've never been here, have you? It's only about six blocks from your house . . ."

* * *

In Paris, when Elizabeth had told him about Larisa's love for Peter, she had also told him that she believed that Larisa had become even more beautiful with that love. And now, as Larisa opened the apartment door to him, Nick saw that it was true. She looked more beautiful than ever, radiant and hopeful, her cheeks flushed a rosy pink and her silky golden red hair caressed by the most brilliant of fires. There was fire, too, in her flashing bright blue eyes. Fire *and* ice.

"Come in, Nick. Would you like a drink? A little Scotch, perhaps?"

"No." *Yes.* "Would you?"

"No." Larisa could drink now, a glass of champagne to celebrate with Peter would be quite safe for her; but she didn't drink, not a drop, because it would not be safe for the magnificent miracle of love that was growing inside her. A lovely smile began to touch her lips as she thought about her baby, but Larisa blocked the wonderful thought and its smile and cast a brilliant ice-blue glare directly at Nick.

"What's wrong, Larisa?"

"What did you do to her?"

"I beg your pardon?"

"What did you do to my friend?"

"What did she tell you that I did?"

"Nothing!" Larisa exclaimed with obvious frustration. "Elizabeth says nothing happened, but I *know* that's not true. Something happened between the two of you in Paris, Nick, and whatever it was, it—*you*—hurt her terribly."

"I never wanted to hurt her."

"Well, you have. She won't admit it, of course. It turns out that when I get hurt—or betrayed—I get very weak and needy and look for ways to float far away from the pain. But when Elizabeth Jennings is hurt or betrayed she simply turns to steel. She's stronger than ever, working harder than ever. . . ." Larisa looked at the dark blue eyes that were obviously deeply troubled by what she was saying and repeated, more gently this time, "What did you do to her?"

"I told her the truth, Larisa. I told her that I loved her, and that I knew our love was impossible. She deserves far better than me."

"Oh, Nick."

"You know it's true, Larisa. You know enough about me to know—"

"That you're beyond redemption?"

"No," Nick answered quietly. "I was redeemed by my son."

And I have been redeemed by this hopeful innocent life inside me, Larisa thought, and by the wonderful love of my miracle baby's father. It was a joyous thought, and yet a shiver of ice suddenly passed through her, a twirl of an icy ghost that would not die, a reminder that she had loved and trusted before only to be brutally betrayed. But not this time. Go away, ghost! Peter would never betray me.

Larisa gazed for a long thoughtful moment at the man who was so nobly and so resolutely denying himself Elizabeth's wonderful love. Finally she said, "You know enough about me to know that I have some deep flaws, too, including the same one that you have—the uncanny ability to betray myself and my own happiness. Maybe I shouldn't be, but I'm trying again, giving myself another chance at love and happiness by trusting Peter . . . and myself." Larisa hesitated a moment then added with quiet urgency, "Elizabeth really loves you, Nick."

"And I really love Elizabeth, Larisa."

454

"You both turn to steel when you're wounded!" she exclaimed to the very cold and very resolute blue eyes. "I hate you for hurting her."

"I hate myself for hurting her, too, Larisa," Nick said quietly, calmly holding her icy glare. After many silent moments, a gentle smile touched his lips and he said softly, "But I'm very happy that you've fallen in love."

"Hi," Peter greeted her with loving surprise when Larisa called him twenty minutes later. "What happened?"

"Elizabeth had to go in for a case, so my plan to force her to talk to me tonight backfired. I did, however, get some information from Nick."

"From Nick?"

"On impulse, after Elizabeth left, I called him and asked him to come over. I wanted him to be here, in this place where she lives, so he could *feel* her sadness."

"I wish I'd known you were going to do that, Larisa," Peter said with obvious concern. "I would like to have been there, in case Nick became angry."

"Nick isn't dangerous, except to himself—and, I suppose, to the people who love him." Larisa paused, and then, to the man who made her feel so free and so safe, who loved her and protected her without possessing her, she added softly, "Thank you for wanting to protect me, Peter."

"You're very welcome. So . . . what did Nick say?"

"That he had told Elizabeth that he loved her, which he obviously does, and that he had also told her that their love was impossible because of what he perceives to be his own lethal flaws. It wasn't a line, Peter, it's what Nick really believes about himself."

"At least now you know what's been troubling Elizabeth. Are you still hoping to talk to her tonight?"

"No. From the description of the trauma that was coming in, she'll probably be there all night."

"Shall I come get you then?"

Larisa curled into the loving gentleness of his voice as if she were curled against him now, safe and warm and drifting off to wonderful dreams in his arms. But . . .

"I'm very tired, Peter." *And your baby and I need our sleep.* "I think I'd better just go to bed—soon—right here. I want to be well rested for our trip."

"All right. I'll be there to get you at nine tomorrow morning. Sleep well, my love."

"I will," Larisa promised. *We both will.*

As Larisa drifted off to sleep, she thought about the days that lay ahead. In just five days, on Monday, *Promise* would be released. At this very moment, the magnificent photographs Emily had taken of her against the backdrop of the meadow were being incorporated into major national magazines and the romantic forget-me-not crystal bottles filled with the enchanting fragrance were being shipped to boutiques and department stores across the country.

Everyone associated with *Promise* truly believed that once revealed the fragrance would sell itself; but Peter had decided he wanted television ads anyway, a celebration of the full-bloom springtime meadow if nothing else, a chance to share the extraordinary beauty of the place where the extraordinary fragrance had truly been created. The television ads were to be filmed next week, beginning Monday and finishing by Friday so that Larisa and Peter could return to San Francisco in time to attend Christine and Stephen's Saturday afternoon wedding.

The coming week would be exciting—and busy—but it was the private days that would come before that Larisa anticipated with the greatest excitement and joy. Tomorrow she and Peter would fly to Boston, and on Friday morning they would begin a leisurely sentimental journey to the places of Peter's childhood, ending up on Sunday at the estate on Cape Cod. Peter had told her that he wanted to share with her the places and memories of his childhood; and, he had added solemnly, there were some other very important things that he wanted to tell her.

There was just one very important thing that Larisa wanted to tell Peter, but it was the most important thing of all: the joyous news about the tiny miracle that lived inside her, the little life that had defied all odds, like the bravest of wildflowers. Larisa believed without question that her miracle baby was a little girl, and she decided that she would tell Peter about his tiny courageous daughter as they sat amid the courageous flowers in the magical meadow of *Promise*.

As Larisa drifted off to a most peaceful sleep, she envisioned the immeasurable joy in Peter's dark green eyes when she told him . . .

Peter had planned to drive Larisa to Concord on Friday and wander through Boston with her all day Saturday; but when he awakened Friday morning, so close to Innis Arden, Peter knew that that was where he wanted to take her first. Because it was there, in the meadow, that he would tell her the truth about his childhood dreams—and the man who had stolen them from him; and it was there that he would tell her the most important truth of all, that he loved her and wanted to spend his life with her.

Peter had already told Larisa a little about the father that he had loved so deeply, and during the drive to Cape Cod, he told her about the dyslexia that had crippled the dreams of the gifted carpenter long before the arthritis had crippled his art and about the wonderful dreams that the father and son had shared.

But it wasn't until Peter and Larisa were at Innis Arden, sitting on a sun-warmed patch of grass in the enchanted meadow amid the fragrance of *Promise,* that Peter told her what had happened to those dreams.

"I told you that I had known Julian briefly at Harvard," Peter began, his heart aching as he saw her lovely hopeful eyes cloud at the mention of Julian's name. Larisa had neither mentioned Julian nor even alluded to her marriage since the day in September when he had asked her to be the model for *Promise;* and Peter had hoped that with their love the painful memories would have long since faded. But as her beautiful blue eyes suddenly became very wary, Peter realized that she had not forgotten Julian Chancellor at all. "There's more to the story, Larisa. I'm sorry, but I think you need to hear it all." *And then, my darling, you can tell me about the pain he caused you too . . . and then, my love, we can both forget him forever and live our wonderful love.* "Okay?"

"Okay," she agreed quietly, barely able to breathe because the invisible chains from which she had so bravely freed herself were suddenly back, coiling tightly, ever more tightly, around her chest.

Peter told her the essential facts of his enmity with Julian as quickly as possible. But still, long before he had finished, her eyes had left his to gaze past the joyous flowers to the vast emptiness of the sea beyond.

458

"Larisa?" he asked when he had finished speaking. He had stopped the story with the day in August when Innis Arden had become his. There was more story he could have told, of course. He could have told her about his discovery that she was Julian's wife and his fleeting worry that she had been sent by Julian to enchant and seduce him as once Marcy had been; and he could have confessed that even if that had been the case, by then it was far too late, he was already hopelessly enchanted; and he could have spoken aloud his still tormenting worry that the fire that might have destroyed the mansion in December had been arranged by Julian. But Peter stopped the story with the day in August—because Larisa was already so terribly far away. *"Larisa?"*

"What was the date in August when you so cleverly tricked Julian?"

Peter didn't answer right away, not because he couldn't instantly remember the date, but because her voice terrified him. It was so hard and so cold.

"The fourteenth," he said finally. And then, because she wasn't going to look at him, he moved in front of her. And when he saw blue eyes that were as hard and as cold as her voice, he pleaded, "Larisa, talk to me!"

"You said you weren't sure if Julian even cared about Innis Arden any longer." Her icy voice spoke beyond the vast horizon to the memory of the night that Julian had lost the estate. "Well, Peter, you'll be pleased to hear that he was very upset indeed."

"What did he do to you?" Peter asked, as an ominous wave swept through him. Larisa didn't answer his question, not with words; but for just a flicker Peter saw in her forget-me-not blue eyes the same look of bewildered disbelief he had seen when she had told him what had happened to her when she was twelve. Controlling his rage enough to speak again, he asked with quiet despair: "He raped you, Larisa?"

"Don't sound so upset, Peter. Julian did what men—*all* men—have always done to me." She looked at him then, with her hard and hopeless cloudy blue eyes and asked softly, "It's what you've done to me, too, isn't it?"

"Oh, Larisa," he whispered hoarsely. "How can you say that?"

"Wasn't using me as the model for *Promise*—with the meadow as the backdrop—all part of your plan to get back at Julian? 'Look, Julian, look what I've stolen from you now. Not only your precious meadow, but your wife too!' "

"Larisa, I *love* you. I brought you here to tell you what I believed you had to know about me and Julian and then to ask you to marry me. Here." Peter retrieved the velvet box from his jacket pocket and extended it to her. And then, because she wouldn't take it from him, he opened it himself. Inside was an engagement ring, *her* engagement ring, a flawless forget-me-not blue sapphire encircled by delicate petals of brilliant diamonds. "I had this made for you."

Larisa looked from the magnificent ring to Peter's loving, and so desperate, dark green eyes; and for a moment she remembered how much she had believed in his love and how nourished she had been by it. It was a wonderful memory, and how she wished she could live in it forever, but she forced it away, and then forced her eyes to leave the loving dark green ones and return to the glittering symbol he was offering her as proof of his love. She had been offered glittering yet meaningless symbols of love before—by the man whose empire Peter wanted to destroy.

"Oh no," she whispered as she realized the depth of

Peter's betrayal of her trust and her love. "Having me model for *Promise*, flaunting me and the meadow together, was just a tiny part of your plan, wasn't it? This, your offer of marriage, was what it was really all about."

"There was no plan, Larisa. I fell in love with you."

"You believed that by marrying me, you would be marrying into half of Julian's fortune," she said, ignoring the loving softness of his eyes and his words, and ignoring too the heart that was crying to her, Listen to him! "Well, Peter, I'm afraid the only money I have is the money you've given me. I didn't want Julian's money, you see, I just desperately wanted to get away from him, to stop being owned by him. This is all such a terrible joke. I allowed myself to be owned by you so that I could stop being owned by Julian."

"I don't want Julian's money, Larisa. And I don't own you, nor do I ever want to own you." Peter's dark green eyes searched the blue ones, and when he spoke it wasn't to the icy surface he didn't know but to the uncertain flickers of love he saw still in the forget-me-not blue depths. "I just want to spend my life loving you."

"I trusted you, Peter," she pleaded softly. "I made a promise to myself that I would never trust again, but I trusted you."

"You *can* trust me. *I love you.*"

Listen to him! her heart cried. Listen to him! Trust him still. *Please.*

I want to trust him, but . . . she said very quietly, "You should have told me about your relationship with Julian."

"Yes, I should have," Peter agreed with matching quiet. "I know that now. But, Larisa, from the very beginning I sensed that you didn't want to talk about him, and frankly that was quite all right with me. All I knew about your divorce was what I read in *People,* and that article

461

implied, more than implied, that it was Julian who had wanted the divorce. I've spent the past six months loving you, and wanting our love so much, but being afraid that you loved him still."

"Oh, no, Peter," Larisa whispered. "I never loved Julian, not really. It was all just an illusion." But your love for Peter, and Peter's love for you, is not an illusion, her loving heart defiantly reminded. Tell him that you know that! Reassure this wonderful man who loves you. Larisa looked at the gentle and tormented dark green eyes and said very softly, "I know now that what I had with Julian was an illusion, a deception. I know that now, Peter, because of you."

"Oh, Larisa." It was a whisper of hope. "I love you."

"I love you, too, Peter." It was a wondrous truth, and a confident one, but there were other truths, terrifying ones—and they prevented her from curling into his loving arms. "You think Julian's responsible for the fire here in December, don't you?"

"I don't know. Maybe."

"Julian never forgives or forgets, we both know that. He's going to be enraged when he learns about me modeling for *Promise,* and if he ever knew about us . . ." Her blue eyes filled with immense fear and her voice lost its hope as she whispered, "Oh, Peter."

"Larisa, listen to me. Julian never needs to know—not about *Promise* and not about us. Why don't we go into the mansion right now and I'll make the calls that will stop the launch?"

"Most of the magazines have already gone to press, and even if they haven't by now more than one publisher will have told the media or perhaps Julian himself that I'm the model. *Promise* is already in the public domain. Julian is going to know, and he will do everything he can to destroy it and us."

"Then, after I get you settled in the mansion, I'll go to New York to see him."

"The damage has already been done, Peter. There's nothing you could offer him at this point that would appease him."

"My intention is *not* to appease Julian, Larisa," Peter said solemnly. "My intention is to warn him to stay away from you and us—forever."

"It's too late," Larisa said softly, speaking aloud the silent thought that had spun in her mind when Peter had asked her to spend the weekend with him at Lake Tahoe. Then, because he had believed she was still mourning the loss of Julian's love, he had gently suggested that perhaps it was too soon. Larisa had known it wasn't too soon, but a knowledge deep inside had warned her, even before their love began, that it was too late for her and Peter. She should have heeded that deep wisdom, but she hadn't—and now a precious and innocent life was involved. Larisa knew that Julian's immense fury about the loss of Innis Arden and even his anger when he discovered that she was the model for *Promise* would pale into insignificance when compared to his rage if ever he learned that she was carrying the baby of his ancient enemy. With sudden urgency she said, "I have to go, Peter. I have to go away now."

"We'll go away together, darling."

"No, Peter, that's not possible. Don't you see?"

"No, I don't see," Peter said with quiet calm, even though icy waves of fear washed through him. Peter London wasn't physically afraid of Julian Chancellor, of course, but there was fear nonetheless. Julian had stolen his dreams once before . . . and now the thief of dreams threatened to destroy the most important dream of all—his lifetime of love with Larisa. "We love each other, Larisa."

"Please, Peter, just let me go!"

Peter gazed at the woman he loved. Larisa was suddenly so desperate, and so fearful—as if she believed he would violently deny her soft plea for escape, as if she still put him in the same category as the evil men who had brutally betrayed her. Peter thought that they had gotten way beyond that—and back to their wondrous and trusting love—but now she was very far away again, and in another moment she might simply turn and run. The keys to the rental car were in his pocket, but he didn't want her driving, this upset, along the unfamiliar winding roads.

"Why don't I go to the mansion and call a cab for you?" he suggested finally, gently. "You can come with me or wait here until you see it arrive."

"Couldn't I make the call myself?"

"Of course. The mansion is open. The housekeeper's name is Ellen. If you like, I'll wait here until I see you leave." Peter's heart screamed with silent pain as the wary blue eyes told him that yes, that was what she wanted. He continued with great control, "After you leave, I'm going to stop the launch and then I'm going to New York to see Julian."

"Please don't tell him that you and I were lovers."

"All right, I won't. But, Larisa, we are far more than lovers. We *love* each other." After a moment he asked with quiet emotion, "Will you take the engagement ring with you?"

"No, Peter, I can't," she whispered to the loving and anguished dark green eyes. Let me go, Peter! But, she realized, Peter wasn't holding her. He was doing nothing to prevent her from leaving, nothing whatsoever to possess her against her will; but nonetheless Larisa felt the powerful call of his heart, wanting to hold her, pleading with her to stay forever with him and their love. The invisible bonds that had bound her to Julian had been punishing, suffocating, and dangerous; and the invisible bonds to Peter were wondrous bonds of love. But she had to flee those wondrous bonds as desperately as she had fled the destructive ones that had bound her to Julian—because now there was an innocent life inside her, a brave flower filled with hope and joy and promise, and she had to find a safe place for her precious little love. "I have to go, Peter. Goodbye."

After the cab that had come for Larisa pulled away from the mansion, Peter made the calls to abruptly stop whatever still could be stopped for the launch of *Promise*. Then he drove to Logan to catch a shuttle to New York. Larisa was at the airport, Peter knew. Ellen had overheard her make a reservation for the two-forty flight for San Francisco. Peter wanted to find her, but he forced himself to focus on what needed to be done, not on what had happened. We love each other, he reminded his aching heart. We will be together. This wondrous dream of love will not be destroyed.

Peter knew that Larisa needed time alone, and it was comforting to know that she would be in San Francisco, in her romantic bedroom filled with images of *Promise*. She would be safe there; and soon, very soon, he would be able to go to her and assure the wary forget-me-not blue eyes that they no longer needed to worry about the specter of Julian Chancellor.

But how could he ever truly give Larisa such a categorical assurance? Peter wondered as he made the brief flight from Logan to La Guardia. He planned to warn Julian to stay away from Larisa, from both of them, but what was the "or else"? He didn't have much ammunition—except for the fact that Julian was in essence a bully, and therefore, like all bullies, in essence merely a coward.

He wouldn't even offer an "or else," he decided. The threat would simply be implied by the icy resolve of his calm and unflickering gaze.

Icy? Calm? Peter's own ability to remain calm and cool in the presence of the man who had so brutally harmed his lovely Larisa was a worry far greater than what words of warning he would speak. How could he possibly control his rage? With love, he told himself. His love for Larisa would enable him to do whatever was necessary.

Whatever was necessary. When he was shown into Julian's office only moments after being announced and met his ancient enemy's mocking dark eyes, Peter's carefully suppressed rage burst into sudden flames. And in the brightness of that raging inferno, a thought presented itself with simple yet brilliant clarity: I will kill him. I will kill Julian Chancellor. Right now. Right this minute. With my bare hands.

Peter welcomed the glittering thought with a sense of great peace—and he let it go with great reluctance. It wasn't possible, of course, at least not practical, to murder Julian Chancellor in cold blood. The peaceful thought vanished, leaving Peter to fight the fires of rage that blazed within him even as he filled his eyes and his voice with the calm steadiness of ice.

"Peter. What a nice surprise."

"Is it a surprise, Julian?"

"You mean did I expect you to inform me in person about your new venture and my wife's role in it?" The smile on Julian's face was as dark and menacing as his

466

eyes. Gesturing to a copy of one of the soon-to-be-published print ads for *Promise* that had been sent to him, he said, "As you can see, I already know."

"Your ex-wife."

"Ah, yes. And your mistress? Unfair question, although I assume that she is. She's really quite lovely, isn't she, Peter? So very willing to please, so happy to satisfy every imaginable sexual whim—"

"I'm here to warn you, Julian," Peter said, his voice icy still and his dark green eyes eloquently conveying their impractical—and yet so appealing—murderous wish. "I know what you did to Larisa. And I also know that you are responsible for the fire at Innis Arden."

"I don't know anything about a fire. And as for Larisa . . ." Julian stopped, smiled a charming conciliatory smile, and said, "Listen, Peter, it's obvious that we need to talk, to resolve some misunderstandings. I have a meeting I really must go to now, but why don't the three of us meet later? Let's say dinner at Le Cirque?"

"Not the three of us, Julian. And not dinner."

"Larisa's not with you?"

"Where and when, Julian."

"Right here. Nine o'clock. I'll have my secretary notify building security to be expecting you."

Something in Peter's solemn expression had given Julian the distinct impression that Larisa hadn't accompanied him to New York. But, quite obviously, Peter and Larisa had been together somewhere very recently, revealing their secrets to each other. At Innis Arden? Julian wondered. Yes, probably. And was Larisa there still, waiting for her lover to return with the triumphant announce-

467

ment that he had warned Julian to stay away from her once and for all?

Because he paid people to keep him informed, Julian knew that there were guards at Innis Arden now, ever since the fire that had done far less damage than had been his hope; and he knew that in the past month a live-in housekeeper had been hired, as if Peter was planning to take up residence in the mansion; and he knew that the telephone number to the mansion had not yet been changed from the number it had been during the years that it had belonged to the people of Cape Cod.

Julian identified himself to the female voice that answered as Carlton Evans, a senior associate with the advertising firm that was handling the promotion campaign for *Promise*.

"I'm sorry, Mr. Evans, but Mr. London isn't here," Ellen replied.

"Well," Julian answered amiably. "It's actually Larisa to whom I need to speak most urgently. Is she there?"

"No. I'm sorry. She's not here either."

"Really? I had understood that both she and Peter were going to be there. I am reaching the mansion at Innis Arden, aren't I?"

"Yes, and they both were here, but they both left earlier today."

"I see." Julian sighed audibly. "This is a problem. I really do need to speak with Larisa as soon as possible. Did she by any chance tell you where she would be? A phone number perhaps?"

"No, no phone number. However, I did overhear her making reservations for an afternoon flight to San Francisco."

"Leaving at what time?"

"Two-forty. She left here shortly before noon, so I assume she was able to catch that flight."

"Wonderful," Julian said with genuine enthusiasm. It *was* wonderful, because it was only four-thirty now, and Peter was in New York planning to meet with him at nine, and Larisa was still en route to San Francisco, and *he* was in control. "I have Larisa's number in San Francisco, so I'll be able to reach her there. Thank you so very much for your help."

Before making the next calls, Julian removed a manila folder from a locked drawer in his desk. The folder contained financial data on Peter London—the detailed information required by the Chancellor family attorneys for the purchase of Innis Arden as well as various credit checks Julian himself had had done. Julian held in his hands extensive confidential information about his enemy; but all he withdrew from the folder now was the information that Peter himself would carry in his wallet—credit card names and numbers, driver's license, home address, and unlisted home phone.

The next two calls Julian made as Peter London. The first was to an airline to make a reservation—paid for in advance by credit card—for the six-fifty flight to San Francisco; and the second was to a car rental company, for which Peter had "express" privileges, which meant the car would be waiting, with no further paperwork required, when he reached San Francisco.

Then dark, handsome Julian Chancellor left his office to travel to San Francisco as dark, handsome Peter London. The casual clothes into which he changed were enough of a disguise. He wouldn't be recognized—his face simply wasn't that familiar to the general public—

and, although he traveled extensively, it was always in his own jet, the same way the wealthy and powerful people who would have recognized him always traveled too.

And if the airline personnel had a vague memory of the dark, handsome man named Peter London who had been on the evening flight to San Francisco? Fine, wonderful, because they could help place Peter London in San Francisco at the time of the unspeakably brutal murder of Julian Chancellor's beautiful ex-wife.

"Oh, yes, Mr. London," the security guard greeted him when Peter returned to the Chancellor Building shortly before nine. "Unfortunately, Mr. Chancellor will be unable to meet with you after all. He phoned earlier to say that he had been called out of town on urgent business. He doesn't expect to return for several days, so he asked me to extend his apologies and offered to meet with you next week in San Francisco."

San Francisco. Peter's mind reeled. Was that where Julian was going now?

"Where is he?" Peter demanded sharply. "Where was the urgent business?"

"I don't know, sir. I'm sorry. He didn't say."

"Is there a phone here that I can use?"

"Of course. You can use this one."

Both the direct and nonstop flights to San Francisco stopped departing New York at about eight every night and didn't resume service again until six in the morning. But there were indirect routes on "red eyes," and Peter finally found one, involving two middle-of-the-night plane changes, that would depart New York at ten-thirty and have him in San Francisco by dawn. As soon as he made the reservation, Peter dialed Larisa's number in San Francisco. He knew she wouldn't be there yet—if on time, the two-forty flight from Boston should have been landing just about now—but maybe Elizabeth would be.

And what would his message to Elizabeth be? Peter wondered as the phone rang unanswered a continent away. That Julian might—*might*—be on his way to see Larisa? Surely he was overreacting, Peter told himself. His rationality and logic had been completely usurped by emotion, his immense love for Larisa and his almost equally immense hatred for Julian. Surely . . .

But still, he decided as he finally hung up the unanswered phone, he would keep calling until he reached her . . . and when he did he would tell her to stay where she was, in her very safe and very secure apartment.

Chapter Thirty-five

Larisa's flight from Boston should have arrived in San Francisco at six-ten Pacific time, but because of mechanical problems discovered during the scheduled stopover in Chicago, the original jet was grounded and its passengers were given seats on a flight that finally touched the tarmac in San Francisco at nine-forty—an hour and a half before Julian's flight from New York was due to arrive.

During that hour and a half, Larisa felt a strange sense of urgency, a restless and ominous feeling that despite her exhaustion, she needed to act tonight on the decision she had made instead of waiting until morning. At first Larisa fought the feeling. But with each passing moment the ominous restlessness crescendoed, and finally, just as Julian's flight was landing, she began to get ready to leave.

Larisa packed hurriedly, as she had once before, when she had desperately fled the Fifth Avenue penthouse. She packed most of the same old friends she had packed then—her jeans and sweatshirt from Berkeley, the tattered nightgown and robe; but one friend she left behind—the romantic beaded gown that Julian had refused to let her wear on the eve of their wedding, and which she had worn the night when she had first met Peter. The lovely romantic symbol of innocence and hope would stay behind this time . . . and in its place Larisa packed a symbol of hopelessness and violence: the gun that Julian had given her. Larisa reached for the box containing the lethal weapon with surprising confidence, even though she knew she would die before ever pulling the trigger.

Still, she packed it.

It was almost midnight, and Elizabeth wasn't home, and in answer to Larisa's call the page operator had told her that Dr. Jennings was scrubbed in the OR with a renal transplantation and would be for several more hours. So, Larisa left her best friend a note: *Dearest Liz, I have to go away for a while. Please don't worry about me. I'm okay. Love, Lara.* She hesitated a moment and then added, *I want you to be okay, too, Elizabeth Jennings!*

Larisa left the note in the kitchen, propped up against the ELIZABETH! CELEBRATE!! mug she had given her on her twenty-first birthday. Then she withdrew from her wallet the small card that Darlene Buchanan had given her in December and dialed the number to the motel in Lake Tahoe.

"Hello, Darlene? This is Larisa Locksley."

"Larisa! Hi."

"Hi. I didn't expect you to be answering the phones this late."

"I take the evening shift twice a week, when Craig is on duty. My night clerk will be arriving any moment, but I'm happy to be the one to have answered your call. Do you need a cottage?"

"Yes, if you have one. I'm in San Francisco and was hoping to drive up tonight."

"It's between ski and summer seasons, so we actually have several available—including, if you want it, the one where you used to live."

"Yes," Larisa answered quietly. "I would like that cottage, perhaps for quite a while if that's okay."

"Of course it is. Melanie will be so thrilled. Not," Darlene assured swiftly, "that she'll bother you."

"She would never bother me and I'm very much looking forward to seeing her again. Since I won't arrive until the middle of the night, I may sleep late in the morning. But please tell Melanie that when I awaken I'll open the curtains and would love to have her—and you, too, of course—come visit."

"Melanie will be there as soon as the curtains are open. Craig and I have a meeting in the morning with our accountant, so I won't see you until later on."

As soon as Larisa said goodbye to Darlene, it was time to say goodbye to the sanctuary of Elizabeth's apartment and her own bedroom of *Promise*. This time, she thought as she reached for her suitcase, she wasn't escaping to a safe haven where she would be rescued by the generosity of a kind friend. This time, *at last*, Larisa Locksley was going to rescue herself.

She would go to the tiny cottage and confront the icy ghosts that lurked there still. She would force them to come out of hiding from beneath the delicate floral wallpaper and she would stare at them bravely until she knew all their secrets and they were vanquished forever. And then, even more bravely, she would stand before the mirror and gaze with gentle love at the woman who had finally conquered her own ghosts . . . and who knew that her love for Peter had not been an illusion . . . and who was going to spend the rest of her life loving and protecting his beloved baby.

* * *

Julian had just brought the car rented to Peter London to a stop across the street from Larisa's apartment building when he saw her emerging from the gated underground garage. Julian might have ignored the car entirely—inexpensive, American-made, not acceptable for his wife—but the glow of a street lamp illuminated her magnificent hair, creating a brilliant beacon of fire that beckoned to him, and betrayed her.

Larisa didn't notice him, of course. He was a dark shadow inside one of many cars parked on the street. And even when he began to follow her, she didn't notice, because he drove without his headlights on until she turned onto Divisadero, brightly lighted and busy on this Friday at midnight.

Larisa drove cautiously, forcing her fatigued mind to concentrate on the long drive, abruptly stopping her thoughts whenever they began to drift with the wondrous reminder that she was carrying a most precious new little life inside her.

Julian followed, at first impatient with her cautiousness, wanting the speed and power of the car to match the pace and power of his racing thoughts; but finally he simply savored the slowness. There was a most delicious anticipation, a most wonderfully titillating tension as he leisurely imagined her terror and his triumph, her brutal murder and Peter's conviction for same.

Larisa was playing right into his plan, leading him to some remote place, perhaps known only to her and her lover; and, Julian decided, by now Peter himself was playing into his hand, too. He was doubtless already making his frantic journey from New York to San Francisco, having perhaps phoned Larisa first—when he discovered that Julian had no intention of meeting with him—telling her to flee and promising to join her as soon as possible.

Wonderful, Julian thought. What could be more perfect than having Peter arrive to find his lover dead? He would rush to her savagely murdered body, covering himself with her blood, incriminating himself even further.

Julian's lips curled with lustful hunger as he imagined that bloody scene and his bitter enemy's anguished horror. How he wished he could witness it!

But he would be long gone by then, awaiting with more delicious anticipation the news of the brutal murder of the wife who, although he had eventually tired of her, the world knew he had always treated like a princess.

Julian watched from a distance as Larisa checked into the motel. His dark eyes followed her to the remote cottage and remained fixed there as she pulled the curtains and finally turned off the lights. Then Julian himself checked into a motel across the street, paying in cash this time and using neither Peter's name nor his own. He had no plans to sleep, of course. His energized body didn't need sleep, nor did he want to miss even a moment of the wonderful anticipation.

Julian could have made his move now, in the darkness of night; but the more he thought about it, the more likely it seemed that eventually Peter would appear. He would wait, he decided, at least long enough to give Peter time to return to San Francisco and begin the drive to Lake Tahoe. Besides, the idea of murdering Larisa in the morning was far more appealing than murdering her now, when she was too tired to plead and struggle the way he wanted her to; *and* she was always so beautiful in the morning, when she had just awakened and the memory of her dreams had left her blue eyes wide and hopeful . . . as if she truly believed that this new day would be better than the day before . . . as if in her dreams she had somehow forgotten the truth.

Julian could have murdered her now, but for many reasons, the morning held far more appeal. Perhaps the most appealing reason of all was that tonight the only weapon he had was his hands—and they were more than lethal enough; but in the morning he could go to the store he had noticed just a block away—with a boldly lettered sign proclaiming it to be a "hunter's paradise"—and he could buy a hunting knife . . . the kind with the jagged edge.

Peter's plane touched the tarmac in San Francisco just as the golden dawn was beginning to lighten the spring sky. As soon as he deplaned he found the nearest pay phone. He had called the apartment throughout the night, whenever he could, from the planes when they had phones, and from the ground as he had made his middle-of-the-night connections.

And always there had been no answer.

But she's there, he told himself. She's there. She's just not answering the phone.

This time the phone was answered.

"It's Peter, Elizabeth. I'm sorry to call so early but I need to speak to Larisa."

"She's not here, Peter."

"Not there?" An immense wave of pure ice stopped his heart and froze his breath.

"She was here," Elizabeth assured swiftly. "She left me a note, saying she needed to get away for a while and assuring me that she would be all right."

"Has Julian called?" he pressed, his heart beating again.

"Julian? No. This has something to do with Julian?"

"Yes," Peter admitted, breathing finally, exhaling the icy fear—and then inhaling pure frustration. Yes, he thought, this had something to do with Julian, whether or not he was anywhere near San Francisco. Larisa was fleeing from Julian—from *both* of them—both of the men whose bitter enmity had shattered her lovely hope for a safe and joyous love. "If he does call, please tell him nothing and let me know right away. I'll be at my place in Sausalito."

"Do you think that Larisa is there?"

"No," he answered with quiet—and anguished—confidence. "I don't know where she is, Elizabeth."

"What *happened*, Peter?"

"Julian and I go way back, a past history that I had hoped had long since been forgotten. I told Larisa about it yesterday . . . and it became obvious that Julian hadn't forgotten about the past at all." Rage washed through him as he thought about the proof that Julian hadn't forgotten, what he had done to Larisa on that August night.

"And that realization upset Larisa," Elizabeth offered into the suddenly charged silence.

"Yes." After a moment Peter asked, "Do you have any idea where she might have gone?"

"No, not offhand. I'd have to think about it."

"Well, if you do think of somewhere, will you let me know? And if you hear from her . . ."

"I'll tell her that you called, and that you're in Sausalito," Elizabeth promised. She could promise that, but even though she knew of Peter's great love for Larisa, and now heard his obvious immense worry, she couldn't promise that if she did think of where Larisa might be that she would tell him—not without checking with Larisa first. Because, as much as Elizabeth knew how much Larisa loved Peter, it was very clear that now, for some reason, she had run away from him. Putting a smile in her voice, because she very much hoped that the love of Larisa and Peter would survive, she said, "And Peter, if you hear from Larisa, please let me know. I'm on first call for trauma today so I'll most likely be at the hospital."

Maybe I already know where Larisa is, Peter thought just moments after his conversation with Elizabeth had ended. As he dialed Directory Assistance, and then the number to the motel at Lake Tahoe, he thought, Maybe I already know where my lovely forget-me-not would go when her world has fallen apart—again.

"Yes, Ms. Locksley is here," the motel clerk said. "But the cottages don't have phones and we make a policy of not waking our guests this early in the morning—unless it's an emergency, of course. Is it?"

"No," Peter answered truthfully as the relief pulsed through him. It wasn't an emergency anymore. He knew where Larisa was now, and that she was safe. Julian knew nothing about the motel in Lake Tahoe. Larisa had gone to a place where Julian would never find her and where she knew—didn't she?—that Peter would. She was safe, and perhaps expecting him, but still something made Peter ask, "Did anyone else check in last night?"

"No, just her. Did you want to leave a message?"

"No. Thank you." *I will give her all the messages of love when I see her.*

Larisa had wondered if she would be able to sleep in the cottage surrounded by all the icy ghosts. But, in fact, she

479

felt strangely safe in their midst. They were well known to her, after all, enemies and yet familiar companions. So she slept, a deep sleep without dreams or nightmares, awakening at nine and opening the curtains to a brilliant sapphire sky.

She showered, and dressed in her sweatshirt and jeans, and was just about to leave to get breakfast for herself and her baby when there was a knock on the door. Larisa smiled as she moved toward it.

It would be Melanie, the little girl she herself once had been. No, that was wrong. She had never been as safe or as loved as Melanie was. Melanie was the little girl who her own daughter was going to be, so safe, so protected, so very loved.

"Good morn—" Her smile vanished and her face filled with pure fear.

"Good morning," Julian answered, calmly stopping the door as she struggled to close it, surprised by Larisa's strength, but truly amazed by his own. He had never been so powerful, so *omnipotent*. He effortlessly stopped her from closing the door and then easily opened it wide and entered the tiny cottage.

"Get out, Julian."

"Sorry, Larisa. I'm afraid I just can't do that," he said, smiling charmingly, menacingly, and arching an approving eyebrow as the door locked automatically as it closed behind him.

"What do you want?"

"Let's see," Julian replied, thrilled by the sheer terror in her beautiful blue eyes. Then, as calmly as if he were in the midst of a negotiation for a piece of property, he explained, "What I want is to very slowly carve up your lovely flesh . . . and then let your lover pay for your murder." Julian extracted the just-purchased hunting knife from the pocket of his jacket and added softly, "And, Larisa, you know I always get what I want."

"Julian, *no!*"

"Larisa, *yes,*" he mocked. "I always get what I want, and I never wanted to let you go."

"Julian," she whispered to the man who was so obviously in control, and yet so obviously crazed with delusions of grandeur. She had seen glimpses of Julian's madness before, but now Larisa saw its full force: the wildly excited dark eyes, the menacingly seductive smile, the terrifying pleasure in his voice as he spoke so calmly about her murder. She fought her own terror, knowing that she could never overpower him, needing to keep him at bay, keep him talking, while her mind searched for a way to escape. She reminded him quietly, "But you gave me the divorce, Julian."

"I had to! I didn't want your *boyfriend* to know that I was upset about Innis Arden." Julian smiled conspiratorily and added, "I had plans, you see."

"The fire."

"The fire. Not an unqualified success, as you know. However, there would have been another fire, some time when Peter was in residence." Julian gave a dismissive gesture with the hand that held the gleaming hunting knife. "But this is better. *Much* better. Aren't you going to scream, Larisa?"

No, she thought in silent answer to his question. Larisa knew that a scream would cause more harm than good. The cottage was too remote for anyone to identify her scream—if they even heard it—as anything more than a vague sound. They would listen for the sound to repeat itself, to pinpoint its source; and when there was no second scream, because Julian's powerful hands would have clamped over her mouth, they would dismiss the sound they had heard as a cry of a bird, or a squeal of a tire, or the joyous shriek of a frolicking child.

A scream would accomplish nothing. It would only bring Julian closer to her, touching and confining her, and once that happened all was lost.

"You never did scream, my sweet," Julian continued when his question had been greeted with lingering silence. "I would have liked it very much if you had. Maybe I just didn't hurt you enough before. Maybe this time you will scream for me."

"I should never have divorced you," Larisa said suddenly, trying to get him to drop his guard, just for an instant, just long enough for her to dash past him and make her escape. It was her only hope. She continued softly, "I was very angry with you, Julian, but if I had understood how important Innis Arden was to you . . . I've been thinking about you, *us*, remembering what we had, what we still could have."

"There is nothing for you but death, *whore*."

Julian lunged at her then, the razor-sharp knife cutting through the sleeve of her sweatshirt as if it were gossamer silk and deeply slashing the delicate flesh beneath. Larisa felt no pain, only the hot dampness of her own blood; and then she felt the calm that had so bravely urged her to keep him talking while she plotted her escape evaporate into pure terror. There would be no escape. Julian's crazed eyes were now filled with a lustful desire that told her he would not stop until his hunger for her agonizing death and his triumphant revenge was fully and robustly satiated.

This is how it ends, Larisa realized with astonishing clarity. This is the full circle. I died here once before, a death of the heart and the spirit, and now I die here again . . . forever.

Julian obviously wanted her to fight him, to struggle valiantly but futilely to save her life. For a moment Larisa decided that her final victory—the only victory she would ever have—would be to deprive him of the pleasure of her struggle. She would simply give herself up to him, a willing victim, accepting her destiny with a sense almost of relief that both the foolish illusions and savage betrayals of her life were finally over.

But then something new filled Larisa, a power as strong as Julian's madness. She didn't know if it came from the heart that had solemnly and joyously promised to protect her baby *always* . . . or if it came from the small precious life herself, the courageous wildflower that had been so determined from the very beginning, putting brave delicate roots where no baby ever had dared to before because she wanted a chance to grow and live and laugh and fall in love.

So Larisa fought, stumbling away from Julian, twirling from the savage blows that became more and more vicious, and more and more calculated, as his pleasure increased. She was wounded, weak and bleeding, but still she fought. Julian liked her brave and foolish struggle, *he loved it,* and he wanted it to go on as long as possible, savoring her terror, marveling at the rich redness of her blood against the beautiful snow-white skin that became whiter and ever whiter as she lost more blood.

Julian let her twist away from him for a moment—it would be so wonderful to see a flicker of hope in her terrified blue eyes!—and watched with interest as she crawled across the small room. Her determined journey wasn't toward the door, a destination she knew he would not permit her to reach, but to her suitcase and to a box inside it. As soon as Julian recognized the box, he felt a rush of exhilaration, and he watched with eager anticipation as Larisa's pale trembling fingers removed the gun.

And then, as she so bravely pointed it at him, Julian laughed, as he had laughed in August and as another man had laughed in this same tiny room eighteen years before.

But Larisa wasn't that twelve-year-old girl anymore. She was a mother, keeping the most solemn of all promises of love—to protect her baby always . . . and to give that precious innocent life a chance for joy, for happiness, and for love.

Larisa was a mother, not the twelve-year-old girl anymore, but in her fading consciousness, she heard a little-girl voice cry, as it had cried all those years before, "Stop, *please*. I'll shoot you! Please *stop!*" Larisa knew her lips weren't actually whispering those brave and frantic words. Her mouth and lungs were fully engaged in the desperate battle to find air to supply her ever dwindling blood supply with oxygen, to keep her awake and conscious. The little-girl screams came from deep inside, from the innocent little girl she once had been . . . or from her own precious daughter.

Then Larisa Locksley did what she had never been able to do before, because before there had only been herself to save.

She aimed the gun at Julian's heart and pulled the trigger.

There was a sudden thunder in the tiny room, and Larisa saw the expression of stunned disbelief on Julian's face—and then the final look of anger. As his dying body fell heavily on top of her, he plunged the knife deep into her flesh . . . and plunged her world into soundless darkness.

Chapter Thirty-six

Elizabeth had never dialed Nick's unlisted home phone number. But she knew it *by heart*.

And now it was that heart that compelled her to dial. "I need you, Nick."

"Elizabeth," he answered softly. *I need you too—so much.* He asked gently of her troubled voice, "What's wrong?"

"I just got a call from an emergency-room physician in Lake Tahoe." Elizabeth drew a breath to try to calm the rush of emotions, but her voice was still shaky as she whispered, "It's Larisa, Nick. She's been badly injured . . . stabbed."

Nick felt a sudden rush of shaky emotion, too, but he forced calm into his voice for Elizabeth, and with that calm sent a quiet reminder that she had called him many times to talk to him about badly injured trauma patients. "Tell me what happened, Elizabeth. Tell me everything. You said the call came from a doctor in Lake Tahoe?"

"Yes. She was at a motel there. I don't know why. She and Peter were supposed to be in Boston all this week, but she returned last night and left me a note saying that she needed to get away. Peter called me early this morning, obviously terribly worried about her. He told me then that he didn't know where she was, but he arrived at the motel just moments after she shot Julian."

"Larisa shot Julian?"

"It was self-defense, of course. He was trying to kill her. That's apparently quite obvious from her wounds, but there was also an eyewitness. The daughter of the couple who manage the motel had gone to the cottage to visit Larisa and saw through the window what was happening. The cottage door was locked so she ran to get the key and call her parents. She opened the door just moments before Larisa pulled the trigger. Peter and the girl's father—a police officer—arrived almost immediately after."

"Is Julian dead?"

"Yes."

"And Larisa?"

"She has lost a lot of blood, although there's no active bleeding now, but as Julian was dying he apparently stabbed her in the left upper quadrant of her abdomen. The physician who called says it's impossible for it not to have gone directly into her spleen. There's no clinical evidence of rupture yet but she needs to be explored. They're sending her here. The Flight for Life team is already on the way." She sighed softly and then simply confessed, "I can't do it alone, Nick. I can't operate again on someone I love—not without help . . . your help."

"I'm on my way."

"Thank you. Nick? There's something else."

"Tell me."

"Larisa is unconscious now, but earlier she was awake just long enough to whisper something about a baby. The physician who examined her in Tahoe thinks she's about four months pregnant. He also said that there are no knife wounds at all in her lower abdomen." Elizabeth drew yet another breath to combat yet another rush of emotion. "She must have kept twisting away to prevent Julian from stabbing her there."

"So the baby seems all right?"

"Yes." For now, Elizabeth amended silently, knowing that Nick was making the same silent amendment. The baby was fine . . . unless Larisa's spleen suddenly ruptured and caused catastrophic shock.

"I'm on my way, Elizabeth."

Larisa's lacerated spleen ruptured in the operating room, a violent and powerful explosion of tissue and blood. Had she been operating alone, or with anyone other than Nick, Elizabeth wasn't absolutely certain that she would have been able to act quickly and decisively enough to save her best friend's life.

But Elizabeth wasn't alone in the operating room, and her delicate and talented hands followed the confident lead of his, dancing their flawless graceful dance as always, calmly subduing the powerful gush of blood and carefully removing the irrevocably damaged tissue—but taking care, too, to leave some of the undamaged tissue behind to continue its important immunologic function of protecting Larisa against infection.

Together, Nick and Elizabeth saved Larisa's life, so swiftly that her unborn baby was never subjected to any of the adverse effects of shock; and after they had gently closed her abdomen, they left the operating room to find Peter.

Before they started the walk along the linoleum corridor to the private waiting room, Elizabeth turned to Nick, her beautiful face very thoughtful, and asked, "What did you think about Larisa's spleen, Nick?"

"That it had been previously injured," he said solemnly to the thoughtful emerald eyes. "Why?"

"When Larisa came here last August, to escape from Julian and her marriage, she was very weak and very pale. She denied that it was anything more than exhaustion, but . . ."

"But it was an injury that probably saved her life," Nick gently assured the emerald eyes that were obviously thinking about that time and wondering if she should have pressed Larisa further about her pallor and weakness. "It was the old scar tissue that contained the rupture until she got here. If the scarring hadn't been there the spleen would have ruptured much sooner."

"That's what I thought, too." She gave a bewildered shake of her dark curls and a soft smile touched her lovely lips.

"Why are you smiling?"

"Because Larisa has always accused me of being able to find the silver lining in even the darkest of clouds. I was just imagining her reaction to my telling her about the lifesaving silver lining to Julian's brutality."

As Elizabeth met the dark blue eyes that gazed at her with such gentleness, such pride in the lovely optimism that enabled her to always find the silver lining, her soft smile faded and the heart that had only survived for the past two months because she had resolutely wrapped it in steel suddenly broke free of its protective armor and cried with anguished despair, *I can't find a silver lining, Nick—not one troy ounce—in the loss of our love.*

"We'd better go find Peter," she said finally. Neither of them had had a chance to speak to Peter before the surgery. He hadn't been permitted to ride with Larisa in the Flight for Life helicopter and they were already in the

OR when he arrived. "You've met him before, haven't you?"

"Yes." *Oh, my lovely Elizabeth, don't look so sad!* "I attended a number of board meetings about the institute and I spoke to him briefly again at the Fairmont ball."

Peter stood the moment Nick and Elizabeth appeared in the doorway of the waiting room, his exhausted dark green eyes haunted, anguished, and searching . . .

"She's going to be okay, Peter," Elizabeth reassured swiftly. "She did have a splenic laceration, but the rupture didn't happen until she was in the operating room and we were able to contain it. She'll have scars, of course. There were deep cuts on her arms and legs—"

"Scars don't matter," Peter said softly. *Only Larisa matters. Larisa and . . .* "And the baby, Elizabeth?"

"The baby is fine, too."

"Thank you," Peter whispered first to the emerald eyes and then to the dark blue ones. Then he returned to the emerald ones, because he knew them the best, and asked quietly, "Where is she, Elizabeth? Can I see her?"

"She's on her way up to the Surgery ICU. The nurses will need time to get her settled in, and even though the anesthesia was kept quite light because of the baby, it will be a little while before she's fully awake."

"I'd very much like to be with her when she wakes up."

Elizabeth hesitated briefly before answering. "Let me talk to her first, Peter."

"To see if she wants to see me?" Peter saw the answer in Elizabeth's sympathetic yet resolute emerald eyes. And how could he blame her? Just a few hours ago he had asked her help in finding the woman who had so obviously fled from him.

"I'm sorry, Peter."

"I should have killed him."

"What?"

"I should have killed Julian."

"I thought you arrived at the motel after Larisa had already shot him."

"I did. I mean I should have killed him in New York."

"Peter . . ."

"Please tell Larisa that I love her, Elizabeth. Please tell her that."

"I will," Elizabeth promised gently. "And I'll come find you in the ICU waiting room as soon as I've spoken to her."

"Thank you. I think I'll go on up now." Peter smiled a soft smile of hope. "Maybe she'll awaken demanding to see me."

After Peter left, Nick and Elizabeth were alone in the small waiting room, and there was no rush to get to the ICU because Larisa was in very capable hands, and even though her heart still screamed with pain at the tenderness she had seen in his eyes moments ago—as if he had somehow forgotten that he didn't love her enough to even try—she had to bravely meet the dark blue just one last time.

And when she did, Elizabeth said, "Thank you very much for helping me, Nick."

"You're very welcome. Elizabeth?"

"Yes?"

"I would like to tell you about a nightmare that I've been having." After a moment he asked very gently of the wary emerald, "May I?"

"Sure," she answered with a shrug. "Why not?"

The shrug was supposed to be light and casual, but how could it be when she was so weighted down with sadness? What was he going to tell her now? Yet another reason why their love was impossible? A stern reminder because he'd seen a flicker of hope in her eyes in response to the tenderness she had seen in his? The sadness was heavy, so very heavy, that it compelled Elizabeth to sit down on the couch.

"Tell me, Nick," she said, her gaze fixed on the floor. "Tell me about your nightmare."

"It's actually a nightmare that's with me all the time, day and night, whether I'm awake or not. And in it, Elizabeth, what I feel is the great emptiness of spending the rest of my life without you, never talking to you again, never touching you, never loving you . . ."

His voice was so gentle, so wondrously tender and loving that her vision of the floor became blurred with a sudden mist of hot tears. But still Elizabeth didn't look up. She simply steeled her weeping heart and waited to hear how the strong and disciplined Nicholas Chase was going to conquer this nightmare.

Then through the tears, he was there, kneeling before her, gently raising her chin until her glistening emerald eyes met his loving blue ones.

"Do I have to spend the rest of my life without you, Elizabeth?" he asked softly as he cradled her face in his talented and so gentle hands. And then, because the joyous answer appeared in the shining emerald before the emotion in her throat allowed her to speak, he whispered, "I love you, Elizabeth. I love you."

"Oh, Nick," she echoed finally. "I love you, too."

Nick tenderly touched the tears that spilled from her eyes, such joyous tears, and then he kissed them, and then he kissed her lovely mouth, and finally, through whispered kisses, he asked, "Where are we going to live?"

Elizabeth pulled away and looked at him with uncomprehending surprise. "Larisa told me that your house was quite large. If you would be willing to share your bed with me . . ."

"Always, my love," Nick whispered, eloquently sealing the promise of his forever love with a gaze of dark blue desire. "But what I was wondering, Doctor Jennings, was where you've accepted a new job."

"Nowhere," Elizabeth confessed. "I haven't actually been looking."

"Because you sensed my nightmares?"

"No. I've tried very hard not to let myself even think that you would come back to me." She frowned and asked very quietly, "What would have happened if I hadn't called you today, Nick?"

"I would have called you. Well, first I would have tried to find out how you were. If you were fine, if you'd obviously put our love behind you, I would have left you alone."

"But you could tell just by seeing me today that I hadn't?"

"Yes, I could . . . but I already knew. Three nights ago your best friend gave me hell for hurting you so much."

"She did?"

"She did. And I've spent every second since then knowing I was going to talk to you—as soon as I could find a time when you weren't on call. According to the page operators that would have been tomorrow. I was going to call you then, Elizabeth, to tell you that I love you with all my heart."

"Such as it is," Elizabeth whispered softly, before Nick

could. "It's a wonderful heart, Nick, and I'm going to take very good care of it."

"And, my love," he promised, "I'm going to spend my entire life taking very good care of yours."

"Peter?" Nick said from the doorway of the ICU waiting room.

"Nick," Peter answered, looking up and then standing up. "May I see Larisa now?"

"I haven't even seen her yet. The nurses have just gotten her settled. They say she's awake, though, and I'm on my way in right now. I only stopped to see if you knew that you were being paged."

Peter would never have heard his name being paged. He had been quite lost in imaginary—and wonderful—conversations with the woman he loved. "No, I didn't know."

"You can answer it on the phone by the couch. I'll be back, Peter, as soon as I've spoken to her."

"Nick."

"Hi." He smiled gently at the beautiful blue eyes. The brilliant blue was very troubled, and didn't seem the least bit confused, but still Nick asked, "Are you alert and oriented, Larisa?"

"I know that it's Saturday, April twenty-fifth, and that I'm in the surgical ICU at the medical center, and that you and Elizabeth operated on me, and," her voice softened then and her troubled eyes filled briefly with deep gratitude, "I know that my baby is all right."

"Yes. And you probably also know that you hurt,"

Nick suggested gently. "You have a lot of very deep wounds."

Larisa shrugged. Oh yes, she hurt . . . but not one bit of the immense pain she felt was physical.

"What happened to Julian, Nick? I know that I shot him, but the nurses won't tell me what happened."

"He's dead, Larisa." Nick saw her eyes cloud then, but he decided not to pursue the topic, choosing instead, for now at least, to try to get her to look forward not back. "You have your work cut out for you. You're going to have to recover in record time because you have a few weddings to attend. Admittedly, Christine and Stephen's a week from today may be pushing it, but June isn't that far away either."

"June?"

"June," he confirmed to the cloudy blue eyes that he was gently trying to lure out of the torment of the past and into the hopeful happiness of the future. "The wedding has to be in June, because Elizabeth's parents won't be back from England until then."

"Nick?" Larisa asked, focusing then, lured as Nick had hoped she would be by her love and hope—always—for her best friend.

"I know she wanted to tell you herself, but on our way here she was paged to the ER." *And I know she would understand why I'm doing this.* "Elizabeth has agreed to marry me, Larisa."

"Oh, Nick," Larisa said softly. "I'm so glad."

"I am, too. And I know that Elizabeth will want you to be her matron of honor."

"Matron of honor?"

"I imagine your wedding will happen before ours, Larisa."

"I won't be getting married, Nick."

"Why not?" he asked, even though he knew now, with certainty, because the bright blue had clouded once again—just as it had when she had learned that Julian was dead. "Oh, let me guess. Because you're a murderer?"

"Yes, Nick," Larisa answered quietly. "I *murdered* a man. I *am* a murderer."

"You shot a man who was trying to kill you. He damn near did kill you, by the way, and he absolutely would have if you hadn't shot him first."

"But I did shoot him."

"Yes, you did. For yourself, maybe, but mostly I think because of your baby. Isn't that right?"

"Yes, but . . ."

"Julian was going to *kill* your baby. You did the only thing a loving parent *could* do," Nick said definitively. After a moment he added softly, "You killed a man who deserved to die, Larisa. And now there's a man waiting outside who loves you very much . . . and who desperately wishes that he had been the one to kill Julian."

"Peter is here?"

"He's here, and he was at the motel. He arrived just moments after you shot Julian. Peter wants to see you, Larisa, and he wants to love you and his baby."

"You told Peter about the baby?"

"No. You regained consciousness briefly after the shooting and talked about the baby yourself."

"I can't see Peter."

Nick gazed for a moment at the clouded blue eyes, and when he finally spoke his voice was dangerously quiet. "You *can* see him, but if you *won't*, Larisa, if you kill Peter's love because of some sense of unworthiness because of what you did to Julian, then, you truly are a murderer."

"Nick . . ."

"I'm going to go get him."

"*No!*"

"This is where the love begins to get really tough, Larisa. I'm your doctor—"

"Elizabeth is!"

"I'm your doctor and what I believe you need most right now is to see the man who loves you." Nick smiled then, and touched her cheek, and then, very gently, he assured the frightened blue eyes, "It's going to be all right, honey, for both of us. It's going to be wonderful."

"Hi."

"Hi," she answered, looking briefly at his anguished dark green eyes and then returning her own to her hands.

"You and I need to talk about a lot of things, Larisa," Peter said softly. "But right now you need to make a very important decision."

Larisa looked up again at his handsome—and so very solemn—face and asked, "What decision, Peter?"

"I just got a call from Craig Buchanan. Larisa, what do you remember about what happened in the cottage?"

"I remember everything."

"Then tell me, please," he said with gentle apology to her suddenly so wary blue eyes. "I'm sorry, Larisa. I know how difficult this is. But, darling, it's really important."

"All right," she agreed quietly, trusting him, *trusting* him.

"All right," Peter echoed gently. "First, tell me where you got the gun."

"Julian gave it to me when we were married. He insisted that I keep it after we were divorced."

"Okay. Now tell me what you remember just before you pulled the trigger."

Larisa gazed at his dark green eyes, and drew strength from them as she relived the horror. "He laughed, mocking me, just like he had laughed in August, and just like that man had laughed years before when he had known that I wouldn't shoot him. I even heard my own voice—my voice when I was that little girl—pleading with him to stop, bravely telling him that I would shoot if he didn't. But he just laughed, and then I pulled the trigger, and there was a loud noise, and he looked so surprised . . . and so angry."

"Julian was very surprised, Larisa. He knew that the gun he had given you to protect yourself was filled with blanks."

"But I killed him, Peter."

"No, my darling, you didn't. Melanie killed him. She had gone to the cottage to visit you and when she saw what was happening she ran back to the motel office to get the master key, call her parents, and get Craig's gun. It was her voice you heard, Larisa, that was the little-girl voice that was pleading with Julian to stop. You must have both pulled the triggers at precisely the same instant because Craig and I were running to the cottage and we only heard one shot."

"Melanie killed Julian?"

"Yes."

Larisa frowned, then asked very softly, "Does she know, Peter?"

"No, not yet."

"Does she ever need to know?"

"Not necessarily. The police record will contain the truth, of course, but it can be sealed and the story that the press already has—that you shot him—could simply never be corrected."

Larisa knew now the decision she had to make.

And she made it with swift confidence.

And with that momentous decision she vanquished forever all the icy ghosts. Because it was a decision that conquered history. With it, she was permitting an innocent twelve-year-old girl to live her life without anguish. "A different kind of hell," Peter had said when she herself had wondered what her own life would have been like had she shot the man who raped her.

It was a hell that Larisa would not permit Melanie Buchanan to live.

"I don't want her ever to know the truth, Peter."

"I didn't think you would," Peter said gently. And then, because he had controlled his emotions for so long, and because he had almost lost this most precious of all dreams, he whispered, "I love you, Larisa."

"I love you, too, Peter. I had to get away because of Julian, because I knew that if he ever learned about the baby . . ."

"The baby," Peter echoed with soft joy. "May I touch her?"

"Of course," Larisa answered. "Her?"

"I just assume she's a little girl," Peter said softly as he gently laid his hand on Larisa's abdomen. "I just assume she's a little baby forget-me-not."

Then, as his hand still rested with loving wonder above the place where the tiny miracle, his infant daughter, was curled safe and warm deep inside, Peter gently kissed Larisa's brilliant tear-glistening blue eyes, and then her lovely trembling lips . . . and then, between tender kisses, he whispered to her all the joyous promises of love.

Look for
ILLUSIONS
Katherine Stone's newest novel of
friendship and love
to be published in hardcover
in February 1994
by Zebra Books

Please turn the page for an exciting sneak preview of
ILLUSIONS

In the beginning, as they sat in the living room at Clairmont while the casserole heated in the oven, Stephanie and Jillian's conversation focused on Annie—how pretty the golden retriever was, how soft, how wiggly, how friendly, how loving; and they talked about Jillian's teaching career and Stephanie's role in *Corpus Delicti*. It was a tentative dance of inconsequential words, a necessary prelude to the more important ones that might be spoken. Each woman wanted more words, but each was uncertain too—and fearful.

Finally, because the smiles and glances that had embellished the inconsequential words had given her courage, and because she had always been the most verbal one, it was Jillian who began the brave journey into more important—and more dangerous—territory: the past.

"What do you think of my new face?" she asked softly, with the honest candor of the shy yet forthright girl she once had been.

Jillian knew that Stephanie had been discreetly studying her face, more revealed now than it had been at the reception, make-up free and unshadowed in the natural light that filtered into the room. Without make-up or shadows the truths of her new face were fully exposed. The scars were thin and delicate, pearly gossamer threads that were just a shade whiter than the fairness of her skin.

"Very beautiful," Stephanie answered with the heartbeat swiftness with which she had always been able to talk to her best friend. The swiftness had returned already, slowed only by the emotion that accompanied it. Jillian was very beautiful, that was indisputable, the tiny thin lines adding interest—and detracting nothing—from her newfound beauty. But there was suddenly such uncertainty in the emerald eyes that Stephanie asked gently, "What do you think?"

"I think that Claudia did a wonderful job . . . maybe too wonderful."

"What does that mean?"

"It means that if I didn't have this face, Chase would never have noticed me." Jillian frowned, her expressive emerald eyes thoughtful and sad. "It was love at first sight, for both of us. Chase fell in love with what he saw, the beautiful cover, not who I really am."

"Chase Kincaid was a gorgeous man, but you fell in love with far more than his stunning good looks, Jillian. I know you did," Stephanie said confidently to the generous girl who had never cared at all about covers. Stephanie was confident that Jillian had fallen in love with the real Chase—with his heart—but it was obvious that Jillian didn't believe that the reverse had been true for her husband. "What makes you think the same wasn't true for him?"

"There was just so much that we never told each other, never shared. I was as guilty as he. I suppose I was afraid that if he really knew me . . . " Jillian sighed softly. "We should have been friends as well as lovers—but when Chase was troubled he didn't turn to me."

"What troubled him?"

"I don't know."

"Who did he turn to? Brad?"

"No. At least I don't think so. He just turned inward. When something was bothering him, he would go sailing by himself or stay up all night playing his guitar. And if I tried to reach out to him, he only withdrew further." *As if he was as afraid of revealing his flaws to me as I was afraid of revealing mine to him.*

"I'm so sorry, Jill."

"Thanks." A grateful smile trembled on Jillian's lovely lips. After a moment, she assured the sympathetic—and concerned—sapphire eyes, "Chase and I had wonderful times, too, Steph. Everything Chase Kincaid did, he did magnificently—including, in breathtakingly romantic moments, marriage."

"You loved him very much."

"Yes. I loved him very much," Jillian confessed softly. Then, and even more softly, she confessed, "That's why it hurts so much that the police officer in charge of the investigation—Lieutenant Jack Shannon—believes that I murdered him."

"What?" As vividly as Stephanie recalled the arrogant Lieutenant's softly hissed reminder that everything matters in murder, it hadn't occurred to her that he thought her gentle and loving friend might be involved in such a crime. "How can he possibly think that?"

"He has reasons, good reasons. He's appropriately bothered by the fact that Chase, who was an experienced sailor, could have been careless enough to have been struck by the boom, and he also senses that I didn't tell him the whole truth about what happened that night." Jillian's honest emerald eyes bravely met the blue ones that had filled swiftly with righteous indignation—for her.

"And he's right, Steph. I told him that Chase and I had had a pleasant dinner together that evening and that afterward he had gone for a sail. The truth is that we had a terrible argument. It was my fault. I started it. Something was troubling him, something deeper and darker than anything that had come before, and it had gone on for almost three months. He had withdrawn completely from me, as if I weren't even there. I felt so desperate, so helpless . . . so worthless." Jillian stopped abruptly. *Just like you must have felt when you tried to help me and I wouldn't even acknowledge that I had heard your words. I just let you stutter and stutter . . .*

"Jill?"

"Anyway, we argued that night. Chase was very upset when he left to go sailing, and . . . Lieutenant Shannon is right. I *am* responsible for Chase's death. Our argument, on top of whatever else it was that had been troubling him, made him so distracted that he wasn't aware of the boom—"

"Oh, Jillian," Stephanie whispered. "Please don't blame yourself. I know you must be tormented by the last words you said to him . . . and by all the words you didn't say." *Just as I have been tormented all these years by the words I didn't—couldn't—say to you.* Stephanie couldn't speak that emotional thought—not now, not yet—but somehow she was able to offer a soft reassurance, "I'm sure Chase knew how much you loved him."

"I hope so." That gentle hope flickered briefly in the sad emerald eyes, but vanished quickly, replaced by somber anguished bewilderment. "I don't know, Stephanie. Maybe I should tell Lieutenant Shannon everything. The case is officially closed, and my father has let him know in no uncertain terms that he won't tolerate any more questions, but it still bothers me that he believes Chase could have been murdered."

"And that you could have been a murderer."

"That doesn't bother me for me, only for Chase. Chase and Jack Shannon once were friends. I want him to know that Chase didn't marry a woman who was capable of murder."

"Why don't I tell Jack?" Stephanie suggested impulsively.

"You know him?"

"We've met." It was obvious that Jillian hadn't witnessed the glowering encounter between herself and the arrogant lieutenant at the reception, so now Stephanie smiled beautifully—as if her past meetings with Jack Shannon had been entirely pleasant ones. "It would be much easier for me to tell him than for you to."

Easy? The word itself taunted. No, Stephanie knew, it would not be easy at all. But, she realized as she saw the sudden emerald hope, this is so important to Jillian . . . and miraculously she trusts me still . . . and she is willing to give me a second chance to prove my friendship. I don't deserve a second chance, but Jillian is willing to give me one. I can do it. I will. Somehow . . .

The somehow came to Stephanie then. It was something she had never tried before, but it would work, wouldn't it? Stephanie Windsor couldn't speak fluidly, compellingly, emotionally to the intense ocean blue eyes. But confident, sassy and articulate Cassandra Ballinger could. She would talk to Jack Shannon in character— homicide lieutenant to homicide lieutenant.

"Let me do this, Jill."

"All right," Jillian agreed with obvious gratitude. "Thank you."

"You're welcome," Stephanie countered, grateful as

well. Thank you for trusting me, Jillian. I won't let you down this time. I *won't*.

The phone rang then and as Stephanie watched her friend's eyes fill with sudden apprehension, she realized that as long as Chase was still missing Jillian held on to the fragile hope that he was alive, that he would return, that at any moment he would walk through the front door.

The call was from Brad, not the police, and as soon as the relief in Jillian's eyes told her that Brad wasn't calling with the news that Chase's body had been found, Stephanie left to check on the casserole and replenish their lemonade.

By the time she returned, Jillian was off the phone, seated on the couch, her auburn head bent, her slender body very still.

"What is it, Jill?"

The auburn lifted, revealing sad emerald. "Brad just told me about Janine Raleigh, that she was killed Tuesday night by the Guitar String Strangler."

"You didn't know?"

"No. After Chase left that night, I just waited here for him to return. In the two days before the police arrived to tell me that his sailboat had been found, I didn't listen to the radio, or read the newspaper, or watch television." *I just waited, as he asked me to. Annie and I just waited—in absolute silence, listening for the sound of his car on the gravel.* "I didn't know that the Strangler had struck again."

"Why on earth did Brad tell you now?" Stephanie asked, her annoyance unconcealed. Why was Brad burdening Jillian with another inexplicable tragedy—especially one that had occurred just hours before Chase had sailed to his death?

"Because," Jillian said softly, "when I told him that you

were here, he wanted me to ask you to reconsider accepting the lead role in *Journeys of the Heart.*"

"You knew that I had been offered the role?"

"Yes," Jillian answered, surprised—and a little hopeful. "It was my idea."

"Your idea?" Stephanie echoed, needing time. "Neither Brad nor Chase ever mentioned that."

"No." Both Brad and Chase had known how much Jillian wanted Stephanie to accept the role, how perfect she was for it, but . . . "Neither of them knew of our friendship."

Friendship. Jillian shivered at the word, at her own betrayal of the word and at her memories of that betrayal. She had heard Stephanie's desperate whispers. She had heard the stuttering words of love, and the great pain those brave utterances had caused her friend, and she had willfully allowed Stephanie to suffer. No, *worse,* she had wanted Stephanie to suffer, as she was suffering.

Fifteen years ago, when their friendship ended, it had been Stephanie who had stuttered. Now, as perhaps, maybe, please, their friendship was getting a second chance, it was Jillian who spoke with halting emotion.

"I . . . it . . . was my idea. The role seemed . . . right . . . for your eight-octave talent."

"Eight-octave," Stephanie murmured. It had been their favorite description as teenagers, eight-octave talents, eight-octave dreams, eight-octave careers, eight-octave romances. They were going to experience the full range of life, they had decided. They were going to bravely sample every note on the scale, fearlessly embracing both the sharps and the flats, the harmony and the discord, the entire magnificent eight-octave symphony.

Jillian drew a steadying breath before admitting quietly, "I'm A. K. Smith, Stephanie. I wrote the role of Elizabeth in *Journeys of the Heart* for you."

For me? Even though I betrayed you? Even though I abandoned you when you needed me the most?

There had been a time, when they had been best friends, that Stephanie and Jillian had been able to perfectly read each other's thoughts. That was what had always made it so easy, so effortless for Stephanie to speak . . . because the words scripted in her own mind were already scripted as well as in her friend's.

But now both the emerald and sapphire eyes were clouded, their messages undecipherable to each other . . . even though their hidden thoughts were remarkably the same.

I wish I had the courage to apologize for what I did to you—to us. But I'm not strong enough, not now, not yet, and I need your friendship too much now to risk losing it again. Someday I will tell you though. Someday I will apologize.

After a few moments, and at precisely the same moment, the clouds vanished. The blue and green were crystal clear again, as were the messages, clear, and hopeful—and identical.

I want to be your friend again. And I promise—oh, how I promise—this time I will not let you down.

LOOK FOR *ILLUSIONS* ON SALE EVERYWHERE
IN FEBRUARY 1994!

CATCH A RISING STAR!

ROBIN ST. THOMAS

FORTUNE'S SISTERS   (2616, $3.95)

It was Pia's destiny to be a Hollywood star. She had complete self-confidence, breathtaking beauty, and the help of her domineering mother. But her younger sister Jeanne began to steal the spotlight meant for Pia, diverting attention away from the ruthlessly ambitious star. When her mother Mathilde started to return the advances of dashing director Wes Guest, Pia's jealousy surfaced. Her passion for Guest and desire to be the brightest star in Hollywood pitted Pia against her own family—sister against sister, mother against daughter. Pia was determined to be the only survivor in the arenas of love and fame. But neither Mathilde nor Jeanne would surrender without a fight. . . .

LOVER'S MASQUERADE   (2886, $4.50)

New Orleans. A city of secrets, shrouded in mystery and magic. A city where dreams become obsessions and memories once again become reality. A city where even one trip, like a stop on Claudia Gage's book promotion tour, can lead to a perilous fall. For New Orleans is also the home of Armand Dantine, who knows the secrets that Claudia would conceal and the past she cannot remember. And he will stop at nothing to make her love him, and will not let her go again . . .

SENSATION   (3228, $4.95)

They'd dreamed of stardom, and their dreams came true. Now they had fame and the power that comes with it. In Hollywood, in New York, and around the world, the names of Aurora Styles, Rachel Allenby, and Pia Decameron commanded immediate attention—and lust and envy as well. They were stars, idols on pedestals. And there was always someone waiting in the wings to bring them crashing down . . .